GODSTONE MAGE

I0563993

By

RICK A. MULLINS

Copyright © 2014 by Rick A. Mullins

Dedicated to Devon Monk. There are way too many books to choose from when I can break away from my obsessive compulsion to write, and Steampunk was a genre I just never had a chance to explore till I read Monk's *Dead Iron*. Within two months I was finished with the first draft of *Godstone Mage*. Thanks for the inspiration, Devon.

I would also like to thank my sister Melissa for the awesome cover and vital computerese. Without her, all my books would be nothing more than lonely files on my computer. Thanks sis.

Table of Contents

Chapter 1

Liam Quinn took a long swig of water from his canteen, draining it, then screwed the cap back on as he surveyed the land ahead. Water was not far away but the canyons and cliffs blocked him from getting down to where he could refill his canteens and ford the river that cut across his path.

He'd had to backtrack twice now and work his way north to find a spot where he could safely get across where the water carved a path through the stone. He gave a twitch to the reins and his horse turned around again and plodded back the way they'd come.

It took another hour and the sun was nearing the horizon when he finally found a way down to the narrow cut in the landscape. Looking at the sky he saw only blue and nodded to himself as he kneed the horse. He had to knee her again to get her moving and she balked at the water's edge but he urged her on and she reluctantly stepped into the water.

They were halfway across when he heard the thunder and looked again at the sky. It was still an uninterrupted blue. There must be a storm to the north out of sight. He urged the horse to move faster but she reared and tried to turn back to the other side. He pulled at the reins and tried to get her to continue across but she turned again, trying to get back to the western bank.

"Come on girl," he said as he leaned down to pat her on the neck. "Quicker we get across the quicker we'll be safe from what that thunder is dropping."

The mare snorted and turned another circle and he heard another roll of thunder that seemed to stretch too long. He jerked the reins and kicked at the mare's sides but she panicked and reared high instead of running, dropping him off the rear as the rising water level knocked her over. He grabbed at the saddle and his fingers locked on the saddlebags as he slid off the mare's rump at the same time the horse stumbled and fell sideways.

The saddlebags came free and both the mare and he fell into the rising water. Before either could regain their feet, the water rose in a wave as the storm to the north fed a flash flood and his feet left the riverbed.

He clung to the saddlebags with one hand and stroked for the eastern shoreline as hard as he could but the thrashing horse struck him as she fell again when another surge of floodwaters washed into the two of them. Clinging to the impromptu floatation device that his saddlebags provided he tried to keep his head above the rushing waters as the flood carried him into the canyons. He clung to the bags as they were swept away, the mare screaming in terror every time her head came out of the torrent.

In seconds they were swept downstream and into the canyon they had spent the afternoon trying to get around.

Choking on muddy water, Liam pushed the saddlebags down to help keep his head higher and he succeeded till the thrashing horse crashed into him and plunged him beneath the churning water again. He felt a kick to his ribs and what little air he had exploded from his lungs and he almost blacked out.

With a last effort he managed to right himself as the blue sky showed dimly through the murk of the floodwaters. The buoyancy the contents of his bags provided pulled at him as his strength waned and he vomited muddy water as his head broke the surface.

Rolling over he plunged one leg over the leather between the two bags and clung to the bag that floated the highest. In the distance he saw a pair of feebly kicking hooves roll into view then sink below the muddy water as the mare drowned.

Continuing to choke up water himself, he clung to the saddlebags as the flood carried him into the canyon till the sky was a thin blue line instead of a wide expanse. The water continued to rise as he was swept around a bend and he saw the churning of rocks in his path just in time to get a better grip on his saddlebags and take a deep breath. In seconds he was plunged through a series of rapids and dashed against the boulders that littered the riverbed as the flood carried him along.

A sharp pain wrenched at his ankle as he plunged through the rapids and he swallowed more water as he gasped. Choking again, he tried to calm himself as he was thrown over a small waterfall and plunged into the swirling waters below. He choked again and vomited more muddy water as his vision began to grow dim.

Then his mind seemed to clear as the world receded and he heard the voice that had visited him every night since he'd spent a night in a shaman's sweathouse on his way westward. Like in his dreams, the voice seemed to calm him and despite his eyes being closed he was able to *see* the mesquite shrub that jutted from the wall of the canyon ahead on the eastern side.

Without knowing how he did so, he lunged upward, his body lifting more than halfway out of the water as he grabbed a firm hold on the trunk of the bush. He barely held on as his arm was jerked violently with the force of the rushing water as another tremendous wave rolled beneath him.

He clung to the shrub with one hand and sought another handhold on the rock wall with his right, while trying to hang onto his saddlebags with his legs as the rushing waters dragged at the weight. The water level rose again and another wave washed over his head just as he gained a hold with his other hand and the mesquite bush shuddered as the floodwaters dragged at him.

The rushing water pulled with such force he felt his hold slipping as the base of the bush grew slick with sweat and muddy water.

The voice in his head again chanted and he found himself muttering words he didn't know and he pulled himself upward by strength he should not have had. The godstone necklace his mother gave him seemed to burn with an icy fire at his throat as the voice grew stronger and his own voice copied the words he had never spoken.

Without being able to see, he still found another bush to grab onto just as the first one fell free and plunged into the raging water to roll away with the churning waves. He reached up and blindly grabbed again and wrapped his fingers around another handhold and pulled.

The godstone necklace at his throat burned and he chanted along with the voice in his head, pulling upward with strength he shouldn't have had, to find handholds he couldn't see as the rushing waters tried to pull him down.

Then he surged upward when the saddlebags he still clung to with locked legs broke free of the grasping water. As his head spun and the grip of the water fell free, he scaled the cliff rapidly, not even seeing the handholds he used to drag himself and his saddlebags upward by arm strength alone.

When he reached the edge of the cliff, he pulled himself onto level stone and collapsed as he continued to cough up muddy water. After a while he stopped his wet hacking and finally breathed deeply of the sweet air, then rolled over on his back to finally open his eyes and stare at the clear blue sky turning darker with the coming of sunset.

The godstone chain around his throat slowly cooled from its icy fire that gave him control of his curse and supplied the power to the one-time spell he'd just used to save his life. There was only one place to renew that energy and he immediately fell into an exhausted sleep, his ankles still locked around the saddlebags that held his salvation and the cure for the dark mage's curse that afflicted his entire family.

Oblivious to their presence, he slept on through the night as several animals crept close to sniff at his motionless form. When sunlight broke the horizon, he gasped and lurched awake, to see the eyes of a mountain lion only inches from his face, the jaws within easy snapping reach of his throat.

Chapter 2

"Gods, sis," he laughed. "Scared me half to death!"

The tawny lion sat back on her haunches, rumbled deep in her throat and licked her muzzle as he lifted himself on his elbows and looked around. The slight spotting that hinted at the snow leopard ancestry their mother spoke about showed beneath the puma lineage that was more recent and in both their parents.

"Well, if you found me then it shouldn't be too hard to get out of here. Have you eaten yet?"

The mountain lion licked her muzzle again, the godstone necklace glinting through her fur in the morning light as she nodded. Then she rose and loped off, stopping after a few yards and looking over her shoulder.

"Yeah, yeah, I'm coming," he sighed, then rose to his feet and stretched complaining muscles before reaching down for the saddlebags lying by his feet.

He opened each bag in turn to inspect the contents to see what remained of his possessions. The tins that held the various ingredients for the supposed cure for his family's curse was the first thing he checked and he sighed with relief as he saw they were still intact and the potions they'd traveled west to acquire were safe and dry.

Next, he checked the oiled folder that held the journal he'd used to record the way to mix and prepare the potions and the words he needed to speak to break the family curse. There was only one mixture and he had to have the entire family together to cure them all at the same time.

Hopefully.

He checked both bags and confirmed that most of his most valuable possessions were safe, mostly dry, and undamaged, then rose and threw the bags over a shoulder and set off after his older sister. She made it a point to walk where she left distinct paw prints so he could follow her and in no time was able to find where he could set up camp with full view of the landscape.

Orlagh rested beneath a stone overhang that would give them shade from the rising sun. He pulled the saddlebags from his shoulder and lowered himself to the ground to gaze across the desert. A dead rabbit lay beside her.

As he sat, she nudged the rabbit toward a small pile of stones then lay down and began grooming herself.

He sat for a moment as he scanned the area, then arranged the stones in a small ring before collecting nearby deadwood. When the firewood was ready, he pulled his godstone knife from the sheath on his left hip and began splitting a selected stick till he had a pile of tinder. Pulling a striker from a pocket he placed the tinder inside and twisted it till the sparks ignited the shavings, then he dumped the tinder into the middle of the pile of wood.

As the fire caught, he skinned and cleaned the rabbit and tossed the meat into the small Dutch oven he retrieved from his bags. Knowing his sister would select a spot near water he rose and looked around, quickly spotting the depression that still held a measure of rainwater. Her paw prints at the edge of the pool showed she'd already drunk her fill.

He filled his spare canteen, the other two had gone down the river with the horse and the rest of his gear, and returned to the fire.

His sister gave him a look and whuffed a breath.

"Yeah," he snorted as he cut up a single carrot and potato, poured half the canteen's contents into the Dutch oven, and twisted the lid on. "I almost blew it. Damn horse panicked in the middle of the river and kept turning in circles instead of finishing the crossing. My fault, though, should have listened to the thunder and spurred her instead of letting her spin me around and trying to get back to the farther bank."

His sister gave another snort and put her head in her paws and closed her eyes as he raked coals to the edges of the fire ring and placed the oven in the middle. He scooped coals up around the sides of the oven then piled more wood over the pot. Then he poured the rest of the water into his other pot, put two pinches of ground tea leaves inside, then placed the pot beside the Dutch oven and piled the last of the wood around it.

Godstone pots heated quicker than copper, iron, or normal steel and the smell of tea quickly filled the air. The tight fit of the Dutch oven lid kept the smell of the stew from escaping till pressure built up but the smell of the tea let him know the stew was ready to be removed from the fire.

It wouldn't do to ruin the expensive oven so he hooked the handle into the rim and removed it from the fire as soon as the vent hole in the lid began to whistle. His stew would continue to cook away from the heat. Retrieving his cup from his saddlebags he poured it full of tea then set it aside and stirred the coals so they would burn out faster. Then he leaned against the stone to sip tea as he looked out over the land, his thoughts going to his near failure at saving his family from their curse.

His family, the Quinns of Ireland, were blessed with a great heritage. But his father had angered a powerful mage when he refused to sell their island in Erie Lake. The result was a curse that stole their sentience when they were in their changeling form of the puma with faint snow leopard spots.

Another mage managed to solve the problem of the loss of sentience during the change but couldn't solve the second half of the curse. His sister and mother were unable to change back into their human forms except during the three days of the full moon while his father and he were forced into their changeling forms during the three days of the full moon.

And the changes at the waxing and waning of the full moon were forced and painful.

The journey to San Diego to meet with the Chinese mage that guaranteed the proper reversal of the curse was what had brought his sister and him out west while their parents battled with their hidden adversary.

When he finished his first cup of tea, Liam poured the rest from the pot then opened the Dutch oven and quickly devoured the stew. Cleanup took only a few more minutes and when the pot and oven cooled enough to put back in the saddlebags, he filled his canteen, dropped in a fresh mage purifying pellet, threw his saddlebags over a shoulder, and set off on foot.

Following the trail left by his sister, he marched across the land on his way home. Three days later on the evening before the waxing full moon they stopped to make camp early so they could switch places.

When the pull of the moon let them know their change was close, his sister padded around behind some large shrubbery. Like most full changelings, until his family was cursed by the mage coveting their property, they could change from human to puma and back again any time they wanted. The curse took that away from them. They were now chained to the phases of the moon and only their godstone necklaces kept them from acting like the animals they resembled while in puma form.

The mage hoped animal nature would result in their being killed and he could then claim their island for himself. It hadn't worked so far.

Liam retrieved his sister's clothes from their wet-bag in the saddlebags and set them out for her, then removed his own, folded them and placed them inside the waterproof wet-bag. He didn't worry about his sister being able to carry the weight as their heritage gave them both more strength than other humans. Then he walked naked around a large boulder to await the moonrise.

The change was also more painful with the curse and he heard his sister moan at the same time he bit back his own reaction to the moon's cracking the horizon to the east just as the sun set to the west.

Most changelings could control their metamorphosis in that they could assume a full animal shape, or only a partial change that kept the best of both forms. His family was gifted with the control to easily assume that warrior form, but the curse had also deprived them of that option.

He fell to his knees as the change wrenched at him, then fell forward and on his side as fierce pain wracked his body. On the other side of their camp his sister's cries went from those of a cat in pain to the stifled screams of a human just as his own cries changed from human to feline.

His bones shifted and muscles twisted to maintain their proper alignments as his jaw stretched into a short muzzle and fur grew thick on his skin. Where his sister was a creamy, tawny color, his fur matched his hair color and was much darker brown, almost black and with a smattering of very faint gray-white spots the size of silver dollars that showed his snow leopard ancestry on his mother's side.

He rolled on his side and squalled in pain as the change took its time because of the curse. He fought the loss of consciousness as the mage's curse wrenched him into shape instead of the smooth, flowing change he remembered when he was younger. This constant pain was even worse than his first change at puberty, changeling puberty at seven, when the family gathered around him to help him through his *awakening* to his full heritage.

When the change was complete, he lay panting for several moments before pulling his legs under him and rising to all fours. He shifted around, stretching till he felt comfortable in his new skin, then padded around his rock to find his sister buttoning up her shirt.

"Bad one again?" she asked as she tucked her shirttails into her flared dress, with the split legs for riding a horse. "Yeah, mine too."

He gazed up at her and snorted, bobbed his head, then padded over to lie next to the fire ring. It had been rough, but then it always was since the mysterious dark mage decided he wanted Puma Island for himself and cursed their family to drive them away from it or kill them since they wouldn't sell.

After a few minutes to rest from the forced change, he rose to hunt their supper while she prepared their camp. He ran free and quick and soon crossed the scent of prey and his heart raced as he began tracking the feral pig. In minutes he found it rooting through shrubbery, oblivious to his presence.

He didn't waste time and was soon gorging on the bloody meat of the hindquarters. When he finished his half, he dragged the rest back to camp and his sister fixed her own meal.

"That was the last of the taters and carrots," she said as she cleaned the two pots and their single remaining mug after she'd eaten.

He knew because he'd gone without after the meal the morning after almost drowning with their horse, but there was nothing they could do till they could find a settler in these parts. He substituted native plants and tubers for the familiar, but both preferred the domestic kinds.

When night fell, he curled up next to her as she used one of the saddle bags as a pillow and the rain slicker he'd been wearing when the flood took their bedroll and most of their supplies, as a blanket. The next day they set off again and he scouted the trail ahead or padded along beside her.

The sun was at its highest when they smelled the smoke.

Chapter 3

Liam looked up at his sister and she made a motion with her hand. "Go!"

He ran.

It took him only a few minutes to find the source, a small homestead on a stone shelf above the bend in a stream where water collected in a wide pool in a horseshoe cut in the stone.

He made a complete circuit of the settlement and determined by smells that there were only four people living in the home, then hurried back to his sister. They had formed a special way of conveying information in their puma forms and it took only a few minutes for her to ask her questions and for him to answer.

She had continued walking while he scouted and it only took her a couple dozen minutes to come into sight of the homestead. They made no attempt to hide their approach so as to give the settlers plenty of time to assess their presence and in short time a large man and a young girl stood awaiting them.

"Rifle in the west window," his sister observed, but his keen puma eyesight spotted the prudent defensive maneuver.

He continued to walk at her side to show that he was either a *well-trained* beast, or the most obvious fact that he was a changeling in his beast form.

When they were about fifty feet away from the pair, they stopped and his sister shouted, "Hello.

My name is Orlagh Quinn and this is my brother, Liam. We lost our horse and most of our supplies in a flash flood. We're headed eastward to home and would appreciate directions to where we could replace what we lost."

The large red-haired man shifted the double-barreled shotgun only slightly as he responded, "Orson Richards. My daughter, Heather."

Liam could tell from her smell that she was not a blood relative to the big man.

At Orlagh's glance toward the house, Orson smiled. "My wife, Elizabeth."

"Kitty!" a shrill voice yelled and a child came running from the small barn straight at Liam. Before anyone could react more than in surprise, the child barreled into Liam and wrapped his arms and legs around the big cat's neck and body as he almost bowled Liam over. "Kitty! *Big* kitty!" And buried his face in Liam's thick fur.

Orson's eyes went wide as Elizabeth ran from the house, abandoning her strategic position. "Fallon! No!"

If it hadn't been for the boy covering the cat with exuberant hugs and rubbing his face in Liam's fur, she might have fired the rifle she carried in her protective panic.

Heather turned with hands outstretched. "Mama! No! He's a human changeling!" Then she deftly removed the rifle from her mother's hands as the woman charged past.

Liam endured the attentions of the boy as his mother skidded to a halt just out of arm's reach and began wringing her hands.

It seemed that everyone was agitated except for the young boy and his sister, the parents for their son and Orlagh for her brother.

Liam could tell by the boy's smell he was the son of Orson and Elizabeth, while the daughter was undeniably the daughter of Elizabeth but not of Orson. Liam began licking the boy's face, then rolled on the ground and let the boy roughhouse him to his content. It only took a few heartbeats for the tension to lesson as the distraught mother saw there was no danger to her son.

Fallon eventually lost his glee at his new discovery and began petting Liam, his hands smoothing the ruffled fur back into shape, as Liam lay on his side as non-aggressively as he could. "Pretty kitty, soft kitty. Look mama, isn't he pretty?"

"Yes Fallon, he sure is. Now come away," she held her hands out coaxingly.

Fallon wasn't having anything to do with that and wrapped his arms around Liam's neck tightly.

"Fallon," Orson said softly but sternly. "Have you finished repairing the tractor? You said you would be before lunch and your mother was ready to set the table before our visitors arrived."

Fallon immediately forgot about his new toy and stood to face his father respectfully. "Yes papa. I was just coming to tell you when I saw the kitty. I even put in the new godstone detector I made. Now it will separate godstone from the ground when it plows."

Orson's eyes shifted to Orlagh and the big cat with a touch of concern. Godstone, the metal that fell from the skies, was more valuable than gold or gemstones. To reveal there was godstone in the land was to reveal treasure to be found on his property. And to reveal his son was a tinker that could devise a way to collect that treasure could also be dangerous.

Orlagh smiled disarmingly. "Do you use magnets, Fallon?" Then she lifted a boot. "I have magnets on my boots to collect what lies close to my footsteps." Then she looked at Orson. "I picked up several small pieces in the last few miles of our walk. If I was on your property when I picked them up, half of what I collected is rightfully yours."

Liam could smell the tension dissolve at his sister's words, till Fallon blurted. "We've got *lots* of godstone!" Then added conspiratorially, "Ours came from pieces of what made the hole in the world over by Diablo Canyon." Then his face grew cloudy. "That railroad man wants papa to sell him our land so he can mine it for his steam locomotives to pull his trains."

The child ignored the horrified looks of his parents as he rambled on, "I built the engine for *our* steam tractor out of part of the biggest piece."

"Fallon!" Orson bellowed. "What did I tell you?"

Fallon's face fell and tears welled up in his eyes. "Everybody already knows papa. You're the only one thinks it's a secret."

Then he rushed to his mother and she wrapped her arms around him as she crooned,

"There, there, Fallon. It's alright. Papa doesn't think it's a secret, just that it's bragging and you know what the good book says about *that*."

"Sorry," the child murmured as he burrowed his head in his mother's dress.

Now that Fallon wasn't wrapped around him like a cloak, Liam could see that the boy was not as young as his actions said. Where Fallon acted like a very young child, and he *was* small and frail, he looked to be *much* older, fourteen or fifteen at least, maybe more.

Orson snorted. "Well, no matter, now you know what that railroad man and everybody else knows. The meteorite that dug the Diablo Canyon crater scattered godstone all over these parts and we found a chunk as big as a draft horse on our land."

"And enough to fill a supply wagon in smaller pieces," Fallon added helpfully then flinched as he realized he was bragging again.

Orson pursed his lips as he tried not to smile, but his wife spoke before he could say more. "We can talk more at the table."

Then she faced her guests. "You are welcome to join us for lunch." She looked at Liam, then Orlagh. "We just butchered a cow yesterday because Heather was going to go to Winslow for some supplies and we were jerking some meat for her journey and to trade." Then she glanced at Liam and changed the subject. "Is your brother linked to the moon's cycles?"

"Yes, he is," Orlagh replied without explaining more just yet.

"Good," Elizabeth said. "Then it's settled. We have fresh meat to satisfy *his* palate," she pointed a chin toward Liam, "and cooked meat and vegetables for the rest." Then she made shooing motions. "Everybody inside so we can eat and talk. I for one am curious as to why the two of you are traveling these parts on foot."

Mindful of her manners, Orlagh removed her gunbelt with the godstone bowie knife despite the fact that Liam had lost the revolver in the river and hung it on a peg by the door and set the saddlebags on the floor.

Elizabeth gave an approving nod, then hustled them to the table while Heather retrieved another set of dinnerware for Orlagh. Orson opened a thin door at the back of the combination kitchen living room and a waft of cool air showed that it led to a mage-cooled closet. He came out seconds later with a large cut of bloody beef that he laid on a tin platter and placed on the table. When the meal was ready, he led the family in prayer before placing the platter on the floor for Liam.

As they dug in, Orson asked, "So, you say you lost your horse and supplies in a flash flood?"

Orlagh confirmed the fact, then told their hosts of their travels from the east to obtain the cure for their curse, not hiding anything in return for Fallon's innocent revelations.

Heather scowled when she finished their story. "Dark mages like that give the rest of us a bad name."

"You are mage trained?" Orlagh asked.

"Yes," the young woman replied, then glanced at her mother, who took up the conversation.

"I was the sole survivor of my own family's encounter with a flash flood and was raised by a Pima father and Mojave mother," she then gestured to her daughter. "Heather's father was my native mother's youngest brother. She was declared *spirit blessed* at her birth and received training from the village mage till I was betrothed to Orson."

"She fixed me so I wasn't locked inside my head," Fallon declared.

Orson scowled as Elizabeth explained, "A Pinkerton mage cursed me when a mine owner accused us of giving aid to native rebels while I was carrying my son."

"All we did was feed some starving Apaches," Orson grumbled. "We didn't know they had escaped from the local cavalry who had accused them of trespassing on their own land by the mine owner."

"I am also mage trained," Elizabeth continued. "I have trained my daughter in everything I know and a local Master has continued that education. Although I do not practice as much as I should I am still considered a powerful mage. My daughter is worth two of me at my best years ago."

"I was stuck in my head and couldn't get out," Fallon said as he gripped his head with both hands. Then he smiled at his sister. "Heather helped me get out and now I can talk." Then he frowned. "But part of me is still stuck."

Conversation lagged for a moment before Orson spoke, "Our son is the best tinker in the whole Arizona Territory and makes things out of godstone metal that defy comprehension." Fallon beamed as his father continued, "He even makes steam into foam that was invented during the War Between the States. It's so light it can lift heavy things."

He gestured to the walls of their home. "That's how we were able to move big boulders and whole logs with just the four of us to make our home so sturdy and strong."

"Only 'cuz my sister can magic it to stay solid," Fallon contributed. Heather blushed as her brother continued, "If she didn't make it *stay* solid it would 'vaporate in a handful of hours if you don't keep chanting it." He thrust his hands into the air with a quick spreading of his fingers. "Poof! Back into normal steam!"

Orson put a hand on his wife's hand and smiled around the table at his family. "My beautiful wife and I are blessed with two wonderful children with amazing abilities."

Chapter 4

Liam lounged in the shade of a tree while Orlagh sat nearby with Heather and Fallon on a red and white checkered blanket, a picnic basket beside them. The two young women talked while Fallon devoured sandwiches meant for all three.

"Fallon! Save some for us," Heather laughed.

"Orlagh said I could have hers," he looked guiltily at their guest as crumbs fell from his lips. "Didn't you?"

"Yes," she answered as she patted her stomach. "I had one and they're so big just the one filled me up."

"See!" Fallon declared, then stuffed the remains of another sandwich into his mouth.

"I will have some more milk, though," Orlagh said, then as Heather filled her mug, added, "I've never seen milk stay so cold for so long without an active cold spell. How do you do it?"

"Mageried steam foam," Fallon mumbled around a mouth full of sandwich.

At Orlagh's raised eyebrows, Heather explained, "The pitcher has two shells, one inside the other. Fallon makes the steam into foam with his godstone tinkering, and I use magery to *lock* it solid for longer and a lot thinner than the normal foam. It melts back into water eventually, just not as fast as the kind that fella in San Fran invented last year. That's why I don't have to renew the cold spell on our freezer closet but once a week."

She jumped up with the milk jug in her hands. "Come on! We'll show you."

Fallon jumped up and started to run ahead to the barn, then turned and ran back to the shade of the tree. "Come on kitty! I'll show you what we can do."

Liam got up when the boy began tugging hard on his ears and loped after him as the two young women headed for the barn at a slower pace.

Fallon rushed by the two women, and ran inside, then back out again. "Hurry kitty, hurry!"

Liam trotted faster and quickly found himself inside the barn where a steam tractor took up most of the room. A pair of draft horses occupied stalls on the right side and a jumble of machine parts and tinker tools on the other. The loft above was mostly filled with bales of hay.

Fallon rushed to the left and jumped up and down excitedly as the others followed. The boy was so excited he could barely contain himself, eyes wide and breath coming in gasps.

Heather went to one knee in front of him. "Calm yourself, Fallon. Remember, breathe deep and slow or you'll pass out."

Fallon began to sway as he hyperventilated, but then took his sister's advice and breathed deep and slow. As color came back to his face he calmed down and shook his head to clear it as he began to speak. "Slow and deep, slow and deep." Then he smiled at his sister. "I'm alright now, I'm alright now."

"Good, now let's show our guests what amazing things you can do."

"Only with your help. If not for you all I can do is make steam foam. *You* make it *special*!"

Heather and Orlagh smiled at the boy and his sister patted him on the head. "But I can only do it with godstone steam foam and *you* make *it* special. Now set up your steamer."

She turned to her guests as she held up the milk jug. "See here. The bottom twists off like this." She removed the bottom of the jug and a few drops of water dripped out, then a few more. Then she held it upside down and shook it. A white tube of foam drifted out and upwards toward the roof of the barn. The foam stayed firm for only a moment then dissipated into normal steam and was soon gone.

In seconds Fallon had a small steam engine chugging away and the two women and the puma moved closer as Heather explained, "I don't know why it only works with steam foam from a godstone engine, but it does." She shrugged. "Steam from a normal engine gets foamy but it only lasts a few hours before it goes back to being just normal steam. Steam foam from a godstone steamer lasts about a day normally, but I discovered a chant that locks it longer if it's inside an airtight container."

Orlagh and Liam knew godstone affected things in odd ways and magery was another thing they didn't know much about so they just accepted the young woman's words as they awaited the proof.

In moments the engine was chugging away smoothly and Fallon's attention never wavered as he watched the gauges. "It's ready." He held a small tube up and put a hand on a release valve.

Heather held the milk jug out. "Here Orlagh. You hold the jug and be ready to screw the bottom back on when I say so."

Orlagh did as instructed and Heather began to chant as Fallon waited patiently. He knew when his sister was ready and with practiced experience, opened the valve just as her chant began to repeat and rise in volume. A thin line of foamy steam began to flow from the end of the tube and Heather placed her hands open around the steam foam as it flowed into the bottom of the jug.

The steam thickened and expanded as it rose, doubling then tripling in size and coagulating and in a heartbeat, Fallon shut off the valve and began bouncing excitedly. Heather continued to chant and the steam began to bulge out of the bottom of the jug as it continued to solidify and expand, the jug actually getting lighter as the foam expanded.

In a few seconds Heather swiped her hand across the expanding foam to wipe away the excess. "Alright, screw the bottom back on."

Orlagh did so and Heather smiled as Fallon bounced excitedly.

"That's all there is to it," Heather said, then swayed before catching herself.

"Are you alright?" Orlagh said concernedly as she put out a hand to steady her new friend.

"Yes. It just takes a little bit out of me sometimes."

"I'll go get you a sandwich!" Fallon said and dashed toward the door, then back again to make sure his steam engine was properly turned off. He twisted handles and released pressure as he secured the machine, then hurried out of the barn. In seconds he was back with the half sandwich he hadn't eaten yet and an apple and gave them to his sister as she sat on a bench by the tinker's table.

She devoured the sandwich and half of the apple before she spoke, "Sorry. It doesn't usually take that much out of me but I was showing off and put more into my incantation than I usually do." She looked embarrassed. "I guess I was trying to impress you too much."

Orlagh started to set the jug on the table and it wobbled unnaturally for a moment then began to drift upward as Fallon giggled. "You sure did! If you don't watch out it will float away and papa will be mad. That's his favorite jug when he and mama go on their *private* picnics."

A shadow crossed the barn's door and they all looked up to see Orson coming in. "Oh, I thought you were all out by the apple tree."

"We showed Orlagh and kitty how we make better steam foam," Fallon blurted. "Heather was showing off and made it so light the jug almost floated away!"

Orson smiled tolerantly at his son. "I'm sure it was just a mistake, son. We all make mistakes sometimes. Remember when we were in Winslow and I forgot to get your mama's yarn?"

Fallon giggled. "Yeah! We had to go back to town and it was way past dark by the time we got home! The sky sure was pretty."

Orson turned to Orlagh. "Heather was going to go to Winslow today to get some supplies and should leave now if she wants to get there before dark. I don't want to run you off, you're welcome to stay as long as you want, but I'm sure she would like the company and you can get another horse and all the supplies you might want while you're there."

"I know you want to get back east, but you can come back here and stay another day or so if you want," he said as he glanced at Liam. "That way you can be here where it's safer when the two of you go through your changes."

"That's a good idea," Orlagh said as she glanced down at her brother, then back at their host.

"Can I go too?" Fallon said bouncing in place.

Orson scowled. "Are you sure? Remember how those other kids called you names?"

Fallon wrapped his arms around Liam's neck. "They won't *dare* make fun of me with kitty by my side."

Orson looked at his daughter who nodded. "Alright, you can go too."

"Hurray!" Fallon cheered and ran out of the barn yelling over his shoulder, "I'll get my things!"

Orson shook his head and laughed. "That boy has more energy than any three people. Alright ladies let's get the wagon hitched to one of the horses. It's already loaded with the goods Heather was going to take to town."

Chapter 5

The rock hit Fallon in the back and the jeers of the children followed. "There's the dummy. Hey dummy, why don't you go to school?"

Fallon buried his head in Liam's fur and wept as Heather patted him on the shoulder. "Just ignore them Fallon. You're smarter than all of them put together."

"It still hurts," Fallon mumbled into Liam's fur.

Liam couldn't take it anymore and shrugged from the boy's grasp, stood up in the back of the wagon and roared his disapproval.

The children following the wagon and taunting his new friend grew wide eyed and stopped in their tracks. Liam lunged to the rear of the wagon and roared again and the miscreants turned and ran. The one that threw the rock ran full bore into a post beside a water trough and fell into the mud around the trough. The two other children stopped and gaped, then pointed and laughed at their friend, forgetting their original target as they now jeered the mud splattered boy.

Liam huffed and sauntered back to a grinning Fallon and lay down beside his young friend who sat straighter as he stroked the large puma's fur.

Moments later, Heather steered the wagon to the blacksmith's building and they all piled out.

The huge black man with the equally huge leather apron standing just inside the door scowled for a moment as he looked up, then roared, "Fallon, my boy, how are you?"

Fallon ran and leaped into the man's arms. "Lucas! Hello! Look, I've got a lion friend."

Then he whispered, loud enough to hear over the pounding of Lucas's apprentice son at the forge. "He roared at mean Billy Johnson after Billy threw a rock at me, and Billy ran scared and fell in the mud."

"He did, did he?" the big man said as he set the boy back on the ground. "Well that serves mean old Billy Johnson right for throwing rocks at people."

Lucas extended his arms and gave Heather a hug as she introduced Orlagh and Liam. "Shapeshifters, huh? Well any friends of the Richards family are friends of mine no matter what they look like," he said as he winked at Orlagh. "Kind of know what it's like myself to be a bit different than most others."

He slapped his hands together. "Now young Fallon, did you bring me those new inventions we talked about the last time you were here?"

"Yeah Lucas. Me and Heather…"

"Heather and I," his sister reminded him.

Fallon looked puzzled for a moment. "You and you? Oh! Yeah! Heather and *I* 'scovered another way to mix magic and tinkering. We can make things *really* small now."

He lowered his voice conspiratorially. "I built a little forge in my secret place so I can 'speriment and papa said I could use as much of our, *you know what*," he whispered loudly, "as I need.

I'm doing just like you said, lettin' my 'magination run wild."

"That's wonderful," Lucas whispered back just as loudly, then stood up. "It's almost suppertime. Why don't you folks come eat with us? Micah! I'll close things up here while you go tell your mama we've got company." He looked at Liam. "Let her know to get a big cut of meat from the cold closet for our four-legged guest too, will you?"

"Sure pa." Then the young man ran off to pass the message while Lucas banked the fire to the forge.

"Heather, why don't you and your friends pull the wagon around back while Fallon helps me here."

"Okeh, Lucas!" Fallon exclaimed in Choctaw.

In minutes the wagon was parked in the barn behind the smithy and the draft horse unhitched, wiped down, and made comfortable with fresh hay and a scoop of oats. In only a few more minutes they were all seated around the large table with Liam by the door as Lucas said the prayer, then they talked while they ate.

While Orlagh stayed in the smith's spare room, Fallon and Micah and Liam slept in the loft above the barn. Fallon showed his friend several of the new inventions he'd tinkered together while Liam napped just out of reach of the lamp's light but in full view of the full moon.

Only one more night and Liam and his sister would go through their forced change and reverse their positions again till the next cycle of the moon.

The next day Fallon showed Lucas the things he'd brought for the blacksmith and Heather renewed the steam foam and cold spell for their freezer closet. Then she led the Orlagh around town to finish the rest of their trading before they went to the stables to purchase a horse.

"You can have the stallion and the saddle for five ounces of gold and two ounces of godstone," the stablemaster said as he darted a look at Heather. "Got him from a drunk savage what needed money to buy whiskey," Heather stiffened but didn't say anything, "but he's too headstrong to ride and has busted out of his stall three times in the last month. He's *trouble*, nuthun' but trouble, but he has already mounted all the mares we've introduced him to and the missus has confirmed all four are with foal."

Heather took a breath to argue but Orlagh put a hand on her arm, then pointed with her other hand. "The stallion and *that* saddle, not the used one, for *three* ounces of gold and *one* of godstone."

The man glared and started to object when Liam sauntered up and sat next to his sister while Heather crossed her arms and glared. "Fine!" He spit in his palm and held his hand out.

Orlagh didn't flinch, spitting in her own palm and holding her hand out. When the stablemaster tried to crush her hand, she exerted her own shapeshifter strength and, locking eyes with him, *squeezed* till *he* flinched.

Heather then led Orlagh to the gun shop where she bought a new pistol and rifle, and ammunition for both. The gunsmith tried to charge more than the weapons were worth but after Orlagh insisted on going behind the shop and showing her marksmanship he grudgingly accepted *her* offer for the cost. Then the two went to the General Store where she bought the rest of the supplies she and her brother needed. Liam had to remain outside because of the sign that forbade shapeshifters and *all* non-whites from entering.

"I hate to do business with them but they're the only place in town that has what you need," Heather admitted in apology, then snorted derisively. "They're still mad their side lost the war. He tried to keep me out too, but Mr. Washington refused to do business with him unless he did and Lucas is the only blacksmith in town. It's only two days to Flagstaff by wagon, but Lucas told pa there's a Jew already bought a piece of land to build another store, and he's not picky about whose money he accepts."

She snickered. "Mr. Smith doesn't realize his kind are already outnumbered and Mr. Goldstein will put him out of business unless he changes his ways." She shrugged. "Or maybe even if he does. A lot of folk around here are impatient to do business with a merchant a bit less openly hateful to so many different kinds of people."

The two women finished their tasks in time to share another fine meal with the Washington family and were on the road home with plenty of time to get back to the Richards's homestead before sunset.

Fallon was more than pleased when Orlagh let him ride the horse while she rode in the wagon with her new friend. Heather was surprised when Liam trotted alongside the stallion and the horse didn't seem to mind.

Orlagh chuckled. "I could tell he was just right as soon as he perked up when he got a whiff of Liam and me. I could feel the aura around him and I'd bet an ounce of godstone he was raised around shapeshifters. And treated a lot better than that stablemaster treated him."

They traveled on and the women marveled at the way the horse seemed to play with Liam as they trotted around the wagon. The draft horse even got into the mood and several times Heather had to calm her down as the mare got too frisky and bounced them along the rough road too much.

"I don't think I've seen Fallon so happy in months," Heather commented when her younger brother's laughter carried back to them as the horse and puma chased each other back and forth ahead of the wagon.

They stopped once to give the animals a rest and snack on the basket of food Hazel Washington filled for them and were soon back on the trail toward home.

Later in the afternoon they saw a dust cloud in the distance and Heather commented, "Somebody must be on the road the railroad is building alongside the path the tracks are going to take."

"Must be riding pretty hard or else there's a lot of them to stir up that much dust," Orlagh observed.

They watched the dust cloud for a moment, then traveled on. After a couple of miles Liam and the stallion stopped suddenly, then Liam turned and raced back to the wagon. Orlagh and her brother had devised several signs to pass information from their puma forms to their human sibling and Orlagh stiffened.

"Liam says he smells smoke, lots of smoke," she said as her brother took off at full speed, the stallion racing after him as soon as he passed.

Heather's eyes grew wide and she slapped the reins on the back of the draft horse. They'd only gone another mile when the smoke grew thick enough they could both smell it. Another mile and they could see the smoke rising in the distance.

Orlagh didn't say anything, but it was obvious the smoke came from the Richards homestead. When they came around the bend in the road that led down to the farm, they could see the flames engulfing the house and barn. Liam and the stallion raced across the stream and they could see Fallon jump from the horse's back and run to a dark shape on the ground between the two burning buildings.

It took another few minutes for them to cross the stream and both women leaped from the wagon as the draft horse came to a stop, foam lathering her sides as she gasped for breath.

Fallon was running back and forth between two still forms in the dirt screaming. "Mama! Papa!

They're *dead*! They *killed them*!" He ran in circles between the two pulling at his hair in despair as Heather and Orlagh raced to the bodies, but before they could reach him, he dashed off behind the homestead, his screams echoing off the cliffs around him.

"Fallon! Come back!" Orlagh yelled as Heather ran to her parents, throwing herself on the ground beside her mother after looking at her father in horror.

Liam was sniffing all around the area as Orlagh knelt by Orson and examined his body. He still clutched the shotgun that he'd tried to defend his home with. She counted at least five bullet holes in his chest and two more in his back. The huge godstone necklace and rings he had worn were all missing. One of his fingers had been cut off to get the largest of those rings.

Orlagh rose from Orson's body to cross the distance to Elizabeth where Heather clutched at her mother, sobbing uncontrollably. As Orlagh approached, Heather looked up and her eyes began to glow as she chanted.

Orlagh backed away as Heather rose to her feet and chanted her Mage's curse. The young girl walked in circles around the two dead bodies of her parents and stopped several times at different spots covered in boot prints.

Orlagh glanced at her brother and his signals told her each of those spots was where one of the murderers had stood. She followed the girl around the grounds of their destroyed home and picked up the scent of each man as she knelt to examine the ground where the boot prints were thickest.

Liam roared at the sky and ran in the direction Fallon had run off, while Orlagh stayed out of Heather's way as the grieving girl chanted her spell as she circled the grounds. In moments Liam came running back and collapsed just as the sun and moon touched the west and east horizons respectively and Orlagh felt the first twist of her body as the change came upon her.

Heather continued her chanting as Orlagh and Liam fell to the ground, their bodies twisting and wrenching them violently from one form to another.

Chapter 6

"You *fool*!" Jack Easton growled, then lost his composure and blasted his hired man in the mouth with a huge fist, the two godstone rings splashing blood from the man's nose.

"Aggh," he muttered in disgust, then bent to where his hired man had fallen to the floor and wiped his hand clean on the man's shirt.

He stormed around his desk and gripped the edge in anger while Abe Harper rose shakily. "I thought I told you to make *damned sure* you killed all four of them *at the same time*, especially the two gods-damned witches!"

"The girl and the tinker weren't there and when Richards pulled the hammers back on his double barrel the boys had to protect themselves," Harper whined as blood flowed freely down his face. "Then the half-breed's squaw mother started chanting and we had to do her before she hexed us."

He brightened. "But we got *all* the godstone *and* the steam tractor. Gods boss, you should see how much we got! If people knew that fat farmer had so much somebody else would have kilt them a long time ago."

Easton fumed, but he had to admit Harper was right. The tractor alone was worth what they risked and all the godstone ingots and raw nuggets were several times more than what he was told the homesteader had.

"What about the big piece?"

Harper beamed through his bloodied face. "It took all of the boys to get it on our wagon, boss. I swear it weighs more than five men."

Jack doubted that, but several locals insisted the original piece was as big as a draft horse and if the ingots were all from the original then the stories just might be true.

"Did you at least clean the place up before you left? If the half-breed is as good a mage as the locals say, then she'll be able to follow you here."

Harper's eyes grew wide. "We picked up all the shell casings like you told us and burned everything down."

He reached up to touch his busted nose and Easton's face grew fierce as he pointed. "What the fuck is that?"

Harper smiled as he looked at the large ring on his finger. "It's a beauty, in't? Had to cut the fat bastard's finger off to get it. Chose this as part of my share and gave the other rings to each of the boys. That big gaudy pendant we saved for you. It's in the bag with the nuggets."

Easton snorted and shook his head. "You're not just a damned fool, Harper, you're a *dead* fool walking."

"Wha?"

"*You let the girl live you brain addled idiot,*" he snarled venomously. "She's a Native trained mage and that," he pointed, "was taken from her murdered father and mother."

Harper's eyes grew wide and he tried to take the ring from his finger. "It won't come off!"

"Well that cuts it," Easton snorted. "The witch has already found her parents and hexed the rings. Now she can follow you wherever you are." He laughed aloud. "You *might* be able to throw her off if you cut your own finger off and ship it to the other side of the world, *with* the ring."

Harper thrust his hand behind his back. "That's my gun hand! I can't cut my own finger off my *gun* hand!"

Easton chuckled and shook his head at the stupidity of wearing a ring on your gun hand. "Then I guess you've only got two choices. Either go kill that girl quick before she can come after you or run as fast and as far as you can, and don't stop very long at any one spot for the rest of your life."

Easton turned toward the silent man in the corner. "Shane, find out which ones of these dead men walking is wearing one of those rings, pay them off with a full month's pay and get them out of here within the hour. Maybe they'll draw her away from us. Then burn everything they've touched, including the bunkhouse and everything in it."

"Boss?" Harper whined.

Easton glared at Harper. "You and your boys have one hour to get your things together and start running as fast and as far as you can. If I catch any one of you in a day's ride away from me *ever* again, I'll have you burned alive. *Now get out of my sight before I change my mind and kill you where you stand!*"

Harper started to put his hand on Easton's enforcer and Shane Gibbs pulled his pistol quicker than the frightened man could move. "Touch me you hexed idiot and I'll blow your brains out."

Several minutes later Shane returned just as Easton finished stuffing the last of his important papers into a bag. "They gone?" At his man's affirmative nod, he sighed. "Should have sent you instead of *those* damned fools. We might not have the godstone yet or the homestead but we wouldn't have to cover our tracks like we have to now. Have some of the boys spread the word that only Harper and one other man were supposed to go out to the homesteader's place and just to make an *offer* to buy. Give 'em some silver to buy drinks with for their story tellin'."

"Yes sir."

Before he could leave, Easton asked, "Is Firecloud still nearby?"

"Yes sir," came the raspy reply. "He's purging the scent from the tractor and the ingots. He claimed the necklace medallion and cut Lefty's finger off for him and claimed the ring *and* the finger, too."

Easton's eyes widened, then narrowed. "So, he's already challenging the witch?" At his man's nod, Easton snorted. "Well, at least he knows what he's up against." He chuckled. "I'd sure like to see *that* duel, from a distance of course."

Shane Gibbs made no comment, but he wasn't fool enough to want to stay anywhere close to dueling Native mages.

"But no matter what we might want," Easton corrected himself, "can't take any chances. Tell him to melt the medallion and ring too if he rides out with us. I don't want that witch having a way to track us. If he wants to challenge her tell him to stay and do it and catch up to us later when she's dead. He can do with the boy what he wants."

"Regardless of what he does I want everything purged and loaded in my train and I want us on the way back to Albuquerque by midnight," Easton kept stuffing papers into the bag as he continued giving orders. "I want as much distance between us and this end of the rail as we can get till this thing is settled and the witch and her brain addled brother are dead."

He started to leave, then added, "Have some of the boys, *ones you can trust to follow orders*, burn this building down just before sunrise. Tell them to make sure they aren't seen. They can catch up to us later when the supply train returns for more rail and workers to replace the ones that deserted or dropped dead."

"Yes sir."

Easton left the building and hurried to his train and his private car.

"Evenin' Mr. Easton," the guard said as he approached.

Easton ignored the man as he mounted the stairs and unlocked the door. He threw the bag with his salvaged papers onto the floor and lit a gas lamp, then pulled the shades down on all the windows to keep prying eyes from seeing inside. He lit the rest of the lamps before heading to the bar and pouring himself a double shot of brandy. He was on his second glass when the knock came. There was only one man with that distinctive knock.

"Come, Mr. Gibbs!"

The bodyguard came inside and his eyes swept the car's interior despite knowing Easton was alone. Easton smiled. That was one of the things he liked about the former Pinkerton man. He *never* took anything for granted and was *always* alert to the unexpected.

In fact, most of Easton's best men were former Pinkertons. Men who had crossed the security organization by failing one of the ridiculous items on *the list* Allan Pinkerton made as his rules for his detectives.

Easton's list was much shorter. Do what he said when he said it without question or hesitation, and keep their mouths shut about anything they might see or hear. It was short and simple, and those that failed to do so were dealt with by Gibbs or Firecloud.

Those who worked for him preferred to have Gibbs deal out punishment because at least then there was a *much* better chance they would live. And if not, their deaths were quick and relatively painless. Firecloud's punishments tended to last for days and resulted in grisly trophies that were displayed openly by the dark mage as a reminder to the rest of Easton's men.

Easton didn't need to say anything as he sipped at his brandy.

"All is ready sir," Gibbs reported after he'd assured himself his master's abode was secure. "Firecloud has completed his magery and the cargo cars are secure. The men not on duty are in their bunk car and the fuel tanker is full of water and the locomotive is building steam. We should be in motion," the car lurched, "any second."

"Good, good, Mr. Gibbs. You are officially off duty. Would you like a drink?"

Gibbs's eyes narrowed. It was drinking too much lost him his position with the Pinkertons. That and his tendency to kill the prostitutes he purchased when he couldn't perform drunk. That would not be a problem now. "Yes, sir. One before I turn in."

Easton smiled. "One it is then." He held out his empty glass. "Pour me another while you're at it, then send that new girl up here so I can break her in for the boys." He liked rubbing the one failure in his security man in Gibbs's face whenever he had the chance and smiled sweetly as he held his glass out to be refilled.

Gibbs was already committed so he poured a small shot for himself and a double for Easton, then waited patiently while Easton swirled the brandy contemplatively as he gazed at his glass. Gibbs waited till Easton sipped, then chugged his short shot and stood.

"With your permission, sir," he said as the short train began to move slowly down the side track and back toward Albuquerque.

Easton waved dismissively. "Of course." And his man exited through the rear door.

As the train rocked when it turned onto the main track the door opened and a young girl of no more than twelve entered the car. Easton's heart raced as he thought, *"So young. So vulnerable."*

He smiled and drained his glass of brandy. "Hello my sweet. Come here and let me show you the tenderness you will never see again."

Chapter 7

This change was worse than most and it was nearly midnight before Liam could rise. He struggled to his knees to see Heather collapsed on the ground between her dead parents. Off to the side his sister was still tangled in her clothing, panting with the exertion of her own *change*.

He rolled to his knees and flinched as he hurt all over. He wondered if it was the magery that Heather had spread as she chanted her curses and the *seekings* that she'd crafted in her grief that caused this change's difficulty. Or was it just another addition sent by the original source to torture his victims more?

Liam struggled to his feet and staggered to the stallion that was calmly resting near the draft horse in companionship with his own kind. Both horses stood patiently waiting to be attended to by their human friends.

Naked, he checked his sister first, then untangled her from her clothing before going to retrieve his own. She finally rose to pad off into the cliffs before he was dressed and went to check on Heather.

He approached slowly to make sure he would not startle her into a defensive reaction that could cost him his life. "Heather. Heather, its Liam. You haven't met me in human form yet. Orlagh is in puma form now and went to find Fallon. He's still missing. Heather, we need to find your brother."

Liam sighed deeply. "Heather, *please*, we need to find Fallon to make sure he's safe and we need you to help us."

Heather's eyes flew open and Liam surged backwards as her eyes *glowed* and she sat up in an instant.

"Liam?" she gasped. "I *hexed them!*" Her glowing eyes dimmed and she smiled a smile that scared him. "I know where they are!" Then more softly. "I can find them, anywhere, anytime."

Her eyebrows creased. "And *HE* is with them! I swear on my parents graves he will pay for what he has done to help those that killed my mother and father!"

"Oh, I hurt all over," she gasped, then shook her head to clear it. "Fallon!"

"He ran off that way," Liam pointed toward the cliffs behind the homestead.

Heather smiled. "He probably went to his secret place. His caves. We both have our own. He'll be safe there."

Then her eyes grew wide. "Orlagh didn't go after him, did she?"

"After she *changed*."

Heather sighed. "She should be okay then, as long as she doesn't push him." She smiled. "If you haven't noticed, he *really likes* kitties."

His chuckle burst out. "Yeah, I noticed."

Her smile warmed his heart like he couldn't believe, then she groaned again. "Oh, I hurt all over."

He chuckled again. "You *did* go into the longest and most intense mage trance I've ever seen without a really long preparation." Then his face fell and he looked around at the burned and smoldering homestead and the two bodies nearby. When he looked back at her the smile was gone and her face was clouded again.

They gazed in each other's eyes for a few heartbeats, then both looked away and rose to their feet and looked at the destruction around them. The house and barn were burned to the ground and all that remained around the stone foundations and first floor half walls was smoldering coals and rising smoke.

And the two bodies.

Liam tried not to console the young woman as she silently wept. After a few moments he bent to Orson's body and gently closed his new friend's eyes, then he moved to Elizabeth's body. He gritted his teeth in anger as he saw she had been hit by several times more bullets than her husband.

Those who killed the two knew she was the more dangerous and her body was riddled by dozens of bullets and several shotgun blasts. One hand, the one she most likely raised to curse her attackers, had been blown from her body just above the wrist and half of her face was gone.

By the looks of the body several attackers continued to blast away at her as she lay dead on the ground. If he hadn't gotten a clear scent of her in life there was no way he could have recognized her in death. He gritted his teeth in anger as he and Heather prepared her parents for their graves.

The sun was halfway to noon before they had the two bodies prepared, and the graves dug beneath the apple tree where the family traditionally held their close picnics.

They lowered the two bodies into the ground, then Heather sighed. "We need to find my brother before we finish this."

Liam looked at her without saying anything as he leaned on the new shovel they'd brought back from their trip to Winslow.

She closed her eyes and sighed deeply, then looked him in the eyes. "Fallon needs to see them one last time before we cover them."

"Is that wise?" Liam said softly. "Can he take it?"

Heather sighed again. "He's stronger than he looks, than he acts. And he *needs* to see what those animals did to our parents so he can deal with them like they *need* to be dealt with when we catch up to them."

Liam didn't comment. It was not his place to tell her how *her* family dealt with those that killed their parents. He had enough problems dealing with how his own two brothers had died in the War Between the States, one supporting each side, and both too young to know what they were *really* fighting for.

That and the curse his family now suffered.

He waited and after a few minutes she spoke again, "He'll be in his secret place, the caves west of here, about three miles." She sighed as she shaded her eyes from the sun, then looked at him. "I just hope Orlagh knew enough to not push him. Under the circumstances he could be as dangerous as those that did this," she gestured toward the unfilled graves.

Liam remained silent and Heather sighed again. "We'd better go find him."

The stallion didn't have one but Liam removed the surviving draft horse's bit so the mare could graze easier, then they set out on foot. It was not a long walk before they came to some cliffs where they found Orlagh resting under a tree in front of a cut in the layered stone.

She rose as they approached and made some motions that Liam translated, then pointed as Orlagh trotted ahead. "He's in a cave a couple hundred feet that way."

Heather smiled. "You two can talk pretty well between beast and human form, can't you?"

Liam snorted. "Kind of like the finger talk the deaf use," he said with a smile. "Just without fingers."

She smiled but it quickly died as she nodded her head. "I'll have to learn it if you stay with us for our revenge."

Liam swallowed as she turned away to walk toward Fallon's cave. Did he *want* to join them in seeking their revenge? He and Orlagh had only spent a couple of days with them and they had their own quest to complete.

Without answering he followed her into the gully that split the cliffs.

It was only moments later he heard the weeping and a few steps after that they found Fallon wrapped around Orlagh as he cried his misery into her fur. It was several minutes later before Fallon released his grip around the puma and wrapped his arms around his own sister's neck and cried till he could cry no more.

When he finally released his sister, Liam picked the boy up and carried him the few steps to the mouth of the cave he called his *secret place*. Stepping into the cave, it took several heartbeats before Liam's eyes adjusted to the dark, and he gaped in wonder.

The cave was not that big, but it was a tinker's paradise. The walls were covered with shelves and each one was littered with tinkers' machinery parts and completed gadgets of every imaginable kind. Liam could recognize some, but most were beyond his ability to identify.

One shelf contained replicas of birds of every kind while another was covered in dozens of metallic insects, both flying and walking kinds and some Liam was sure never existed in the real world.

Several of them whirred and moved and focused glass eyes upon him as he stood gaping at their wonder. More than one poised dangerous looking talons or stingers in readiness for defense or attack.

Three insects and a bird began to hum, then whirred and their wings fluttered and they lifted from their perches.

Liam took a step back with the weeping child in his arms, but Heather spoke a phrase and waved a hand that caused the tinker toys to settle back to their perches. Liam noticed none of them turned themselves off as their eyes followed Fallon's every movement.

After a few heartbeats he stepped further into the cave and found a place to sit as he cradled the child and rocked him. After a few minutes Fallon lifted his red face from Liam's wet shirt. "Mama and papa are dead. Why? They didn't hurt nobody. What did they do to be killed?"

Liam's thoughts went back to the war that killed his two younger brothers. One fought for the north against slavery while the other fought for the injustice of mechanical over forced manual economics. No bodies were ever identified but neither had returned home after the war ended and both were listed as dead.

Now the nation spread west and both versions of economics competed with each other. Men still toiled till they died and the mechanics of industry advanced at a rapid pace, spurred by the competition of war and profit.

Coal was giving way to gas and gas to the wonders of steam power fueled by water cracked to hydrogen and oxygen, but it was still steam power that drove the world. Even with the wonders that tinkery and godstone and magery provided, it still took the muscles of men to break the way.

Where black slaves had been freed by the victory of the north over the south, now the native red man and the yellow man from across the Pacific broke their bodies to advance the technology that advanced the European white man's search for power and money. The black man was free, but that freedom was tenuous and the economic distinction between whites and the other three groups was still evident to any with eyes to see.

And it was the wondrous metals that fell from the sky, godstone, that fueled that greed for money and power. The white man had a leg up on that search for power, but it was a struggle that was equalized by the metals that fell from the sky without concern for whose land it fell upon.

Liam's memories dictated his answer. "They didn't *do* anything wrong except to have something evil people wanted for themselves. Evil, greedy people that wanted something someone else had, so they *took* what they wanted." His arms clenched around the quivering body in his arms. "Evil, greedy people who killed your mama and papa because it was easier to *take* what they wanted than to…"

He stopped as he thought about what he was saying. It was no different than the mage that cursed his family to obtain Puma Island by having others kill his family when in beast form to get their island. Those that killed Orson and Elizabeth were no different than the mage that cursed his family.

He grasped the young boy by the shoulders and held him at arm's length as he looked him in the eyes. "Fallon. The men that killed your mama and papa will pay for what they did. I pledge to you I will help you find *every one of them* and make them pay."

He gazed around the cave at the level of the mind that could tinker such wonders he saw on every shelf that lined the cave's walls.

"Fallon, I give you my word I will help you and your sister find those that killed your parents and bring them to justice." He looked around the cave at the wonders created by a mind that surpassed the abilities of any tinker he had ever known. "If you agree to help me, we will bring these men to justice."

He looked over at Heather and the puma that was his sister. "Are the two of you with us? Will you seek out this evil? Will you help us rid this world of those that would kill innocent people to steal wealth to gain power over others?"

Heather looked down at the mountain lion she had a hand on the shoulder of, and then back at Liam. "Only if that seeking starts with those that killed my parents *first*. After we bring *them* to justice my brother and I will continue to help you bring justice to others like them."

She looked at her brother. "Do you agree, Fallon?"

Fallon stood tall and confident for the first time since Liam and Orlagh had met him. "Yes!" Then he whistled a few notes, and several of the tinker toys on the shelves around them whirred and came to life.

Firecloud staggered, then lashed out and the nearest guard gasped and clutched at his throat, gasped again, then fell to the floor of the train car's stoop, blood streaming from his mouth and ears. His body twitched and shuddered for several moments before lying still.

"What the hell?" Gibbs exclaimed as he gaped at the Native whose face showed the first signs of fear he'd ever seen. "What the hell was that all about?"

Firecloud took several deep breaths, then regained his composure. He kicked the dead body over the rail and the train continued on. Taking another deep breath, he turned black eyes on the former Pinkerton man. "*Never* tell anyone what you just saw and I will allow you to live!" Then he stormed into the private car that held his and Gibbs's private quarters.

Gibbs leaned on the rail to look over the side and back at where parts of the mangled body of the dead guard tumbled out from under the wheels of the private train. "Gods! Now I'm going to have to wake another guard to finish this watch!"

Chapter 8

When the sun rose over the eastern horizon Liam was placing the last stone around the cross at the head of Elizabeth's grave. It was another full day after the massacre and the fire had finally consumed the last of the house and barn, leaving only smoldering ash inside the stone. The other draft horse died in the barn and the only thing standing was the lower half of the house – where Orson had used heavy boulders – and the sturdy chimney. The rest burned completely as had the entire barn.

Heather and Fallon stood nearby in silence as they watched Liam finish the graves. Liam looked at them and couldn't believe the changes he saw. Where both had been happy and full of life only a day earlier, now they burned with a veneer of grief barely covering contained anger and resolve.

Heather was composed but he could see the glow in her eyes as she silently chanted her *seeking* spell.

The change in Fallon was more pronounced. His happy, carefree innocence was gone. In its place was a focused intensity that scared Liam.

The tinker's machinery that surrounded the boy scared him even more. A small metallic owl perched on one shoulder, while an insect that didn't exist in nature perched on the other. It was almost as large as the owl and sported a stinger that was as long as Liam's pinky finger.

Several other mechanical insects and birds perched on tree limbs and fenceposts nearby. A couple of them leaked steam from old, cracked gaskets, but all of them hummed smoothly and quivered with anticipation. Several others scampered nearby on four, six, or eight legs, one of them a scorpion almost as large as a coyote, the stinger a revolver with six shots.

He rose from the graves and turned toward the others. "Ready?"

Heather nodded, turned and pulled herself up on the loaded wagon. Fallon simply turned and walked away heading down the path that led to the nearest road. In seconds Orlagh padded up beside him and paced herself to his steps. After a couple dozen feet, he hopped up on the wagon beside his sister as the wagon passed him, then let out a series of whistles.

Immediately all of the mechanical devices not already stored on the wagon ran or flew to him and found a perch somewhere near his seat.

Liam shook his head sadly then mounted his horse, patting the stallion's neck. "Okay, Trouble, let's see if we can make those that killed our friends pay for what they did."

Trouble snorted and threw his head in apparent agreement, then followed the wagon.

When they came to Winslow, they noticed several people running for cover as soon as they were recognized. Liam particularly noticed the ones that *didn't* run but walked with purpose. A pair of those paralleled them as they moved down the street, then stopped and one kept an eye on them while the other ducked into the saloon.

Several boys started to follow the wagon and began collecting stones but scampered for safety when they saw Fallon's face. Billy Johnson came into view and sneered as he bent to pick up a rock. He didn't see the mechanical bug lift from Fallon's shoulder and fly in a circle around behind him, but Liam did.

"Fallon," Liam said as he brought Trouble up beside the wagon. When the young boy turned his clouded eyes toward him, Liam simply shook his head minutely and said softly, "Direct your anger elsewhere."

Fallon glared a moment then lowered his eyes. "Yes, sir."

Liam smiled as Fallon gave a measured whistle and the stinger bug flew a circle back to the wagon.

"Hey dummy!" Billy Johnson yelled then drew his arm back to throw.

Just then Orlagh rose from where she'd been lying behind the bench seat and let out a fierce puma roar. Billy dropped the stone and turned to run, running straight into a hitching post and flipping head over heels and landing on his back. Rolling on his stomach and thrusting his hands against the ground, he rose quickly, banging his head on the hitching post and falling flat on his face.

Fallon started to laugh, stopped, then looked at Liam and smiled. When Liam nodded approval, he put his arms around Orlagh's neck and whispered his thanks.

Heather steered the wagon to the front of the blacksmith's building and set the brake just as

Lucas Washington came out of the large front door wiping his hands on his leather apron. His eyes went to the large load on the wagon and the determined faces of the four of them then back and forth between Liam and the puma of a different color than the one he'd met.

He kept silent as Liam dismounted and handed Trouble's reins to Fallon when the boy jumped down to the ground. Fallon led Trouble to the water trough while Liam introduced himself, then spoke softly with the blacksmith.

Lucas's eyes grew sad as Liam recounted the deaths of Orson and Elizabeth, then he turned and bellowed. "Micah! Come out here boy!"

Micah came through the wide doors with a horseshoe hammer in his hand. "Yeah pa."

"Close the shop and show Miss Heather around back, then take care of these folks' horses. Tell yer mama that we'll have company for the night."

"Yes sir," Micah replied and did as he was told.

Just then a scruffy looking man with an axe handle for a cane came storming up with the sheriff and Billy Johnson in tow. He pointed at Orlagh sitting tall behind the wagon's bench seat. "That animal attacked my boy sheriff. I want it caged till the magistrate gets here, then I want it destroyed!"

Liam nodded to the sheriff. "Sheriff." At the man's return nod, Liam continued, "Kind of hard to attack a boy thirty-feet away while sitting in a wagon."

The sheriff turned to look at the accuser. "That true Hyrom?"

Hyrom turned to glare at his son. "Boy?" When Billy flinched and cowered, Hyrom backhanded him. "You lie to me boy?" Then he turned and glared at Liam, lifting his axe handle cane threateningly. "We don't much like yer kind 'round here animal man. I'm gonna let this go fer now, but you mark my words, watch yerself or I'll have me a big cat pelt fer a floor mat!"

"Brave words for a man who beats children and carries a big stick," Liam said softly, then sniffed openly. "Smells like you had a whiskey breakfast for courage to back up big words."

Hyrom sneered. "Drop that iron and let's see if I c'n teach ya some manners animal man."

Liam looked at the sheriff, who smiled, shrugged, and stepped back. "Man makes a challenge, another man might need to accept or back down. Not my concern as long as the fight's fair."

Liam knew what the sheriff meant. The axe handle just *might* even out a fight between a normal man and a changeling. He nodded and unbuckled his gunbelt. Knowing exactly what he was doing, he turned his back on Hyrom as he handed his gunbelt to Lucas.

He was ready and when he sensed the belligerent man swing, rolled forward as the axe handle hit him across the shoulders.

"Not so tough, are ya, animal man?" Hyrom sneered as Liam rolled and stood slowly just out of reach, then swung again.

Liam stepped into the swing, grabbed the axe handle and twisted it to ram it into the man's stomach, once, twice, then wrenched it from his grasp as Hyrom fell to his knees gasping for breath. Billy turned and ran.

He glared at the man for a second then snorted as he handed the stave to the sheriff. "In my experience, bullies do what they do because they've been bullied, usually by bigger bullies." He bent low to glare in Hyrom's face. "That would be *you* Mr. Johnson. I'm going to give you some advice you probably won't take. Quit drinking your breakfast and see if you can be a better father to your boy so he grows up to be a better man than you're teaching him to be."

He straightened and nodded to the sheriff. "Sheriff, we done here?"

The sheriff smiled. "Yeah, we're done." Then he lent a hand to the gasping man. "Come on Hyrom, let's go get you some coffee and a lunch you can chew.

Chapter 9

"I can't accept that!" Lucas declared as they sat on the stoop of his cabin behind the blacksmith shop, their chairs separated by a small table with a pot of tea and two mugs. "It's too much even if the land wasn't covered with godstone."

Heather shook her head. "We've already collected all the biggest pieces on the surface and Fallon has had his tinker toys scouring the property for the past couple of years picking up every nugget not buried. There's more, sure, but not as much as some people might think."

"Still, I can't let you just *give* it to me. It just ain't *fair*."

Heather sighed. "Mr. Washington, Fallon and I are heading east to bring justice to those that killed our family. It could be years before we come back if we even live that long. We would rather have someone we know have our place than let scavengers fight over it."

Lucas looked at Heather, then at Liam for help. Liam shrugged a shoulder noncommittally.

Lucas snorted. "No! I can't just *take* it for free. I'll make you an offer. I'll *trade* you a bigger wagon and additional supplies to fill it properly *and* another draft horse so you got a pair, to *watch* your land for you and I'll put half of every ounce of godstone we find in escrow for you for *when* you return."

Heather looked at Liam, then nodded. "But only for two years, then if we don't return it's all yours."

Lucas shook his head. "Five years and you have to send a letter a month to keep us informed on your," he smiled, "*progress*."

"Three years."

"Four."

Heather shook her head. "Three. Any longer and either we'll be dead or we're not coming back anyway."

Lucas scowled. "Okay, three years and half the godstone we mine. But you'll send a letter every month and you have to wait at least three days for me to make sure the wagon is done right."

It was Heather's turn to scowl. "Three days and the murderers will be scattered all over the country."

Lucas glanced at the talisman hanging from her neck. "We both know ain't none of them getting away from you, girl. And if you go running off unprepared there's more of a chance they'll get you before you get them. Your mama was the best mage I've ever met next to you and she couldn't stop them 'cuz she wasn't ready. Three years and you have to send a letter saying you're *not* coming back and we write the papers up to say that."

Heather scowled for a moment then spit in her hand and held it out. "Done."

Lucas didn't hesitate, spitting in his palm and holding it out. "Done!"

They shook and rose from their chairs as Lucas spoke, "You'll find a couple of those you're looking for in the saloon and a few more out at the rail head's construction site." He snorted. "Course, you probably already knew that."

Heather smiled and touched the talisman at her neck, then looked at Liam.

"Right," he said, "let's get started."

He looked at Fallon. "Can you stay with Lucas and help him while your sister and I go take care of business?"

Fallon looked like he was going to object, then Lucas nudged him. "Going to need you, boy." Then he smiled and winked. "Got to make sure the wagon is built right."

Heather's eyes narrowed but Liam had already turned to go and she had to hurry to catch up. They cut through the blacksmith shop and headed straight for the saloon just as the sun touched the horizon, Orlagh padding just behind.

When Liam pushed through the hanging doors the barkeep looked up from wiping the countertop. He jabbed a finger and hollered, "We don't allow yer kind in here! Get out afore I call the sheriff!"

Liam looked down at his sister and she huffed and walked out to stand just outside the door.

The barkeep glared at Liam for a moment, then at Heather, but wisely said nothing more as several patrons chugged their drinks and slunk out of the door – making sure to give the puma outside plenty of room. Others moved away from a trembling man at the end of the bar.

Heather headed directly toward the cowering man as Liam scanned the room for other dangers before following.

Lefty looked left and right for support, then chugged the whiskey on the bar in front of him, poured the glass full from a nearly empty bottle and chugged it as Heather came up next to him. Then he shut his eyes and waited to die.

Heather reached out and lifted the quivering man's right hand to look at the old scars where he had lost his pinky and ring finger years ago. A bloody bandage covered the stump of the middle finger, leaving just the thumb and forefinger intact.

Lefty almost swooned at the touch.

"So," Heather crooned, "that's why they call you Lefty." Then she dropped the hand and reached over to pour another drink in the empty glass. "Tell me, Lefty, you got something that belongs to me?"

Lefty shook as he looked her in the eyes, then he grabbed the glass and downed it in one gulp. With shaking hands, he poured another drink and stared at the glass and shook.

Liam heard a click and looked in the mirror behind the bar to see a man on the second floor aiming a carbine. He snatched his pistol from its holster and fired one shot.

All eyes went to the man on the landing whose face looked surprised, his carbine fired into the ceiling as he tumbled forward and fell, landing on his back on a card table. Cards and coins went flying as the table shattered and the men at the table jumped up or fell backwards in their chairs. The man gasped once as a trickle of blood dripped from between his eyes then he exhaled his death rattle and was still as several other patrons scampered through the door to safety.

Lefty reached out to grasp the whiskey glass with a hand so shaky he spilled more than half before downing the rest. Then he reached into a pocket and pulled out a pouch that jingled with the sound of metal and held it out.

Heather smiled and took his left hand in hers, plucking the pouch away and tucking it in a pocket. "Thank you," she whispered, then she kissed Lefty's left palm, whispered a few words and blew softly on his fingertips.

Lefty gasped and clutched his hand to his chest a moment, then held it out to see all five of his fingertips turning black.

"The black will reach the hand in a day if you don't cut the fingers off and the wrist in another day if you don't cut off the hand. It'll reach the elbow in another two days and the shoulder two more after that," she smiled and reached out to empty the bottle into the glass. "If you wait till then you won't have anything else to cut off. I think we're even. Goodbye, *Lefty*."

Then she turned to go just as the sheriff burst through the saloon doors. He looked at the dead body tangled in the shattered table, then at Lefty who was staring at his hand in horror. He looked at Liam with his smoking pistol hanging at his side, then at the barkeep and raised his eyebrows.

The barkeep looked at the sheriff, then at Liam, then at Lefty, then at Heather, then back to the sheriff. "It was a fair kill," he stuttered. "Bart was getting ready to ambush them from the second-floor landing," he pointed as the words tumbled out. "He's been bragging about killin' some homesteaders and spending more godstone than he's ever had since he came to town."

The sheriff walked over to the dead man and patted him down, pulling out a bulging pouch and looking inside. He pulled out a small godstone nugget and tossed it to a black-clad man standing to the side of the room. "This should take care of the body, gravedigger."

The man nodded and another man helped him haul the dead man away.

The sheriff walked over to Lefty and looked at his hand. "Better take care of that before it gets worse, Lefty."

Lefty reached out to take one last drink but his fingers couldn't grip the glass and it fell to the bar and spilled the last of his whiskey. He looked at his hand in increasing horror, then ran from the bar moaning in misery.

The sheriff shook his head and snorted in contempt, then handed the pouch of godstones to Heather. "This yours Ma'am?"

Heather nodded and accepted the pouch.

"You folks leaving soon?" he asked as Liam exchanged the empty casing for a new cartridge then put his pistol back in its holster.

"Three days," Liam replied.

"You staying at the blacksmith's place the whole time?"

"Got some business at the railhead first thing in the morning while Lucas gets things ready for us to head east."

The sheriff nodded. "That should take most of two days. Would appreciate it if you take your time coming back so you're not in town long enough for hotheads to get ideas about causing the kind of mischief that gives the gravedigger more business."

Liam smiled. "I think we can manage that."

"Thank you for that," the sheriff sighed, gave Heather a respectful nod as he touched the rim of his hat. "Ma'am, your folks were good people. My condolences to you and your brother," then he turned and walked out of the saloon.

Chapter 10

"You have *got* to be kidding me," Heather fumed as she planted her hands on her hips, then slashed one hand toward the object under discussion. "You call *that* a wagon?"

Lucas looked at the *wagon*, then back at the young woman and shrugged. "Got wheels and it's pulled by horses, so yeah, it's a wagon."

Heather looked at Liam who tried unsuccessfully to hide his smile. Then she turned and glared at Lucas. "You expect two draft horses to pull *that*?" she pointed at the huge contraption.

It was a rail car, a *large* rail car. The two draft horses looked small in comparison. It had four equally huge wheels that looked bulbous and sturdy. The *wagon* looked like something that would need a thirty-mule team to pull.

"Well? Tell me how two horses are going to pull that?" Heather fumed.

Lucas bent down and pointed underneath. "Look there, it's a locomotive steam engine. There's another one between the rear wheels. When the horses pull, it engages the locomotives and *they* drive the wagon."

He stood up and beamed with pride. "Yer brother designed 'em and we built 'em in two days.

Heather looked around. "So where is the coal car?"

Lucas beamed wider. "Don't need coal, or wood."

Heather snorted. "Then what's it run on?"

Lucas laughed uproariously. "It runs on water!"

Heather glared at the big black man. "Of course it runs on water. All steam engines do. Everybody knows that. But what does it *burn* to make the steam?"

Lucas laughed heartily. "Water! It burns water to turn water into steam!"

He ignored the young girl's glare as he continued, "You know how the war made tinkers invent all kinds of war machines? Well, I was showing young Fallon a paper about a tinker from Ohio."

He looked at Liam. "You might have heard of him. Fella by the name of Edison."

Liam nodded. "Yeah, Samuel and Nancy's boy. I've met him. He's about my age. Has a young apprentice named Tesla said to be just as smart, if not more."

"Yeah, that's him. He invented all kinds of things to help the north free my people. One of his ideas people can only make with godstone, and turns water into gas that burns. I showed the paper to young Fallon and he said it was easy so I dared him to tinker one up for me and he did! Then we made three big ones and put two of them underneath your wagon to drive the wheels. I'm keeping the other one so I can use it to make more. Micah put the little one your brother made on a bicycle and drove it out to your place and back in under two hours on a half-gallon of water with about a half pint left over."

The big man rubbed his hands together and literally giggled. "Already got people in town wanting me to build motorized bicycles and wagons for them. Let me show you the inside!" He waved for them to follow him and climbed the stair at the front of the wagon.

Inside the smell of freshly sawed and polished wood assailed them.

"Lucas!" Heather started, but he cut her off.

"Don't worry Miss Heather. It's all already paid for," Lucas assured her, then hesitated. "Or will be as soon as we dig up some more godstone from your place. The carpenter is out there now with my boy prospecting for his pay."

He gestured at the opulent interior. "Most of this was already in the car I bought, and the rest only took a couple of days to finish." He chuckled. "And the railroad man I bought it from is out at your place with Micah digging up his own pay, just like the carpenter." He spread his hands, palms up. "So, *you* paid for it all fair and square."

He showed them the front sitting room with its small kitchen and freezer closet, then the two sleeping compartments in the middle third, one long thin cabin each for Heather and Fallon on either side with the narrow hallway down the middle as they walked back.

Heather took a breath to berate the big man but he put a finger to his lips. "Young Fallon stayed awake for over two full days while you were at the railhead dealing with those other murderers. He's only been asleep a handful of hours so we should probably try not to wake him."

Heather glared and Liam tried hard not to laugh aloud as Lucas continued the tour of the opulent *wagon*.

The rear third held boxes and crates of supplies and led to a small porch stoop that was large enough for all three of them to stand without crowding. Then he led them up onto the rooftop deck where more crates and bags of supplies were tied down under canvas tarps.

"Young Fallon wanted some curved hoops like Conestoga wagons use to hold up a canvas roof, only bigger," he pointed at one side. "There are the iron hoops and they attach at those frames there and there," he pointed again. "Have to buy the canvas tarp to cover the upper deck later."

He led them across the jumble of supplies to the front of the roof of the railcar wagon and back down to the ground where he showed them how the horses were hitched. "They don't actually *pull* the wagon. In fact, the wagon pushes *them*."

Heather's eyebrows creased and he laughed nervously. "Well, our deal included another draft horse so I couldn't very well go back on my word, now could I Miss Heather?"

Heather finally admitted defeat and laughed as her face went from disapproving to a warm smile at the tragic look on her friend's face. "Okeh! You were true to your word in every way. You told me a *bigger* wagon." She looked at the object in question and shook her head. "And it sure is bigger than what we came here in. And you *did* say another draft horse," she gestured, "and there she is."

She sighed deeply. "And you *did* say additional supplies to *fill* the new wagon *properly*." She glared at him. "I *am* tempted to change our deal despite the fact you *did* go a bit over what I expected, but I won't."

She shook her finger at him. "But you can bet that at the end of the three years I'll be sending a note to the bank that *finalizes* your ownership of *your* property."

He held his hand out tentatively and she slapped it aside and lunged forward to give him a fierce hug instead.

It only took him a moment to relax and hug her in return.

When they finally broke apart, she said, "Now, let's go to the bank and finalize the paperwork so we can get going to hunt down some murderers and get justice for my ma and pa."

It didn't take long and they were soon signing the last papers and shaking hands all around. Lucas left first as Heather signed more documents.

When the three of them came out of the bank it was to see the sheriff and four Pinkerton men coming toward them. Lefty cowered behind with his rotting left arm in a sling.

Orlagh snarled and moved to the side as Liam moved slightly away from Heather so they were not all three in a bunch.

"Sheriff," Liam said when the nine of them stopped in the middle of the street in a spread-out group.

"Miss Richards. Mr. Quinn." He looked at Orlagh and nodded. "Ma'am."

Then he looked Liam in the eyes. "These men are from the railroad. They have some questions for you about three of their former associates that seemed to have died out by the railhead."

Liam looked at the apparent leader of the group, but Heather spoke first, "They murdered my parents and stole valuable property. We went for justice and justice was served."

"That true?" the leader of the Pinkertons asked looking at Liam.

Liam nodded. "Yes sir. The three men in question admitted as much before we killed them and retrieved Miss Richards' stolen property."

"Any witnesses to this confession?" the Pinkerton man asked.

Liam looked at Heather then back at his questioner. "Not in front of anyone living to say except Miss Richards, my sister," he nodded at Orlagh, "and me."

Two of the Pinkerton men moved a few steps to the side while the leader spoke, "I'm sorry but we'll have to have more than that. We knew these men and they were not honest enough to remain one of us, but that don't mean they don't deserve justice."

Liam nodded toward the cowering man behind them. "You talk to Lefty yet?"

The Pinkerton man looked behind him at the wretch. "Said he might know something, but said he needed to talk to the mage first."

Liam looked at Heather as Lefty came forward hesitantly. She glared at the cowering man and said nothing.

"Please Miss Heather," he pleaded as he held out his rotting arm in its sling. Two of the Pinkerton men closest curled their noses and stepped away from the shivering man and the smell of rot from his arm. "I'll tell them everything but please. It's my only other hand. I don't want to cut it off. I done gave another finger to that Native mage and you got all my pay. I swear on the Lord's Name that I didn't put a bullet in your kin. I was in the barn getting the tractor. Please."

Heather pointed her chin at the Pinkertons. "Tell *them*."

The Pinkerton man turned toward Lefty and raised an eyebrow. "It's true sir. The three what were at the railhead were at the Richards place and kilt this girl's parents. I was in the barn and when I came out, they was all laughing and collecting trophies, rings and jewelry and such."

"They gave me a ring to keep quiet about the murders, but they's dead now and I'm not, and that Native has the ring and one of my fingers." He held up his bandaged right hand. "I got nuthin' left but my life," he gazed in horror at his rotting arm, the blackness halfway to his elbow, "and this."

The Pinkerton man nodded. "Okay, justice has been met." He tipped his hat to Heather. "Good day Ma'am." Then nodded to Liam. "Mr.?"

"Quinn," Liam replied.

The Pinkerton man looked at the sheriff. "Sheriff, if you want to return to your office, we can finish the paperwork and be on our way."

"Right this way," the sheriff said with a gesture, then turned toward Liam. "You said you'd be gone by today."

"Leaving shortly," Liam confirmed then jerked a thumb over his shoulder. "Miss Richards was just finishing some land ownership paperwork of her own before we left."

"Okay then," he tipped his hat to Heather. "Miss Richards, good luck with your search." Then he turned and followed the Pinkertons.

As they walked away Lefty approached with tears streaming down his face. "Please, Miss Heather. I done what you asked. Please?" He held out the rotting arm.

Heather looked at Liam then reached up and took the putrid arm gently in her hand and blew softly on it and whispered... and it was whole and healthy in a single heartbeat.

Lefty looked at it like he couldn't believe what he was seeing then broke down in sobs and collapsed to the ground. "Oh God, oh God, thank you Miss Heather, thank you so much." Then he curled around his whole arm and cried in gasping sobs as Heather marched toward the blacksmith shop.

Liam caught up with her in a few steps and paced quietly beside her.

She gave him a sideways look and smiled. "There was nothing wrong with his arm. It was all in his mind. If he'd cut anything off it would have stopped the curse, but if he didn't, he would have been sick as hell for a day after it reached his shoulder and woke up whole again, nothing more."

Liam stopped in the middle of the street and laughed. "It was an illusion?"

"It was an illusion," she confirmed with a devilish smile. "If he could have stood the sight and smell for a week he'd have been as good as new." She shrugged. "If he'd cut anything off above the curse before the end of the week, he'd have done it himself and lived with the choice."

"Now let's go get the rest of them so my parents can rest in peace."

Chapter 11

"Where are all of your tinker toys?" Heather asked as she and her brother sat on the padded seats behind the draft horses as they rode along the road beside the tracks. Liam rode Trouble a hundred yards ahead, Orlagh scouting out of sight.

Fallon shrugged. "Had to take 'em apart and melt down their godstone metal for the locomotive engines and the," he waved a hand negligently, "other things."

"Other things?"

Fallon smiled. "Yeah. Mostly the locomotive engines. The parts I needed to break the water down so I could burn it for fuel." He shrugged. "Couple other things, nothing important. I did keep some of my favorites." He whistled a few notes and an owl hooted from the top of the wagon behind them.

He perked up. "I was able to melt some of them down and make new ones using that invention Mr. Edison made."

"From what I hear, Mr. Edison only thought of it and *you* invented it," Heather suggested.

"Naw," Fallon insisted. "Lucas showed me papers that showed some already made, and that railroad man had one on his private train. There's not many of them, but enough I can't claim the *idea* as my invention." He smiled. "But I might be able to claim mine is better."

Heather nodded her agreement. "Yeah, Fallon, you're probably right. How is yours different?"

Fallon's eyebrows creased. "His is built into the steam engine's boiler inside the firebox and mine is inside a godstone pipe between the water tank *and* the boiler's firebox both so the boiler is smaller and lighter to get the same heat level. Makes the whole thing about half the weight for twice the power output."

Heather nodded as if she understood then gestured toward the draft horses. "You might want to pull back a little so you don't push the horses too fast."

"Oh yeah," Fallon said. "They do look like they're getting tired." He adjusted the lever he called a *throttle* and the wagon slowed enough the draft horses were able to slow to a comfortable walk. "You know," he mused, "I don't really think we need the horses except to steer."

His face bunched up in thought. "Maybe I could make a lever or a wheel or something like that to aim the wagon where we want to go. That might be better than, them," he gestured toward the draft horses.

Heather smiled. "I'm sure you'll figure out the best way, Fallon."

They sat in companionable silence for a few miles while they rode beside the finished railroad till they came to a small group of people camped. It looked like a small village was in the process of growing near the tracks and a crossing trail with a small stream nearby.

Fallon made some adjustments to the throttle and the rear locomotive cut out while the forward one cut power till they were moving at the pace of a man's slow steady walk. They passed through the camp where several large tents and the beginnings of a wooden building stood on the same side of the tracks as the road they traveled. As the sun set and darkness fell around them, they rolled on a couple hundred yards till they came to a gathering of wagons before they stopped.

Liam rode Trouble up as Fallon set the brakes and released the last of the steam from his locomotives and the draft horses huffed in relief.

Orlagh bounded up and leaped on the rear stoop, then from a water barrel to a support brace and up to the upper deck. Several people nearby looked around as if they were unsure what they'd just seen, then went about their business.

After a few minutes it seemed like many of them made a point to venture close to the railcar wagon to get a closer look. Orlagh made it a point to stay on the upper deck out of the way of curious eyes while Liam and Fallon tended the horses, then checked out the railcar wagon to see how it had fared on its maiden voyage.

Heather spent her time inside the wagon preparing a late supper while Fallon showed Liam the workings of their transportation.

"Those gaskets are wearing too hard," Fallon said as he pointed. "I think I might have to replace them every couple of weeks till we can get some of that new *vulcanized rubber* invented by Charles Goodyear before the War Between the

States." He pursed his lips. "In fact, I think it would be best if *all* our gaskets were made of rubber."

The boy looked at Liam for support. "What do you think Mr. Quinn? You think we can wire for sheets of rubber instead of using leather for gaskets?"

Liam made as if to think seriously as he stroked his chin. "Don't rightly know Fallon. I'm not as experienced as you are in this matter. You don't have much leakage with the leather you use, do you?"

Fallon copied Liam's chin stroke as he thought. "Leather works real good, but it wears out too quick. I read where rubber lasts a lot longer without cracking and leaking."

Liam smiled. "Then it sounds like this rubber this Goodyear fella invented might be better. Why don't we wire somebody to see if we can get some rubber sheets for gaskets and test them and see for ourselves if they're better or not? Seems to me the best way to find out is to test each and see which is better."

Fallon smiled broadly. "Sure sounds good to me!"

Liam nodded. "So, the next time we come to a telegraph station we send a wire and see what we can see."

Fallon smiled and lunged to hug Liam. Liam accepted the hug and when Fallon let go, he said, "So, what do we do about pushing the horses so hard they have to run till they sweat just to keep up with the wagon?" His face grew serious. "Not fair to the horses to make them run hard just to keep up."

Fallon's face mirrored Liam's serious look and he nodded. "You think we should run the locomotives slower, or should we just sell the horses and run the wagon at the speed it'll go?"

"Could do either," Liam replied. "We could go at the best speed the horses feel comfortable with, let them pull a little weight but not all, or we could sell them and run faster on your mageried locomotives."

He stroked his chin. "Course, if we sell the draft horses to go faster, then Trouble would have to run harder to keep up."

Fallon pondered that thought a moment. "Yeah. Course we could move supplies around and make a stall for Trouble on the back stoop of the wagon or on the top deck. That way he could ride and we could still sell the draft horses."

His face scrunched up. "But what if we can't get enough water to run the locomotives? We still have to cross the divide and we might need the horses to help us get across the steepest high passes."

Liam smiled as he acknowledged the young man's concerns. Concerns that many had neglected to their peril. "The good thing is, if we get caught in the snow we won't have any trouble getting water for the locomotives."

Fallon smiled broadly. "Yeah. Don't matter how deep the snow gets. Snow is just frozen water and it'll burn for heat and locomotive power all the same."

Liam smiled in return, then the two continued inspecting the wagon as Fallon taught Liam about the machinery of the locomotive.

Later in the evening Liam built a small campfire close to the wagon and several local campers joined them for drinks of free coffee and companionship.

"You folks heading up toward Denver?" one scraggly old man asked as he sipped at the coffee Liam provided. "I hear some men what feeling loose with godstone fer whiskey were headed that way."

Liam glanced sideways at Heather, who sat on the back stoop of the wagon away from the campfire but still within earshot. "We're going to Albuquerque to get around the south end of the Rockies where the passes aren't so high, but our main path leads us east."

The old man glanced in Heather's direction sitting in the dark just out of sight. "Mage don't need my rumors ta know where ta git her revenge. Just saying what the talk is in the whiskey tent."

Liam nodded and refilled the old man's coffee mug as he continued, "Fellers I hear about are following the railroad east same as you. Following that fancy private train what went through here a few days ago but going north after they get through the pass. Same as you most likely if yer mage tracks 'em up that way."

The old man sipped again at his mug. "Five of 'em by my count and all of 'em carrying enough guns fer twice that number. Looked ta be a couple of them long guns used in the war what shoot a man through the eye at near a mile away. Big tinker tubes on top ta see where ta shoot, both day er night."

Liam nodded and sipped his own coffee as another man spoke. "Fellers in a hurry, too. Ride faster than a wagon can roll. Won't catch 'em less'n they stop fer a couple days or more. Longer if'n they ride hard all the way ta Denver."

He looked at their wagon and gestured with his coffee mug. "Easy ta see you got railroad wheels on yer wagon and tinker engines underneath. Could catch 'em afore Albuquerque if ya got off'n da road. Hear dere's a fella in camp what got a small rail car ya c'n use ta haul yer horses. Feller wants ta head east but can't git his car hitched to a locomotive ta pull him."

The man snorted. "Damned railroad people don't like regl'r folks using their rails. Made him take his car off'n *their* rails. Threatened ta dump it on its side ta git it off'n the side rail even though it weren't in nobody's way. Folks in camp helped him take it off. Could be this feller could help ya catch yer murderers before they git too far 'head 'a ya."

Chapter 12

Liam sat beside Mason Phelps as their train rolled down the tracks faster than any horse could run. Ahead of them the supply train for the railhead west of Winslow grew closer as it moved slower than them.

Mason pointed his chin. "Railroad people don't much like regular people using their tracks, do they?"

Liam smiled and shrugged as they passed a caravan of Conestoga wagons headed westward. "Don't want regular folks using the roads they build beside their tracks, either, but that don't stop people."

Mason snorted. "Tried to charge wagon trains but a few dead folks on either side put a stop to that when Pinkertons refused to enforce their arrogance."

Liam nodded in agreement. Allen Pinkerton's security firm had some black marks when they backed big money against their own workers, but they didn't hold with those same big money people running roughshod over folks they didn't already own.

That was why Liam waited till a supply train went eastward before leaving the side rail and following. If they had come up on a train heading west, they would have had to back up or leave the track, but as long as they had a train in front of them heading the same way they were safe from Pinkerton justice.

"Pa, Ma says coffee's ready." They looked around to see Mason Jr. poking his head up through the trap door in their rail car. "Want me to bring it up to you?"

"No Jay-Ar," Mason replied, standing. "I'll come down." Then he looked at Liam as his son ducked back down into their car. "Want some coffee?"

Liam rose from his chair. "Yes, thank you. I should check on the horses too. Let me tell Heather."

He walked around where Orlagh lay dozing and walked to the front of the upper deck of the car and called down where Heather and Fallon sat at the controls. "Heather, Mason and I are going to the back car for a bit. I'll come back soon so you can visit with Mrs. Phelps."

"Okeh," Heather said with a smile then turned to Fallon. "I think I can handle things myself. Do you want to go back and visit with Jay-Ar for a while?"

Fallon brightened a little at that. He was still in the throes of his grief but he was young and had enjoyed the company of the younger boy in the few days they had traveled together. "Make sure this gauge here stays between those two marks," he pointed, "and let me know if this gauge here moves more than two marks either way."

Heather smiled tolerantly at her brother. "Okeh, now you go play."

"Okay, but we're not playing," Fallon said seriously. "I'm teaching him tinker things so he can help his Pa turn their car into a locomotive wagon like ours." Then he scampered up the ladder to run past Liam to join his new friend, stopping long enough to ruffle Orlagh's fur, then smooth it again before running across the upper deck and down to the Phelps' car.

Liam smiled after him then turned back to the boy's sister. "I'll come back to take the conductor's seat in a half hour or so."

At her nod he turned and followed Fallon at a more leisurely pace. He took the ladder down to the back stoop and stepped across to the Phelps' car where Mason waited, then the two entered the small half-car living quarters.

Mason Phelps purchased the fire-damaged car and cut away the half that had burned. The half that remained contained two rooms, a bedroom for the adults and a sitting room that doubled as a bunkroom for the children.

Liam and Mason passed through the bedroom and entered the sitting room where Patricia was pouring coffee. "Thank you, Mrs. Phelps," Liam said as he accepted the mug.

"You're welcome, Mr. Quinn," she replied. "Give me a moment and I'll take Pearl into the bedroom so you and Mason can talk."

"No, no," Liam said. "I need to check on the horses, so I'll take my coffee there."

She nodded and smiled, then gave her husband a peck on the cheek as she handed him a mug.

Liam opened the door and stepped out of the car's cabin onto the flat cargo deck of the altered rail car where the two draft horses and Trouble stood.

Mason had purchased the car back east and hitched a ride with a man driving a small locomotive delivering cargo up and down the rails from Texas through the New Mexico and Arizona Territories. Mason had dreams of doing the same but had yet to get his own locomotive working.

The partially completed steam engine sat at the front of the flatbed cargo half of the car, where Mason Junior and Fallon were huddled in noisy animation. The rest of the cargo deck around the three horses was cluttered with what cargo Mason commissioned as soon as he'd accepted Heather's offer of a pull eastward.

Liam drained his coffee and set the mug in a railed shelf on the wall of the cabin beside the door, then began cleaning the area where the horses were tied. He mucked the area behind them, sweeping the road apples over the side, then gave the animals fresh hay to eat.

Next, he checked to make sure all three were secure before brushing down each horse as he talked to them. Lastly, he gave each a dried apple and a carrot while Mason checked the rest of the cargo to make sure all the lines were secure. Finished, they moved to the end of the car where Jay-Ar and Fallon were working on the steam engine.

"How's it going boys?" Liam asked.

"Hi Mr. Quinn," Jay-Ar said as he looked up. "Really good. Fallon almost has this old steam engine working and he's taught me how to fix it if something breaks."

He held up a notebook. "I'm making a repair manual so I don't forget anything and so I can teach my Pa how to fix it too."

"Good idea," Liam replied with a smile as he accepted the manual. The pictures were rough, but easily interpreted and the notes were done in neat, precise letters. He handed the manual back to the boy. "By the time we get to Albuquerque you should have it up and running, then you and your Pa can go into business."

"Yes sir," Jay-Ar replied with a smile. "And Fallon says we can put big wheels on our car and turn it into a wagon like yours. Then we can go where we want so we don't have to be beholden to the railroad people for using their tracks."

Liam nodded. "That's a good idea."

He turned to Mason who shrugged. "First I heard of it, but yeah, it *is* a good idea." He looked at the boys working on the steam engine. "Maybe I should start training on this thing myself so I know what I'm doing."

"Well, if you're going to do that then I might as well relieve Heather at the controls so she can take a break and visit with your Missus."

Mason nodded and bent to listen as Fallon continued his work on the steam engine. Liam turned and retrieved the two coffee mugs and knocked on the cabin door before entering to thank Patricia for her hospitality. In moments he was sitting at the controls to the train car and Heather was heading back to the Phelps' car to visit.

A couple of hours later he smelled the odors of supper being cooked and soon after Heather brought him a steaming plate. She took the controls while he ate, then took his plate back to clean up while he returned to his driving.

After completing his evening chores Fallon joined Liam up front and they talked while they chased the railroad supply train eastward.

"That's a good thing you're doing for the Phelpses," Liam said. "Especially tinkering them that water fuel device."

Fallon smiled. "It only took four ounces of godstone and it'll free up lots of room for cargo so they don't have to carry so much coal or wood. And they can still carry a little bit of coal or wood if they run out of water to burn instead of what they have to have for the boiler."

The unnaturally serious boy shrugged again, and said, "They are helping us go faster without selling the draft horse, and we have plenty. Giving them a few ounces of godstone didn't cost that much for getting them free of the rails after they put some dirt wheels on their car."

Liam smiled warmly at the boy, then they sat and watched the rails go by as they drove eastward. An hour later the sky began to turn with the setting sun behind them and not long after they saw the lamps of the train ahead being lit. Minutes later Heather lit a couple of their own lamps inside their car's sitting room, the glow through the front windows just enough to let them see the area of the front stoop while not ruining their night vision for the track ahead.

Not long after that Mason came forward and took the driver's seat while Liam went to the upper deck to sleep. Heather took the mid-watch then Liam was driving when the sun cracked the horizon ahead of them. They ate breakfast together and an hour later they began to see the greater traffic on the road beside the tracks that indicated an increase in local population.

Heather and Fallon were up front and Liam was napping on the upper deck when they passed the first buildings. By the time Heather delivered lunch to Liam and Mason in the driver's seats there was always a building or wagon or some other sign of habitation in sight.

An hour after that Liam pulled their train off the main rail onto a side rail and they hurried to build the road wheels that would make the Phelps' car independent of the rails.

When the railroad supply train passed them heading west the next morning, they said their good-byes to their new friends. The Phelpses headed back west with another load of cargo and four road wheels hanging off the sides of their car. The steam locomotive pulled them along smoothly and they were soon racing after the supply train loaded with paid cargo.

Liam turned to look at Heather who was gripping the *seeking* talisman hanging from her neck and raised an eyebrow.

"They're close," she said. "*Real* close. I didn't say anything because we were helping Patty and Mason finish their road wheels, but they were here last night. Got here a couple of hours ahead of us. They're on the move now, heading north, probably to Santa Fe."

Her eyes flashed as she looked at him. "If we take the rails we'll beat them."

Liam pursed his lips. "Then we best get around town and see if we can get back on the rails."

Her smile held no hint of warmth, only the anticipation of the justice to come.

Chapter 13

It didn't turn out to be that easy. They were able to get to the side of town where the new rails led north, but a southbound train was scheduled so they couldn't take the rails yet.

They did decide to sell the draft horses and used one of Fallon's steam-foam hoists to lift Trouble up to the upper deck now they had used some of their supplies and delivered the small amount of cargo they'd agreed to carry. The southbound train was late and it was dark before they could transfer to the rails so they waited till the next day when that same train made its northward run.

"We should still beat them to Santa Fe unless they ride really hard," Liam said as they steamed along behind the northbound train.

They ran into more trouble when they came to a spot where their raised road wheels were still too low and wide to pass through a narrow section cut through the landscape. By the time they removed the wheels and stowed them on the upper deck, then put them back on where the cut widened again, they had to pull off on a side rail to wait for another southbound train to pass before they could continue.

"They've stopped," Heather informed him as she clutched her *seeker* talisman. Her smile didn't reach her eyes. "They have the feel of whiskey in their gullets."

Liam nodded. That meant they were planning on staying the night. "Maybe we should lower the road wheels and find us a place to set up off the rails."

Heather's mind was elsewhere so he got Fallon to help him lower the road wheels to lift the car off the tracks and they steamed off at a road crossing. By the time they skirted town and found a place to camp on the road toward Denver it was nearly dark.

"There!" Fallon said as the balloon swelled with the steam foam and the ropes tightened where they were attached to the sides of the upper deck. He turned the valve to shut off the steam as Heather chanted the last repetition then wiped the excess away and quickly screwed the cap over the opening.

They attached the balloon to the harness around Trouble's belly and Liam spoke softly to the stallion as Fallon held tight to the ropes tied to a stake pounded in the ground. In seconds they attached the balloon and it lifted Trouble a foot from the car's upper deck.

Heather smiled with satisfaction as the balloon bobbed. "I'm getting better at judging weights," she glanced at the mists leaking through the seams of the canvas balloon. "Even if we let Trouble fly free, he'll lose enough steam foam to touch down in fifteen, twenty minutes."

Liam smiled and winked at her, then loosened the ropes on the far side, pushed, and Trouble drifted sideways. When he was almost clear of the wagon Liam gave slack to the ropes on the near side. Then he grabbed hold of the sling and his weight pulled Trouble downward gently toward the ground while Heather let the secured rope feed out slowly and Fallon pulled from his position on the ground.

In seconds Trouble was on the ground and Fallon was releasing the valve that let the steam foam dissipate. He closed the valve and they let the balloon rise and in moments had lifted the saddle and the locomotive bicycle that Fallon tinkered over the past few days down to the ground.

"Fallon," Liam said, "there're only three of us. Your sister and I need to go into town to take care of business, but we *need* you to guard the wagon and you're all we have to do that. Can you accept that duty?"

Fallon's smile was innocent on the surface, then he gave a measured whistle and the owl on the rail above them hooted. He gave a different whistle and a wolf-sized mechanical scorpion scampered out from under the wagon and brandished the revolver on the end of its stinger tail and clicked its claws.

"I can accept you and my sister going after those that killed our Mama and Papa if you can accept I'll keep others from thinking they don't have to fear me if they come to plunder our wagon while you're away."

Liam pursed his lips to keep from smiling and nodded. "You have the charm Heather made for you?"

Fallon tucked a hand under the pendant hanging from his neck. "Anybody with bad intent comes close I'll know to hide and send my tinkerings to deal with them."

Liam nodded. "Good man."

Fallon's chest expanded with the confidence shown by the man he was coming to look at as the father he'd lost to evil profiteers. He nodded and gave several distinct whistles and several tinkerings nearby gave responding clicks and chirps.

Liam nodded in return then turned to Heather. "You ready?"

She started the locomotive cycle she straddled and it chugged with quiet efficiency as it built up steam. When the gauges reached the right spots, she looked up. "Ready."

Liam swung up into Trouble's saddle and nudged the stallion into motion. Seconds later Heather followed as the cycle built up enough steam to power the rear wheel.

The two of them traveled the couple of miles into town as the buildings grew thicker where a greater number of people congregated. As the tents on the outskirts of town changed into wooden buildings, then to stone and adobe mixed with wood, the number of people also increased.

Santa Fe was not as big as Albuquerque, but it was much larger than Winslow. Wagons and horses soon crowded the road through town and dozens of people walked the boarded walkways that lined both sides of the main street. Not many of them noticed Liam on his horse, but most were curious about the young woman that rode beside him on the steam powered bicycle.

As they made their way, Liam could *sense* the few that were shapeshifters like him. Most of those could tell he was like them but only a few could sense he was somehow different, *cursed*.

He could tell those few that had also crossed a mage that left them with their own differences. He ignored those that projected no animosity toward him, both changelings like himself and the bigoted full humans he was used to sensing after a lifetime of interactions and the charms he'd accumulated for just that purpose.

He kept an eye on Heather and when she steered her steamcycle toward a hitching post, he kneed Trouble in that direction. The stallion responded to the body language almost as if he read his rider's mind.

Liam swung a leg over the saddle and draped Trouble's reins over the horizontal post while Heather released the valve that let steam escape from her cycle, then closed the valve that fed water to the small steam engine. She then disconnected the short pipe that held the water cracking godstone tinkering, waved it in the air to cool it off, and tucked it into her shoulder bag.

After giving Trouble an apple and a carrot, Liam looked at Heather and she nodded toward the saloon across the street with the second and third floor rooms above. He nodded back and the two of them headed away from the building for a few dozen feet before crossing the street between the wagons and horses going both ways.

They went inside a General Store and Heather took his arm as they looked at some scarves and Liam bought her one that matched her hair. Liam tried on a hat but it was too big, then Heather bought a band for the hat he wore that was made of tiny beads in a Native design. Both paid with silver coins.

They exited the General Store and Heather grasped the talisman hanging from her neck as she whispered. "Three in the saloon. The other two have mage charms that are covering their location, but they're nearby." Her eyebrows creased. "One of those is on the move away but I can't tell which direction just that he's getting further away. Maybe getting into position for a long shot."

Liam nodded as they walked closer to the saloon. "Do we go in?"

Heather concentrated as she gave a silent chant. "The one is heading away but I still can't tell what direction and the other hidden one is still nearby but I can't tell exactly where. The three are in the saloon and close to each other."

Liam nodded as they continued down the boardwalk toward the saloon watching everybody in sight. When they came to the saloon Heather let go of his hand and began her chants as she palmed one of her three-inch godstone darts in one hand, and her three-shot mini pistol in her other.

With a quick chant, Heather took the arm of one of the *working girls* returning after giving a client a farewell kiss and shared a laugh as they entered together. Liam followed immediately behind, beside another man staggering through the hanging doors after getting a breath of fresh air.

They both went different directions after entering the saloon and Heather released the arm of the woman she'd entered with and headed toward the piano player. She bent to whisper a chant in his ear and he began hammering out a raucous tune and singing loudly as Liam moved toward the bar.

Liam used the scents he'd gathered at the Richards massacre to identify the three men he was looking for, then raised a finger and pointed as he positioned himself where there was no one behind him. "*You three men!* I accuse you of the ambush murder of Olson and Elizabeth Richards and the thievery of their honest property! I call you to now surrender and defend yourselves in a court of law from my accusation!"

The saloon went silent except for the singing piano man for only a moment, then all three spread out as they reached for their pistols.

Liam had to wait for that reaction before he could draw his own pistol, but changeling reactions were quicker and Liam ducked to the side as two of the men drew and fired. A third shot rang out as the slower man fired but by this time Liam had drawn his pistol and fired three shots.

Two of his rounds impacted flesh but the third missed as the fastest of the three darted to the side. That man fired again as the other two fell, but immediately sprouted a godstone dart in his eye as Heather chanted and threw.

Then she screamed, "*Down!*" and Liam dropped to the floor without hesitation as the wall behind him shattered with the impact of a heavy round fired from across the street. Two more rounds shattered the wall as Liam rolled while Heather ducked behind the piano. A fourth round pierced the wall and an innocent bystander screamed as his arm blossomed a spray of blood.

"He's reloading!" Heather yelled and snatched another godstone dart from a hoop sewn into her vest and rolled toward a window shattered by a customer crashing through to escape the carnage.

Liam dove toward the front door as other patrons scampered for cover and began firing in the direction of the sniper. As he fired his pistol, Heather rose with a chant on her lips and slung the dart underhanded just as another shot rang out and she spun to her left and fell to the floor.

"Heather!" Liam yelled and ran to her side, his pistol empty and useless in his hand.

He grabbed her and pulled her toward the thickest shelter he could find but there were no other shots fired. He looked frantically for her wound and saw blood on her shirt, but when he looked closer, he saw that it was only a flesh wound that was barely seeping blood.

"Got him," Heather whispered, then her eyes grew wide as she clutched the charm at her breast. "Fallon! The fifth man is after my brother!"

Then she fainted.

Chapter 14

Fallon turned the screws that held the owl together and smiled. He twisted another screw to open a port and poured a couple ounces of water into the fuel tank.

"There," he crooned to his mechanical friend. "Now you can fly more than a few minutes at a time."

He closed the fuel port and screwed it shut then set his tinkered friend on its feet. He adjusted another set of controls then turned a striker to ignite the hydrogen gas the water cracker provided.

It took a few moments for the steam to build up but then the owl's eyes began to glow and Fallon lifted the tinkered mech and whistled a special note. The owl shifted and spread its wings and he smiled as he lifted it up in front of him… and it shattered in his hands and blasted forward to hit him in the chest.

He gaped for only a heartbeat then scurried to the side just as another sniper's bullet impacted the wagon behind where he had just sat. On hands and knees, he scurried around on the ground as another round impacted beside him, then he changed direction as another round hit in the direction he'd been moving.

He rolled under the wagon and gasped in fear as his heart beat so fast he thought it would fly out of his chest. He tried to whistle up some defense but his mouth was so dry all he made was farting noises with his mouth. Trying not to whimper like a baby, he crawled further under the wagon where godstone tinkering would stop a bullet fired from a mile away, day or night.

He'd read about some of the snipers that gained glory and fame on the battlefield in the War Between the States. Most of them succumbed to the skill of their contemporaries, but that still left hundreds after the war ended, all of them looking for employment and only one skill to their credit. If he hadn't raised the owl tinkering at just the moment he had, he'd have been another notch on the barrel of one of those surviving snipers.

A round ricocheted from a stone and up into the lower frame of the railcar wagon and down to splash into the dirt next to his foot. He scurried further back as he tried to think what to do and another round ricocheted under the car and snatched at the fabric of his shirt and his whimper couldn't restrain itself.

The dark mage Firecloud had been a Pinkerton for only a short time before he'd been exposed for what he was. Allan Pinkerton hadn't wasted any time terminating the license of the Native mage, but one like him never had much difficulty with employment, whether his own or that of someone with more resources to defend than scruples.

It had been Firecloud that cursed Elizabeth Richards. And it was Firecloud that locked Fallon inside his head before he was born through curse. His sister had created the first crack in that curse and the death of his parents widened that crack.

Since the murder of his parents Fallon had begun to emerge more from the cage of his mind. The walls of the curse weakened in the past few days and his mind raced with the new freedom as this new stress caused him to emerge further from the trap inside his skull.

But his time he didn't just emerge… he *burst free*!

His eyebrows creased as *everything slowed* and he saw the *exact angle* of the rounds that entered the narrow space beneath the railcar wagon. He saw the impact points and the angle that led to the upper frame and back down again to almost hit him.

Just as another round struck a different spot he moved and the ricochet hit *exactly* where he anticipated at the instant it hit. He smiled as the last barrier split the fifteen-year-old curse asunder. In a second that had thousands of distinct segments, his mind was completely free for the first time in his short life.

He smiled and gave a measured whistle and the scorpion in its niche between two water barrels on the left side of the wagon stirred as its internal engine built steam.

"Wow! I tinkered that!" he thought, then remembered every bit of that process in a fraction of the time that he'd tinkered the scorpion. In a second, he *remembered* several hours of tinkering in every detail with perfect clarity and eidetic recall. He also knew exactly how to improve the already magnificent tinkering.

He gave another specific whistle and the scorpion that was inside the light of the wagon's lamps came alert and faced the direction Fallon determined the shots to be coming from. He easily moved to a position that was outside the ricochet angle of the sniper when another round hit in an unexpected angle and blew the heel from his boot.

Instead of whimpering, this time he chuckled as he thought to himself, *"On the move. Two hundred yards closer and twenty degrees to the left."*

He mentally went through the landscape he'd passed through just before they made camp in his freed mind and in less than a second knew *exactly* where the sniper had run to, from his original position four hundred yards away, for his new angle of attack. Judging how fast the sniper could run and where his next best position was, Fallon moved a few inches and held out the wing of the owl he was still holding.

Seconds later another round hit the ground under the wagon, ricocheted up into the frame from above, and back down to smack the wing out of Fallon's hand... and he smiled. Then he heard the sniper's footsteps as the man ran toward him again for another angle of fire and Fallon knew how that position lined up with his hiding place and he shifted again.

Somehow the snapping of the curse that had locked his brain sped his thoughts up and increased his cogitation to the point he could examine each and every second of time at his leisure. The last twenty seconds seemed almost like hours as he *calculated* the angles of the sniper rounds shot at him and the sounds of the man's footfalls among the other sounds of the night.

He took his time, all ten seconds of it as the man ran closer, but more stealthily, to shift position again as he whistled another measured tune. The outer scorpion guard scampered toward the incoming sniper and settled into position. Several seconds later Fallon whistled another tune just as the sniper should be reaching his next best position to shoot under the wagon.

Fallon could hear the noise of the man running and judged his position when he stopped just in time to move to another position under the wagon. With another portion of his mind, he wondered to himself why he didn't just dash under the edge of the wagon and up into the enclosure that had weapons and godstone plating for safety.

But he knew why. This was one of the men that killed his Mama and Papa.

He knew it was wrong, but he decided to play with this man. He whistled another tune and the scorpion that had lain in wait moved much slower than it should as Fallon used it for *evidence* of his weakness.

The sniper had run closer and closer, knowing this was a devious tinker with dozens of dangerous tinkerings that several of Easton's employees and dozens of locals had seen and described. At the first noise he saw the wolf-sized scorpion rise out of the grass and turn its tail-mounted revolver toward the sound of his running boot steps.

He was surprised at how slow the stinger moved to track him and was able to skid to a stop and put three rounds into the tinker's mechanical guard before it could fire. He noticed the whistles in the distance, but the tinker couldn't control his defender and it slowly collapsed in a hissing of steam from the rounds he'd pumped into it.

The sniper sneered. The owl was down by his scope's evidence and now the scorpion up close. The intelligence he'd gotten said the flying stinger bug thing had been melted down with all the rest of the idiot boy's non-lethal tinkerings so the quarry could tinker together other devices with the godstone metals.

There was one more scorpion but the sniper knew the boy would keep it close for a last defense. If it moved as slow as the first one, he would have no trouble beating it if he saw it in time. All he had to do was take it out and he had the biggest pay award in his career as soon as he could deliver the boy's head to Easton.

Despite his success so far, he didn't overestimate his quarry as he ran the last hundred feet toward the circle of light around the railcar wagon. He slowed as he neared the edge of light. Ducking down slightly he could see the shadow of the idiot boy as the scrawny tinker cowered underneath the wagon just outside of a good ricochet angle. As long as he watched out for the second scorpion machine and its revolver tail, he would have his trophy.

The man slowed as he cautiously came to the edge of the wagon's lamplight and tentatively called out. "Come on out boy. I'm not after you. I'm after that animal man and his cat, not you. Just want to ask some questions, then I'll let you go. My word of Honor."

His words were almost unrecognizable as they slowed with Fallon's stretched time

Orlagh! In all of the excitement, Fallon had forgotten about Orlagh! What should he do? Then he *remembered* the stealthy movements on the upper deck of the wagon. Orlagh was up there waiting for her chance to move.

No! She'd tailed Liam and Heather!

Wait! No one had said what she would do in the stalking of the murderers in town! Or did they? Concentrating on the *now*, he was not sure. Where was she? Then he heard a small scuffling on the deck above him. If it hadn't been for that he wouldn't have known it was her since he hadn't whistled up any of the last of his tinkerings stored up there.

In his hyper state he judged where she was and what she was preparing to do. To stop her he whistled a tune he hoped she would interpret, and the scratching he heard settled to a big cat at rest, but ready to pounce. He whistled a comforting tune then waited.

The sniper didn't let his guard down as he swung the big rifle around every time Fallon whistled, looking for the second scorpion.

Fallon smiled, and whined. "Please Mr., don't hurt me. I'll tell you anything you want, just don't hurt me." All Fallon could think of as he spun his web with dozens of minutes to plan for each second that passed, was how good it would feel to get his revenge.

He whimpered in feigned fear, interspersed with a whistling tune that brought the second scorpion closer and positioned it just right but out of sight. Stepping out from under the wagon and raising his hands in surrender, he put just the right quaver in his voice. "Please Mr., what do you want?"

The sniper sneered and his eyes darted left and right looking for the second scorpion as he moved closer, stepping into the circle of light. A few more steps and he could shoot the target in half from the hip with the full cylinder he'd reloaded as he ran down to point blank range. But getting a little closer wouldn't hurt.

The man was so close Fallon could see his face when he stopped a couple dozen feet away and his eyes shifted to the most likely spots for the second scorpion to be hiding in ambush.

"I'll tell you anything," Fallon whined, then couldn't resist and stood tall. "As soon as my scorpion blows your murdering guts out!" Then he gave a measured whistle as the man took two more steps forward.

The second scorpion surged out from behind him where it had been cuddled up to the underside of the wagon, then time *slowed* and Fallon sagged just as he began the proper whistle to fire at the angle that would cut the sniper down.

The scorpion attained its last command position and stood at the ready, aimed in the proper direction but lacking the final notes from Fallon giving it the order to fire.

The whole sequence of events had happened so quickly the sniper was caught off guard and the scorpion froze before he realized he was dead, then wasn't.

Of course, he laughed and taunted his target. "So, dummy, the Native was right. All it takes is a little stress and you'll fall in a heap and I don't have to waste a bullet to get my trophy, just hold you up by yer hair and cut yer head off while you scream. Then I can collect my pay."

The man shuddered theatrically as he calmly walked closer. "No offense kid, but I really don't think I need to know what you wanted to say before your body shut down."

He tucked a free hand under the medallion of godstone hanging from his chest. "Firecloud said this might turn you off like releasing a steam valve if I got close enough. Guess he was right."

The man stopped a few yards away and raised his sniper's rifle. He didn't bother to use the long-distance scope since he was only a few steps away from his target. "On second thought, don't want to take the chance you'll come up with something so I'll just end this quick." He leveled the sniper's rifle at Fallon's chest.

Fallon thought he heard Orlagh belatedly crouching to spring when she realized that something had gone wrong, but the sniper would have plenty of time to put a fifty-caliber round into his midsection before she could do so. His earlier signaled assurances to her had delayed her just enough to ensure that.

Time sped up again just enough for Fallon to *hear* the sniper's tendons flex against the trigger.

Then a shot rang out and Fallon *flinched*. Then another shot sounded, and another, but Fallon didn't feel anything. In his hyper fast time sense the sniper took forever to assume a surprised look. Then he crumpled to the ground just as Fallon looked to the side to see Liam rushing into the light of the wagon's lamps riding a foam-flecked Trouble.

Then his mind retreated to its former hiding place and he crumpled to the ground.

Chapter 15

Heather sighed as she tried again to explain it to Liam. "He broke the curse Firecloud put on my mother that trapped him in his mind, but then he did something that caused him to rebound *back* further than he was before."

They looked at the nearly comatose boy rocking back and forth on the ground between them, as Heather continued, "It also has something to do with the cursed talisman the sniper had around his neck. I can feel Firecloud's magery inside it."

"Can you do anything with it?" Liam asked.

She pursed her lips. "I think I can crack its incantations and might be able to use it to break Fallon back out again, but it's going to take some time."

Her brow creased. "If I'd have gotten here sooner it wouldn't be so hard to do."

Liam left her in the saloon when he jumped on Trouble to race back to their camp and she'd been further delayed when the sheriff had called the local Pinkerton agent and Heather had to explain her case a second time. The sheriff finally let her go but only after she gave her parole to return to his office tomorrow to finish the paperwork. Only then would their actions be documented as legal so they could reclaim the stolen property the men possessed.

Finally released by the authorities, Heather raced into camp on her steam cycle nearly two hours after Liam shot the sniper at the wagon. By this time Firecloud's mage talisman signaled the wearer's death to its maker and its energy began to dissipate.

While Heather tended to her magery investigating the evaporating curse, Liam tended to Fallon who was completely unresponsive. Orlagh paced nearby, body language and muttered snarls signaling her disgust with herself for failing to react differently. Liam took the boy in his arms and rocked with him as he spoke comfortingly and was encouraged when Fallon relaxed enough to put his arms around Liam's neck.

It was nearly an hour later when Heather approached. "I think I have a solution, but I don't like the cost."

At Liam's look, she gazed sadly at her brother, still clinging to Liam's neck but without the clenched and rigid body language. Fallon seemed to be listening but kept his face buried in Liam's shirt.

Looking back into Liam's eyes, she explained that cost. "I was able to learn *most* of the curse before it dissipated and I can bring Fallon's mind back."

Liam started to smile, but the look on her face stopped him. "There is some sort of time function that was linked with the original curse that did something to renew it when the amulet came within a certain distance. The curse in here," she held up the amulet, "contacted what was left of the curse in Fallon's mind and strengthened it."

Her face fell. "But somehow Fallon had already broken the original curse and was in state of hyper awareness that changed his perception of the world. That caused some sort of feedback loop into the amulet and back into Fallon, back and forth and back and forth in an instant till he burned out."

She breathed out an explosive breath. "I was able to catch the curse and add my own chants and change the way it worked, but every time Fallon uses it, he will *perceive* time at a greatly increased pace. But he will also *age* at that same increased pace by orders of magnitude."

Fallon relaxed his hold on Liam's neck and slowly turned. "I'll be smart again?"

"Again?" Heather sighed. "You always *were* the smartest person I ever knew little brother."

He smiled at the words as she continued, "You just lost that *speeded up* brain, it's still the same brain."

Fallon shook his head sadly. "No, I lost something. Even though part of me was still locked up I could think about things *ahead of time*. I could think about something with everything I knew and *anticipate* how to get my tinkerings to do what I wanted to ahead of time."

His voice cracked. "Now I still know what I already *did* but I can't think how to make *new* things." He whimpered and buried his head in Liam's shoulder, his voice muffled as he wailed, "I lost all my future thinking!"

Heather put her hand on her brother's back. "Fallon, this new charmed amulet will let you get all of that back, but there's a heavy price to pay. I need you to look at me while I try to explain that cost the best I can."

She waited and after a moment Fallon released Liam's neck, swiped a sleeve across his face as he turned, and nodded. "Okay. I'm ready."

Heather smiled with unfeigned love, then began explaining, "From what Liam was able to get out of you and Orlagh before I showed up, you were in that hyper-speed spell for two minutes."

Fallon's face crumpled. "It seemed like hours and my brain worked so good that I could think ahead so *fast*."

Heather nodded. "But it wasn't just your brain that was working fast. So was your body. Fallon, in that two minutes you aged nine or ten days, maybe more, it's really hard to say at this point. If you activate the charm in this amulet now," she held it up, "you'll age about ten or eleven months an hour."

Fallon's eyes grew wide as Liam gasped and Orlagh squalled a feline yowl. "You mean if I put it on, I'll die an old man in a couple of days?"

Heather shook her head. "Not *exactly*, unless you left it *activated* that whole time, even while you slept."

"I can turn it on and off?"

Heather nodded. "Yes, you can turn it on and off and it will automatically turn off if the amulet is more than a couple feet away from your brain. And every time it shuts off there will be a few moments or a few *minutes* of that weakness you felt before, depending on how long it is activated."

"There's another danger that I anticipate," she cautioned. "The hyper-speed takes a lot of energy and it can only get that energy from your body. That's why you were so tired after only two minutes and why you were so hungry after you came out of the body faint Liam found you in. You have to make sure to eat a big meal before you activate the charm *and* eat while speeding *and* have a big meal waiting for you when you deactivate it."

She snorted. "You actually wouldn't live two days at the hyper speed otherwise. In fact, if you fell asleep with it activated, you'd starve to death before you woke up."

Fallon's eyes were huge as Heather explained, but then he got a determined look on his face. "Show me how to activate it."

Heather hesitated. "Fallon, are you sure?"

At his nod she wrote down the chant for him and had him practice it till she was sure he could say it properly then she chanted a *memory* spell as he read it in the properly measured way. Hoping the memory spell would hold through the rest of the curse's effects, she repeated the process with the deactivation syllables.

When they were ready, she had him hold the amulet against his forehead and chant the activation syllables while she chanted her spell with a *hold*, then repeated the process with the deactivation code. Then she gently took the amulet from him and changed her chant to release the *hold* and then *locked* the spell into the amulet and sagged against Liam's quick support as her chant ended.

After a few heartbeats she regained her feet and handed the amulet to her brother. "You are as close to being a man as any other fifteen-year-old, so I am going to trust you to keep this."

She shook a finger at him as he looked at the amulet in his hand. "You be careful! I don't want to wake up and find out you've died of starvation in your sleep!"

She waved a hand about. "Make some sort of alarm you have to reset every minute while you're speed tinkering, something that'll wake everybody near the wagon in case *you* don't wake up!"

She shook her finger at him again. "I mean it little brother! You better be careful with that thing," she pointed at it, then put her hands on her hips. "I want you to activate it now and show me you can turn it off when I say so."

Fallon gulped as he gazed at the amulet in his hand. Looking up at his sister he whispered, "What if it doesn't work?"

Heather gave a slight shrug. "Then you'll just have to stay a normal boy with that small part of you still locked inside your mind, just like you have been for fifteen years and I'll love you just the same as I always have."

"But I can't do the things I did before," he whispered. "I lost more than I got back after Papa and Mama were killed."

"Fallon," Liam said softly, "you may not remember most of it but you didn't lose it." At the boy's confused look, Liam explained, "The manuals like the one you helped Jay-Ar make for his Pa's steam engine. Before we even met them, you made a whole set for Heather and me to use when you're not around. You still remember how to read, right?"

Fallon nodded yes.

"See?" Liam said with a smile and gestured toward the amulet. "If that thing doesn't work then all you have to do is study those manuals and I bet before long you'll start thinking how to do things better and then you'll realize you can *still* think ahead. In no time you'll be Master tinkering with the best of them again."

"You think so?"

"I do," Liam replied. "But it's going to work and while you use it maybe Heather can see how to fix that aging thing."

"Can you?" Fallon wondered hopefully as he looked at his sister.

Heather gave Liam an appraising look before replying. "Maybe. I would have said something before but I didn't want you to get your hopes up too soon, but yes, maybe."

She sighed and gestured toward the amulet. "But I won't know till I can examine the spell while it's activated."

Fallon took the ends of the leather thong laced through the top of the amulet and tied it behind his neck. Then he stood nervously and muttered the syllables that activated the amulet's spell… and smiled.

Chapter 16

Fallon sulked. "But I *was* doing something."

"You were simply staring at the world going by," Liam reminded him, again. "For two whole minutes *after* you dropped the owl and with your alarm blaring away."

Fallon slumped. "I was memorizing everything I could see and hear and smell and just got distracted."

Liam tried to remember that Fallon still had a child's emotions, despite its being in a growing adult body. He put a hand on the boy's shoulder. "Maybe that's what you have to concentrate on, learning how *not* to be distracted so much you go into a trance and lose track of time. It's good you've learned how to memorize things for after you turn the speed off, but you have to limit those things to what you really *want* to remember. Things you can write down or sketch while you're seeing them whether in the real world or in your mind."

The young man brightened. "I bet if I had some colored paints, I could paint the whole thing *exactly* the same as it was when I saw it. Every cactus flower and mesquite bush, branch, and leaf, and every stone layer and pool of rainwater *exactly* the right shades. And the sky and clouds in all of their shades and their reflections in the pools of water, too, and all of the birds and insects and Orlagh chasing a rabbit. I could use a tinker's glass to see real small and make every detail just like I still remember it, every stone and leaf and feather to scale."

Liam smiled as Fallon went into one of his *motion stops* that plagued him since Santa Fe. Heather assured them the new habit was not a bad thing, as Fallon's mind seemed to be processing the memory being focused on, catching up on what he'd seen in such intricate detail.

"It *was* a beautiful scene, wasn't it?" Liam snorted. "And if you *did* paint it just like it looked and had Heather magery it so it lasts for centuries, then people would pay a lot of money for that painting. And by the looks of the pencil drawings you're making on your tinkering manuals, you'd be a great painter."

He stroked his chin in thought. "Maybe we can get you some paints when we get to Little Rock, and a lot more pencils."

Fallon smiled with the ease he'd almost lost those first couple of weeks after Santa Fe. They experimented as much as Heather was comfortable with until she was convinced she had adjusted the spell as much as she could and they were all adjusting to the two new Fallons.

She was able to slow the aging process some, down to just under four days per minute while not slowing Fallon's mental capacity. She also found a way to help him retain more of what he learned while under hyper speed. The result was that her brother was quickly getting back what he'd lost and more.

There was now a growing stack of notebooks in Fallon's bunkroom and every night he added to them with tinkerings in precise detail. Each notebook showed how to build all kinds of mechanical devices Fallon thought up while he was under the amulet's hyper speed spell.

In one hour-long, hyper speed session he'd tinkered together a small paper making machine that wove a hemp sheet – a couple inches more than a foot wide – in a continuous roll as long as the base material was fed into the hopper. Hemp rope could be found in almost any General Store and Fallon made enough of the silky paper he was able to trade two fifty-foot rolls in Oklahoma City for some paints.

Not everything went well. Trouble didn't like the smell when Fallon fired up his tinkered paper fabric making machine and it threatened to take up the entire upper deck not occupied by the stallion. Then Fallon asked if he could make it bigger, making the weaving port a yard or more wide so he could adjust it to make hemp clothing fabric as well as paper. But there was always something else more important when he spent his allotted time hyper tinkering and he hadn't made that change as yet.

The hard part was getting him to limit his time *enchanted* and it showed in his haggard features after an hour inventing new tinkerings. A hearty meal and a few hours of sleep always brought him back but a couple of weeks on the trail since Santa Fe had aged him. He was only fifteen, but he could easily be mistaken for a small man of eight or ten years older. And his withdrawn episodes were getting longer, periods when he simply rocked and stared.

Heather finally talked him into a single five minutes or less hyper tinkering after each main meal of the day so he could live longer. She hoped she could cut that down in the future by getting him to study the manuals he penned while under the amulet's influences more. She hoped to get him in the habit of only hyper tinkering when he really *needed* to, but Liam understood she had to take that restriction slow so her brother wouldn't rebel and overdo it just to prove he could.

They were traveling through a sparsely populated area west of Little Rock, following an eastbound train when they passed by a large gathering of people south of the tracks.

"I'm ready to stop for the day a little early if you are," Heather called up from her turn in the conductor's seat at the front of the railcar wagon. "You want to pull off the tracks and see what the party back there is all about?"

Liam leaned over the front rail of the upper deck where he and Fallon were lounging and talking about their supper stop the night before. "Sure!"

That was all it took and Heather quickly turned valves and made adjustments with the practice of weeks on the rails and road. In seconds the railcar slowed and soon came to a stop. The three of them moved with equally practiced speed and in minutes all four road wheels were lowered and jacked up to raise the rail wheels from the iron rails.

Heather was still in the conductor's seat and expertly engaged the steam engines and turned off the rails at the crossing they had stopped in front of. A family in a rickety buggy gawped as they sat watching the tinkered transformation from railcar to road wagon. As the railcar wagon passed by the amazed family heading toward Little Rock, Trouble let out a loud greeting from his perch on the aft end of the upper deck.

"Hi! Hi!" Fallon waved and shouted, momentarily excited and reverting to his less mature persona.

The family's two children waved back tentatively then the youngest one yelled out, "Nice wagon! You going to Little Rock?"

"Yeah!" Fallon hollered back as they steamed past the stationary buggy. "Saw a party back that way and wanted to say hello."

The faces of the family grew wary and the father spoke brusquely as he glanced at Heather. "Might not want to take the young Miss to that particular party while they're stringing up a dark fella with a young wife looks just like her."

Before they could say anything, they were past the buggy and the man lashed his team and ran them hard to put distance between his family and an increase in trouble.

Liam whispered a few words to Fallon and leaped down to sit beside Heather. "You hear all that?"

At her nod he continued, "Told Fallon to mount one of those two sniper rifles we claimed on the forward right deck brace we built and look through the scope. When he gives the *ready* whistle stop us where we can get out fast if we have to where the sniper post has a line of sight to the, *party*. Fallon will whistle you his best choices from up top."

She nodded as he continued, "I'm going to lift Trouble over the side and you might want to take the steamcycle and the other sniper's rifle to a second position."

He didn't wait for a response as he moved to do his part. They had practiced several of these emergency scenarios when they camped on the road or as distractions during the boring rail interludes and everyone knew their part.

Fallon seemed able to coerce the rail schedules out of every attendant at every stop they made and that helped them plan their time on the rails and the road. Bored station managers and willing conductors were eager to share knowledge with an eager young man of such a pleasant demeanor but not seeming to have the intelligence to understand what talkative people had to say. As a result, they not only knew where every train was that might interfere with their chasing of Easton's private train and all of their time schedules, but where Easton was ahead of them, too.

Their path was now marked only by Easton's and Firecloud's movements, and both of those seemed to be together. As they traveled, they were also collecting a disturbing pattern that was also following the Easton train, a string of missing children from babes up to the age of twelve. There were several gruesomely mutilated bodies discovered close to the tracks, but they were too far from where they disappeared to have gotten that far any other way.

They were also compiling a record of Easton's public purchases and there were several deliveries that were waiting for him as his train traveled eastward. They were able on one stop to match the godstone ingot used to purchase specific metal beams and pipes, plus heavy, coated and uncoated wire as they had numbered each of their ingots before the theft and made pressed paper impressions to match the markings.

Heather retrieved all of the missing pieces of jewelry her parents had worn, except for the two intact pieces that traveled with Easton's train. Easton had wisely had Firecloud purge the rest by melting but he didn't know about the challenge the Native mage had given Heather in the form of the ring taken from Lefty and the large medallion that Orson had worn.

She knew most of the personal items made with godstone were melted down to destroy Heather's ability to track them, so she presumed that Easton ordered the melting. But why all but two pieces?

There could be no other explanation for Easton to allow Firecloud to stay with him. He didn't know the Native mage had defied his sensible order. If he lacked that level of control over his employee maybe he *wasn't* directly responsible for the death of her parents. That didn't absolve him of his actions after the murders, but he may not be her primary target.

Her vengeance was now focused on one target. Firecloud, the Native mage who originally cursed her mother and Fallon before he was born. And the mage that now taunted her by openly carrying two of her father's possessions. Easton was second on her list, but it was convenient to have them both still together when she finally faced Firecloud.

They were still on a trail of vengeance, but first they were going to see what worried a man with a family as he gave them a warning of danger ahead.

Liam hurried to put the emergency lifting harness on Trouble. The stallion stomped impatiently, as he knew this meant he usually got to run hard and fast on a surface that didn't move under him.

Liam put the two canvas tubes and their sling over Trouble's saddle and flipped through the small pamphlet Fallon inked for him. He read each item on the checklist and performed the directed acts as he attached a tube to a release valve and fed steam into the first tube hanging on Trouble's right side. As foamed steam filled the tube, he chanted the syllables printed on the next item of the checklist and the foam swelled almost explosively. In seconds the balloon rose to bob at the end of its lines.

Liam rounded Trouble and threw a leg over the saddle as he moved the line to the left tube while continuing the chant. In seconds the left tube balloon filled with steam foam and the two tubes swelled as he closed off the intake and shut the valve on the end of the tube. He jerked on the tube as he and Trouble lifted from the deck and the force of the pull caused them to drift over the side of the wagon just as it stopped at Fallon's signal whistle.

As soon as they were clear, Liam stopped chanting and opened pressure valves and the balloons began venting foam, which immediately turned to steam and wafted away. Trouble drifted gently towards the ground and when his hooves touched down Liam tucked the amulet Heather provided with the imprinted spell for making steam foam into a pocket as the two balloon tubes continued to deflate.

On the other side of the wagon Heather was repeating his actions with the steamcycle to get into position for her part in their hastily crafted plan.

In seconds the two, hemp canvas balloons deflated and were hanging like twin blankets on either side of the stallion. Liam quickly tightened straps to pull the left tube up to the same level as the one on the right. He checked his pistol and the carbine in the saddle holster and touched the reload pouch on the other side to ensure it was full of rounds for both his weapons. Only when he was ready did he kick at Trouble's sides and race toward the gathering of revelers. He pushed Trouble just enough to look like he didn't want to miss anything, but slow enough to not startle those watching his approach. When he got to the main crowd, he pulled the horse back to a steady walk.

As he walked Trouble into the middle of the group of people, he studied the situation with a critical eye. The more he saw the more he hoped

Orlagh was being careful and Heather and Fallon were watching his signals closely… and Fallon wouldn't go into one of his episodes.

Then he wondered if the young man was enchanted and starving to death while he took his time trying to save a man's life and not getting killed in the process.

A man separated himself from the others and came to greet Liam as he rode up to the heart of the celebration.

"Liam Quinn," Liam identified himself openly.

"Mayor Percival Granger," the portly man responded. "Ya come to enjoy the festivities?"

Liam nodded toward a Negro standing on the bed of a wagon with his neck tied to a stout limb above. "That the guest of honor?"

Mayor Percival Granger turned and laughed. "Escaped slave. Gonna hang him then send his half breed squaw and their muddy spawn down ta Kitty's place ta fill some vacancies the last group of miners passin' through made."

He turned back to look up at Liam. "You want some good local brew there's a tent over that away," he waved a hand negligently, sloshing some of said brew from the mug he held. "Might want ta hurry if'n ya want ta git a good spot cuz we're 'bout ready ta have the main attraction."

Liam looked at the man for a moment in sheer wonder the drunken mayor completely missed. "Thought the war was over. Man his color can't be escaped slave because there ain't no slaves no more."

The mayor looked affronted. "Maybe ya aught ta have more loyalty ta yer kind. Some kind of men, half men I should say, will always be nuthin' better'n slaves. Besides, got a warrant says he escaped before the end of the war so he's still an escaped slave." He shrugged as if it were obvious. "Darkie got ta pay for the old crime."

"Cut him down," Liam said as he calmly leaned forward in the saddle.

Mayor Granger started to take a deep pull of the mug he carried, then froze a moment with a confused look before lowering the mug. "What did you say?"

"I said, *cut him down*. Your fun is over. You scared him good and proper and I'm willing to bet a godstone nugget he'll take his wife and daughter and get out of your sight just as fast as he can," Liam said calmly, then he gave the mayor a non-threatening, neighborly smile.

Several men moved closer and began to scowl at Liam and put hands on pistols as they converged on him.

Liam continued to smile as he reached slowly for an object tucked in a strap of Trouble's harness. "Easy now, I just want to show you something."

He pulled out a flat paddle of wood with markings on one side and held it up.

"See this," he pointed, speaking a little louder so those around could hear him better. "About the size of the mayor's head. Even got a face marked on one side, see, here're are the eyes and the nose, and here's the mouth. It's even got the front teeth missing, just like the mayor. Now I'm going to hold it up real high like this."

He did so and two seconds later the paddle jerked in his hand and a hole pierced one eye. Liam quickly turned it ninety degrees and two seconds later it jerked again and the other eye was pierced. Seconds later the echo of a faint shot rang out, then another from a different direction.

Liam showed the paddle with the two holes to the growing group around his horse. "I've got two really good snipers a few hundred yards away with scopes on all of you," he pointed with the paddle then held it up high. "If I drop this paddle for *any* reason people all around me will start getting their eyes shot out. Now, *cut that man down*!"

The men around him muttered angrily and came closer and he lowered the paddle a foot. "Who wants to die first?"

"You'll never git out alive," Granger sneered. "My son is on rifle watch an'll take you out afore you c'n kill more'n me. And if you're still alive when you fall, we'll have some more fun afore we let a race traitor die easy."

There was a squall and everyone looked to see a large mountain lion on a stone promontory with her jaws clamped around a young man's neck as a rifle clattered away uselessly. One hard jerk and the man's throat would be torn out.

"That your son there?" Liam asked as he pulled his pistol with his free hand. "I'm going to start counting. I'm not even going to tell you how far but at a certain point I'm going to get tired, drop this paddle, and just start shooting people."

He pointed his pistol at the mayor's red face. "You get to be first, then my sister, oh yeah, we're not your kind either, will rip your boy's throat out. By then the snipers will have started culling the rest of your disgusting herd." His eyes raked those around him. "Then we'll start killing everybody at this party till we run out of bullets."

He smiled. "How many of you are that committed to this party?" He waited only a heartbeat. "Not many of you if truth be told. Now, please, somebody cut that man down before my arm gets tired. My two snipers can't hear our friendly talk. They're just waiting for me to drop my arm so they can rack up notches on their stocks and earn some extra pay."

One man close by took that challenge and raised a carbine. "Don't matter how fast ya c'n move beastman. I'll put a bullet in yer brain afore the mayor dies." He gave the man in question a short glance. "Sorry mayor, we gots to stand up to halfmen and any one of us c'n be the first to die. You and yer son will hold honorable spots in our town's history so folks know what we sacrificed to be of pure stock."

The mayor looked stricken and inhaled to plead for another solution from his fellow purebred white, but while the man with the carbine had been talking Liam spun the paddle in a series of dots and vertical dashes.

Finished apologizing to the mayor the man then turned toward Liam and sneered. "I aint gonna' count." He cocked the hammer on his carbine and took aim, then his left eye disappeared and the other side of his head sprayed bone, blood, and brains all over the man on that side of him.

Chapter 17

"We was headed west but twice now I was almost killed by people mad about their side losing," Blackie Lincoln explained. "We was trying to get down to Mexico where we might be better accepted by Native kin, but it sure is hard passing through land full of angry folks."

The black man shook his head sadly. "Wonder how long that mad is going to last? Sure do appreciate you and yours saving my life and my wife and daughter from whoring to survive, but we still got a rough road to travel if'n we want to be safe."

He gave Liam a sideways glance as he sat the right-hand side at the front of the wagon. "Might be best for you if you shed us quick so people leave you alone."

Liam snorted. "Folks at your party back there probably already know who and where we are and where we're going. Might need another gun if there's too many coming at us at one time."

He gave Blackie a smile as he steered the wagon on the road into Little Rock, then pointed his chin toward the man's bandages. "Wasn't going to let you walk out beat up like you were. Heh-heh, if you weren't already standing in the back of a wagon it would have taken two men to put you in the same spot. Was only the rope holding you upright and when they cut it you just dropped. Thought you was dead at first."

Careful not to twist the splint on his right forearm or bump the left arm in its sling, Blackie rubbed at the bandage around his throat. The mob had taken turns beating him before they dropped the rope over his neck. He had mostly hung limp more than once before getting his feet back under him, only the shock of choking waking him from his faint.

"Was the second closest to dying I ever got, Mr. Quinn," Blackie said seriously then continued at Liam's raised eyebrow. "Back before I escaped, my master's wife was real lonely and made me bed her a whole month while he was away making money before the war. He got back in time we all thought, hoped, it was his when her belly started to grow but we weren't that lucky.

His face took on a haunted look. "A week after the baby was born, he had me build this big fire and heat water to a boil in the biggest iron pot I ever saw. Then he threw his wife's and my baby boy into the pot of boiling water and cooked him alive."

The big man's eyes teared at the memory as he continued, "Most horrible thing I ever saw, then he caned me almost dead while telling me I was next in the pot. Woke up north of the Mason Dixon line being cared for by my future wife. She said my old master's wife had saved me just to spite her husband for killing her baby, no matter its color. Thought that kind of thinkin' was over and done."

"Well, I'm not sure a family like yours with nothing but the clothes on your back is going to get to Mexico without a rough road. You might want to re-supply first and to do that you need a job." Liam smiled and gave Blackie a sideways look. "Might be in a position to offer you work till you're in better shape. You got any crafts or skills?"

It was Blackie's turn to snort a laugh then he flinched as his broken ribs grated. "Heh-heh-OW!" It took him a moment to catch his breath. "I was the foreman for all the house slaves, fourteen in all from six years up to old master crafters. We did a bit of everything what needed built or repaired at the main house, the guest house behind it, and the tinker's barn behind that."

"I had to make daily written reports to the Missus, the master's wife. Each foreman met with her alone at the end of each day and my report was always last. I gave her all my reports on *my* back that month the master was gone. Had to keep my hands over my eyes so she wouldn't have to look at me while she rode at her own pace for what her man couldn't give her."

He gazed at nothing for a moment in memory before continuing, "I spent all my spare time in the family library reading anything and everything I could get my hands on, on all the tinker's machinery we had at the three buildings of the main compound. Got twenty years of hands-on experience as a tinker's apprentice and about six, seven years of book learning on other things on my own."

Liam nodded, impressed. "Well then, how about a dollar a day plus room and board for you and your Missus and daughter? Fallon already gave his room to your wife and daughter because he sleeps up on the upper deck with Trouble and me most nights anyway. You can sleep up there with us."

"That's mighty generous of you after saving my life and all this," he displayed his splinted and bandaged self as he took short breaths to keep from stressing his broken ribs. "Might be a day or two before I can do much but Maria can help Miss Heather and Rosa can tinker some. She's only twelve but she was starting to be a good apprentice to me before neighbors still mad about the war drove us off. If'n your young Fallon needs any help tinkering I can tell Rosa what to do and be her eyes of experience till my wings heal," he gestured with both arms and flinched at the resulting pain.

Liam laughed. "If you don't stop flapping those wings, it'll take till winter for them to heal. So, what do you say? A dollar a day with room and board for you and your family till you feel well enough to resume your journey." He shook his finger at the man next to him. "But if Maria and your daughter do much work, though, they'll have to accept a dollar a day for each, too."

"Don't know," Blackie mused, "dollar a day riding *the wrong direction* while healing, *plus* room and board. Or get dumped alongside the road with just the clothes on our backs and angry locals looking for someone to take out their hatefulness on."

He snorted. "My old mammy used to whack me upside the head and say, 'Blackie, boy, you got a brain like any other man! Use it! You'll do stupid things, you're a man, you won't be able to help it. But boy, don't ever do something stupid twice'."

He gave Liam a smile and sat back comfortably. "I *know* what will happen if I get off this wagon. The last time I took this road out of Little Rock I almost died and my family sold to a whorehouse. I believe I'll accept your offer of employment till we can obtain a wagon of our own and maybe a guard or three instead of traveling with the stagecoach."

Liam laughed. "Wise choice! Now, you say you grew up apprenticed to a tinker?" At Blackie's cautious nod to keep from self-inflicting more pain, he continued, "Fallon is just about the best tinker I've ever seen in my twenty-two years and half the time he has to show me what to do before I can do what he wants. By the time he shows me what to do he could have done it himself so I'm really not much help."

That had been true at first but the length of time he'd spent with the young man the more he'd learned. He was only slow about half the time now on new tinkering projects, but he was his best on maintenance checks using the manuals Fallon had inked.

Blackie looked around as they steamed down the road. Twice in the last couple of miles they had passed other steam wagons hauling some farmers' early produce. "Don't know how much help *I'll* be. Never seen about half the tinkerings I've seen since I woke up and my Missus told me to haul myself up front here to sit and talk."

"Oh, I'm learning they're all the same as most other tinkerings that do what they do, just smaller," Liam said with an airy wave.

"The steamers between the wheels don't look like they could roll one of those," he pointed to a small two seat steamer sitting in front of a large house and barn a hundred yards back from the road. "But each one can roll this wagon faster than a horse can run full out or down a level track faster than most railroad locomotives can pull a six-car train."

He grinned broadly as he continued, "And they run on water! Just water. Fallon read about the new war machines the Army and Navy tinkerers from both sides made during the war and just by reading about them and seeing pictures knew how to tinker one."

"He put his first water fueled steam engine on the frame of a bicycle and that's what Heather gets around on instead of a horse. Him and another friend made three more and put two of them on our railcar wagon. Lucas is using the third one back home as a template to build more just like it."

Liam snorted. "Wanted to call them Richards-Washington steamers, but Fallon insisted Washington-Richards was easier to say and made him promise to call them all by that name."

As they traveled, talking easily to get to know each other, the population grew and more eyes followed them as they steamed by on the increasingly crowded road.

"Maybe I should go back inside where eyes attached to flapping tongues can't point you out to anyone that asks to anyone what might be following us."

"Nonsense!" Liam said vehemently. "You got a coat over most of your bandages and the one around your neck could be a dust storm scarf and you've got a wide brimmed hat covering most of your face. Lots of folks of means have employees for heavy labor. You look just like any wealthy man's hired hand."

Then he snorted. "And anybody seeing this wagon steaming down the road or tracks is going to know that it is owned by wealth."

He snorted again. "If fact, you won't actually be working for me. Miss Heather will be paying your wages. All I actually own is Trouble and my saddle, and a few other odds and ends. I'm not working for a wage, but I am racking up a considerable amount in recovery shares. Since we're both seeking the same man, men, our paths have coincided and will continue to do so for the near future."

He didn't see Blackie's knowing smile as he continued, his eyes on the crowded road ahead. "Anyway, you work for Miss Heather and we all sort of work for young Fallon sometimes. Most of the time I just pass messages and make suggestions."

"Well then, that would make you my foreman and absolves me of all responsibilities of the *officious* kind," Blackie said with a disarming smile as he shifted in his seat to get more comfortable. "For my first contribution let me tell you the best place to park this obvious wealthy heiress's lavish steam castle where it can be best defended near folks that might be a bit more accepting."

Chapter 18

The next morning Liam was on watch on the upper deck when the sun cracked the horizon, the waxing moon settling in the west and the pull he had been feeling the last couple of days washing away. Orlagh lifted her head where she'd been lying on a hemp canvas, puma sized mattress, and rumbled sympathetically.

Liam smiled at his sister and turned to view the horizon in front of their camping spot. Facing eastward with the city's lights to their left, they were mostly hidden from view of the railroad tracks that ran along the south side of Little Rock. As the sun rose, he saw the several hoe-boys that had gathered around a small fire to their right and out of sight of railroad people, had disappeared. They were already probably trying to avoid the bulls and hitching rides both east and west.

The lamps of the growing city had winked in the night as fog engulfed the lowlands. The thickest part of Little Rock was a couple of miles away and their small hill gave them a good view while allowing them to stay isolated enough anyone looking for them would be unable to find where they'd camped. Those that did know of them mostly ignored their presence unless prodded into useless actions by their employers to do so.

Blackie spoke from experience in explaining the hoe-boys that rode the rails for free and the few families that frequented this small isolated shelter would be the best watchers they could hope to find.

Of course, instead of using the time to rest, Heather, Maria, and Rosa had cooked up several pots of rice and beans and served the transients while Blackie introduced Liam and Fallon to dozens of people *he* didn't even know.

The night stretched well into Liam's Watch and if not for the *wakening* charm Heather mageried for him, he wouldn't have been able to stay awake for his watch after the excitement of the day. It was only after Heather brought him a plate of breakfast, he turned his watch over to Fallon, who immediately began checking out all of his tinkerings instead of staying on the upper deck and actually *watching*.

"I'll take the Watch," Blackie said as Liam hesitated before going to his hammock in the cargo room now that an open space had been made by supply usage. Liam looked at him blearily for a moment, then nodded his acceptance of the offer, then released the *wakening* charm with a series of magery syllables as he headed for his hammock.

In his mind he was planning the supplies they would have to replace for the run to and across the Mississippi when the blackness of exhaustion overcame him. He came awake slowly and stretched in luxurious health of his changeling anatomy and smiled at the light breeze coming through the corner window of the wagon. Then a scent wafted in with the breeze and he rolled out of the hammock and dashed through the doors, grabbing his pistol belt on the way out.

He crossed the extended back stoop, now almost a small deck, and jumped the rail to land on the scree on the left side of the wagon and slid down to the even ground. Rising more slowly and dusting his breeches he approached the renewed fire in the ring of larger stones.

Heather looked up and smiled as their eyes locked. He smiled back as Rosa said from the side, "Morning Mr. Quinn. Got fresh bacon and eggs and buttermilk cornbread almost finished."

At his look she added, "Farm boys know where to get what they want. Miss Heather gave them silver coins to buy with and every one brought back signed receipts for what they bought. None spoke names or the look of the wagon."

She nodded toward the ragged group waiting to eat and his brows creased. "I hope there's enough for everybody?" At her nod, he continued, "Then it won't matter if these folks eat first, will it?" At her surprised look, he added, "You got an apron I can wear so I don't get grease splatter all over my clothes?"

There were murmurs around the camp of those without homes or more than the clothes on their back as Heather took off *her* apron and put it over his head as Maria seemed to *bump* her from behind. The motion brought them closer together and she looked up into his face as she felt his arms steady her.

Her face grew red and she stammered, "Oh! Uh… here… take mine," then she hastily moved away and turned to glare at Maria. "Maria, could you come with me a moment, *please*."

"Just a minute Miss," Maria said as she rubbed at an ankle. "Stepped on a rock sideways and almost twisted my ankle. Sorry I bumped you like that, but you did keep me from falling, so I thank you."

Then she added with complete innocence, "Mr. Quinn caught you from falling so all's well." Then she waved her hand. "You go ahead and I'll be up in a couple heartbeats." She cautiously put her foot down and tentatively put her weight on it as Blackie tried valiantly to keep a straight face.

Heather's face grew even more flushed as she looked around at everyone watching her, then she turned and tried to look natural as she walked to the wagon.

Liam looked over at Blackie and shrugged. "Looks like we're the servers my friend." Then he looked at Blackie's obvious limitations. "Or maybe just me."

He turned with a smile to the startled people around the campfire. "Folks, you form a line right here," he pointed, "and we'll see how long this batch lasts, then we'll cook up some more and see how long *that* batch lasts."

When no one moved he pointed to a couple hovering over three children not yet with two numbers to their ages. "You five! You're first! Come over here and hold out what you got to put some of this in!" He gestured toward the big platter of eggs and another of bacon while Blackie tried without success to wield the iron skillet with the cornbread till his daughter rescued him from embarrassment.

Liam finally helped him out about the same time they noticed the family of five had only one plate for all of them to share from. It took a few moments for Liam to whistle a few notes and in seconds Fallon was running up with a stack of tin platters.

"Told you," the young man said then gave Rosa a shy look.

Liam smiled. "Yes, you did, and this shows why. Now people can start to rebuild their lives with things they own. Why don't you go get the other things?"

Fallon smiled with innocent pleasure and ran back to the wagon and quickly returned with a mug for each of their guests to add to their own new plate. In moments the line formed and nearly two dozen men, women, and children filed past as Liam served up the breakfast whose smells had awakened him.

They were still serving when Heather and Maria came out of the wagon together carrying individual crates and laughing as if they were free of care. As they came closer Heather looked at him in a different way and he felt a shiver run up his spine.

He turned to look at Blackie but Blackie was shaking his head in sympathy. "Sorry son, choice has been made and you got no say."

Liam looked at the two women in panic and then back to the black man. "But... but, it's only been a day, *less* than a whole day!"

Blackie shook his head sadly. "That's one of the things what got us thrown out of our home. Maria's peculiar magery gift. People would pay her money to read them then get mad when she told them what she read. When wives didn't love husbands, the husbands blamed my Maria and when husbands cheated on the wives, the wives got mad at Maria for *telling* them what they paid to know."

"She's had enough time to read both of you and that little scene earlier was to deep read *both* of you together," Blackie said, and shook his head in sympathy. "You fight it and you'll just make both of you miserable."

Liam glared for a moment till he realized one of the starving children was staring at him in fear. "Oh, sorry little one. Oh look, there are two eggs left and a whole strip of bacon. You're just in time!"

"You sure, sir?" the waif whispered. "My pa's sick and he was too weak to get up to get his own. I would sure like to bring him a bite. It's jus' me and him and I got to take care of him till he gets better."

Heather overheard and in seconds urged the young girl to lead her and Maria to her father.

They buried him at high noon, explaining to the stricken girl that her pa had most likely died in the night. Fallon and Rosa walked the girl back to the wagon while the others stayed to finish.

"She'll sleep with me in my room tonight," Heather explained as they arranged stones and a cross around the dirt mound. "Maybe later we can clean the back storage room and make it into two more bunkrooms. That way Liam, uh Mr. Quinn can still have his hammock by the corner window and she can have the other side."

Maria simply raised an eyebrow and smiled, then both women giggled and looked at Liam, who scowled at Blackie. The broad-shouldered black man laughed openly and Heather glared at him till Maria poked her, then they put their heads together and whispered and giggled as they finished the unknown man's grave.

Before they were finished another group began digging a second grave nearby. They helped the second group collect the plentiful stones they used to line the bottom and sides and cover the dirt mounds. Then they scoured the area and transplanted several types of wildflowers between the stones on top of both graves.

Later in the day Liam rode Trouble into town, Heather on the steamcycle beside him as they looked for the businesses Blackie and Maria suggested. They returned with saddlebags and panniers loaded with absolute vital supplies, Liam with ammunition and Heather with women's toiletries for their growing female population.

By the time they returned from that first scouting trip, Fallon and Rosa, with Blackie's experienced supervision, constructed a rolling cargo box they attached to the side of the steamcycle. With its own small steam engine, even fully loaded with supplies, the steamcycle easily adapted to the three-wheeled design. The small side cargo box allowed Liam riding Trouble to be mostly free of bulky supplies while he provided an obvious guard.

On their second trip into town they met with several people who had seen Easton's private train two days straight on a side track, and there were always several more men guarding it than was normal. Another informant told them what supplies the Easton Train purchased in their layover while a third regaled them with the stories told by the private train's hired hands when they weren't starting fights in the three largest saloons.

At one point a pair of men flashing Pinkerton badges confronted them, furtively hinting their nearest Mississippi crossing might be problematic and where it might *not* be. As they left one of the men mentioned loudly to his partner about not liking defending *certain people* that *used to be* a Pinkerton, or the kind that might hire that kind of unsavory *person*.

The conversation was not said *to* him but was plenty loud enough for his changeling hearing and direct enough Liam knew they were being as helpful as their code allowed them to be.

"Firecloud seems to make an impression on everyone he meets," Liam commented after piling the last supplies into the sidecar and strapping down the canvas tarp.

"Evil is always noticed," Heather said as she threw a leg over the steamcycle's saddle and engaged the boiler. As the warm boiler built up steam, she added, "It also leaves a stench I could follow blind. Elizabeth and Orson Richards will soon be able to rest easy."

"Now, let us get back to camp so we can tell the others we will have to travel north to get another railroad bridge across or find a boat to ferry us to the other side."

She sighed. "That means our crossing will be several days longer at the best while Firecloud has more time to prepare for our meeting."

Liam looked at the lowering sun. "Orlagh and I will be changing places tonight. That will leave only Blackie and Fallon as men to discourage those too stupid to know certain women can handle themselves."

"Oh, you'll still be around," Heather said, just as a release valve let her know the cycle had built up the proper level of steam.

"Race you," she said with a mischievous grin as she fed steam to the actuators that spun the rear wheel and the cycle sprayed grit behind its wheel then chugged away down the street.

Liam laughed, then leaped atop Trouble and trotted after her. They returned to camp and found a young man they had never met standing guard. The young man had another younger boy beside him that simply sat and stared blankly at the ground in front of them. Both looked at them when they approached then returned their gazes to the area around the campfire ring, or the ground.

Liam and Heather unloaded the supplies then returned to town one last time before sunset to get more supplies as they calculated what they might need for their increased numbers.

Each time Heather or Liam took turns exchanging godstone for gold and silver coins in smaller denominations – at different banks to make their future purchases at other businesses less memorable.

Between the second and third trips to town collecting supplies and information on their quarry, Fallon got lost in a hyper tinkering spell and was dead asleep when they returned to camp.

"How long was he tinkering?" Heather asked.

"Little over two hours," Maria said nervously. "Rosa had to stumble into his arms and accidentally tear the amulet away from his neck and he just fell dead asleep. We've been able to get him to take some thick broth and his color is coming back but he hasn't woke up yet."

Heather nodded. "Tell Rosa that was good thinking and thank you both for saving my brother's life." Then her face grew cloudy. "Now let me know where he is so I can *kill* him for doing something so stupid!"

Liam grabbed her arm. "Heather!"

He worriedly looked around at the growing crowd around the Hoe-boy's Camp. "Orlagh and I are going to change soon." He glanced at the sun. "About an hour. *Trust* my sister! She'll stand by you and give you good advice."

Then he blushed. "Don't believe all of her stories about me, she tends to exaggerate sometimes."

Instead of answering, Heather pulled her arm so they stood close and she gazed up into his eyes. "You forget, we already had two days and three nights together. I'll believe every word and am anxious to see you in your warrior form again."

"I won't be in my warrior form," Liam replied. "I'll be in the shape of an animal."

Heather put a hand to his face. "Only a different warrior form. There are chants my people have taught me that might allow you to decide which form you take during this forced change, but if I perform them on you, you will not be able to break the curse with the rest of your family. You would still be forced into the change on the three nights of the full moon and not be able to select the time and place of your change like your heritage allowed before your family was cursed."

She smiled warmly. "But I will know more tonight when I witness your sister and your changes while performing a mage *seeing*," she said, then smiled. "For all we know, I might be able to break your curse before the night is out."

Chapter 19

Liam rested on all fours on the puma mattress he now claimed for three days and nights while Orlagh tried to convince the others she knew what she was talking about.

"But I told you. The whole time I was a cat I still knew what I was seeing. I didn't get the chance to actually turn wrenches and twist screwdrivers and swing hammers, but I *know in my mind* every turn, twist and swing. I watched every maintenance check every one of you did, well, when I wasn't napping to save energy for hunting."

"Please! Just tell me what to do and I'll show you I can do it without being watched. Please? I want to *feel* the world for three days, something different than just riding a horse or a wagon with my hands laced together unmoving."

She looked from one woman to the next, from Heather to Maria and back, then to Rosa. On the other end of the upper deck Blackie tore one of Fallon's tinkerings apart to replace a broken part while Fallon rocked silently in one of his silent, introverted episodes.

Liam was about to close his eyes and nap when a modulated whistle came from the woods in the direction of the road to town. Another whistle sounded and the guard with his staring shadow stirred and rose.

Several minutes later a couple of men Liam recognized as Pinkertons nervously rode their horses slowly into camp. Both men wielded sawed off, double-barreled shotguns as if they expected to have to use them at any moment. Orlagh and Heather faced the two men side-by-side without hesitation after they dismounted.

"Uh," the apparent leader stammered as he looked around at the suspicious faces in Hoe-boy Camp, "we was told to inform this camp no boys will be allowed on any train going east for ten days. Girls, uh, women going east will be allowed to employ themselves appropriately, but they can't take any male kin east with them," the man finished and gulped.

"Must be the last two men on the rolls," Orlagh commented sympathetically. "Okay, Pinkerton man. We know sometimes you have employers that give you stupid assignments, so we're not going to hold you personally accountable for your message."

"Pass on up to your *real* bosses we thank them for their possible assistance in the future. Other agents have already confirmed the original crime and we have positive identification. There are already high-level politicians calling in favors to protect an influential *suspect*, but too many credible people have identified the men we are following for them to avoid trial. They will legally submit to our warrant or defend themselves."

The Pinkerton man firmed his resolve. "Those that currently employ us do not recognize that additional evidence and would refuse to *admit* its credibility if they were to stumble on those facts and see them as what they were. I," he looked at his partner, who nodded once, "*we*, will pass your resolve up our chain of command to the ears willing to listen."

He looked more benignly at the homeless families and adventurous farm boys that had become a mobile source of both trouble and hardworking, innovative thinking to those willing to listen, and nodded. "We've given you the message we were paid to deliver and now we'll take our leave."

He looked around at the crowd already beginning to dismiss them and return to their tasks of survival. "I'll ask the bulls to leave this spot off their rousting-out parties till you can build something out of that scree rock after you leave."

Heather smiled and Liam could smell her amusement at the obvious hint. "Thank you for the advice, sir."

But the Pinkerton man missed it. "Uh, there was another man here before, wasn't there?" He looked at Blackie with his arms still immobilized or wrapped in casts despite rapid healing magery, then over at Heather.

Liam chose that moment to lunge into view, snarl once, then relax into a sitting position, then flex his massive feline shoulder muscles before yawning wide.

Normal pumas weighed about a hundred forty pounds on average with only the biggest males reaching two hundred, but changelings weighed the same as their human form. Liam was well over six-foot tall and the type of muscular that showed the results of a changeling metabolism and hunting skills combined with over a year of hard travel. He weighed more than a dozen pounds over two hundred in both human and puma form.

Liam as a puma was a *big* cougar. When Liam darted into the area where the Pinkerton man was talking, he flinched and began to raise his sawed-off shotgun. He caught himself and put both hands in the air. "Sorry, surprised me for a second. Nothing to get riled about."

"Evening sir," he nodded toward Liam. "Uh, I guess I'll say bye then, sir, ladies. Uh, bye."

Then he calmly and with much dignity turned and walked with his companion to their horses, mounted, and rode back around the hill toward town. Coded whistles sounded as they passed each of the impromptu guards on their way out of Hoe-boy Camp.

When a distant whistle told them the Pinkertons were on the last road into town, Heather turned to Orlagh, then looked at Liam crouched nearby, then back at Orlagh. "What do you suggest?"

Orlagh looked at her brother, then smiled. "I say we stock up on supplies for as long as we need to drive where we need to go to get across the Mississippi." She flexed her shoulders. "I have three days to stretch my muscles and I want to *do something constructive* so when my brother and I switch places again he won't think I just laid around scratching myself in places I couldn't reach as a cat."

Then she looked surprised. "I can't believe I just told you that."

Heather quickly hugged her, blurting, "I want to know you better, but I want him back too," she whispered the last, momentarily forgetting that changeling senses were more acute than those of the natural creatures the changelings copied. "I *tingle* all over when I touch him, even when he's like that." She thought she was being discrete as she twitched her chin in Liam's direction where he lay dozing on a roll of hemp canvas.

Orlagh smiled knowingly and pitched her voice at just above the level he couldn't hear, "Felt something like that a little bit a couple of times. Tell you what, I promise to tell you all the bad things so you can know just what you're getting yourself into."

Liam whuffed loud enough they knew he was listening, then yawned widely and lay back down to doze as his sister and the woman he was beginning to realize he *did* love with all his heart, whispered low enough he couldn't hear. He fumed in silent frustration at not being able to tell what they were talking about after his traitor sister helped Heather adjust her voice for privacy as the camp discretely settled into the deepening night.

From where he lay Liam could see the rest of their extended camp in their small private camps just outside of the light of the central campfire. They came west looking for nothing more than a chance to better themselves and fallen on hard times. Other than the clothes on their back and maybe a coat or blanket, most of them now each owned a plate with cutlery, and a mug.

The Pinkerton visit set Heather on a tear and she made a shopping list with Orlagh, then the two of them left camp with Heather driving the steamcycle and Orlagh riding Trouble. They returned an hour later with the cycle and sidecar overflowing with packages and bundled everything into the wagon and shut all the shutters.

From the sounds Liam guessed they'd bought and were now trying on new dresses. He mewled a small feline chuckle and went back to sleep.

The next day they were serving another community breakfast when a wagonload of heavy wood was whistled in by the perimeter guards. Blackie explained the security system wasn't special for them. The hoe-boys and migrating vagrant families did it for their own protection, as this particular Hoe-boy Hill was their near permanent camp away from the railroad bulls. The hill was nearly always occupied by more than a dozen, but no one group stayed longer than a week.

The wagon driver held up a sheet of paper. "Says right here. One wagonload of seasoned, twelve-foot, two by six oak planks and four by four posts. One keg of five-inch bolts with one nut and two washers each. One gallon of wood polish and four horsehair brushes."

Then he pointed at the railcar wagon. "That the wagon, huh? Nice." He gestured at the four young men still in the wagon. The family resemblance was obvious. "Those're my boys, they'll have your wagon finished in twenty-four hours like we promised."

"Wait… what?" Heather started then one of the new guards, the one with the brain-wounded brother sidled up.

"Uh, Miss Heather, your brother gave me a list and some papers with pictures and such and some godstone nuggets the last time he was different. You know, all fidgety and smart and always tinkering real fast."

He gulped. "Anyway, he gave me that list and those other papers and a pouch of godstone nuggets. I made sure to bargain hard but fair and would have given him the pouch with the rest of the nuggets back, but he was in another of his faints so I just tucked it under his pillow."

Heather turned to the carpenter as his sons began collecting tools and eying the wagon. "You say my *younger* brother hired you to make some changes to *our* wagon?" When that fact sank in the man became more attentive. "Exactly what kinds of changes are we talking about? If I may ask."

The man pointed. "We're supposed to extend the rear stoop to about three times as big as it is now and do the same to the front where we'll put in a wet water ship's style wheel to steer with and enclose it a bit more. Then we'll round out the top deck the same amount fore and aft and add four more iron hoops for the longer canvas coming tomorrow."

He rumbled a deep laugh. "Like to give the tentmaker fits getting the shape right."

Then he slapped his hands together. "But that's of no account. Me and my boys been paid a handsome sum to do a *quality* job in one exact day and I better make darn sure my reputation ain't tarnished by my boys taking shortcuts."

With that he rumbled off and soon all of them were cutting, sawing, and shaping the new back stoop and forward driving cabin around the railcar's frame. It didn't take long for Liam to make himself scarce but he was close enough to hear when Heather got Fallon to spend a couple of minutes hypering so he could tell her what he'd tinkered up this time.

When they all gathered for their midday meal together, they invited the carpenters and were pleased when the man and his four sons took staggered breaks so at least two of them were working all the time. By the time the sun set the railcar was nearly fifteen feet longer. The rear stoop was now big enough to hold both Trouble and the steamcycle with its sidecar and the longer overhead contained an extendable steam powered hoist.

The forward wheelhouse grew by morning and the polishing and finishing was completed with nearly a half hour before the deadline. Then they all turned toward an approaching steam powered wagon.

"Ah, here it is," the large carpenter exclaimed. "Pull it out and put it up, boys." He rubbed his hands together in anticipation as his sons pulled the large roll of canvas from the wagon and wrestled it onto the upper deck.

"Uh, you've put the canvas on the inside of the iron support hoops," one of the hoe-boys observed helpfully.

The carpenter smiled hugely as one of his boys fed a tube of canvas down through the hatch door. Another boy fed another tube to a pump and turned some valves and began pumping the canvas bag full of air. It swelled as it filled with air and within minutes it was bulging around the half hoops of iron that restrained it. The four brothers continued to pull at the ropes that held the canvas balloon into place snuggled up against the planking of the upper deck until the balloon was evenly situated. The pump continued to fill the hemp canvas, but the weave wasn't that tight and they had to keep pumping or the balloon would sag.

The carpenter turned to Heather. "Ma'am, I'm supposed to tell you it's time for little brother to do his tinkering thing."

Heather's face clouded, then she sighed and turned to Fallon as she pulled the amulet from a pocket. After his last episode of extended wear, she doled out his speed tinkering herself. She put the amulet in Fallon's hands as she recited the activation syllables and her brother's eyes came alive.

Chapter 20

"How is he?" Orlagh asked as several people looked on in wonder at the apparition.

"Asleep," Heather replied as she came out of the wagon to join the others. "He had to stay hyper the whole time to get it right. An hour and a half of hyper tinkering today after doing two hours just yesterday. His body can only take so much in big doses like that."

She scowled at the wagon. "Shouldn't have let him talk me into it."

"I thought he explained it pretty well," Orlagh said. "It would only work if he was in his hyper state and spraying the godstone paint on the canvas from the inside. Only he would be able to *see* where every pass of the sprayer needed to go to get the most even coverage with the right amount of godstone paint. Only he would be able to see the thin spots as the paint soaked into the canvas from the air pressure to keep the steam foam from leaking out."

They all stood and looked in wonder as the carpenter and his sons and the driver of the steam wagon packed up their tools and equipment.

The big man came over when they were ready to leave. "Balloon's not near big enough to fly with hot air or that new steam foam that fella from San Francisco invented." He shrugged helplessly and gestured. "Looks pretty, but... why?"

Before Heather could answer one of the self-appointed security men came running up. "Miss

Heather, they's some folks coming this way that say you harboring a criminal and that makes you a criminal, too. They's a lot of them and they's all got long guns and a mage to stand with them."

He looked panicked. "They's too many for us to defend Hoe-boy's Hill. The rest of us is going to scatter till they gets tired and goes home."

He shrugged. "Happens three-four times a year when the bulls roust us out. Once more by lynch mob's not much different, less'n you some other color than white."

He looked in the direction several had already fled. "Anyways, thanks for being such sharing people. Good words on you already traveling the rails. Hope you make it out alive but I'd be hurrying if'n you want your odds to stay good."

Then he turned and ran in the direction that would be hardest to travel, because that was the only direction their silent stalkers were *not* coming from.

"Well then, I guess we'd better go too," the carpenter said, then over his shoulder as his wagon followed the other, "Sure hope you folks know what yer doin'. Good luck!" They rode off without much worry, being fully white and lacking any shapeshifter auras.

"Orlagh!" Heather yelled as soon as the two wagons entered the forest. When Orlagh came within earshot she tried to maintain her calm. "I hope you can keep up with what tinkering you said you could do because Liam's got no hands and

Fallon's out cold from hyper exhaustion. It's just us, you and me and Blackie and his wife and daughter."

She looked around. "Where are they? I hope they didn't go to town."

"No," Orlagh replied. "Blackie was resting in the back of the wagon after the balloon spraying and Rosa was studying one of Fallon's tinker manuals in the sitting room while Maria sewed."

"Good. Go get Rosa to help you set up the foam steamer. It's the one about half again as long as it is wide and high. Have Maria go fetch two five-gallon buckets of water while Rosa and you set up the steamer."

She looked around where Trouble was tied between two trees so he could forage at his leisure while the wagon was being remodeled. She started to head that way when another of the guards approached.

"Miss Heather, Miss Orlagh needs to ride the stallion out of here so they can both be safe," he looked around with a measuring eye. "It's too late to drive the wagon out, but maybe we can hold them off if we hole up inside and pick 'em off. If'n you have a spare rifle my brother can reload for me while I help."

Heather hesitated as she tried to remember the young man's name. "Sesco is it? Sesco Lawson?"

"Yes'm. And my brother Revis."

The young man wrung the hat in his hands as he looked at the edge of the forest. "He got beat real bad in the head by a drunk bull and don't think real good anymore. He gets loud when he's scared and makes it hard to be quiet when hiding. He reloads real fast though and I can shoot fair straight. You might need another barrel spitting bullets at attackers."

He gave a look at several frantic whistles. "Sounds like some others waited too long too. They's a handful of folk coming back this way."

The young man looked her in the eye and stood straighter as his brother shuffled up and took his arm shyly, whispering loudly, "Go! Go! Scared!"

Heather didn't hesitate. "Revis!" When the brain hurt young man focused on her, she said, "You go into the wagon and make sure Fallon doesn't fall out of bed! He's been tinkering hard and is in his dead sleep. Okay? Can you do that for me?"

Revis bobbed his head fiercely for just a few seconds. "Not let him bump *his* head!" Revis promised as he hit his own with a palm slap, then ran off to perform his duty.

Heather looked into the grateful eyes of the other young hoe-boy. "Sesco, you say more of our own are coming back here?"

"Yes'm. Whistles say two groups, that family with three little'uns and a group of three."

"So, we have ten more bodies to lift," she half muttered to herself as she looked back at the railcar wagon with the stiff, too-small hemp canvas balloon painted with godstone hardener. The silvery color of the cigar shaped balloon lay in contrast to the polished wood of the railcar wagon beneath it.

She turned back to Sesco. "I want you to take Trouble to the back of the wagon and wake up Blackie if Orlagh hasn't already done so. Get the horse on the back stoop and lower the storm shutters, then take down the carbine hanging over the door inside the storage room and stand aft guard. You'll have to do your own reloading."

"Yes'm," the young man said and hurried to do what she said.

Moments later, Liam ran into the clearing and moved in practiced signals to report. Reading the newly learned body language, Heather was prepared when the young couple with three children under the age of ten came running into the clearing.

"Quick, get in the wagon. Go into the front sitting room and close all the storm shutters. You sir, I forgot your name. There's a carbine in the driving cabin just above the door. It's already loaded and there's another box of ammo in the niche on the right. Put the storm shutters down and don't plant your face in front of the slot windows. You're on forward guard post. Do *not* fire unless you're absolutely sure you're going to be shot at first. Shoot *only* those that are shooting at us."

The man nodded and herded his family into the wagon just as three men rushed into the clearing from another direction. "You three!" Heather pointed. "Into the wagon. Any of you have a weapon?"

One man held up an oversized derringer with a three-shot cylinder while another displayed a large Bowie knife. The third brandished an axe handle.

"Into the wagon," then she looked around and put a hand on the last man's arm. "Are there any more of ours inside the cordon?"

"No, Ma'am. Everybody else got out afore they closed off the southeast path. We's the last." He looked nervously in the direction of the growing din as beaters slow-walked through the forest, driving everything in their path.

A couple of deer bounded into the clearing, darted back and forth at the sight of the humans and Liam in cougar form and then dashed back into the forest. Then an older bear cub dashed into sight then ran straight for them and the man with the derringer lifted it and aimed.

"No!" Heather shouted and knocked the man's hand away just as he fired.

The bear cub skidded to a halt in front of them, bawled in terror, and turned to run back into the woods, then skidded to a stop again at a gunshot in the distance and sat down and bawled in racking sobs. Then a female bear bounded out of the woods and raced to her cub. As the mother bear consoled the cub with low mutterings, Heather approached slowly.

She put her hand on Liam's head as he walked up next to her. "Welcome friends," she gestured toward the wagon. "We seem to be getting a bit crowded, but there's still room if you want to avoid irrational bigotry."

There was only a moment's hesitation, then two more shots rang out closer than the first. The mother bear nudged her cub, then more forcefully till he rose and hurried to the wagon. Heather and

Liam quickly followed and in moments all of them were inside.

Heather positioned two more men in the larger driver's cabin and another in the sitting room with the bear people, then hustled the children into her cabin. "It has thicker walls for soundproofing, but they stop bullets better too," she explained to the mother. "That way you can reload without having to worry so much about them."

The woman nodded with confidence. "I'm sure we'll all be fine, Miss Heather. Now you go help that other lady create a miracle and save us all."

Heather snorted a laugh. "Okay, I'll do just that!" She smiled and turned to help Orlagh, muttering softly. "I hope."

She hustled the children into her cabin, then looked in on her brother in his. Revis was sitting on the floor with his legs wrapped around the bunk's center support beam.

The young man smiled. "I'm ready if we get jostled, Miss Heather. I won't let him get tossed out of bed."

Heather beamed at him. "Good man, Revis. Thank you."

The young man smiled and turned back to talk with his sleeping friend, telling him everything would be okay.

Heather stepped through the door to the aft storage room to find Orlagh ready. The foam steamer was hooked up to the hose that led up into the rigid balloon attached to the upper deck.

Blackie looked in through the door to the back stoop. "Trouble's secured in that harness thing on the back stoop and my Maria is manning one of the sniper rifles while that Sesco boy has the carbine."

He snarled his frustration as he gestured with his wounded arms. His injuries had improved quickly with mage healing, but he was still far from able to withstand a rifle's kick. "Can't do much more than reload for the others and be an extra set of eyes, but I'll do what I can."

"That's all anybody can ask," Heather said, then nodded to Orlagh.

Orlagh engaged the steam engine and it began feeding in the boiling water and turning it into foamed steam it pumped through the godstone tube leading up into the balloon. As it passed through the tube Heather chanted and the foam expanded explosively, piling up inside the balloon and forcing air back toward them in a growing wind, continuing to expand as it reacted to the mage chant and the otherworldly metal humans called godstone.

In moments the first five-gallon bucket was emptied and Maria poured in the second. Halfway through the second bucket the wagon shuddered and they could hear Revis' bellow of fear over that of the bear cub, but just barely.

They kept at their task just as Sesco challenged a man entering the mostly abandoned camp. "You there. We are prepared to defend ourselves if'n you display evil intent."

"I am Mayor Percival Granger," a loud voice proclaimed. "I have come for those what murdered one of my citizens and freed a criminal convicted to hang."

"You got a warrant?" Sesco hollered back from inside the heavy wood storm shutters with the narrow window that doubled as gun slots.

"Don't need no warrant," another voice yelled. "And I want the pelt of that animal bitch what embarrassed me at my bachelor's party."

Orlagh giggled as she fed the last of the steam into the tube while Heather tried to maintain her steady mage chant. Otherwise, they ignored the drama building in the abandoned camp. When the second five gallons drained out of the holding tank to form steam, Orlagh shut off the steamer and disconnected the tube, Heather put a hand on the godstone painted iron brace that wrapped around the godstone balloon and continued her chant. She winked at Orlagh and nodded her head that she had it from there as she continued chanting. Orlagh nodded and handed her the bag that held the energy drink Fallon had tinkered for his own nourishment while hypering.

"So, you don't have a warrant, just an angry boy and a mob of hate," Sesco commented, stalling. "I don't see the sheriff from Little Rock with you. He know you folks out here intent on killing people?"

"Ain't people," the mayor's son insisted. "Animals and, and, *mud people*! Their kind need to be put in their place and sometimes ya got to make a few examples so's the rest can see justice done right,"

The young man looked to his father for confirmation and got a nod of approval for his practiced words but his face didn't match his words and the approval only increased his frown.

"So, did ya get any beast people or other *real people*?" Sesco seemed to be able to draw the spokesmen for the growing crowd as Heather chanted the steam into foam so devoid of substance it weighed as close to nothing as it was possible to weigh.

The wagon lurched again then steadied firmly against the ropes tied to four iron stakes pounded into the ground.

"Sheriff accused *us* of being the criminals and threatened to arrest us if we didn't get out of *his* town," the young Granger sneered loudly. "And the damned Pinkertons wouldn't take our coin, but we got enough of our own folk to get justice back like it should be. Give us the animals and the mud people and the rest of you c'n go free."

Orlagh rose and began wiping excess foam away as it continued to swell with the magery Heather performed. Outside the confrontation continued as the wagon lurched again, creaking in a new way. After a few moments the seepage increased the foam coming out with more force but dripping less water in the process. Heather continued to chant, growing dizzy from the effort while examining the texture and consistency of the foam by watching Orlagh wipe it away.

"One more question," Sesco called out. "Did you catch anybody in the woods or was all that shooting and hollering just from braggards to feel good?"

The mayor didn't have a chance to lie as his son spouted off again, "Shot a big buck deer. Was a full animal, not a half animal. Gonna eat good tonight when we finish the party you folks interrupted."

"Don't know of any deer changelings, but you never know," a voice taunted from the front of the wagon. "So, you folks are cannibals too."

Ignoring the background noise of laughs and angry mutterings from inside the railcar, Heather waited till Orlagh swiped at the foam still emerging from the tube and when her hand came away dry, she cut off her chant.

Orlagh was ready and screwed the cap on the end of the tube. "You go up front, I'll distract them back here."

Heather nodded and Orlagh secured the tube then stepped out on the rear stoop. To her right, Trouble nickered and she reached into a bin the horse couldn't open and gave him an apple and spoke a few comforting words. She stepped around the steamcycle as she checked her pistol then put it back in its holster.

"Okay, Sesco, go ahead and raise the shutter."

"Miss Orlagh? They's a lot of guns out there. Might be better if'n we keep the shutters down to parley."

Orlagh smiled and turned to the side. "Rosa honey, you just duck down below the rail and be ready to help your mama use that sniper rifle if the shooting starts."

"Yes'm," Rosa replied as Maria folded the sniper rifle up on its extendable arm attached to the overhead hoist rail and locked it in place.

Securing the weapon facing the crowd, Maria dropped down to sit with her arms wrapped around her daughter and the support post for the aft rail. The new rear stoop's heavy oak planking was thick enough to protect both from any bullets.

When she was sure they were both protected, Orlagh nodded to Sesco. "Go ahead and raise the shutter, Mr. Lawson."

Sesco did so as Blackie moved back more in the shadow of the wide overhead. He held the pistol awkwardly in his right hand, the cast locking his elbow in place heavy but not interfering with the hand. He could hold his gun hand steady, just not aim very well. If he was needed it would be because they were being boarded. He didn't like it but he accepted Miss Orlagh's order, standing over his Maria and Rosa with his pistol ready.

The motion of the storm shutter caught every eye and when Orlagh stepped to the edge of the rail the half ring of people took notice. "Hello mayor, and the son. Never did get your name boy," she made a face and a distasteful mouth sound. "Got your taste, still there, maybe road apples will get it out."

"You! Pa!" The young man gaped at his father then whirled and pointed. "It's *her*!"

Then he looked startled. "She's… beautiful."

"She's an *animal*!" the mayor screamed at his son then turned toward Orlagh. "You keep yer devil magic to yerself girl! Don't you go hexing my boy!" His finger quivered in abject fear as he pointed it at her threateningly.

"My, my, mayor, I'm not doing anything but standing here wondering what could make civilized men act with such, *intensity*." She gestured around the mob's arc as she smiled down at the crowd.

Then she placed both hands on the rail and leaned forward far enough to look all around the camp on the north side of Hoe-boy Hill. "Tsk-tsk," she clicked her tongue as she scanned the camp with practiced eyes. "So many angry men intent on mischief."

"Thought we'd have gotten all that angry out already with so many on both sides dying in war." With the practice of a lifetime aided by her changeling ancestry, in a single one-second glance she counted twenty-four people on foot and two large wagons with a driver and a boy in the back of each banging a big drum.

Scattered among the rest were a dozen men on horseback. Except for the mayor and the drummers, every one of them brandished a weapon, including the mayor's son.

"War might be over, but a lot of scores still left to settle," the mayor regained the top speaking part, now the human form of the puma that had held his life in her jaws mesmerized his son.

Orlagh wasn't paying much attention and aimed her eyes at the taught rope that was all that held them down on the left rear corner, then caught

Sesco's eyes meaningfully. Sesco leaned over and blanched as he realized the wheels were not touching the ground.

He'd felt the wagon's tremors as the steam foam swelled to less than nothing but didn't realize they had lifted from the ground when the motion stopped. The motion stopped because the wagon was secured to long iron spikes driven deep in the ground, but the wheels were each more than a foot from the ground and the mooring ropes taught.

The mayor pompously rambled on with all of the self-importance he claimed for himself, thinking he had his quarry trapped. "Should have built a bigger balloon or a less fancy wagon," he crowed. "Then you might have got away from my justice." He sneered as he continued, "But you picked the wrong man to cross."

Continuing to ignore him Orlagh quickly gave Sesco some whispered commands and he rushed around Trouble to the other side of the stoop and leaned the storm shutter out and looked along the length of the wagon. He turned and shook his head and leaned back out, then he started loosening the rope and the wagon lurched as the right side moorings were loosened.

Orlagh turned back toward the mayor just as he yelled, "Are you listening to me?"

"Oh yes, mayor," Orlagh said sweetly. "And I'm so sorry I ruined your son's bachelor party. I bet the lucky lady is beautiful."

"Not as beautiful as you," the young man blurted, then looked aghast as a lumpy, bulbous-nosed man near him on horseback glared and shifted the aim of the carbine he held.

Nobody else seemed to notice but Orlagh and the mayor's son as she continued without pause, "I'm sure several of you men have beautiful wives and daughters you'd like to get home to." She glanced behind her where Sesco was comforting Trouble, then she leaned out and nodded as she unwound the mooring line but did not release the last pressure.

She caught several sets of eyes. "We have a dozen gun barrels inside an iron framework wrapped in thick wood and you're all packed into a bunch out in the open."

She smiled as several of the ones at the back nearest the forest began to look over their shoulders and move toward the cover of the trees behind them. Their concentration was on their silent retreat instead of the wagon – taking a dozen guns out of a quick response time.

She was waiting and when Heather blasted the locomotive horns mounted by the carpenter, she snapped the mooring rope the final bit loose and the wagon leaped for the sky.

Chapter 21

The hemp rope sang as it fed through the wooden cleat and over the side, feeding through the hoop of the spike buried in the ground. The wagon lurched with alternating resistance points as the ropes caught briefly at each corner but continued its leap into the sky. There was a harder jerk, then another, then they were lifting free, the four mooring lines dangling below them.

They were surprised to hear no gunfire, then there was a scream and Orlagh pushed the storm shutter out to see a man strike the rocks below. Another figure dangled from the rope below her and she saw that it was the mayor. She could just barely see the end of the rope behind her and it flapped free.

She started to call out to the mayor but before she could speak, he lost his grip and fell screaming to the rocks below, then the rail beside her shattered as a sniper's round hit. She pulled her pistol and reached out to fire downward, emptying her revolver and stepping back to reload.

Before she could dump the spent casings and reload, Maria shoved by and unlocked the sniper rifle and swing it to the rail. The rifle was fitted within its mechanical arm with an iron shield and Maria leaned out over the circular firing platform and gripped the rifle with steady concentration.

A second later another round from below streaked by and they heard it impact the balloon above them with a metallic whump. Maria took a breath, held it, then squeezed the trigger, then shifted her aim as the shield around her rifle's body and scope rang and a round ricocheted into the overhead planking, still wet with wood polish.

Without flinching, she resumed her position, took aim, took a steady slow breath, held it, and squeezed, then shifted her aim. The third time she had to follow her target around till she relaxed and pulled the sniper's rifle back into the standby position. "Out of range."

Finished reloading, Orlagh darted a look over the rail to see they were well out of the range of any sniper firing upwards. Maria could have shot into the crowd below, and muzzle flashes showed the frustrated mob was still firing upwards, but none of the bullets from below were going to reach them. It was most likely that bullets falling back down would strike within the mob.

She also marked the two dead snipers and the third abandoned rifle where the third sniper dropped it to run for his life.

She watched as they continued to rise and after a few more seconds their rising slowed perceptively and they began to move horizontally with the few clouds around them in a northeasterly direction. Holstering her revolver, she moved to each one of those with her. "Everybody okay? Nice shooting Maria. You okay Rosa? Blackie?" She leaned around the big black man and smiled. "Trouble doing okay, Sesco?"

"Yes'm," the young man replied as he fed Trouble an apple. "Told him if he didn't kick me, I'd give him an apple."

The young man smiled. "He was so good I gave him a double handful of oats too." Then he patted Trouble on the neck and jerked his head over his shoulder. "Oh yeah, we got a rider still hanging on over this side."

Orlagh rushed to look over the left rear corner of the airship, to see the mayor's son dangling below. Her brief look showed her that he hung by some tinker's contraption that gripped the rope firmly. The device was attached to the young man's forearm securely.

Orlagh gaped and the young man smiled up at her as he dangled by his left arm. "Hi. Uh, could you pull me up?"

His smile only flickered a bit when Maria, then Blackie, then Rosa joined Orlagh at the rail. "On second thought, I'm good right here for now."

"Okeh," Orlagh replied in Chaktaw, "you let us know when you're ready to come up. Oh, you got a name?"

"Mathew, Mathew Granger."

"Okay Mathew Granger, you just hang on and think about what you've gotten yourself into. When you want to come up here and face us with the numbers on our side, you just holler."

"Yes'm," Mathew muttered morosely and looked at the ground far below as the railcar flew with the wind.

She hid a smile then moved away from the rail. "Blackie, could you please stay here and if Mr.

Granger asks nicely you can pull him up if you want."

Blackie gestured with his whole-arm cast and the left arm still in its sling. Mage healing had done him wonders in a short time, but it would be a while before he could use *either* arm effectively.

Orlagh simply smiled. "Well then I guess you'll just have to explain to Mr. Granger how much you'd *like* to pull him up, but you're still recuperating from his bachelor party."

Blackie beamed. "Right you are Miss Orlagh. Might want to remind him that if I *could* pull him up, I might be well enough to see if a man might want to go one-on-one instead of kicking me in the ribs *three* times while four men held me spread-eagled at kicking height."

Orlagh raised an eyebrow. "He the one broke your ribs?"

Blackie's brows creased. "Actually, no. Come to think of it his kicks hurt the least of all. I whuffed and moaned out of habit just like my kind have learned to do all our lives when being disciplined, but he didn't hurt me at all. Even hit in such a way only *looked* hurtful."

Then the large black man took on a thoughtful look. "Looked at his pa every time he said something hateful, too, like he was always being tested."

"Hmm," Orlagh mused. "Tell you what, you might want to ask him about that. See what he says. Maria, Rosa, could you please raise the shutters and use the sniper scope to see if any of our persistent stalkers are still coming after us?"

They turned to their task as she turned to the hoe-boy. "Sesco, could you please take care of Trouble and be another set of eyes and ears. And remember we're just like any hot air balloon up here. Sound travels so it might be best if you have to talk, to whisper softly and *listen* to what people are saying below us. If *we're* quiet, they won't realize how loud *they* are. I'm going forward to see what's happening."

They nodded and scattered to do their tasks without comment, already being quiet as the wagon flew free in the sky at the mercy of cloud high winds.

Orlagh entered the supply compartment with her hammock swinging near the left rear window, just behind the foam chanting station. Actually, it was hers only three days out of every lunar month, the rest of the time it was her brother's. She had to admit, though, he'd claimed a perfect spot in the luxurious vessel they'd ended up traveling on.

She ducked through the next door into the narrow hall between the two main cabins, looking inside Fallon's room to see Revis still sitting with his charge. "How's he doing? Revis? How is Fallon doing?"

Revis turned his head. "I didn't let him fall. He did wake up fer a bit when the shootin' started. Stuck his head out tha window and looked all around fer a bit, then fell back tah sleep and I held him agin." Then he fell backwards, his legs still wrapped around the support post and his arm and chest covered in blood.

"Revis!" She rushed into the compartment and bent over the young man looking for the wound.

"It's okay Miss Orlagh," he said slowly then held up his arm where a bandana was tied. "Blood's all mine. Waited till the shaking and shooting stopped before I wrapped it but it ain't bleedin' no more." He scowled down at his chest. "Ruined my shirt. Hope Sesco don't get mad."

"Oh you wonderful boy!" Orlagh said and gave him a kiss on the forehead where he lay then rose to her feet. "You wait right there and I'll get somebody in here quick."

"Yes'm. I'll just lay right here and rest."

"What happened?" Fallon said weakly as he stirred on the bed.

Orlagh snorted. "You slept through the maiden launch of the greatest airship in the world is what happened."

"Had a dream," he muttered with a baffled look as she explained.

"Revis said you woke up long enough to take a quick look out of your window, but you were out the rest of the time after you sprayed the inside of the balloon. That bunch of race purists came back and we were surrounded. We had to make steam foam and Heather chanted it till it hardly even existed anymore, and well, it worked. A balloon of godstone painted canvas no bigger than the railcar it carries, and it flies. It flies near a mile high with a full load and thirteen unexpected passengers."

Fallon blinked as he came awake and his mind quickly caught up. They found he was lucid for the first few minutes after waking from any deep sleep after speed tinkering. Depending on the length of the hyper tinkering session, for that first few minutes he was as normal as anyone. His awareness diminished and his focus drifted and he was addled within a half hour, but at first, he was a normal young man.

His forehead creased. "I don't hear the fans."

It was Orlagh's turn to look confused. "Fans?"

Fallon had spent a long time in a hyper state to spray the interior of the canvas balloon. As a result, his awareness dissolved more rapidly after waking from his hyper sleep. He lost track of what he was going to say, then recovered. Shuffling through the shelves beside his bunk, he pulled out one of his many tinker's manuals and held it out.

"This shows how to assemble the fan blades. We have all the parts you need on board to make two complete fan and rudder frames. Otherwise we'll just drift with the wind." He pursed his lips. "That's what we're doing now, isn't it?"

"Yes," Orlagh confirmed. "But we're high enough we're not likely to run into anything and we're heading in the right direction. At least now we're above sniper range."

Fallon's brows creased again as his thinking started to get harder. What did he just want to ask? Oh yeah! "Did we get any holes in the balloon?"

Orlagh nodded. "Yes, I'm sure we did. I know of at least two rounds that didn't hit the rail and I'm sure I heard at least one solid hit. But we don't seem to be leaking."

Fallon worked his mouth but nothing came out. So quick this time. Usually it took *at least* ten or fifteen minutes before he went dumb again. It wasn't fair, just when he thought he'd gotten through that cloud in his mind he'd caused a greater one. He wished he'd never gone fast that first time, the sniper would have put him out of his misery.

"Patch kit," he stammered. "Last chapter of second maintenance manual." It was getting harder to focus as his attention was caught by so many things at once. He pointed shakily. "Patch sprayer there."

Then he dropped his arm and turned toward Orlagh. He smiled pleasantly. "Can I have my paints? I want to paint. Painting makes me feel good."

Orlagh sighed. This lucid period hadn't lasted very long. She would have to tell Heather. It wasn't something that could be hid because it might help Fallon's sister find a mage cure for the dark mage's curse. And any help with breaking *that* curse could aid in learning how to break her family's curse.

"Yes, Fallon. Remember? We put them right here with this easel we built right into your wall. Here, see, all your tubes of paint and your brushes."

"How many pages?"

"Just two at a time, remember? And you have to finish one before you can get a clean sheet. Remember? You were the one suggested that rule."

"I 'member," Fallon muttered shyly then pointed. "Who's he?"

"That's Revis. He held onto you while we we're getting away from the bad men and got shot. He's okay, just sleeping."

"*Real* sleeping or the kind that don't stop?" Fallon wondered, then said, "Must be the real kind. The kind that don't stop don't make that noise."

Orlagh almost bit her tongue. "Well, you paint to help you relax and say hi to Revis when he wakes up."

"Okay," then he rose from his bed and started looking through the tubes of paint for the colors he wanted.

Orlagh watched for a few seconds then ducked out and headed forward, into chaos. The sitting room was packed, all the chairs and benches full and several other people sitting flat on the floor. In the center a bear cub almost too big to be called a cub hung close to a suffering mother bear.

Orlagh sympathized with the mother. "First forced change at puberty?" she guessed softly as she scratched the cub behind the ears.

The mother bear sighed and bobbed her head.

"Hey there young man," Orlagh said. "My name is Orlagh, I'm a cougar. That's my brother over there those children are crawling on."

The cub turned and gave a couple of bear-sized sniffs and looked at Orlagh mournfully. His mother had taken him into the woods so he could fully enjoy his first time in forced, full bear form and he gets chased by race purists and almost killed for what he'd turned into. He couldn't even speak in this form and he was miserable down to his core.

"You do realize we're flying, don't you?" His ears perked up. "Yes, that's why nobody's shooting at us, we're over a mile high…"

She didn't get any further as everyone spun to open all the shuttered windows to gape at the ground a mile below them. The bear cub ran back and forth and was looking at Orlagh piteously when a boy tugged his paw and moved to the side so the bear could see.

"Orlagh, three holes… oh," Fallon stood and looked at the people lining the sides of the air wagon, gazing in wonder at the ground below. He went into one of his trances and his eyes scanned the car's interior with a slow speed that made it look like he was staring at the same spot for several seconds at a time.

Orlagh saw the steady pace of the young man's head as he *memorized* the entire scene. She waited as the others ignored him, entranced with the scene out their windows. After several moments he focused on her face and smiled.

"What was it you wanted, Fallon?"

"Huh? Oh, nothing… just memories," then he turned and went back to his room.

Orlagh sighed, then went forward into the expanded driver's area at the front of the air wagon where she approached Heather and handed her the manual. "That's supposed to show how to make fans that can push us where *we* want to go instead of where the wind takes us."

"Fallon?"

Orlagh shook her head sadly. "He was only awake for a few minutes this time before he wanted to paint. He's doing that now. Before he left us again, he gave me that," she pointed toward the manual. "It shows how to build frames that will hook into the main wheel and steer us wherever the driver, pilot, aims us. He also mentioned *patch kits* after I told him we'd been hit by bullets from below."

Heather nodded. "Yes, we'll get some steady leakage through the holes."

She looked over the side and along their flank. "In fact, I can see we're already losing altitude and I think I see at least one hole leaking steam."

She looked around in the direction the wind was taking them and pointed. "I'm going to try to set her down on that open field." Then she got busy with valves and watching the angles the wind was taking them.

Orlagh watched with fascination as they drifted close to the right direction.

"Everybody move left!" Heather shouted then ran to the left side of the cabin and motioned frantically. The others up front moved to the left side of the cabin and the weight caused the air wagon to tilt in that direction. "Back to center!" Heather shouted, then did so, everybody else copying her movements slightly behind her. The air wagon leveled out and Heather released more steam from inside the balloon and they dropped faster. "Going to be a little short. Might scrape those trees."

Orlagh watched as the line of trees around the open hilltop grew closer, then her eyes grew wide and she turned and rushed back through the railcar. She dashed through the sitting room lined with backs on both sides as their passengers gaped out of the windows, soaking in every instant of an experience they would never in the world believe they would ever have.

She ran through the sitting room and darted down the hallway between Heather and Fallon's private cabins and into the rear storage room. She burst through the door to the rear stoop and worked her way around Trouble to look over the side. Mathew Granger was hanging limply. Was he dead? Then he yawned and settled down again.

"Hey!"

He jumped and began swinging in a slow circle. On one slow turn he saw what lay ahead and he looked up in shock.

"Can you climb?"

He tried to move but only flailed and spun in a faster circle. "No! Left arm won't move. It's all numb and tingly."

"Oh for…" she snorted.

"Hang on," she said and began pulling the rope up hand over hand. It was slow and if not for her changeling strength she would not have been able to do it but she got him high enough he only broke a couple of branches on the very top of the tree they hit. By this time Sesco realized what she was doing and grabbed the rope before the force of hitting the tree tore it from her grasp and looped it around a cleat.

Then they struck the ground and bounced – and so did Mathew – then he was dragged behind as the air wagon rolled on its huge ground wheels. When they finally stopped, he lay unmoving.

She leaped over the rail and ran back to him and turned him over. His head in her lap he slowly opened his eyes to see her head surrounded by the glow of the sun behind her.

"Beautiful," he muttered, and fainted.

Chapter 22

"No," Mathew shook his head, then flinched. His left arm had been dislocated at both the elbow and shoulder and was now in a tight sling, but not too tight because he had two broken ribs. His right arm was broken and the elbow separated when they crash-landed and was in a full cast to keep them rigid.

He looked at Blackie, still recuperating from almost identical wounds. "I'll rent a buggy and drive back to town to bury my Pa. He wasn't much and made me do things I didn't want to do to please him, but now he's gone and I can do what I want. At least I won't have to marry Bertha Adams."

He shuddered at the thought.

He looked around at the people seeing him off, many of them with decidedly less than friendly faces. He looked at Orlagh instead. "Mrs. Lincoln took out two of the snipers and you already shot Mr. Yoder's head off."

He hung his head. "My Pa and Mr. Ginrich both fell to their deaths. That's five out of the seven or eight that were always the first to get people riled up. Maybe with them dead, things'll have a chance to settle down to normal."

"Yeah, maybe," Blackie growled.

Mathew blushed. "If it don't, I intend to sell my Pa's land, well, I guess it's mine now, and go where folks might allow me to be able to let folks be different. I'm tired of doing wrong to please the people I'm supposed to look up to, but don't."

Blackie snorted, then shuffled forward and offered his right hand. It was awkward for both of them, their elbow-locking casts keeping them from getting the right angle They worked at it till they could clasp hands, then they smiled at each other through the pain their contortions caused.

"Think he'll change?" Orlagh asked as Mathew Granger walked down the road with the family of five and the three other members of the former passengers.

"I'm more wondering if the others take all he owns and leave him in a ditch," Heather pondered.

Orlagh put a hand on her pistol. "They wouldn't!"

Heather laughed. "Actually, I put a charm on the three men so they want to protect him as long as he buys them the hot restaurant meal, heavy rain slicker, kitchen backpack with basic provisions, and a good pistol he promised each."

Orlagh laughed. "How about the family? You charm them too?"

"No," Heather beamed. "He promised to buy them a cart big enough to haul all three kids, a full kitchen kit with a week's supplies, and a donkey to pull it. I did give the wife a charm to compel one promise and told her if he didn't keep his *freely offered* promise to use it on him. If he does keep his promise then she's got a future charm to use as needed if they ever get in a tight bind."

The small group passed out of sight and the two young women turned to look at the downed air wagon.

"You want to do it?" Heather asked.

"Oh, may I?' Orlagh replied eagerly. "I'm going to change soon and it'll be another experience I can remember when I don't have thumbs for another cycle of the moon."

Heather smiled. "Okay, you do the inside and I'll roll them from outside."

They went to the air wagon and Orlagh helped Heather into the steam foam hoist and tied all the safety ropes to the rail, then they filled the hoist's balloon with steam foam and Heather lifted to pull herself around the side of the air wagon.

"I already found two bullet holes," she called down as she displayed her roller. "I'm ready."

Orlagh nodded then dashed into the wagon and grabbed the patch kit and the small hand sprayer. Sesco held the ladder as she climbed up to turn the wheel on the hatch the carpenters put next to the feeder tube. There was a small whuff of air as the seal cracked, then a couple drops of water fell as she threw the hatch open inside the godstone-painted canvas balloon.

As she pulled herself up and into the interior of the balloon her eyes adjusted to the gloom. Three lines of light pierced the darkness, each of them on the same side of the balloon's shell. The bullets that had pierced the outer hull plunged through the nothingness that was mageried steam foam and stopped. All three bullets would be lying on the bottom of the balloon where they fell when the foam dissipated with the opening of all pressure valves.

Orlagh moved over to the nearest hole and yelled, "Okay, I'm going to see if I can work this thing!"

She was fidgeting with the sprayer when she finally found the on switch and twisted it hard like the directions said to do. The tiny engine caught and it chugged to life, vibrating in her hand as it built steam. In moments the tiny plug of godstone began to melt and she yelled, "Almost ready."

"Okay," Heather yelled from outside, hanging from the steam foam hoist near the bullet hole Orlagh was getting ready to patch. "I'm ready too!"

When the godstone pellet was melted and drained into the sprayer tube, Orlagh yelled, "Okay, I'm getting ready to spray the patch!"

"Okay, I'm ready, too!"

Orlagh raised the *patch*, a tiny circle of canvas sewn onto a larger circle than the bullet hole. She waited till the hand steam sprayer leaked a tiny drop of melted godstone from the tip and yelled. "Spraying!" Then she sprayed the tiny patch and held the patch further away and swept the sprayer across the canvas a second time, only a little getting on her leather glove. Then she positioned the patch with the tiny circle over the hole.

She released the patch and grabbed the roller and yelled, "Rolling!"

Through the balloon shell she faintly heard the responding. "Rolling."

Then she yelled, "Spraying!" And she sprayed in as even strokes as she could till the sprayer sprayed air and she called out, "Empty!

Rolling!" She didn't hear the response through the balloon shell but she could feel the other roller's resistance when she lightly rolled the patch. She counted the dozen and a half rolls, then inspected her efforts in the light of the other two holes. The blackness was so great and her eyes adjusted so well those two tiny shafts of light were all she needed to see what she was doing.

All three holes were in the lower bulge of the balloon where it extended past the edge of the railcar below, the bullets coming from below as they were. None of them pierced the foam far enough to exit the shell at the top of the balloon.

In minutes they moved to the second hole, moving faster with experience, then quickly patched the last one by the light of one of Fallon's friend Tom's tinkered candles. The two young women finished the repairs in less than an hour once they got going and were relaxing in the railcar's sitting room with mugs of tea when Sesco called out from his watch down by the road. They all walked down to meet the cart with the family of five all smiling.

"He bought us a bigger cart 'cause it was the only one for sale," the father explained. "Then he had to buy *two* burros 'cuz he said the cart was too big for one."

"They're a mated pair," the wife whispered excitedly. "Gonna give us youngins to sell or give to our three when they git older."

"Oh, Mr. Granger said to give you these." He dug four iron spikes with rope rings on the end out of the cart. "Said they're in trade for the four you left back at that hoe-boy's camp."

He shook his head. "Amazing how one day he's the evilest man you can know next to his Pa, and the next he can be downright *civil* once his Pa's dead."

"Not so amazing, I'd say," Orlagh opined. "Sometimes bad men are following the only example they think they have to follow. Once you give them a chance to be who they want to be you find out they're not the man you thought they were."

Heather snorted. "Not always to the good. Sometimes you think you found a winner only to have him come up lame!"

The two women laughed and joked as they dug out the crates and packages Fallon had delivered along their planned trail up to Little Rock. In a couple of hours, they had the first of the huge steam fans attached to the aft end of the wagon.

"This thing would feel real good blowing across the stoop on a hot muggy evening," Orlagh commented.

"I would rather be inside a closed room with steam foam insulation and a chilled glass of tea," Heather commented.

"A sitting room sized freezer closet!" Orlagh exclaimed with a gay laugh. "Now *that* would be decadent!" The two of them laughed and began assembling the second tinker's fan.

By the time the motor and support frameworks were assembled on either side of the aft end the sun was setting. It took all of them with workable arms and a steam hoist to lift the fans into place as darkness settled and attach them to the frame of the wagon directly above the rear ground wheels.

"That's what those tubes with the springs inside are for," Orlagh commented.

"What?" Heather asked, as she looked at the wagon settled down more on the back end.

"Those four tubes in the supply room under my hammock," Orlagh explained, thrilled she had figured out their purpose. She pointed at the frame of the air wagon. "They attach at two spots on the frame on each side and on that frame around the axle. They absorb the shock of the wheels and raise the heavier, back end half of the frame level with the front."

Heather leafed through the manual in her hand, turning pages till she found the one she was looking for. "Yes! There they are! Spring levelers!"

She pointed at the manual page, then looked up at Orlagh and chuckled. "My brother built an entire air wagon with pusher fans and patches for the balloon and mechanical arms to hold the weight of a sniper's rifle so a child can defend us. And he built a ground vehicle capable of carrying the air wagon across any landscape *and* he wrote it all down in manuals with detailed pictures so any half-educated man could follow the directions."

She glanced in the direction of Fallon's cabin. He was probably still inside engrossed in his latest painting. She held the manual out for Orlagh to see. "See here, this last picture doesn't look like what the wagon looks like now. The *inside* looks the same, but it's bigger, wider. The wheels are inside an outer walkway with a high rail. See, it goes around the pusher fans and around the wheels to this big patio deck on the aft end."

She pointed at the detailed pictures in the manual. "He even drew in small doors right where they would be at the back end of the sitting room, one on each side." She stabbed the page with a finger. "*That's* what our wagon will look like the next time my brother gets hold of his amulet." She put a hand on the pocket holding the magical device.

They still did their best to make the attached pusher fans match Fallon's pictures and when they brought him out to see, he smiled broadly. When they took him back to his room, they found him mostly finished with two complete pictures, each on a three by two-foot canvas sheet. One was a vertical picture of the air wagon lifting from Hoe-boy Hill surrounded by angry people, and the other showed the distant ground through windows crowded by the backsides of a dozen saved refugees with a grizzly bear mother and cub in the center ready for battle.

Orlagh smiled, knowing one person that would be *very* glad this version got more exposure. And it would because Liam had been copying the large oil paintings on his paper paged diary as much as his skill allowed, in colored pencil. On each left page he described every exciting day in detail and on the right supplied his own rough sketches of the *Fallon Richards* originals.

He sent three sections with sketches home by post and locally and the dime novels they commissioned were being sold faster than they could be printed. They were repairing the air wagon from its inaugural voyage when people hired to make those repairs marveled they were already reading about the adventure only days after it happened and meeting the heroes of those adventures.

It was inevitable more than one of those insisted on getting a *picture* with the air wagon in the background. As it happened those pictures ranged from the newly crashed vessel to the proudly standing version with the impressive steam powered, twin, counter-revolving pusher fans mounted inside barrels.

When the full moon waned and their curse again reversed along with the two bears, the mother bear abandoned her newly pubescent cub.

"That's the way it is, son," she said as she walked away. "You get to stay with me till you turn full bear. If you was a girl you might get to stay a couple years more, but that's only so I could teach my daughters how to ditch male cubs as soon as they turn."

She waved a hand over her shoulder. "You want company go find your father." With that she walked away, the grain sack she'd accepted as a dress sashaying with every swing of her ample hips.

Orlagh's tail lashed as Liam tried hard not to laugh aloud. Before the change his sister had been sure the mother bear hadn't been taking her newly turned son out to the woods to ditch him. It was obvious how wrong she was. As soon as the moon had waned and the bears had changed, along with Orlagh and Liam, the obvious was, well, obvious.

Bear changelings were pretty much like their animal likenesses. Male bears were solitary and generally antisocial while the females ditched a newly pubescent male bear cub during his first full, forced change at human puberty.

The abandoned cub, a pimply boy of about fifteen or sixteen, it was hard to tell through the dirt and grime with only a grain sack for a sort of kilt, gaped at where his mother disappeared into the woods. After a moment he turned toward the small audience. "She left me. She just walked away and told me to stay away from her."

He sounded miserable, then a rumble sounded from the direction of his midsection. "Anybody got anything to eat," he wondered hopefully.

Chapter 23

"Last chance!" Heather stated as they stood around the air wagon. "Anybody? No? Okay then, all aboard."

Those that had decided to stay with the Richards Air Wagon scampered aboard. They included the brother and sister that owned the air wagon and another brother and sister that switched changeling bodies each full moon.

In addition to those four was a pair of brothers, a husband and wife and their near adult daughter, and two orphans of sorts. One was a true orphan while the other just acted like one till he got his mental attitude shifted to accept his lot in life.

The eleven of them included three shapeshifters, one Master Mage and four casual mages of increasing experience, one sometimes Master, Master Tinker, and ten tinkerers of varying growing capabilities.

They climbed the ladders up to the deck that wrapped around the former railcar and headed for their duty stations.

Since it was an odd numbered day, Blackie and Rosa took the forward watch post and backup drivers while Sesco and Revis took the aft deck. Orlagh and Brutus napped in the sitting room while Fallon worked on another pair of paintings – he always did two at a time.

Liam operated the steamer while Heather chanted the foam till they gently lifted from the ground just as the sun set. Rosa initiated the fans as they slowly rose and turned them into the wind while Heather chanted the steam foam into further nothingness. When Liam wiped away a dry film of steam foam, she stopped her chant and he screwed the cap over the tube and stowed it.

The two of them hurried forward and Heather took the wheel from Rosa while Liam walked from one end of the air wagon to the other checking everything on his mental list. When he sat back down in the seat beside her, he reported.

"Sesco and Revis have aft watch and Fallon's painting," he ticked off fingers as he talked. "Maria, Brutus, and Orlagh are in the sitting room and the waif is on the side opposite my bunk huddled against a wall and…" he gestured where Blackie and his daughter were looking over the rail at the anchor point below, "and you and me," he ticked off eleven fingers. "All crew accounted for Cap'n," he said with a smile as the air wagon drifted on the end of its tether with the air fans keeping them hovering into the wind.

"Release the tether, please," Heather called out and Blackie let slack into the forward cleat and the rope whistled through and away to curl around the tree they were anchored to.

They rose quickly as the line fed out around the limb of the tree below. He leaned forward to watch. "Mooring line free." Then he started pulling it up and coiling it below the forward cleat while Heather turned the large wheel.

Heather got the feel of the twin fans behind her, turning with gusto and pushing them in the direction indicated by the flat compass mounted atop the post in front of her. When she was lined up, she fed power to the fans and their speed increased along with the wind in their faces.

Looking around she spotted Fallon gaping in wonder as if he hadn't been the one that had built their wondrous air wagon in his mind and drawn specific schematics of each and every part. He performed this amazing feat while under the mental hyper speed that was aging him four days a minute, but in his current state he was no more than any other awestruck observer.

He had created some miraculous tinkerings, but at a cost that showed every day. He started out as a boy just crossing that line into manhood, but a month later looked a decade older. Heather finally took charge of the amulet and rationed its use to keep him from literally burning out, but even she had to admit that without his sacrifices they probably wouldn't be alive now.

She continued to adjust their speed and angle as she watched the compass and after an hour switched places with Liam. "The wind's on our right and she keeps pulling left."

"Okay," he said as he took the wheel. After a few minutes, he said, "I see what you mean. I can just feel the correct pressure to keep on the wheel to stay true to the compass."

He took his eyes off the compass for a second to look her in the eyes. "Your brother is a genius, you know?"

"Yes, he is," she smiled in return and placed a hand on his arm. "And he's much more aware and easier to get along with when you're around. I can't say enough how thankful I am to you for the way you treat him. Much of the healing to his heart has been because of you."

Liam smiled and looked back at the sky in front of them. He adjusted the wheel minutely and the air wagon turned back into the wind till the compass was pointed exactly where calculated.

The young man had created another manual training lesson and penned it on several pages of hemp paper. Then Heather created a memory charm on Liam, Sesco, Rosa, and herself while he gave an intense enchanted course in stellar navigation. Now the four of them could all plot their position every three hours all day with a glance at the sky using the teaching manual as a reference.

An hour later they switched seats again, this time Rosa taking a turn at piloting while Liam went aft to check things out. He checked the water feed line and gauge readings to the pusher fans and entered the numbers in the log book after topping off the water reservoirs. After he initialed Sesco's navigational readings, he went to the aft deck to watch the world pass by beneath them for a few minutes to visit.

"How's your arm, Revis?"

"All better!" Revis exclaimed then winced as he moved it too quickly. "Miss Heather gave me a new shirt to replace the one what got all bloody."

Liam smiled. "That was a brave thing you did."

"Not brave," Revis objected. "Only had to hold Fallon onto bed so he won't fall." He chuckled nervously. "Not brave, *easy*."

Liam put a hand on the brain-hurt man's arm. "Not that. I mean staying with Fallon while *you* were hurt. *That* was brave."

Revis looked at him skeptically. "Didn't bleed that much but okay, if you say so Mr. Quinn."

Liam laughed and patted the man on the shoulder, then pointed at the world below. "Looks beautiful from up here, doesn't it?"

Revis simply nodded and they looked on companionably for several minutes. Occasionally someone below would yell up to them and they would yell back down, but at their height most words were hard to understand. Revis was best at getting those on the ground to understand them with his hands cupped over his mouth and yelling single words at a slower pace.

He was also best at yelling his and his brother's names. Liam let the lack of other names go so as to help confuse any tracking of their movements. After a few more minutes he left the aft deck and passed through the storage room on his way to check on Fallon.

The waif, whose name none of them had gotten out of her yet, lay in the spare hammock from storage, set opposite to his own by the starboard corner window. She nodded as their eyes locked and he nodded in return and continued on. The right side pusher fan whirred just outside her open window, but she'd tucked cotton in her ears to muffle the sound. She'd silently handed him his own cotton ball earlier. It was still tucked in a pocket ready for use when he returned to his hammock. The ideal quiet place he'd chosen earlier not looking so peaceful now.

Reaching Fallon's cabin door, he knocked and when Fallon opened the door, he almost burst out laughing. Fallon's face was covered in several different colors of paint. His eyes lit up. "Liam! Hi!"

He looked at the mess in his hands and wiped his face. "I forgot to put the caps on some of my paints." Then he went into an intense study of his hands. "The colors are so… *colorful*."

"May I come in?" Liam prompted to break Fallon out of his building trance.

"Oh! Yes, come in, come in," the young man stepped back and gestured. "Look!"

Liam stepped into the room and looked in wonder at the boy's latest creations.

The left canvas was turned so that it was taller than wide. It showed the air wagon from an angle of the front deck surrounded by men brandishing guns and ropes and torches. The wagon was in the process of slipping its mooring lines and three of the men with longer rifles were firing up. Liam leaned in close and saw the exact spot of one of the bullets hitting, where a small puff of steam could be seen in the picture. Fallon's face filled a window in the middle of the railcar while the others could be seen on the fore and aft decks.

The other picture showed the backsides of everybody in the sitting room as they looked out of the windows after they first launched. In both pictures the colors were bright and vibrant and every bush and bird, and grain of wood or fold of cloth was as lifelike as he could imagine. Both pictures had a three-dimensional look that made them seem more of a scene through a window than a painted picture.

"As soon as Heather charms them so they last longer we can put them in frames and, and, so can I start two more now?"

Liam chuckled as he put caps on paint tubes that looked like they matched. "Yes, we did promise you could only get new canvases if you finished the ones you had, didn't we?"

Fallon answered by rapidly shaking his head up and down, his mop of hair flying every which way.

Finished capping paint tubes Liam wiped his hands on a relatively clean rag then stroked his chin in thought and Fallon copied him, smearing more paint on his face in the process. "Your sister is kind of busy right now flying our air wagon and can't charm these," he gestured to the two pictures, "yet. You still have a lot of paper, don't you?"

"Yes," Fallon said, pointing. "Got two rolls under my bunk."

Liam spread his hands. "There you are! While you're waiting for Heather to charm these two canvas paintings you can use the pencils to draw more pictures on paper sheets." Fallon's eyes lit up and Liam tried to slow him down some. "Remember, we don't have the paper making machine anymore because we didn't have room. Those two rolls of hemp paper are all you have so don't use them all up too fast."

Fallon's eyebrows creased as Liam continued, "What I would suggest is you do the same as you did there," he pointed toward the two pictures, "but with colored pencil drawings. Do one at a time till that one is finished before you start another."

Fallon's eyes were bright and he was more animated than in a long time between his enchantments in hyper tinkering. "I could make a picture book of all I've seen since," his face fell. "Since Ma and Pa got killed."

He swallowed at the memory as he looked back up at Liam, then he blurted, "I'm going to need more colored pencils."

Liam snorted a laugh. "Just go easy on the ones you have till we can buy some more. Can you cut the pages yourself, or do you want me to help?"

Fallon's smile warmed his heart like he couldn't believe as the innocent face beamed. "Will you help me? I could do it myself, but it's more fun with somebody else."

Then he whispered conspiratorially, "Revis likes to help but it takes too long to get him to understand and by then I get distracted, then he gets bored and goes away."

Liam smiled as he pulled out one of the rolls of silky hemp paper. The roll was bigger than he expected and had enough paper to keep Fallon busy for quite some time. After getting out the roll of hemp paper, he went to the storage room and retrieved the paper cutter Fallon had tinkered together just for this purpose.

The waif ignored him as she materialized behind them and selected one of Fallon's manuals, nodded at Fallon who nodded back, then darted back out the door.

"You might as well keep this in your room so you can cut your own sheets if you run out before anybody else can help you." Liam said, giving the departing waif a glance.

"Okay," Fallon mumbled as he began to get excited.

"Fallon, watch your breathing," Liam cautioned. "Slow and deep, slow and deep."

Fallon repeated the words on Liam's second time as he calmed himself. "Slow and deep."

Liam readied the cutter and Fallon pulled the sheet out flat on the measuring pad.

"How big?" Liam asked, then added, "The roll is eighteen inches wide. Why don't you make each page twenty inches long so you have a border to sew together for the spine to make a book? That would give you square pages one and a half feet on a side"

Fallon beamed. "Okay! Twenty inches long." Then he stuck his tongue out as he measured the first length precisely and pressed the page flat. "Okay, cut."

They cut ten pages before Liam said, "That should be enough to start with, don't you think?"

Fallon looked at the cut pages critically. "Can I use both sides?"

Liam made a face. "I don't see why not." He held up a cautioning finger. "But remember Heather can't lock the pages one side at a time and if you try to lock it with only one side finished the other side won't stick. So be careful you don't smear one side when you're drawing and writing on the other."

"Okay. Can I start now?"

Liam laughed, wondering if Fallon heard a word he'd said. "Sure, let me put the roll of paper back under your bunk and cover the blade on the cutter. We can put it under your bunk too, so you can cut more sheets if you need to."

Fallon had completely forgotten Liam before he'd even started doing that and in seconds he got a quick glimpse over Fallon's shoulder as the boy-man started the first picture.

"I'll just let you be, Fallon," he said with a smile as he opened the door to the room. When Fallon waved a pencil-filled hand, Liam snorted softly and quietly backed into the passageway, shutting the door softly behind him.

In the sitting room he looked around at the occupants. Brutus had his knees planted on the floor with his head shoved squarely through the nearest open window with his grinning face facing the wind of their flight.

The only other person in the room, Maria was knitting and keeping an eye on the bear boy. "Can't believe she just *left* him." She shook her head sadly. "What kind of mother could do that?"

"Actually," Liam explained, "that was the whole point in taking him to the woods for his first forced full change. She intended on leaving him in the woods anyway. It was only happenstance that she got caught up in Mayor Granger's lynch mob."

Maria's face reflected her shock but before she could say anything he hurried on, "They're bears, Maria. It's their way, just like their animal cousins. "The males are solitary and don't even much like to spend time with humans when they're in human form. The only time they come around is when a female is in heat or to find something to eat. They're really hard workers but not very good at socializing unless you keep them fed."

"The females keep a male cub around till the forced change at human puberty, then drive them off cause a male cub going through puberty is a trigger for the female to go into heat. If they drive him away, they might go a whole year before they go into heat again."

He gave a half shrug as he continued, "They keep a female cub around a couple of years longer because females going through puberty *inhibit* the mating process. It only takes a couple years of that before the two are ready to kill each other and they go their separate ways."

"Brutus's mother was going to ditch him anyway because if she goes into heat and another male comes around, he might kill the boy trying to get to his mama through him. And Brutus would die to protect his mama even though the act of protecting her is not needed and will get him killed."

"Even in human form the bear nature will take over. His mama would be in heat and any male bear changeling that gets a whiff of her will kill Brutus to get to her and she won't *be able* to care once she gets a whiff of *both* males' battle scent. By then her son's scent will just be that of another male in battle for *her*."

He shrugged. "She'll feel bad afterward, but not *that* bad if he couldn't extricate himself by then. It's their way. In fact, it'll only be about a year or two at the most before he," he pointed his chin at the oblivious boy with his head hanging out of a window in innocent glee, "will be more trouble than he's worth. He'll know before the rest of us and one day he'll just be gone."

He looked at the boy's back with a sad smile. "It's their way."

Chapter 24

"What's this?" Liam asked as he watched the fishing line. Relaxing with a pole in his hands he had a stringer of fish beside him in a canvas tube. The tube allowed water to enter to keep the occupants alive but didn't allow scavengers to get in and steal his catch. He was proud to say it was *his* invention and since they had a considerable amount of canvas, he was able to test his theory.

"It's a book," Heather explained as he looked at the thick stack of papers. "A picture book."

"Where did you get it?" Liam asked, then his stomach sank as he *looked* at the first page.

"Fallon said you told him to make it," Heather's voice was frosty.

Liam looked down to see the scene buried in his own nightmares, Fallon crouched weeping over his father's bloody body and Heather with arms raised in full mage chant. He noticed that Elizabeth's hand was blown off and her face half missing from shotgun blasts. There was not as much detail as the oil paintings but only by degree.

All of the faces were in the sharpest detail.

Fallon had used black and gray to make precise lines, then used the colors in such muted ways they only accented the lines. It looked like a painting but done so evenly it was hard to see any brush marks. It was a painting using colored pencils instead of oils.

He looked at Heather. "How?"

She planted her hands on her hips. "He said you *told* him to."

"What, make a hundred page…"

"*Two* hundred pages," she cut in.

"Uh, yeah, a two-hundred-page book of hand drawn pictures." He turned pages and stared in wonder. "He did all of this since him and I talked… oh."

"Yeah… *oh*!"

He flinched at her tone.

"I was so busy charting where we were going and learning the manuals he made, and he was so quiet," he stopped. There was no excuse.

He realized he hadn't seen Fallon in two days. The fact that everybody had been extremely busy was no excuse. He continued to turn pages, seeing scenes continuing on from the moment they'd found Orson and Elizabeth murdered and their home burned to the ground.

The pictures showed every scene in Fallon's life from the moment he'd found his murdered parents. Each picture was a frozen scene that told a story to each of their growing number that experienced it as it happened. And each of them was drawn with the same detail as any of Fallon's other drawings or paintings.

"Turn it over and look at the last page," she suggested.

He did so to see a strange design. "What's that?"

"Don't know," she replied. "But that's not the last picture."

He turned the last page back to see a close-up of the bow of the air wagon with Fallon and Heather and him together, with Orlagh standing on an equipment chest near the rail. There had been no time since they'd left Hoe-boy Hill where all four of them had been on the bow alone.

He looked at the next picture back and it showed Revis collapsed and bloody with Liam holding Fallon. The two previous scenes showed Mathew hanging from the left rear mooring line and Maria's snipering of the ones on the ground shooting at them as they flew skyward.

There were two hundred pages with two sides each and only the last page didn't have a second picture, unless you counted the strange design that covered most of the back page. And the picture it did have he couldn't remember happening.

Liam closed it and held it up. "This isn't all of it. This only goes up to when we got away at Hoe-boy Hill. So, that means he's still painting."

"Yes," Heather fumed. "He shuffled up to me and said you told him to make a picture book and that I would charm each page so it would last forever. Then he said he was going to forget more memories, or something like that, and went back to his room. Probably to paint more of those," she pointed at the bound stack of hemp paper paintings.

Liam shocked her by smiling and rising from where he was fishing. He reeled in his line with the device Fallon tinkered and bent to pick up the canvas tube that held his line of fish. When he picked it up by the strap attached on either end it drained out within seconds. "Let's go see what he's up to."

"What *he's* up to," she fumed. "What are *you* up to?"

Liam looked down at the tube of fish. "Got bass and walleye here, threw everything else back. Tired of catfish after one day and wanted something different." He pointed a chin to the side. "Should be some clams over there, lot of clams in this part of the river. Might want to have a fire on the ground and have fish and clams."

At her stormy look, he added, "At least, that's what Fallon as much as suggested to me. I was just about to tell everybody I decided to throw a late party since we're in a spot few can get to us at. Then you came up while I was trying to get just *one more fish.*"

"How?" Heather started then her face took on a knowing look. "Your clock."

"Yes, my clock told me. Gave me all the hints that led me to think I was thinking of it myself."

Heather snorted. Fallon had given each of them a small steam clock he made them promise to never let run out of water and each of them contained hidden messages. Fallon insisted on giving each clock a checkup when he was hyper tinkering. The clocks had a tendency to extend rolled letters from Fallon to his two favorite people when he was in a less mentally capable condition.

Her brows creased as he continued, "And he worked on me to get the paints, then we let *him* make out the order and give somebody else the coin to pay with. And we just accepted it as an honest mistake when he got enough oils and pencils to start his own art shop."

She began to fume and he had to hurry to keep up with her as she stormed toward the airship tethered to several large trees even though the wheels supported all the weight. "He's been badgering me till I made a charm so any one of you can stabilize one of his paintings or drawings so he would bother one of you instead of me. Ooh that little, wait till I get my hands on him."

Liam laughed and pulled at her arm till she stopped. "Don't you get it? *This* Fallon doesn't know anything about it. It's the other one that's pulling the strings. The question is, why?"

"There's one sure way to find out," Heather said, then stormed on toward the air wagon.

The air wagon sat amongst several large trees on an island in the great Mississippi between Arkansas and Tennessee. There was a braid of similar islands all up and down the banks of the great river. Most were transient islands made up of accumulated debris washed down from upstream, but a few had existed for hundreds of years and were covered in thick forests.

Heather alone decided they would camp for a two-day layover while they prepared to make the final push to catch their quarry. She detected the stopping of Easton's train in Memphis and under gentle hints from Fallon through her message clock had chosen to land to prepare.

They'd picked an island where they could land the air wagon in amongst trees old enough and tall enough their silvery gray balloon was hidden from passing riverboats. Nestled within a large clearing there was enough open space on the landward side for a large fire and the trees around them were thick enough to mostly hide the light of their fire. There weren't rocks to be found so they dug a fire pit into the rich wet soil, heaping the sod around the pit to raise its edges.

As they approached, Sesco held up a string of fish. "Look what Revis and I caught. Got enough for everybody and more."

"We found a whole bed of clams," Rosa said as Blackie and Maria filled their biggest iron pot with water and some herbs and wild spices they'd collected nearby. "We were thinking with all this food we should have a little celebration."

Heather looked back at Liam who smiled in return and shook her head. "He's been a busy boy."

Liam swung the canvas tube of fish to Sesco. "Bass and walleye. Heather and I are going to have a word with Fallon."

"Oh, tell him thanks for telling us he saw that clam bed. There's enough there to take a few bushel baskets to town to sell when we fly there tomorrow."

"I'll be sure to do that," Heather snarled and Blackie gave her a puzzled look.

When he looked at Liam hurrying behind the increasingly furious girl, Liam quipped in passing, "Fallon's room." Then hurried to catch the boy's sister.

He made it just in time as Heather banged on Fallon's door, then again before even the fastest person could have responded. She was raising her fist to bang a third time when Fallon opened the door.

His bright and innocent smile was replaced with one of shock and surprise as Heather almost hit him in the face with her fist in door-banging position. "Uh… hi?" he stuttered without a trace of guile as Heather glared.

"Heather, he doesn't know."

She darted a glare at him, then deflated. "Okay, okay, I know." She blew an explosive breath through her nose, then took a deep breath and blew it out slowly and looked at Fallon.

He flinched. "Did I do something bad?"

Heather melted and consoled her brother. "No, Fallon, you didn't do anything bad. Somebody else did. Well, we don't know if it's bad or not, but something sneaky and we want to know what he's doing and why."

"Oh-h-h," he nodded his head knowingly, but with a confused look on his face. "Anybody I know?"

Heather smiled warmly. "We're about to find out if we can get the two of you together."

He immediately forgot about what they were talking about and as soon as he saw the book of pictures in Liam's hand, said excitedly, "Oh-oh come here and look. I've got the rest in here. I was just finishing the last one."

They came into his room to see another stack of pictures almost as large as the one in Liam's hands. Dozens of other painted sheets littered the floor and chairs and bunk.

Fallon walked over to a small steam compressor – yet another new tinkering – that sat quietly chugging away in a corner. Several tubes led to small long thin cylinders. Fallon picked up one and pressed a button on the side and swiped at the sheet of paper in the frame. He replaced the paint pen and swiped at several spots with another colored spray pen. He ignored them as he continued to fill in the color to the pencil drawing.

Liam and Heather moved over to watch the final strokes as Fallon painted a beautiful picture of them all having a fish and clam banquet by a roaring fire in front of the grounded air wagon.

"There," he declared. "All finished!" Then he turned toward Heather. "Okay, I'm ready to go hyper."

Heather looked at her brother then at Liam, then back at Fallon. "You *knew*?"

"Knew what?" Fallon asked simply.

"That we were going to ask you to go hyper."

"Is that what we're going to do?"

Heather sighed. "Fallon what happens when you finish the last picture?"

Fallon thought about it a moment as he stroked his chin, then smiled and said, "I don't know."

"How did you know we were going to ask you to go hyper?" Heather spoke patiently.

"That's what you always do when you come to my room all flustered," he explained simply and she snapped her mouth shut on an angry retort as he continued.

"Anyway, I was 'sposed to finish the last picture and then I could forget all these memories." He gestured toward the stacks of pictures. "Then you came in all flustered like you do when you want *him* to do something for you and I just figured I was going hyper."

He finished and smiled with his own simple brand of infinite patience as she looked in horror at how it sounded coming from his lips. It took her several seconds to process the images it put in her mind.

"Heather?" Liam said from behind her. "He set this whole thing up for a reason. Maybe it's time sensitive."

Heather shook her head to clear it and pulled out the amulet. "Go ahead and put it on," she told Fallon as he took it with the absolute trust of his less cognitive self.

He tied it behind his neck as he chanted the activation syllables and when he put his hands down his face was different. He looked around and Heather was just taking a deep breath to start in on him when he said, "Wait! We have to hurry. How long has it been since I finished the last stroke on the last picture?"

"What? Wait a minute!" Heather started.

"Two minutes, maybe three at the very most," Liam replied.

"Good, plenty of time," Fallon opened a drawer next to the painting easel and pulled out a small roll of paper that turned out to be a thin sheet a foot and a half long and an inch and a half wide.

"Sound out the syllables written there just like this," then he demonstrated.

With an exasperated growl she did so and he corrected two of her attempts and got her to speak them again. "Good, good, now do a memory charm on me and alternate that line of mage syllables between each repetition. Go, now, do it!" And he waited.

"What? Wait! What is this?" She looked at the line of mage-speak. "This isn't a spell I've ever…"

"*Heather!*" Fallon yelled. "I was able to take all of those memories out through the pictures to make room for more of *me*, but you have to hurry or it'll start leaking back in," his eyes pleaded with her. "*Please!*"

"You better be right!" Then she started the memory chant and inserted the new line of syllables at the end, then repeated the memory spell again, then the new lines, then again. By the fifth repetition she didn't need the paper, chanting the syllables by memory. On the tenth repetition Fallon opened his eyes and smiled and Heather stopped her chant on the last syllable a second later.

"Fallon?" Heather asked tentatively.

"I got it all," Fallon said with a vacant look then his eyes focused on his sister. "It's all there. I didn't know how much would fit, so I trimmed and spliced till I had as much as I *thought* would fit. I misjudged and there's room for more."

"What are you talking about?" Heather said explosively – then softer, "Fallon. What did we just do and what are you talking about? In that order."

"Oh, those," he gestured at the hundreds of pages of pictures, "are memories. I was flooded with them and couldn't concentrate because they were all in my head all the time and at the same time. Every time I got distracted and went into one of those staring fits my mind was chugging along just fine, absorbing *everything* I saw and heard and smelled and tasted and felt, and filling my head so much there was no room for anything else."

He pointed at the scattered and stacked pages of pictures. "I put those memories in there and you locked them out of my head and put my other memories back in the empty spaces at the same time."

Heather looked shocked – then even *more* shocked. "How in the Gods' names did you do that?"

Fallon smirked. "Well, magery is a form of science and I just translated the language and put together the syllables I needed you to say. I couldn't do it because I'm not a mage, but you could. All I had to do was give you the right chant to get the result I wanted. Simple really," he said smugly.

"Of course, I had to invent two new syllables to get it to work... but it did. Now! All I need you to do is make me three amulets so I can do the rest myself."

"What? What are you talking about now?" Heather sighed with exasperation.

Fallon gave his own sigh, one of borderline patience. "I need three amulets. One to put the other memories, the smell and sound and all the rest into the pictures to make more room in my brain, and I need another one to put *new* memories away. Oh, I didn't tell you, I'll still probably go into those staring trances, they just won't be as long or as total... maybe. I'm kind of new at this magery tinkering thing."

"Anyway, I'm still in hyper and I'm not *totally* sure I'm going to be good enough to finish what you started when I come down. All I put in the empty spaces is the knowledge how to shed myself of the rest of the memories I picked to make room in my head for more of *me*."

He rubbed his hands together then reached behind his neck to untie the amulet. "I've only been hyper seven minutes and twenty-four seconds. We should know shortly if it worked." Then he sat in the only space not covered with pictures and tossed the amulet to Liam, who caught it by reflex as Fallon sagged into his hyper crash.

Chapter 25

Firecloud was baffled by the loss of the link he'd had for so long. He wondered if the source of that link had finally found a way to die, but the echoes didn't indicate that. Just to be safe he began his special preparations. He'd been collecting the items he needed for his challenge ever since he'd acquired his bait and was ready for this last contingency.

He studied the sky as he prepared, letting the world give him its message as he dissolved the last bits of several innocents. He'd made sure to dispose of their bodies far enough away from the rails their eventual discovery wouldn't lead to him through his employer. Most of them were hidden so well it would be long enough before they were found even the best magery wouldn't be able to tell when they died – much less the purposes for what parts of theirs were missing. Scavengers would dispose of enough more to hide what was taken before death.

He tied a leather strip on another amulet, this one wearing the eyes of a young girl who no longer needed them. The emotion she'd expended while he removed them gave them much power to see for him. Tucking the amulet into the snake hide pouch hanging from his neck with the other three, he began picking up pairs of ears to make his next weapon.

Standing in the shadow of Easton's train, Gibbs watched the Native making magery by himself a couple of hundred feet from the railcars and prying eyes. He was getting nervous. He knew the Native had challenged the girl and her addled brother but he expected them to die quickly chasing those that he'd set behind to face them first.

By all accounts the two changelings that had been seen with the whelps in town before the homestead was sacked were still with them. All four had united and made a clean path through the bait he'd left behind despite their supposed skills learned in war. The four were even making their names known by others of respectful standing, like the Pinkertons that had declined to renew his contract and asked him to return his badge and identification papers a few years ago.

His sources told him there were newspaper stories of the four. Stories that made them seem heroic enough people were beginning to build them into something they weren't. He knew they weren't! He knew they'd just gotten lucky with magery and some fancy tinkering that was just new, not different or special.

That damned Native was up to something and it could only be concerning the gaudy pendant and ring he'd neglected to melt down. Gibbs couldn't say anything to Easton about the items now without admitting he'd always known they hadn't been melted with the rest. He'd never told because he knew which of the two was the more powerful in the real world.

He might not be able to safely warn his employer as yet, but he could prepare *himself*. If the Native was getting ready to have a mage duel with the daughter of the two they'd had killed then he should prepare for the tinker. He smiled at the thought. Let the Native have the girl and her magery, he would be satisfied with the tinker. He never saw a tinker's machine that could move as fast as a man and this brain addled child tinker seemed to carry an abundance of godstone Gibbs could loot from his dead body.

He would be ready when the two and their animal friends came after the Native and Easton while he stood off to the side and waited to see who the winner was. Then he would kill the winner when they were at their weakest.

Sure, he would have to start all over again, but he'd done that before. Several times in fact.

The air wagon lifted silently in the growing dark an hour after sunset and pointed its nose across the wide Mississippi River.

"No, and that's final," Heather said with force. "This is not your fight and I will not have you throw your lives away."

Liam steered the air wagon across the river as Rosa hauled in the second mooring rope while her father argued for them all.

"But what about your lives. If all of us added to your numbers will just be throwing our lives away, what does that say about your chances without us?"

Heather sighed. "The magery Firecloud and I will be wielding will be orders of magnitude more than the simple charms I've taught you in only a few days."

"But you said brute power was nothing beside clever use of minimum power," Rosa put in as she coiled the mooring line.

Heather glared at the girl. "Still, no! We will put the balloon down on the other side of the river and close enough to Memphis to reach on horseback and the steamcycle with its side car. Fallon has filled it with tinkerings and I've made all my battle charms."

She smiled warmly at her friends. "We need you all to stay with the air wagon and there's nobody else we can trust to do that but you."

"Now, I've penned some papers you should open if we're not back by tomorrow sunset. Your orders are to open the papers and follow the instructions. The first one will include the magery chants to make steam foam light enough to lift. Remember, the dryer the steam foam the higher you'll fly."

She smiled at them. "Just because we're not back in one day doesn't mean we're not coming back. Moving is a precautionary thing to help protect the air wagon from unfriendly hands. Lift at sunset and move to another spot far enough away nobody can reach it on horseback. Wait a day and move again the next night."

"If we haven't found you by the third night you can start looking to see if we're hiding or incarcerated," she smiled at them as Liam aimed the air wagon toward a likely landing spot on the eastern bank of the river.

"We're here," Liam said as he brought the wagon around in a wide loop. They all moved to that side to look. "There's a good road into town and it looks like it's private, a dead end. It goes by that little, bare peninsula and it's another mile before it connects to the main road into town."

Blackie pointed. "That one there? Yes, you can see the main road and the bare point at the same time from there."

"Okay," Liam said as he steered the air wagon in to put them low over the small peninsula.

Blackie took the controls while the rest went to the aft end and put Trouble and the loaded steamcycle with its redesigned sidecar over the side on steam foam hoists.

"Where's the seat?" Heather asked.

"In the way," Fallon replied.

"What's that in the big bag with our supplies?"

Fallon smiled. "A surprise."

He grew serious. "All the reports of us tell of a side *car* that another person rides in. I'll be getting off before the rest of you get where people will remember a passenger so the seat isn't needed. I made some other changes so you'll look more like a wealthy nobody with a fancy ride."

Heather looked at the altered cycle critically. It did look more thrown together to carry excess luggage that a woman of the means to have such a machine would require. But due to Fallon's *special* modifications it wasn't actually going to look the same when she finally got to Memphis. She stood out of the way as Sesco and Revis reeled Trouble's hoist in and attached it to the cycle's frame and fed a refresher shot of steam foam into the lifting bladder.

She had to smile at the proficiency with which they recited the mage chant, even Revis chanting with the proper cadence and volume. The bladder filled with steam foam and lifted the steamcycle and they stopped their chant and let the feeder tube drop. They gave the bobbing cycle a push over the rail and the steam foam leaked out of the open tube with calculated speed, dropping the fully loaded steamcycle to the ground softly. Free of the weight of the cycle the hoist bobbed upward, was stopped by the attached rope, and the brothers hauled it back down.

Orlagh was next and Heather smiled as her friend squalled at the indignity of being manhandled by the two brothers as they put her in a sling below the smaller hoist. They filled the bladder and eased her over the side and down to the ground. Liam released his sister from her entanglement and the brothers pulled the bobbing hoist back down again when it flew upward without any weight to hold it down.

All the while Sesco and Revis worked, Blackie kept the air wagon stable above the bar peninsula.

Heather was checking her last strap and Sesco was ready to feed steam foam into the tube when the waif rushed out onto the aft deck and gave Heather a fierce hug. "Maddy," she whispered.

"What?" Heather asked softly.

"Maddy," she repeated, then stood back to look up into Heather's eyes. "My name is Maddy, Madeline Darwin. Here, you might need this."

Heather reached out by reflex and found herself holding a cage of godstone wrapped around a massive, silvery white pearl.

"Honey, Maddy, do you know what this is?" Heather could feel the power as it rested in her hand.

"It's all I got left in the world till you took me in," she replied. "My mama and papa said it came across the spice road to our kin two hundred years ago. Mama said it held the wishes of all our ancestors. My wish is that you have the power to defeat your enemy so you may come home safe."

Heather felt the surge of power with the words and smiled. She knew the young girl had no idea what she'd just done, or what the ancient power amulet gave her with the demand Maddy had just put in motion.

She pulled out a special woven strand and put it through the opening made just for that. Tying the braided cord around her neck she tucked the pendant inside her shirt, its warmth spreading out through her from where it touched.

Oh yes, this unexpected gift made her think she just *might* live to see another sunrise. "Thank you so much, Maddy Darwin, my friend," then she gave the girl a fierce hug. "I'll see you tomorrow. I want to explore Memphis with you, maybe go shopping for some new clothes."

Maddy smiled with genuine pleasure. "I would like that."

Heather nodded to Sesco and he opened the valve and Maddy joined them in chanting the steam into foam. In seconds she was over the side and being lowered to the ground as the foam vented through the open tube. On the ground Liam quickly attached the deflated heavy hoist and Heather's together as she stepped out of it.

The combined weight was too heavy to lift more than a few feet but that made it all the easier for the Lawson brothers to pull the combined hoists up by hand. As soon as it was out of sight, they saw Fallon spring off the side of the air wagon's rear deck feeding a rope through something on his waist, the hum audible as the rope slid through the device. Then at the last seconds he gripped the rope and in the last ten feet slowed to a stop so softly he stood naturally as the rope went slack.

Liam and Heather looked at him, then at each other and both chuckled.

"What?" Fallon wondered. "The skill might be needed at any time, why not practice it every chance I get." He disconnected the belt that held the rope around his hips and thighs and Sesco and Revis pulled it back up to the wagon.

While they were pulling it up Maddy gave a series of whistles and Blackie turned the air wagon around and headed for the spot they'd agree he would land and wait.

As the air wagon disappeared in the gloom of night, Liam commented, "Looks like low clouds settling in over the city. Going to be easy to hide."

Heather smiled. "Fog can be used as well as anything else in nature. I have ways to use and defend against the use of that and other gifts from nature." Then she touched her breast. "And another gift of such power as I've only heard rumors of."

At his look, she said, "The waif. Her name is Maddy, Madeline Darwin. I could never read her cause she was surrounded by a wall I couldn't pierce. It was an ancient energy resource and Maddy gave it to me with a command. It contains generations of power given to it by the energies of those that have carried it."

She smiled. "And, apparently," her eyes took a faraway look as she touched where the amulet hung, "it's been over a hundred years since anybody's *used* any of that power."

"So, what does that mean?" Liam wondered as Orlagh crawled onto the side car frame next to Fallon.

He was muttering about nobody having any fun as Orlagh yawned in his face.

Heather moved over to feed the boiler and start building steam as Liam checked Trouble. "It means I have a well of power that makes me think I might just live to see the sunrise."

"Oh?" Liam mused. "And what do you think your chances are now?"

"Oh, definitely fifty-fifty now," she replied happily. "It wasn't anywhere *near* that before Maddy told me her name and gave me her family's legacy."

"Fifty-fifty, with an amazing new source of power, which means your chances were not very good before. And you're just now telling me this?"

She shrugged as the tiny whistle indicated the steam at optimum level. She looked at the cycle. "It warms up faster. You do something to it, Fallon?"

"Yeah," he replied as he lounged across the bundles on the side wheel's frame. "Sprayed the inside of the boiler with godstone paint. Gets hotter quicker and holds heat longer. You should get about half again as many miles to a quart of water. The new springs should make it ride a little less bumpy too and the new design is more stable."

Liam waited patiently, not mounting Trouble despite the stallion nudging him.

She sighed. "Firecloud would be concentrating on me and I might have distracted him just enough for Fallon and you to kill him. With him gone the rest of them wouldn't be that hard for you and Fallon to bring to justice."

"Wait," Fallon stepped off of the stack of bags. "You mean you didn't plan on living through this and you're just now telling us." He looked at Liam. "Can you believe this?"

"Apparently she's only telling us because she just got the one thing that brings her up to a fifty-fifty chance with this Firecloud mage."

Heather pulled the pendant free of her bosom and Fallon's eyes grew so wide white showed all around. "Is that? It is! Oh, can I look at it in hyper? Please? I'll make you whatever you want."

"Hey you two," Liam cut in. "We have a job to do and the longer we sit here on a private road the more likely we are to be seen and remembered."

"I want to study that thing, so you better live through this," Fallon said in a stage whisper as he crawled back on the wheel frame.

Liam shook his head in wonder at the two. Since Fallon broke the curse a second time, he was a completely different person. By his own account he'd succeeded in transferring more memories to the pages of the book of their adventure since the murder of his parents.

Apparently, that freed up brain space gave the hyper Fallon room to transfer the memories of his hyper intellect into the empty spaces. Those memories were then accessible when Fallon was *not* in a hyper enchantment.

The result was that Fallon was now as normal as any genius, almost sixteen-year-old man. He could still go into hyper at the cost of four days aging per minute and he would still have the hyper crash afterward, but when he awoke, he would be normal emotionally and intellectually.

The bond the brother and sister had always shown seemed to grow stronger now that Fallon had the emotional confidence to match his intellect. They were easier together and seemed to enjoy verbal banter.

Liam patted Trouble's side. "You ready big fella?" At Trouble's snort and tossed head, Liam laughed. "Me too."

He grabbed the saddle horn and threw a leg up and over. He settled into place as he put a hand to the carbine in its saddle holster and then the new weapons Fallon foisted on him, then on their reload pouches in front of the saddle horn.

He made one last check of his saddlebags and looked over at Heather. She nodded then turned a valve and the steamcycle spun its rear wheel in the dirt beside the road and in seconds Fallon was holding onto Orlagh to keep both of them from being thrown free.

Liam just shook his head, wondering if it was wise to let a woman operate such a dangerous machine. Then he wondered what man would be stupid enough to mention that thought aloud.

He patted Trouble on the neck. "You feel like stretching your muscles my friend?"

Trouble didn't say anything, but he did give an exciting chase after the cycle without any further prompting from his rider. The race ended at the main road where Heather pushed the cycle to its top speed with Orlagh and Fallon covered as if they were lumpy bags.

Liam let Trouble rest from his loosening run as the others drove off. Heather would take her two passengers further up the road where they could assemble Fallon's newest tinkering. When even the muted sound of the steamcycle couldn't be heard over normal night noises he slowed Trouble to a ground eating trot toward Memphis.

Chapter 26

"You can stay here if'n ya want to, but I'm going to help them!" Maddy crossed her arms defensively.

"How you going to do that, girl?" Blackie challenged her. "We're on an island."

"So!" Maddy threw the challenge right back at him. "Those foam hoists can lift more than a horse or a steamcycle. I bet one could carry me no problem and then I could fly to Memphis."

"Wind would take you where it wanted girl," Blackie scoffed and Maddy didn't see Rosa hide her smile. "How you going to fight the wind?"

She thought quickly. "Fallon made spare fans for the air wagon and his room's full of tinkerings. There's more than enough to make a steam engine to turn a fan blade."

"Miss Heather went to die and I can't just wait here to get word she's gone," the young girl said as she looked around at them all. "She even said she left papers to give us this wagon. Even gave us *orders* to keep us busy for a few days after she's dead to let it sink in."

"She said herself she was giving us the wagon. Well then, since she thinks she's going to die, let's go ahead and claim it now." She gripped her hands tightly into fists at her sides as she continued, "Let's go ahead and claim it now and since it's ours she can't tell us we can't come to help her."

Blackie smiled. "I was hoping somebody would make sense out of us just sitting here doing nothing. And you're right girl, Miss Heather went to die. I don't think she intends for young Fallon or Mr. Quinn or his sister to die. I think she intends to be bait so *they* can kill this dark mage while he's distracted killing her."

He slammed a fist against a support beam and it creaked in protest. "I say we open those letters a little early and take advantage of this overcast sky!"

"Hurray!" Revis yelled. "What can I do?"

"We'll chant the steam into foam!" Sesco explained hurriedly. "Blackie will have to be pilot, he's the best and Maria is our best sniper. Revis is the best chanter. He holds the proper cadence every time and he's easy to synchronize with. Blackie, you'll have to dip down out of the fog sometimes, then move back up again. That means somebody will have to be ready to vent foam to descend and chant foam to rise every second."

He pointed back and forth between him and his brother. "You know I'm right and we're the best two to do it. We'll be ready for anything else we need to do, but we'll man the foam chanting station."

Blackie nodded. "That's a good idea. You two on foam chanting and be ready to hit the aft deck and wield the sniper gun or the hoists."

He turned to his wife and daughter. "I'll fly us and Maria can wield the forward sniper gun. Rosa, you'll be my backup and main deckhand"

"Don't forget me," Maddy reminded him. "It was my idea first so don't try to give me something easy."

Blackie smiled. "Oh, your job won't be easy. We're going to toss you overboard with some of young Fallon's tinkerings and let you find out things."

"What?" Maria yelled, turning on her husband. "Are you out of your mind? Send that little thing," her finger was like a spear, "out into the back streets of a city the size of Memphis?"

"I could go with her," Brutus said, raising his hand as if to show he was volunteering and they'd heard right. "I'm not that much older than her but I'm bigger. People that might bother her won't bother me. If they try I'll *hit 'em*." He smiled at the prospect. "Haven't hit anybody in a while and might need to soon or be hard to get along with."

"You might be big but you're still just a boy," Blackie reminded him. "If you could turn bear it would be different, but you're locked into the phases of the moon, your mother said so."

"Oh that," Brutus waved a hand negligently. "We're only locked into full bear form during the three days of the full moon. All the other time we can go into a warrior form whenever we want."

He smiled big, all of his teeth showing. "Want to see mine? Fallon told me it was okay to practice it when nobody was watching and I'm getting pretty good."

He didn't wait for them to approve, or not, and stood tall and clenched his face. In seconds his torso and head *shifted* and in moments he was several times as hairy where his head and hands stuck out of his new shirt and his ears had moved upwards while his jaw extended slightly. It was too short for a normal bear but too long for a human.

"Kigh ob hod oo tak, bu geh be-be-be, good 'i pacis." Brutus moved his mouth around some to better settle the muscles and tried again as his muzzle shortened a bit. "Kind of hard to talk but I'm getting better with practice." The words were somewhat mushy in the toothy mouth, but they were much easier to understand.

"Yeah," Blackie admitted as he looked at the clawed fingers. "That would sure make a few more people leave you alone. Can you change back just as fast?"

No sooner had he asked than Brutus was morphing back in human form. It took a few seconds longer than the change into the warrior form but it was smooth and didn't seem to hurt. "It takes a little out of me, I should probably eat a big meal now and again before we leave to make sure I can do it as easily when I need to." He thought for a moment. "I should probably take a large bag of jerky along, and maybe a few of those sandwiches you made for me before, just in case."

Blackie smiled as Maria got up to fix the boy some sandwiches and a snack pack to take with him. "That covers that. So, we're all agreed? Sesco and Revis are steam chanters and aft sniper team. I'm pilot with Rosa as co-pilot and chief engineer and Maria is forward sniper. Maddy and Brutus are special intelligence and ground scouts."

The youngest two smiled.

"Now, let's get those letters opened to make everything all legal like so we can get this wagon back in the air where she belongs."

The first letter was opened and they learned how Heather had planned to safeguard the air wagon. Using the *language* of magery Fallon had written phonetically combined with special amulets, they had all been practicing every aspect of the operation of the flying railcar wagon as soon as they were added to the growing crew. They found those specific chants were all they needed to fly their balloon without a Master Mage aboard.

Not many people had the ability to do magery under original influence, but – apparently – a greater number could use amulets and talismans *created by* Master Mages. Most of the workings onboard the new airship, were simple tinkerings Fallon wrote and made illustrated manuals for, while many others were much more complex and incorporated magery.

As a Master Mage, Heather was easily able to implant learning charms into the manuals, then memory spells on other amulets she gave to each crewmember. Using the combination, each of them took only two or three practice sessions to become expert in any particular duty, but each also showed themselves to be better in certain duties than all of the others.

Sesco and Revis were the best foam chanters. They could fill the balloon the fastest with the greatest buoyancy, while Blackie seemed to have almost instinctive control of the piloting. Heather told them the reason was both had a *very small* amount of natural magery that just happened to add to their efforts. The same was true for Maria and Sesco in the ability to unconsciously adjust for natural conditions when snipering.

Rosa and Maddy were exceptional tinkerers that could diagnose any tinkering almost by sound or feel. As a team they could take apart, repair, and put back together any of the tinkerings onboard in half the time of any other team, with the exception of any team including Heather or Fallon.

They studied the papers and decided that if their employers died, they would be the sole owners of the airship with each given an equal share. Then they opened the second envelope and discovered some of Fallon's newest inventions that had been machined at each of Fallon's hyper tinkerings. There were also packages in the cargo crates that held parts ordered ahead of time and picked up along the way as they traveled eastward.

They discovered that during his hyper tinkerings, Fallon's mental abilities anticipated the need for certain materials and those packages were waiting for them at every stop if not available locally. They hadn't questioned the packages they were sent to collect from each stop's post office or train station, the designs presented to blacksmiths, or the other purchases made at local shops. The errands had been just another part of the jobs each was offered upon joining the core crew.

Reading from the second envelope's thick sheets, they discovered that many of those packages contained the parts that assembled into amazing devices. There were also several pages to a special weapons manual that included amulets and talismans created and charmed by Heather.

Hurriedly assembling the packages retrieved from cargo and a few *special* packages stored in Heather and Fallon's cabins they laid out an impressive array of tinkerings. Using the charmed manual, they quickly assembled the tinkerings on the empty aft deck.

"It's going to take them till midnight to get to their target." Blackie told the others after they'd gone through most of the papers. He raised the one he'd been studying. "Fallon has tinkered some things that would do an army proud, but we're all the army he and his sister's got."

He took on a solemn look. "Every one of us would probably be dead if not for Miss Heather and Fallon, and Liam and Miss Orlagh. We have about two hours to get there ahead of them and give them all the help we can to repay that debt. Are we all agreed on what we intend to do?"

There were no dissenters, each of them more than ready to give aid to the four they owed so much to. Then they looked at the array of *unique* tinkerings that Fallon bequeathed to them.

"He planned it this way," Maddy commented as they stood in awe of the devices. When they looked at her, she smiled. "Fallon, he planned for us to open the letters early so we could make our own decision to help them or not."

The others started to get suspicious looks on their faces as they realized she was telling the truth. If young Fallon had planned so much for so long it all came together for their final confrontation with their nemesis – why wouldn't he be able to plan for their reaction?

Then they all remembered the urgings and promptings Fallon had verbally made to learn their best magery attempts and tinkering abilities. Then they looked at each of the devices laid out in front of them and how each had been given a specific tinkering that most suited each of them. The tinkerings also matched exactly their current agreed upon assignments in the rescue they planned.

"You're right, girl," Blackie said as Sesco snorted and Maria glared while Revis looked confused till Brutus whispered in his ear.

Blackie snorted a laugh. "Well, since Mr. Fallon Richards has presented us with the means to level the battlefield, so to speak, we should get this tub off the ground."

He looked up at the lowering sky. "Looks like we'll have all the cover an air assault could hope for."

Chapter 27

Liam rode on and an hour later caught Heather and Fallon where they pulled off at the side of the road. The packages that had covered the side frame were all on the ground nearby. Orlagh was nowhere in sight.

He slowed Trouble to a walk as he approached then looked ahead to see why they'd stopped. There was a light on the road in the distance that didn't appear to be moving, so he walked Trouble up to a tree and dismounted. He draped the reins over the end of a low branch. He never used a bit and Trouble immediately began cropping the good grass within reach as Liam went to help the others.

Fallon was almost finished with the transformation of the steamcycle and side cargo frame. The frame had been disconnected then reconnected with angled brackets and now the front and rear wheels were out of line. Liam walked up just as Heather held the cycle steady while Fallon disconnected the last bolt holding the side frame to the cycle's frame.

Liam bent and grasped the side frame opposite the young man and they released the pressure of its weight and lifted it free of the cycle. They twisted it around and lined it up and Fallon attached the bolts that affixed the single tire to the right side of the cycle. The cycle now had three wheels, the rear two spaced the same distance from the cycle's adjusted centerline as Heather released her hold and let the trike settle on the tinkered shocks. The two rear wheels now flanked each other three feet apart.

Fallon and Liam dragged the remaining frame to the side and Fallon quickly unbolted, then reassembled the pieces of the frame and re-bolted them into a new configuration. While he was doing that Liam untied the largest bundle and began to unfold the contents.

When he was finished, he gave it a skeptical look. "I'm glad you'll be flying this thing and not me."

Fallon smiled in return. "Cats don't care much for heights, do they?" When Liam gave him a mock glare, his smile broadened. "Admit it, if it wasn't for the firm deck under your feet you wouldn't be able to fly with us."

Liam shrugged. "So? Your wagon is a bit different than *that*!" His finger jabbed at the odd shape.

Fallon looked with pride at *that*. It was two, sausage shaped balloons side-by-side with an angled gap between that held a series of four small steam propellers arranged in line. One side of the angled tube of open canvas around the frame holding it all was wider than the other end, giving it a funnel shape between the two balloons – wider in front and narrower in the rear with a steering rudder.

Fallon turned toward the trike. "Let's get Heather finished so I can test it."

"You haven't even *tested* it yet?" Liam snorted.

"It'll work," Fallon was smugly confident as he looked up into the low cloud cover expanding outward from the main city. "And we couldn't have asked for better weather."

"As long as there's no lightning," Heather mumbled as she checked over the frame they were attaching above the drive pistons between the rear wheels.

They quickly finished attaching the new addition then placed Heather's smaller bags and travel supplies around the central package behind her. Sitting astride the steady trike she moved around to get comfortable then leaned against the backrest the front of the addition created. "Can you move it forward a bit?"

"Say when," Fallon said as he twisted some bolts with a tinker's wrench.

"When," she exclaimed, then added, "Go back two turns on the left and one on the right." After he did so she said, "There! That feels comfortable with where I hold the steering bar's handles.

Fallon looked at her critically. "Wait a second. Lean forward." She did so and he made several adjustments to the angle of the backrest. "Okay, now settle in again."

She did so and her face beamed. "That is *much* better!" She sat tall in the trike's saddle with her hands on the ends of the steering bars. "I could ride like this for hours with those new spring and cylinder shock absorbers you tinkered."

Fallon waved a hand. "Somebody else thought 'em up, I just copied the drawing I saw in a book." He moved his tinker's wrench around the frame, checking every bolt, then stood up. "There, all set."

"One hour will have to do," Liam interjected as he looked at the glow of Memphis showing on the underside of the clouds. "Our targets still in place?"

Heather touched the seeker talisman at her neck and closed her eyes. "Still in the same place, on the south side of town, probably on a side track headed toward Jackson," she said, then smiled evilly. "I get the sense Firecloud is preparing himself and is sure Easton doesn't know what's coming."

"You can tell all that?" Liam was surprised. He didn't realize she was *that* good.

She smiled in return and touched Maddy's gift in her bodice. "I have this, plus he's not trying to mask himself or the two links I have." Her smile grew ironic. "He's openly calling me to him. He's *allowing* me to track him and he *thinks* he's hiding his thoughts. But this," she touched the pendant again, "allows me to read his emotions without him feeling me."

Her eyes blazed. "I'm getting a lot more than he ever expected me to be able to read or detect me doing so through my father's stolen possessions."

"But he doesn't know about the rest of us," Liam reminded them.

"Firecloud won't know where *Orlagh and you* are, but he will still be able to detect Fallon through the echoes of the spell he threw on our mother so many decades ago. Maybe in a few years the echoes will have died away, but they are still too loud for such as him to not be able to detect."

Liam nodded his acceptance of the observation. "He'll be able to detect the two of you, but not my sister and me. Be careful. I'll see you soon." He took a moment to gaze at her before breaking eye contact, hoping he *would* see her soon.

Behind him she adjusted the trike's steam and started out slow to get the feel of the new configuration. In seconds she was chasing the beam of the directed lamp on the front of the vehicle down the empty road faster than a horse could run.

He turned and walked over to where Fallon was standing beside the frame they'd assembled from the parts of, and carried on, the sidecar. In moments they were attaching the last parts, then Liam lifted the backpack steam engine and Fallon shrugged into the harness. Then he moved under the row of enclosed fans while Liam held the fans up.

Fallon put bolts in place and held the weight while Liam moved around to his back and attached the frame pieces he couldn't reach. With the two outboard balloons hanging down on either side, Fallon braced himself as Liam checked the backpack.

"Everything looks good. Go ahead and start it up."

Fallon turned a valve, then waited two seconds before turning a striker and he felt as well as heard the steam engine engage.

Liam continued to monitor the engine since Fallon could only rely on gauges he could see.

"Okay, you have full pressure and everything looks good."

Fallon nodded, then turned two valves as he started his foam chant. Steam fed into the twin balloons and turned to a nebulous foam that was lighter than air and solid at the same time.

He continued his chant and as the two balloons lifted out of the way Liam quickly dragged the frame with the attached water bladders next to Fallon. Fallon bobbed a couple of times as he stepped on the ballast and fuel frame and Liam quickly attached the straps he could use to adjust the height of the ballast to sit straddled upon or down to stand on, or open a valve for emergency lift.

As Fallon continued to feed steam into the twin balloons and they swelled to their full size a silvery sheen began to form on the outside of the canvas.

"Godstone is starting to harden the shell of the balloons," Liam reported as Fallon continued his chant, then added in amazement. "It's working."

"Of course, it is," Fallon replied smugly after finishing his tenth repetition of the chant. "I'm mixing the godstone mist in with the foam and what doesn't soak into the balloons as they leak the infused steam through the canvas will form a thicker foam inside that will resist leaking if I get hit with any bullets. The foam feeder runs through the core of each balloon tube so the next time I inject clean foam without godstone it will compress the godstone foam outward, re-heating it as it goes, till it melds it to the interior of the balloon to thicken and finish the coating."

"Well, it's definitely soaking into the canvas. I only see a couple of spots on this balloon where steam is still leaking out, and now that has stopped," Liam reported as he inspected the balloons as they expanded to a stubby wing shape on either side of the air funnel. "Let me check the other one." He did so and gave his approval of the new tinkering as Fallon resumed his chanting.

Then the odd contraption bobbed once and rose gently from the ground. A breeze made it sway but Liam was easily able to hold it down as he turned it into that small amount of wind.

"Starting pusher fans," Fallon said as he reached up and started the small steam engine attached to the fan blades between the outrigger balloons.

Steam pressure quickly built and soon the fans were keeping the craft hovering over one spot as it rose further into the sky. Trouble looked up casually with green grass hanging out of both sides of his mouth, and munched contentedly as he watched Fallon lift up above the height of the nearest trees.

Liam looked up as the flyer continued to rise and Fallon turned it to head cross-country directly at the lights reflecting off the low clouds. In moments he was swallowed by the gray blanket, his feet dangling on either side of the ballast rail's saddle the last thing to disappear. Liam continued to watch and twice more saw Fallon's feet appear as the young man adjusted his height to be as out of sight as he could be and still see out of the bottom of the cloud cover.

Liam turned and saw Trouble looking at him expectantly. "Yeah, big fella' it's our turn." Then he retrieved the stallion's reins and lifted himself into the saddle. He didn't need to knee the stallion, Trouble simply moved off down the road before Liam was even settled.

Their timeline was set to Trouble's speed and another hour later Liam entered what would be called the business district of the city of Memphis. There was still some war damage apparent, but some places would never be rebuilt to the glory they possessed before troops battled in their streets. The owners of those properties died in the war, fled elsewhere and hadn't returned, or simply no longer had the means to repair their possessions even if they would have had the inclination to do so.

Liam walked Trouble through streets that went from, lined with night-shuttered businesses and homes, to a stretch where several well-lit saloons, casinos, and hotels lined both sides of the main street with dozens of pedestrians despite the late hour. He continued to walk Trouble through town, casually looking at the variety of steam vehicles parked or rolling along around him.

They were mostly four wheeled vehicles for both passengers and cargo and even one with the star of a sheriff painted on the side. He also spotted several two wheeled steamcycles parked together in front of one noisy saloon and even a three wheeled version with a wide bench seat between the rear wheels behind the driver. The rest of the night's traffic ignored him as the city dwellers went about their business.

Seeming to ignore them in his turn, Liam watched the streets as he made his way slowly. He watched a pair of constables patrolling, one of them openly in his warrior form of wolf changeling. He saw another puma, or rather, he scented a puma changeling in human form and nodded his head as the young man crossed the street in front of him.

"Evening brother," the man said as he stepped in front of Trouble just close enough to hear but not be run over by the stallion. "Got a silver coin for a drink?"

"Might," Liam conceded as he gave his legs a twitch and Trouble slowed to a near stop. "What have you got to earn it with?"

The puma man studied him openly. "Yer not from around here, maybe information, advice maybe, too."

Liam pulled out two silver dollars, tossed one to the man and held the other up to see. "Little bit of both. You get the second coin if the second bit is worth it."

The man eyed the coin in his hand, then the second one, calculating what might get both for just words. "Folks are a bit riled hereabouts concerning strangers. Couple of babes gone missing from their cradles yesterday night. Nobody heard anything but mage with the sheriff said dark magery been done at both homes. Folks fear the kind of mage would kidnap and kill babes to do whatever it is they please."

The man eyed Liam. "Been some folks want to put all strangers to the test with mage truthsayers despite fancy words in the Constitution."

Liam waved the second coin. "Getting closer."

The man looked thoughtful for a moment. "Heard some fella in the saloon talk about all the hoe-boys on the south side being offered bounty for our kind, dead or alive, don't matter. Me and a couple others like us thinking of heading north in the morning. Heard there's an island up in one of the Grand Lakes where our kind is more accepted."

Liam smiled as he tossed the second coin. "Thank you, brother," he started to knee Trouble, then pulled around in front of the man. "There's more where that came from," he pointed a chin at the coins in the man's fist. "Got some business with a man owns a private train. Suspect he's laid over on the south side railyard. Pretty sure he knows I'm coming and just might even be the kind to offer bounty on those like you and me without regard to the danger they are to him."

The man's eyes grew wide, then he said cautiously, "Read a newspaper story about some people chasing some thieves and murderers. Master Mage and her Master Tinker brother out to avenge their murdered parents and take back stolen treasure. Story said two puma changelings ride with them in a railcar wagon what can ride normal roads too."

He gave Liam a measuring look, then continued, "Story said Master Tinker made his wagon fly 'cuz railroad people won't let 'em use rail bridges across the Missip'. Can you imagine that? Making a whole railcar fly? People in Little Rock claim to have seen it," the man said as he looked around. "Don't see nobody but you, but did hear about a new girl in town the last hour or two."

He smiled nevously. "Couple of the boys wanted to go to the south side to check her out but didn't want to chance the bounty."

Liam dug into a pocket and threw the man another silver dollar. "Anything else?"

"Uh," the man said as he looked at his fist closed around the three coins, six times what he'd been paid a day in his last job. "Heard this railroad guy ain't the one putting out the bounty but his entire guard is up to something, mostly their mage and the guy what bosses the rest."

"Heard about a leopard china-man that was the first to provide drinking money from the bounty. Chinaman went to pick up the laundry at the train, then told his wife about what he'd heard. The next day when he returned with the laundry he was forced to change, skinned alive, then the bounty went out."

The man looked at his hand, then back at Liam, and waited. Liam fished out another silver dollar and raised his eyebrows as he held it up.

"Leopard man's wife said he told her the mage and the bodyguard aren't telling this Easton fella what they're doing. They haven't even told him they're preparing for a city-sized war tonight. He thinks all his guards are just getting a last night on the town before they pull out for Jackson tomorrow morning."

"Word is, instead of drinking and whoring they're being scattered in hiding in a four-block radius around the train on one side, and the mage has been chanting all over the rail yards on the other side. Reminds folks of when graycoats were waiting for a bluecoat attack, only a smaller area of defense."

He smiled evilly. "For enough coin each to stock up properly for a trip up north to check out this Puma Island, I'm pretty sure I can get at least three more cats. There's also a couple of puma sisters, twins about your age, who might lend a paw, if the price was right."

Liam reached into a different pocket, drew out an object and tossed it. "Half now, the other half on the other side. Could probably use some help evening out the odds."

The puma man stared at the large godstone nugget in his hand. "Uh, this should get five more for sure, maybe even some other folks of a different form." He looked up at Liam and his brows creased. "How do I know you're not just luring folks into a trap?" He held up the nugget. "Could easily take this off my dead body after I'm skinned."

Liam smiled again and reached into one of the pouches in front of the saddle horn and pulled out some sort of tinkering attached to a small horn. He aimed the device upward discretely while pointing his chin toward it, then where it was aimed, then he looked in that direction. He moved it several times before Fallon's legs dropped below the clouds for just an instant then he flowed back into the low clouds and back out of sight.

He looked back at the man standing beside Trouble and the fellow changeling's eyes were round as he stared at where Fallon had flown out of the clouds just enough to reveal himself and then floated back up and out of sight.

"That would be the Master Tinker you might have read about," Liam commented as the man gaped at him. "And my sister just might be the new girl in town."

The man looked around, knowing there were four people being written about, with a growing group of followers.

Liam smiled again. "She's already here." Then he glanced at the sky again. "We're still waiting to see if some others are going to make it."

Then the horn-tipped tinkering beeped and he smiled at his fellow changeling, then looked up at the light of the city reflecting off of the low clouds. "And here they are."

Chapter 28

"Welcome to the party," Fallon said as he matched position with the bow of the flying railcar wagon. Blackie scowled at him but it was hard to see through his smile. "The children ready?" He didn't quite ignore Maria's glare as she fingered the stock of the sniper rifle hanging from its support arm.

Blackie snorted and shook his head, then jerked his thumb over his shoulder. "Back on the aft deck waiting for the drop. Excited as hell 'cuz they too young to know what kind of danger they're getting themselves into. But they got as much right to repay the debt we all owe as us older folk." He gave a purposeful nod. "They'll do good."

"I'm sure they will. There's a small wooded area about a half mile in that direction on the hill with the graveyard. The cloud cover has lowered itself over the cemetery hill," Fallon said then expertly flew down the side of the air wagon to see Maddy and Brutus standing with Sesco and Revis. Revis waved gaily then mouthed silently that he was being quiet so people on the ground wouldn't hear. Fallon smiled in return and mouthed his silent 'thank you'.

Blackie turned the wagon toward the cemetery hill, Fallon keeping pace with seemingly no effort as Blackie vented steam foam and they drifted down. Just as they saw the tallest headstones on the top of the hill through the cloud that was fog at this level, Fallon steered closer to the rail as Sesco opened the rear stoop's side access door.

Maddy and Brutus stepped close and grabbed onto the ropes hanging down on either side of Fallon's harness below his feet, wrapping the ropes around the forearm gauntlets with the hooks that held the rope in an unbreakable grip. Copied from Mathew's design the small hooks could be reversed to act as additional weaponry.

As soon as the two secured themselves to the rope, Sesco and Revis hurried back inside to chant some foam to lift them back into the sky while Fallon activated his hyper amulet as the weight of the two pulled them earthward. They could faintly hear Sesco and Revis chanting foam for lift as the air wagon disappeared into the fog. In seconds Fallon's hyper senses told him exactly how to alternate venting and chanting to set Maddy and Brutus on the ground so softly they barely noticed they were standing easily.

"You can disconnect now," he reminded them softly from above as his hyper senses kept him hovering motionless.

Embarrassed, both pulled down on the rope to disengage it from their forearm grapplers and twisted hooks a hundred eighty on their gauntlets as they stood back out of the way while Fallon dropped lower and released the hyper spell. "Look inside the bottom bag on the ballast pack," he instructed, as he felt sluggish for just a moment from the short hyper experience to land them all three safely.

"Blackie told us we couldn't have guns," Brutus said as he examined the tinkering while

Fallon drew deeply on the nutrient bladder he'd prepared to renew his energy.

"Isn't a gun, actually," Fallon knew he would have to explain and was being patient as he recovered from his short time hypering. "Stick the barrel against somebody and pull the trigger repeatedly and it'll shock them so hard they'll drop after two, three pulls, maybe four for somebody like you Brutus."

"Huh!" Brutus snorted as he handed the shocker to Maddy. "Won't need no gun, even if it don't shoot bullets. *Yeoww*! What was *that*?" he complained loudly as he rubbed his arm. It hung rather limply.

"That was one pull," Maddy said matter-of-factly as she admired the shocker. "Could be a girl's best friend. I'll keep it. What else is in there?" She stood on tippy-toe as Fallon hovered with the ballast pack saddle at Brutus' head height.

"Two necklaces like the one Miss Heather gave to Liam and Orlagh," Brutus said as he reached in one-handed and wriggled the shocked hand as if he were trying to awaken it. He handed one to Maddy, then let her tie the other around his neck loose enough it didn't bind but tight enough it wouldn't come off as boy or bear as he flexed his shocked arm more naturally. "So, she can always find us."

Nobody mentioned that if *she* lost and Firecloud captured her alive he could find them just as easily as she could.

"Anything else?" Maddy wondered.

"Some odd-looking trousers," Brutus said as he held the apparel in front of him.

"Special made for a growing bear," Fallon said. "The belt will hold the trousers on and you can unfasten the flap and tie it in the back out of the way when you're in full bear form without hands. There are ten pouches sewn into the waistband in front. Four of them hold a half dozen, quarter ounce coppers and four of them hold a half dozen quarter ounce silver coins. The other two each hold a couple of silver dollars, a couple of tenth ounce gold coins, and a single godstone nugget just in case of emergency."

"Anything else?" Maddy said, craning her head.

"Just this, whatever it is. Some sort of funny shaped vest. Too small for me, must be for you," Brutus said as he handed it to her.

She took it and looked at it for a moment, then smiled up at Fallon. "I won't need this for a few more years." She looked at it critically, adding softly, "Hopefully."

"No, but you will. That's especially from my sister. It has about twice the coin and nuggets as Brutus' trousers, but a tinker girl might need more than a bear boy to stay alive long enough to grow into that," he pointed at the vest and she inspected it more closely.

A long slender throwing dagger was tucked into each side above the tiny coin pouches and below where her breasts would grow if she lived a few more years. Between the two points of the sheathed daggers was a targeting charm that would help her hit her target, with little effort.

"You're cutting us free and paying us off," Maddy was indignant.

"No," Fallon objected with a tolerant smile as he had anticipated even this last accusation. "We're going up against some ruthless people and many of us may die before sunrise." He pointed toward their gifts from his position above them as he continued to hover. "If you are separated from the rest or if you are the only survivors, those gifts will help you live longer."

He pointed at his throat, then at them. "If the necklace burns throw it away as soon as you can, preferably in something moving, and go as fast as you can the other way. The rail yard where Easton's private train is currently parked is three miles in that direction. Do you have everything?"

Each held up the signaler Fallon tinkered for talking together. A tiny hand crank powered a horn that could be set to blow one of two notes too high for normal hearing. Using simple Morse code each device would repeat any pattern of dots and dashes it *heard*. The signalers could pick up the constant signal coming from the wagon and they could send their message, then the wagon would locate others on the ground and relay all updated information.

"Good, and just before you arrived Liam signaled me he recruited a handful of local shapeshifters of his own kind and maybe some others out for revenge for the loss of one of their own to our target to increase our odds. Brutus, you're the shifter sensor so keep your nose on alert."

At the boy's serious nod of assent, Fallon continued, "Get as much information as you can and signal it up to the wagon. They'll take it and relay it to the rest of us, me included, and I'll do short looks at it in hyper and send the results back to everybody."

Maddy and Brutus both nodded attentively, looking up at him floating with the small flyer held with his eyes only slightly higher than Brutus' as he continued, "My sound detectors are picking up what might be a wagon pulled by four horses. You're both dressed well enough you won't scare people away, but not so well you'll draw unwanted attention from undesirable individuals. If you hurry you might get a ride into town."

They took the hint and dashed off through the graveyard in the direction he pointed. After a few moments he said, "You can come out now."

There was no response for a few moments, then a large wolf moved just enough forward to be seen by the normal human. Then another wolf, this one a female, stepped into view, then a human boy about the same age as Fallon.

"Hello," Fallon called out as he resisted the urge to chant a few feet of altitude. "I am Fallon Richards, and I greet you as friend."

"So, the stories are true, not just the adventures of a dime novel put in newspapers to expose the gullible," the young man was very articulate and confident as he faced the man from the sky.

"Some of them are true, others are not," Fallon replied then shrugged. "Some truths grow so large they no longer resemble their origin, and sometimes the truth is more wondrous than the myth."

He reached into a pocket in his hanging curtain of supplies and pulled out a small wrapped package and tossed it to the ground. "Be careful with and wary of that. It is a charmed book with eight select memories of my sister's and my journey for justice for our parents. The last three are what we plan to do tonight but there is no ending. Yes, I am *that* Fallon Richards as you already know."

The boy picked up the package and opened it as Fallon alternated his eyes between the dominant male and female of the pack and the boy who was acting spokeswolf for this encounter.

He threw an arm in the direction Maddy and Brutus had gone. "Those two *children* go to risk their lives to help us. It would be a shame if a pack of your size allowed them to travel through other changelings' territories without an escort."

The spokeswolf looked in the direction the two ran, then at the wolves on either side of him. "I see only three. There are two territories between the city's rail yard and a third claims it as their turf."

"I see three here," Fallon said then held up a tinkering, "and five more in close concealment, there, there, there, there, and there," he said as he casually pointed. "There are four more on the outer limits of my detection."

The boy looked surprised and the female growled.

"Do not worry, mother, your cubs are safe from me. The nanny has not brought them any closer than safe, it is just that my device," he held it up, "can hear farther than any safe distance to spy from without equally advanced tinkerings." He smiled disarmingly and the dominant female settled down while keeping her eyes locked on him.

"My sister and I and our companions come to right a wrong done to my family first, but we plan to continue our quest to root out and expose, then capture or kill any pocket of evil we discover."

"We have suffered our own level of evil this past day," the boy said as he continued to maintain an aura of confidence. "A bruin mother to the west in a farming community has lost her female cub born just this last spring. And another child, this one a 'panzee baby from the sharecroppers' barracks out by the railyard, has been taken. There are others as well, suffered by those with better protections than the others could provide."

Fallon digested the information without the use of his hyper spell. "Our collections of information from every town and village along the path of our quarry includes missing and murdered children in the same time period of Easton's train's schedule. We have signed witness reports putting him in every stop where a child went missing and their body found further along the trail at one of the next stops."

He vented just enough foam to settle closer to the eye level of the pack's dominant leaders as he straddled the saddle on the water tube. "I fear it is too late for the missing children, but if my sister and

I do not kill the one that cursed me before my birth, then more children will be used for Firecloud's dark magery."

If he didn't convince them to help at least Firecloud's name would be known. "To get to him we have to go through the ones hired to protect the ones that killed our parents, but there are many of them. Easton has a personal guard troop of twenty men led by a former Pinkerton agent and six more train crew that will fight as well as any of the security men to protect their locomotive."

"They have hired twice that many locals to infest the whole 'panzee territory but the 'panzees don't dare say anything 'cuz folk's memories of the war are still too raw," the young man passed on that bit of information then took a deep breath and looked down at the dominant male. "What if it had been one of ours got took, Pa? Would we let somebody else fight for us, or say it don't matter 'cuz it weren't our kin? The bounty don't specify cats."

The big male sniffed loudly then put his head back and let loose a battle howl that echoed across the mist shrouded cemetery. An echoing call came from the direction of the nanny and the spokeswolf explained. "The cubs will be hidden with some humans we trust. The rest of the pack will join the hunt."

He started to follow as the dominant pair melted into the fog. "Wait!" Fallon said. "Take this."

He pulled out a box-shaped tinkering with a small horn on one end and a pistol grip with trigger on the other. "Pull the trigger and point it at the sky and when the horn beeps push one of these ten buttons. The message each button sends is printed on the side by each button."

The young man read some of them silently in the darkness, his lupine vision using the minimal light. "Pack retreating? Trapped need help? Need mage healer?"

Fallon smiled. "There's also, 'enemy routed', 'guard neutralized', and 'area secured'."

"And dark mage located," the young man read warily. "That one is fourth to last before pack retreating, trapped need help, and need mage healer."

"Yes, it is," Fallon agreed. "If you give that signal you should retreat fast and hope he doesn't follow or you'll need the last two."

He shook his finger at the young man's affronted reaction. "Do not allow your pack leaders to challenge the dark mage! He is far greater than anything you may have faced before and he has gained power through the murders in his wake. If you openly move against him *maybe* one or two of you will live but even if you flee to the other side of the world with the cubs, he will hunt you down and kill all of you as a lesson to any other that might challenge him."

Fallon smiled and pointed toward the booklet in the boy's hand. "If I live to see the sunrise, I will paint this scene on page six." As the young man opened the small condensed memory journal, Fallon opened a valve and put steam into his balloons as he chanted it softly into foam, and the one-man flyer lifted him smoothly into the mist. His last sight was of the wolf-boy running to catch up to his pack.

As Fallon rose, he aimed his detector tinkering and marked when the pack reunited and swarmed into a ball of greetings and sniffings. He detected the sounds of the spokeswolf explaining the signaler and demonstrating the small memory journal with its first page a miniature copy of the scene with Fallon and Heather and Liam and Orlagh discovering the bodies of Orson and Elizabeth Richards.

Fallon could tell by the silence that came over the pack when the memory charm activated and each one that saw the picture *experienced* a small measure of the feeling of the moment. Then all of the wolves howled and howled and dashed toward the south side rail yard.

Fallon nodded to himself and aimed his flyer toward another area of Memphis. He used his detector till he heard what he wanted, then lowered his flyer toward the chanting as he initiated his hyper awareness.

The chanting stopped just before he came into view of an elderly man standing at the ready with chants on his lips as several acolytes formed a line to either side of the Master Mage. Several sets of eyes widened at his appearance from the thickening fog. The old man snapped at one of those he'd been instructing and a curse died on the student mage's lips.

Fallon adjusted his venting and the pusher fans and came to a smooth stop just yards from the line of mages. "Greetings Master Mage. I am Fallon Richards. My sister Heather and I have come to Memphis to avenge the murder of our parents. One of those we seek is the dark mage, Firecloud."

At the name three of the acolytes blanched as the Master responded, "What is it to us if he passes through our city without doing us harm?"

"Firecloud has been abducting and killing children from Winslow to Memphis preparing for this battle. He has already abducted at least two children from this city since arriving here in Memphis in order to create his final incantations and spells for his battle with my sister."

Fallon was able to hear and read the lips of three of the acolytes, two of them female. "So, one of your children is missing as well." At the reactions of most of those flanking the Master – he knew he'd guessed correctly.

"Does *that* make it part of your problem?" he taunted the old Master, watching the muscles of his face as he continued, "From what my sister told me he tortures his victims to death as he dismembers them, and uses their body parts to make amulets and talismans. As a final insult, he puts curses on their relatives that steal the life essences of those yet unborn, robbing them of their most vital abilities."

He saw the old man's eyes flash to the active amulet at his neck. "Yes, he cursed my mother and I was locked inside my head till the murder of my parents cracked the curse enough for my sister and me to bend it more to my control."

"You'll kill yourself boy," the Master Mage said as he relaxed his battle stance. "I can see you growing old before my eyes."

Fallon smiled. "I'm living every minute of that to the fullest in my quest for vengeance."

"The cost is great, but it is not up to me to judge," the Master said. "I see the cost catching up to you as we speak. Would you accept my offer of sanctuary till you recover?" He gestured toward his students. "We must plan our response to this affront to our territory from one that has grown too arrogant with the knowledge our teachings sometimes reveal."

Fallon smiled and took a large swallow of the energy drink he'd concocted, then deactivated the hyper spell. As lethargy overtook him, he mumbled, "Just tie that rope hanging below me off to something, so I don't blow away. I'll wake up in a couple of minutes and be on my way."

He was out before anyone could move.

Chapter 29

Rat was watching as another group darted toward the rail yard on the south side of town. There had been a lot of activity around one specific private train ever since it arrived. Then that old leopard chinaman was chanted into beast form, skinned alive, and a bounty put out for any changeling found within a mile of the rail yard.

Rat was well inside that cordon but he wasn't about to give up his burrow. He smiled his feral smile as he listened to one of that former Pinkerton man's guards patrolling above his burrow. The fool didn't realize how close he was to having his guts ripped out before he could raise the useless shotgun he carried.

Weak little human, Rat could spring out of the concealed entrance to his den and taste the man's lifeblood in a heartbeat. But then he would have to abandon the burrows he'd spent nearly five years digging just the way he wanted.

Rat wasn't really a rat changeling. He was a wolverine and his burrows ran from one side of the refuse pile near the rail yard to the other with several entrances. He got the name from his favorite living food and wasn't ashamed he kept a cage of fresh samples on hand whenever the opportunity of abundance presented itself. He didn't care that the city of Memphis piled all of their rotting trash on top of his home. In fact, he kind of enjoyed some of the offerings that sometimes came his way. There were dead bodies of all kinds and vegetables that snooty humans let sit too long for their own tastes but were just fine to eat.

Then he saw another shape dart across the spaces between the parked railroad cars awaiting the locomotive that would take them south to Jackson or west to Little Rock or Oklahoma City, or east to Atlanta.

Then another slunk between two rail cars. "Damned cats," he muttered darkly, then calmed himself as he remembered the feel of snow in his fur as he reveled in his changeling form in his home territory. Maybe protecting this smelly hole under a trash pile wasn't worth risking his pelt to keep.

In fact, since the private train arrived fewer and fewer people brought good refuse for him to search through and he hadn't gotten a good meal in two days. Plump, well-fed rats were tasty, but even the best food could get boring after too many meals in a row.

He darted back into his deepest den and lit a small candle as he gathered his few most coveted and necessary belongings in a backpack. There wasn't much, but what there was meant all the world to him, or was useful in a necessary way.

There was a beautiful mug of silver with embedded gems that had been thrown away by mistake. He smiled as he remembered the master of that house making his butler and maid go through the trash for two days before he'd allowed them to return home and clean themselves. He'd purchased time with the maid in her new job in the brothel *and* found a gold tooth the master had missed before disposing of the mistakenly suspected butler thief.

He'd also enjoyed getting revenge for the two unfairly treated employees and dined in an expensive restaurant for three days on the coin the wealthy master had so blithely carried on his person.

Then there were the other bits of gold and silver and small gemstones that occasionally ended up in people's trash and lost forever. Rat had three medium sized pouches full of these treasures, wealth accumulated over the five years he'd been in this self-exile while he recuperated from the last time he'd worked for another.

He filled the pack with the few things he owned that he couldn't leave behind, shifted into warrior form and stuffed the last of the rats he had caged for just such a time into his mouth squealing. He chewed furiously, spit out a few bones and tufts of fur, then swallowed the rest as he looked about in the dim light of the small candle to make sure he had everything. Satisfied he had all that mattered, he darted into another tunnel and raced along in the dark to the hidden entrance.

Popping his head out at the entrance, he sniffed and caught the pungent smell of 'panzee. What were they doing away from their sharecropper shacks this late at night, especially with the bounty Easton's man had put out? Did they know the dark mage prowling about had taken one of their whelps? Rat had avoided the remains of the mangled body when the dark mage had discarded what was left after his dark magery.

Rat shuddered as he darted out into the night. He could usually eat just about anything that hadn't aged to runny, but what the dark mage discarded even he wouldn't touch. Rat ducked and darted through the newly crowded rows of railroad side lines for storing railcars being loaded and unloaded and prepared for journeys east, south, west, and north.

Orlagh trotted across the railcar line with the local boy keeping up with her as she jumped from car to car, then she flattened herself as the young showoff continued jumping, then casually trotted back to see why she was not running with him. She batted at his muzzle and hissed a warning and he flattened himself to the top of the car.

"Did you hear something?" a guard walking by asked his partner.

"Don't be so jumpy," another man scolded.

"Boss said to be extra watchful tonight."

"Boss been saying that since we left Winslow," the second voice sneered. "Getting' tired of *'be alert'* all the time. After a few watches of *'be alert'*, ain't no alert left in me. Come on let's finish this round so I can get some coffee."

The other guard grumbled but didn't object and they continued on.

Orlagh rose cautiously, then swatted her young suitor on the snout again and snarled a warning. He looked properly abashed and hung back a proper distance as she continued her scouting circle. She smelled a wolverine scent on one round that seemed fresh, but it was going away from the target train so she dismissed it from her mind as she continued circling, marking the locations of hidden guards bored and losing their focus.

She noted the pumas that stood silent vigil in ambush positions near many of those hidden men, themselves lying in ambush for justice to come for their employer and the greater evil he employed.

She slunk by those men, each of them thinking they were a match for changeling senses, her companion learning several scouting tricks as he watched her with more attention. They left the railcars to run around the mound of the city's growing refuse pile where she detected older scents of the resident wolverine changeling.

She hoped he'd gotten out alive. His kind were rare even in their home range, but almost unheard of this far south. His pelt would be a prize for the kind of man that would put a bounty on changelings even after the change in laws after the War.

She completed another circuit of the area with Easton's private train in the center and started another circuit in closer. This time around she saw more of her own kind, an entire pack of wolves, two coyotes, and a trio of bear females, one of which had the smell of a lactating mother. Then she skirted a handful of mages, the oldest covered in the same kind of old power in the necklace the waif, Maddy, had loaned to Heather.

On her fourth circuit of the battleground she scented her brother and let herself be seen as he rode his horse into the trap awaiting them. When he noticed her, he nodded and loosened the carbine in its saddle holster, drained the prepared bladder of energy drink, and activated the deflector charm

Heather created for him, chanting it into existence softly as he rode toward death.

Herm and his best friend watched through their tinker's scopes as shadows rippled between the railcars they could see. "I tell you, those are *big* cats, not the kind that infest homes and alleys looking for scraps and keeping down vermin," he said to his partner, Potter.

"So, ya want ta put a bullet in one?" Potter answered. "Jes remember, once we start shooting any decent war veteran will be able to mark our spot and try to take us out. I say wait for a good bounty to cross our sights afore we reveal our hiding place. Jes one round each to share the bounty, take the head, then we hightail it over to that second spot we already picked out and wait till mornin' to collect.

Just then Herm stiffened. "Hey! Ain't that that cat man?" He pointed and Potter swung his scope in that direction.

"Yeah, that shore looks like him," Potter settled in and put his finger near the trigger. "I'll get him as soon as he clears the other side of that last car, then we collect his head and take it to Gibbs for our bounty."

He smiled as he waited for the target to come back into sight, his finger closing on the trigger of his sniper rifle. The target was just coming back into sight and he was taking his steadying breath when Herm turned at a noise and gasped.

Potter turned just enough to see a pair of pumas with pink leather collars leap out of the darkness. He tried to get the sniper's rifle around but it was too unwieldy to move quick and he had time only for a muffled cry before the cat closed its jaws on his throat and ripped it out.

Liam chanted the deflector spell as Trouble plodded steadily on, going closer and closer to Easton's train when the sound of a distant scream pierced the night. The scream cut off suddenly just as the signaler hanging from the saddle horn beeped. He lifted it and pulled the charging trigger to spin the magnets inside the cylinder as he turned it till the beep was loudest but still soft enough to not carry far and alert watchers.

He switched the receiver knob on the side of the tinkered box and as the indicator light flashed in Morse code, he read the message the air wagon was sending. When it started to repeat again, he switched the knob back and pushed the *'message received'* button and his signaler beeped at the air wagon circling within the low clouds as Trouble plodded on.

More than once he saw changelings lurking in the shadows and he tapped Morse code signals upward so Rosa could build the battle map at her station in the command balloon. Twice more he received messages that allowed him to skirt heavy concentrations of Easton's first line of defense, the hirelings that were in this more for the bounty in changelings.

He smiled inwardly as every report he got indicated the elimination of those bounty hunters by the very people they were supposed to be hunting. It seemed the cats and dogs were competing to see which clan could neutralize the most ambushers without being noticed. One report from Maddy indicated the wolf pack that now escorted her and Brutus were moving into the cordon manned by Easton's core security team and he whispered, "Be careful girl," as he rode toward the private train.

Trouble snorted and looked to the left as they came around a crossing in the access road beside a parked boxcar and Liam put a hand on his pistol grip.

"Don't want any trouble, friend," a voice came from inside the boxcar. "Just trying to get out of the way of impending violence."

Liam kneed Trouble to a stop and with body language turned the stallion in a slow circle to appear to be deciding which way to go. Smelling the scent from inside, he said, "Don't want to join the party?"

Rat stepped to the open boxcar door so he could be seen, a ragged pack on his back and another bag in one hand. "Dyin' ain't no party, young feller."

He pointed a chin toward Liam's goal. "That's the party you talkin' 'bout?"

Liam smiled as he turned Trouble again as if deciding which road he wanted to take. With the changeling standing just inside the line of the shade and not visible to any but him, Liam continued his quick conversation. "Name's Liam Quinn. Looks like you've been here a while and kind of late leaving. Got any suggestions which way is best if I want to get to the party whole?"

"Folks call me Rat. Ain't my name, but don't want to give that to a man fixin' to be tortured out of all he knows, ifn' he lives that long."

He pointed a chin down one road. "That way has three fellas in a boxcar just like this one on the right." He put his free hand on the side of the door as he stepped out into the light reflected off the clouds by the city's street lamps.

He twitched his head to the side. "That way has two fellas on top of the wood pile in the fuel car of the first locomotive you come to." He snickered. "They's kind of bored and I snuck a bottle from them whilst they was *distracted* by a bear boy stepping on a crunchy rock."

Rat pulled the bottle out of the bag in his hand and held it up, then pointed with it. "They's also a couple more fellas that way with that dark mage."

He pointed back in the direction Liam had come from. "I'd go back that way ifn' I was you. But I ain't so I won't burden you with my 'pinion."

He smiled as if he hadn't already done so, then added as he stepped fully into the light. "None I know of can see this little split in the access road so you can stop actin' like you confused and trying to not *rat* on ol' Rat whilst we converse."

He gazed piercingly at Liam. "You ain't gonna take the advice I didn't give, are you boy?"

Liam stopped Trouble in the direction Rat had *not* advised him to not take. "Bear boy and the girl with him are two of mine," he snorted. "Accumulating a local wolf pack along with them."

"Pride of cats, like you, too from what I've seen."

Liam snorted as he reached for the signaler. "You seem to know more than a whole passel of folks. Could use that skill." Then he turned the signaler toward the air wagon and tapped out the new information.

"Wha'cha got there sonny?" Rat craned his neck and leaned out from the boxcar door with a curious look.

"Tinkered signaler," Liam replied as he tapped out the message.

"Beeps sound like Morse code," Rat observed, adding, "You spelled two words wrong."

Liam looked up with raised eyebrows. "Shortened to take less time. You know code?"

Rat made a wry face. "Good deduction Mr. Obvious. That tinker what I been readin' 'bout tinker that for ya?"

Liam kept his face poker blank. "What tinker?"

Rat snorted. "Now yer insultin' my 'telligence boy. I'm an *ar-kee-all-gist*," He poked his chest with a clawed forefinger at each syllable. "Best place to larn 'bout folks is ta go through their trash. Been studyin' Memphis folks for some years now. They like most other folks, and their trash always includes books and newspapers."

He leaned out and looked both ways before saying in a stage whisper, "You folks bein' writ 'bout all over from coast to coast. The vengeful Master Mage and Master Tinker and their trusty puma sidekicks battlin' evil on the rails and from the sky no less." He snorted as he peered at the low cloud cover and high fog settling over the rail yards. "Kind of thought that was farfetched, up to now anyways."

"Make ya an offer," he one-eyed Liam and Liam nodded his go-ahead. "I'll trail ya and pass on information if ya let me play wit that thing," he pointed a gnarly clawed fingertip as he morphed into an impressive warrior form of his changeling clan.

Liam gave the wolverine man a look. The laws of physics pertained to changelings despite the otherworldly magic involved. Wolverines didn't grow to the size of a normal human, but humans could be wolverine changelings. Where a small human could masquerade as a normal puma or maybe a wolf, no normal-sized human changeling could masquerade as a real wolverine.

Wolverine changelings were some of the most dangerous creatures alive. A normal sized wolverine was not something many animals of *any* size would mess with. A wolverine with the size and sentience of a human was several times more dangerous, and Rat in his warrior form was a sight to see – in a nightmare.

Despite this fact, Liam didn't hesitate to knee Trouble over to the side of the boxcar, and within reach of some of the most dangerous claws in the known world. He didn't really worry because he could smell Rat's scents just as well as Rat could smell his. They both could tell the intentions of the other and combined with their animal cores could also read body language preternaturally.

"This switch turns it from receive to send. These small holes have wires inside that glow when heated and reflects through the colored glass windows. The red one is dots and the blue one is dashes. The buttons next to each lamp where your thumb can reach sends the same, left one is dots and right one dashes when you hold it with the horn pointed up. The trigger spins the magnet inside that cylinder there," he pointed, "to power the thing. There's some sort of other tinkering inside that holds that power for a half-hour or so, so you have to pull the trigger every time it just beeps once to let you know the charge is almost dead."

"It beeps to let you know when to charge it. Ingenious, simply ingenious," Rat muttered without any trace of his previous uneducated speech patterns as he inspected the signaler rapturously.

Liam could hear him muttering things about *focused sonics*, and *electro-magnetic* something or other and a thing called a *battery*. Words he remembered Fallon using when talking about his idols, Thomas Alva Edison and the more reclusive Nicholas Tesla. Then Rat looked up. "You really going to trust me with this? And to pass information to you while you go deeper into that," he held up the signaler first then pointed it in the direction of Easton's train.

Liam reached back and pulled another signaler out of the saddlebag behind him. "Fallon seems to think it's always wise to carry a spare." He kneed Trouble. "I would say try to keep up, but I'll settle for a warning of sorts where needed."

Rat smiled, his warrior's teeth bright in the glow of the night as the fog settled lower when Liam rode away.

Chapter 30

Brutus froze as the slag stone crunched beneath his foot. Beside him Maddy froze at exactly the same time. Several shapes around them melted into the shadows as the nearest guard spoke loudly.

"Dij'ya hear sumpin'?"

"What?" another voice complained. "Yer always hearin' things Shorty, but ain't no tellin' ifn' the boss ain't testin' us so why don't you go check things out whilst I stand guard with muh rifle."

"Believe I'll do jest that!" Shorty loudly exclaimed, and stood up from this seat on a stack of cut wood for the locomotive's boiler.

He was trying to navigate the loosely piled wood in front of his watch position when the other man exclaimed. "What was that?" Shorty looked back and his partner was looking around him at the side of the wood car they were sitting on with their night's supplies, including a bottle of whiskey for when it got chilly in the hours before dawn.

"What, you hearin' things now, Jackson?" Shorty cackled then stumbled on a loose log and almost fell and Jackson laughed at him.

"Oh, har-har, you worthless son of a halfman polecat!"

The two men glared at each other for a moment, then Shorty made his way to the other side of the locomotive's wood car and peered into the night. "Fog's settling in real thick. Can't see more than the car on the track next to ours." He turned and looked over his shoulder. "Maybe we should'a picked a spot where we could see further."

"Hah!" Jackson spit contemptuously. "Then *we* could be seen from further off. Would rather us surprise somebody sneakin' 'round instead of givin' 'em a long shot we don't see comin'."

Shorty was shaking his head in agreement when his partner's eyes went wide and he fumbled at the rifle hanging loose in his hands.

Shorty turned to look behind him just as a large form rose up from the side of the wood car and huge hands with sharp claws wrapped around his shirt and snatched him from his feet. Before he could make a sound, he was thrown and his arms and legs tangled in the arms and legs of his partner. By the time they unwrapped themselves, they were surrounded by several wolves, a large bear warrior, and a small girl festooned with tinkerings.

It was the girl, no more than eleven or twelve years old, who spoke. "Good evening gentlemen. I hope you don't mind, but we would like to ask you some questions. We don't want you to think we don't trust you, but one of you will be questioned over there," she pointed to the furthest end of the wood car then at her feet, "and the other here. Then we'll match the two stories. If they match you live, if they don't," she shrugged and the bear man drooled as he spoke through a mouth full of finger long teeth.

"Hu-u-n-ngry-y!"

Several minutes later Maddy was sitting on the edge of the wood car when Liam rode up. "Hello Mr. Quinn." She held up her signaler. "Just sent in my report and said you were in sight and I'd pass it to you directly."

Liam nodded when Maddy was finished. "Good job, both of you." He gave Brutus a nod and the boy, back in full human form and eating the last of the guards' supplies, blushed. "Hold this position and don't let anyone in or out you or your escort doesn't know without getting their name, likeness, and other particulars recorded."

He looked at the wolves patrolling the perimeter. "Nobody gets in, but anyone you let go out is stripped of powder weapons, all magery, and strange tinkerings, but let them keep knives and other such weapons so they're not completely defenseless when they go through the territories of people they've terrorized."

Maddy scowled, but replied respectfully, "Yes sir, Mr. Quinn."

"What if we don't want to stay put or let anyone from inside live, *cat*?" the young man with the wolf smell challenged.

Liam shrugged. "Every man, or woman, has to decide what kind of person they really are and whether or not they want to show that person to the rest of the world."

He glanced around at the wolves in sight. "I know the pleasure of the hunt and the thrill of prey in my jaw's grasp, and the taste of fresh meat still hot from life. But when I am in my beast form, I still only hunt to eat, never for sport."

"How about revenge?" a wolf in warrior form asked as he approached out of the near fog tugging on a pair of hempcloth trousers. "Isn't that why you're here? To kill for revenge?"

Liam acceded to the point. "Yes, but only those directly involved. Proved through magery that Lefty wasn't part of the actual murders, only the thievery after the murders. Let him live after a scare and retrieving property."

"Read he lost another finger, though," a woman came out of the fog in human form, her trousers tied and a modest vest barely covering her impressive bosom.

"To the dark mage we aim to kill above all others except Mr. Easton himself if he doesn't surrender for a legal trial. His bodyguard might be another but we don't have facts enough to prove either one gave the order to kill, only the pressure to sell the property."

He smiled. "I'll give any man the chance to surrender and give him respect afterward with *my* word of that respect."

He shrugged. "If you don't want to give a surrender respect that is your burden to bear. If so, at least do it openly so other people can see what kind of person you *want* them to see."

The dominant female changeling smiled. "I like you, *cat*! You not like most folks who just talk big. You talk big *ideas*! Most wouldn't know the difference."

Liam tilted his head in acceptance. "So, what are you going to do?"

The pack's dominant male walked up and wrapped arms around his mate possessively. "We gonna capture and question those that surrender peacefully and kill and eat the rest."

The female elbowed her mate in the gut and he blew air out explosively in surprise, then glared at her. She batted her eyelashes and he melted into a nervous smile, then she turned to Liam. "*Just* the livers for humans or other changelings who don't surrender, no other body parts, just the liver, just like the pact President Lincoln signed at the end of the war says. We claim it as our right, but that don't mean we *will* claim its power."

Liam nodded. Along with freeing the negro slaves and ending the genocide of the changeling forms, the changelings' animal forms were allowed one concession to their bestial natures. It was scientifically proven a changeling gained life essence from a challenge to the death survived and the eating of the fresh meat of that defeated challenger.

By offering surrender or not defending till *actively* attacked, any changeling could *legally* kill and claim the defeated foe's liver as a proper trophy. There were those pure humans, and even a few changelings ashamed of the fact, that objected, mostly the same ones that objected to allowing magery or tinkery, but they would have to go through the new Congress and the increasingly race and species inclusive courts to change the new law.

"All a man can ask," Liam said as he kneed Trouble around so he could face Maddy again. Brutus looked up from rooting around in the guards' small pile of possessions, then found something to eat and stuffed it in his mouth.

His eyes moved across the two captives tied up and looking miserable as wolves yawned nearby. Liam smiled devilishly. "You want to have some fun with those?" He pointed his chin at Shorty and Jackson and continued when Maddy looked interested. "Ask them if they got drunk on watch then make them show you their bottle *after* they claim having one, to prove they didn't drink any of it."

At her raised eyebrow, Liam chuckled as he waved a hand negligently. "Light fingered local I talked to just before you assumed your current guard post." He pointed his chin at the signaler in her hand. "Goes by the name of Rat and has one of those now."

Just then a shot rang out, then another, then the sound of several long guns followed just as both of their signalers beeped. They were so close together that both tinkerings picked up the message and the lights on the sides blinked out the message.

Liam kneed Trouble without a word and took off along the access road between the lines of parallel railcar parking rails as Maddy yelled. "Don't you let her die Mr. Quinn!"

Heather rode the trike into the rail yard slowly, looking neither left nor right as she followed the scent of her quarry. He smelled of her mother and father, through the pendant and ring he'd *claimed* as trophies to draw her to him in challenge. Along the way she passed changelings in beast, warrior, and human form. Most of them seemed to be from the largest local clans, the wolves, and pumas like her friends Orlagh and Liam.

Liam. Her mind did some sort of twist every time she thought of him getting hurt helping her bring justice to her parents' murderers and the man that had cursed her brother for so many years. He and his sister *just happened* to be passing through on their own quest for justice when they got entangled in her and her brother's lives.

They weren't beholden to her or Fallon, but had both risked their lives several times since then. Liam seemed to be aloof to her fumbling advances, or she was doing something wrong. Her mama told her she couldn't be *too* aggressive with a man she wanted or all men would think she was a trollop.

But what was *too* aggressive? Liam seemed to be leaning closer and touching her arm more when they were close, but it always seemed so *proper* when he did touch her. It was frustrating as hell! And Maria's kind of magery insisted they were meant for each other! What was she doing wrong?

She shook herself out of her reverie when her special signaler twitched against her right wrist. It moved a stick to touch her wrist, touch left for dots and touch right for dashes. The only way her brother had been able to make it so small was having the booster unit in the trike as part of the special cargo package. She could operate it with her left hand or through two, tiny extendable keys she could tap with the fingers of her right hand.

Her brother rode above her and the message was directly from him, bypassing the air wagon. He'd stayed up high when the clouds were only low, but as they continued to drop until the rail yard was engulfed in fog, he'd had to come in lower and closer to observe from on high.

The trouble was that one of his messages reported he'd felt Firecloud probing him and she should be prepared for him going offline if Firecloud was still able to curse him through the old pathways. She kept her composure and not turned and fled when he said he was afraid to go into hyper tinkering within a mile of the Native mage for fear of being brain stunned, and this fog made it necessary for him to do just that.

Trying to keep her mind on her task as she felt the dots and dashes that came almost steady as Fallon gave her a running report, she followed the path her brother scouted out for her from above. The steam trike was nearly silent as she rode the shortest distance through an obstacle course of guards to duel to the death with the Native mage that had done her family such evil. She put a hand to the source of power that now nestled at her breast hoping it was enough to offset the power Firecloud had been accumulating through a baker's dozen dead children.

She passed by a solitary shape hiding on top of a railcar she passed that gave a smell she hadn't scented since her days as an acolyte under her Master's training and wondered what a wolverine was doing mixed up in this. A little later she got the message through her wrist coder that the outer ring was secure and all but about ten guards remained in the area around the train, including the two that accompanied their primary target.

Following the directions, she turned her trike right at the next access road and crossed two more roads before turning left. She stopped immediately, the feel of death strong just ahead.

She chanted a few lines and her anger grew. How *dare* he do *that* to innocent children merely to gain a dueling advantage! She touched the item in her hip bag. Well, she was prepared for that as well. She engaged the trike as she reached into a vest hoop and drew forth one of her throwing darts, chanted a line, and threw, and the dart pierced the amulet directly between the plucked eyes of a child.

Firecloud grunted and threw his head back and almost killed the guards at his side. With great effort he regained his composure as the two men stepped another half foot away from him. He would need them for shielding and they would do that with their lives anyway, so he held back since it would be wasteful if done to salve the pain of his distant eyes being darkened.

He tried not to massage between his eyes as he *felt* the pain of those eyes' harvesting, in a magery recoil because he hadn't been ready for his opponent to be able to act so swiftly or accurately.

"You alright sir?" one of the guards asked and Firecloud touched an amulet and chanted a phrase and the man choked and grabbed at his throat.

Firecloud *almost* broke the man's neck. Didn't the fool already know he should *never* point out a weakness? The Native mage inhaled deeply through his nose, breathing the man's fear as he was kept from taking a breath of his own.

He released the man. Soon, soon, he would make this one hurt when he finally used him. "No, no, I'm okay, I was working magery and you broke my chant is why I reacted the way I did. Please don't do that again. It is not always possible to realize you are not attacking me."

The guard wasn't sure what the dark mage was talking about or what he did, so he just nodded his head up and down vigorously.

"Do your jobs!" Firecloud snapped. "I'm not the one you're supposed to be watching." He was still glaring at their backs when the other set of distant eyes blasted him with a recoil of the pain of their harvesting increased combined with a magery backed increase that doubled the pain and he went to one knee. Luckily for the two guards neither witnessed this second display of weakness and what he learned from it.

He had seen the *challenged* and watched her destroy one set of his eyes and now the other was destroyed in a spot she could not have reached so quickly *and* that destruction had been done by a Master.

Firecloud smiled. If he could add the essences of both the girl along with the new power she seemed to wield *and* this new Master's essence, then he would be powerful enough to stand up to any other Master of his Craft.

He took out one of his more elaborate talismans, one that had consumed four innocent lives to make. Then he sought out the one he wanted, *there*, and he initiated the spell without hesitation and the power of four life forces surged into the sky above.

"The one that shot our sister will never do so to another on this world," the puma warrior stated as he approached Liam. "Can't she change to heal faster?"

Liam looked up with Orlagh's head in his lap. Several cougars prowled the near vicinity, half of them in warrior form. His sister mewled in pain as she tried not to breathe too deep. "Mage's curse. We're both locked to the moon's full phase. I go into forced beast form on the three nights of the full moon and she goes into forced beast form all other days," he pursed his lips. "We are without our warrior form and it's only with these," he put fingers under his necklace of godstone links, "we even have our sentient wits in control of our beast forms."

Normally Liam wouldn't think of telling them this, but his sister couldn't heal herself without being able to control her own *change* and healing was one of his worst accomplishments with the amulets Heather had distributed. If she didn't get some healing fast, she would drown in her own blood.

The young puma with fresh blood on his warrior's muzzle and both sets of claws stepped close. "I know a healing chant, but I don't have enough power to do it without borrowing power from another."

"Can you share power with another?" Liam asked.

"I don't know, I've never tried. I was always the strongest in our pride and everybody else gave me their power."

Liam smiled as he used his free hand to fish an amulet out of a vest pocket. "We can try. Put your hand over my hand that's over her entry wound. What is your healing chant?"

The puma warrior told him as he morphed into full human. "Okay, change the quaternary syllable to these two syllables," he spoke them and the puma didn't even mention the fact the chant now had eleven syllables instead of the traditional ten or less. Liam made the young man repeat the adjusted chant twice before activating the amulet and joining him.

It only took a few repetitions for the blood flow to slow, and another to stop altogether. Orlagh took a shuddering breath and relaxed in his arms. "You say the one that did this has already paid?"

The young puma changeling wiped a bloody hand across a bloody mouth and held the blood out to be smelled. "He is dead."

Liam did so and nodded his thanks for the honor shown.

The young man scowled. "She took that bullet for me." Then he stood tall. "Leander Fleetfoot Miller, at your service sir."

Liam smiled. He had seen the Native features dimmed by European blood, just like his sister's and his own. Although the *Old Families* of Native changelings still held millennia old tracts of home territory, there were many new changelings with European features intermingling their bloodlines and going where jobs and companionship took them. Liam detected several conflicting scents from the pumas that stalked around where his sister had been shot. Besides his and his sister's traces of snow leopard blood, he detected traces of African lion, Asian tiger and South American jaguar.

Fleetfoot was probably this young man's Native heritage and Liam took that route. "Okay, Fleetfoot, are there any more in your pride with some measure of magery in them?"

Fleetfoot looked panicked. "It's not *my* pride!" He nervously looked around for one of the older females that seemed to be running things most of the time in larger cougar populations. Not seeing one in hearing range he turned a glare on Liam. "There are two others I sometimes work with to, uh, heal headaches, and, uh, things like that."

Liam smiled. He and his two buddies would probably drink all night and use what little magery they had in them to cure their hangovers. "Well if you could bring them here, we might be able to finish this. All we've done is stop the bleeding into her lungs, now we have to work our way along each path the bullet took out to the skin. You up to that?"

Before the young puma man could answer an elderly man approached with authority. "That won't be necessary, young man." Liam could feel the magery around the old Master as the mage waved a hand over his sister. "Huh! Not as bad as I thought." Then he turned his gaze on the amulet in Liam's hand, then at Liam and Fleetfoot.

"You don't have enough magery in you to do this level of healing." He glared suspiciously at Liam, then gestured toward the healing amulet. "That *girl* did that, didn't she?"

When Liam agreed that Heather had created the amulet and it had saved his sister's life, the old man began muttering about being put out of a job by newfangled inventions while he went about finishing what Liam and Fleetfoot started.

After wiping blood from her muzzle, Liam gave his sister one last pat and fur stroke, then moved out from under her head as Fleetfoot slid in to take his place. He was fine as he was getting settled without jostling her, then she looked in his eyes and he froze.

Liam laughed as he rose. "Ponder on what you just got yourself into young man," he continued to chuckle as he grabbed Trouble's reins and mounted. "Thank you for tending to my sister Master Mage."

"Humph! That tinker boy sure is persuasive. Got a string of facts he tied up nice and neat with what we've seen since Easton's train arrived three days ago."

He bent over Orlagh. "Can feel the evil now I know what it is and a most likely location. I'll be with you shortly, young man, as soon as I finish here." Then he added over his shoulder, "Don't die on me before I get there." Then he started his healing chant and Liam could *feel* the strength of the old Master's magery.

"I'll try not to," Liam assured him, then softly kneed Trouble around and headed toward where another amulet drew him.

"I go any lower and we'll land on top of a building or a railcar!" Blackie grumbled.

"I don't think so, Papa." Rosa repeated, then held up one of the signalers. It was different. "I altered one of the signalers and now when I aim it down, it hears the echo and I measure the time between pushing the button and the sound bouncing back."

Blackie looked from Rosa to Maria, then to Revis and Sesco, then back at his daughter. "And?"

"We're still over four hundred feet above the rail yard."

"And?"

"And Fallon is no longer responding. He has three different signalers with him and another private one with his sister. There's no way that many failed to operate at the same time. She reports he hasn't contacted her since he told her she was almost in sight of the primary target."

"How we gonna find him in this soup if his signalers won't work?" Blackie gestured at the cloud around them.

Rosa held up the altered signaler. "With this. I put a smaller horn on it and that'll make a tighter beam to bounce back. That should make it so I can hear a double echo as the beam hits something in the air above the second, louder echo when it hits the ground."

Blackie looked at his wife, then at Sesco. "You understand what she said?"

Before either could answer, Revis raised his hand and waved it. "I do! I do! She means we fly around and she aims her signaler at the ground and when she hears a little echo before a big echo we'll know that it's Mr. Fallon!"

He looked at Rosa and she shrugged and nodded yes and he smiled brightly.

Without a word Blackie returned to the controls while Sesco and Revis hurried back to chant foam. "Rosa, signal Heather and tell her to see if she can give us a general direction so we can get closer."

Rosa did that without wasting time and read the response before speaking. "She says a quarter mile generally northeast of our position and about half our altitude.

Blackie nodded and watched the compass as he added power to the pusher fans and he turned the rudders behind the fans. When he was lined up, he gave the pushers a burst of power, then cut them back and began to coast. "Okay!"

Rosa nodded and reached over the bow rail and began pushing the button on her handheld, echo-measuring device. Then they waited, then after they'd flown another quarter mile Blackie turned the air wagon about and they made another pass. Then Rosa suggested another angle to compensate for the direction the fog had rolled in from and they got the double echo she'd predicted.

"Tell Heather we have her brother," Blackie said as Sesco and Revis manhandled the limp form over the rail. Fallon's eyes were open, but his face was slack despite the gentle rise and fall of his chest.

"She thanks us and is moving on alone," Rosa replied.

"Tell her Orlagh is being tended to by a Master Mage and Liam is moving into position," Maria said as she read an incoming message.

"Done!" Rosa said. "How is he?"

Sesco looked up from waving a healing amulet over the addled young man. "He's awake and all his parts are whole, but he's asleep too. It's kind of like that hyper sleep he goes into, but he's awake."

He looked imploringly at the big man piloting the air wagon. "He needs that Master Mage."

Blackie thought furiously. He knew the longer a curse had to set in, the harder it was to get back out. "Rosa! Get me Orlagh's position! We're taking her down!"

Rosa used one of Fallon's signalers to aim down with a tighter beam than their fixed array of horns gave them. "There!"

Blackie put power to the fans and vented foam. Rosa began pointing to indicate the direction as she read her distance echoer and called out numbers. "Two hundred feet… one fifty… one hundred feet."

And Blackie leveled them out and cut the fans back just as they saw the tops of dozens of railcars.

"There!" Rosa yelled and pointed.

Blackie looked over to see mage-light in a pool with a bloody form in the center. She was alive, but Orlagh had lost so much blood it would be a couple of days before she regained enough strength to hunt. If she could change, she would be healed in a couple of hours at most and wouldn't have needed the Master Mage's help.

Blackie expertly maneuvered the air wagon around and set it between two lines of railcars. Blackie vented foam and the big land wheels creaked as they accepted the weight. When they'd settled enough a strong wind wouldn't buffet them, he closed the valve and told Sesco to take aft deck watch.

He didn't have time to say anything else as Rosa and Maria were already over the rail and running to Orlagh's side. A brave, or foolish, puma changeling stood in their way for only a second.

"Sesco!" Blackie bellowed. "You and your brother fetch that hoist so we can get Miss Orlagh safe onboard."

Blackie looked around to see everyone, including the Master Mage, looking at *him* in awe and wonder as his commanding voice. He stabbed at the mage with a finger. "You sir! Young Fallon has been bewitched with a spell that has addled his brain. You're needed up here, *now* if you please sir!"

The Master Mage reacted automatically to the voice of authority even though it came from a man who'd grown up a slave. He did have a little trouble with the narrow access ladder, but he was soon inspecting Fallon with his expert magery. "I can see what was done and can slow the damage, but it'll take time to break the curse completely."

Blackie was too busy after they got Orlagh on a couch in the sitting room to notice the extra crewman onboard when he had Sesco and Revis chant foam so they could lift. He held position at two hundred feet while Rosa donned Fallon's tiny wrist signaler and contacted Heather.

"She says she's in position," Rosa reported as Blackie eyed the shirtless puma warrior standing nonchalantly beside him inspecting the air wagon's controls. "I told her Liam is between the primary and Easton's train," she said as she read another report coming from a different direction. "Rat reports a core group of eleven guards have pulled back and the crew is separating the first three cars and the conductor is firing up the boilers."

Blackie didn't hesitate. "Tell all ground troops we are going after the train. Sesco! Can you operate that thing?" He pointed at the one-man tinkering Fallon had flown.

Sesco smiled. "Young Fallon trained all of us on so many of his tinkerings just about any one of us could fly it, even my brother." They both looked toward the supply room where Revis sat ready to chant foam in case they needed to gain altitude quick.

Then Sesco started strapping himself into the flying harness. Maria brought water to fill the ballast and fuel bladders, then put a couple of large sandwiches in the supply bags hanging on either side of the saddle.

Rosa handed him a bladder of Fallon's nutrient drink. "Don't know what he puts in it but it's better than anything else I've ever had to stay awake and alert. Take a big drink or two every time you chant one of the tinkered amulets."

Sesco looked skeptical but took the bladder and one of mage-purified water, then he sparked the tiny boiler on the one-man steamfoam hoist. In seconds the godstone boiler was spewing steam into the tube as he chanted it into insubstantial foam. In seconds more he was lifted from the deck and pushed outward to drift over the fog bank, ready to help his two friends somewhere below getting ready to face a dark mage that had killed hundreds, many of them children not even into puberty yet and babes still in swaddling.

As Sesco checked his weapons and aimed his flyer toward the south side rail yards, Blackie pushed the air wagon at full speed to keep Easton's train from getting away.

Chapter 31

"We're *what*?" Easton fumed as he gripped the snifter of brandy and scowled in growing anger.

"We have to leave *now* sir. I've already given the orders and the crew is separating everything back from Firecloud and my car so we can move faster," he explained patiently as he looked out of the curtain of the nearest window.

"We're *WHAT*?" Easton screeched, sloshing brandy on his expensive nightwear. "What do you mean we're leaving now and we're cutting my train in half?"

He looked at the stain with disgust then glared at the head of his security. "What the hell is going on?"

Gibbs thought fast. "It's Firecloud, sir. He did something to rile up a whole bunch of locals and they've come for him and anybody associated with him."

"What did he do this time?" Easton's voice was cold.

Gibbs pitied the man. Easton was convinced he had control of the Native and Firecloud would do whatever his *employer* said. Easton even thought the Native would stand for the kind of *punishment* Easton thought he could enforce.

"Don't know as he did *anything* sir, but locals have come up with three or four missing children and seem to think blaming our mage is convenient," he tried to let Easton imagine the worst with the fewest hints.

"But why do *we* have to leave. We've got twenty men and you told me you hired some locals to patrol out further to secure our perimeter."

"Yes sir," Gibbs kept feeding his employer bits of information to get Easton to think leaving in this way was really his idea. "But there are a *lot* of locals up in arms, all kinds of cats and wolves and even a whole bunch of mages led by some old geezer nearly a hundred years old and still spry. Mages that old usually don't let anybody associated with the one that riled them live. We already lost half of our men."

"And you waited this long to tell me?" Easton accused. "What do I pay you for? Never mind! Get us moving! Do you think we should dump Firecloud's car too?"

Gibbs tried not to remind Easton he shared that car with the Native, then thought about what might be in Firecloud's cabin and how an angry, hundred-year-old Master Mage could use that to track them. "You're right! I'll go back and get what I can of mine out, and when we get out to the main track a ways, I'll cut it loose and set it on fire so nobody can follow us on the rails."

Easton was impressed. "You think that'll work? I've got enough problems with all the damned newspapers saying I'm implicated in murder just 'cuz stupid men can't follow simple orders."

"Of course, sir," Gibbs replied. "Once the mob gets Firecloud they'll forget all about us." Then he added as if it weren't important. "And by then Firecloud will have taken care of the rest of what those fools caused by not being able to follow your orders."

It was subtle, but Gibbs hoped Easton would remember those words. Gibbs would show his loyalty by not reminding Easton, thus appearing to take the blame on himself. He smiled as Easton gulped the last of his glass of brandy, then muttered, "Should have listened to you when you told me to send Firecloud back to clean up his own mess. Then I could have fired him by wire with a generous severance pay and maybe he wouldn't hunt me down and kill me."

Gibbs tried not to show he'd caught his employer muttering true feelings with a gullet full of brandy. Easton actually *was* smart enough to fear the Native. But at least *he* was covered. Now Easton would be easy to convince that leaving Firecloud was *his* idea.

Then, if Firecloud survived and came after them he could prove he was just following orders and they had barely got out alive even so. Easton's car lurched and Gibbs wondered if they *would* get away. "I'll go back and make sure everything is okay."

Easton waved a hand negligently as he poured another glass of brandy. As Gibbs went toward the back of the truncated train, he realized the man had been drinking a lot more than normal since he'd first read about the brother and sister finding their parents murdered and the start of their revenge.

Gibbs passed back through the hall behind Easton's sitting room as the shortened train began to gather speed. Before he passed out of the room, he saw Easton drain the glass and pour another. He ducked down the hall before Easton could turn to sit in his favorite chair and get drunker.

Gibbs ducked through the kitchen car, giving orders as he passed the cooks. "We're leaving fast, secure for battle, you two come with me." He pointed to the cook's two assistants but didn't wait to see if they did.

When he passed through the short hall past his cabin and into the central sitting room he shared with the Native mage, the rest of the crew and security were waiting. He pointed at two men. "You two on the roof of Mr. Easton's car and keep your eyes open for *anything* coming at us from the sky."

"The *sky*, sir?" one of the men questioned.

"Yes, Noah, from the sky," he replied seriously. "You boys been hearing about that Master Tinker what been chasing us?" When more than one nodded yes, he continued, "Well boys, that newspaper story ain't no imaginary dime novel story. That Master Tinker and his Master Mage sister are the two those fools left alive when we acquired all that godstone we been dragging halfway across the country and they're coming at us from the sky in a fancy railcar that flies under a mageried godstone balloon."

"Keep yer damned eyes *on the sky*, not the rails behind us," he told their gape-jawed expressions. "The rest of us will take care of that. Now go!"

He turned to the others as he dug out some keys. "The rest of you get every bit of ammo and spare rifles out of the lockers and into the gun room in the kitchen car. Every rifle and every single box of ammo, but only the unopened crate of dynamite, leave the one that's half full."

He pointed at the two cook's assistants as the train rocked as it gained speed, then two of the guards. "You two and you and you, each of you grab a rifle and a box of ammo and come with me." As they passed through the narrow hall beside Firecloud's cabin, he said, "If you value your life do not *touch* that door."

The two assistant cooks, with eyes wide pushed up against the other wall of the narrow hallway as they shuffled by the dark mage's cabin door, then out the back door to the small stoop at the rear of the two-cabin private car.

Gibbs pointed at the two cooks. "You two watch the rail and road behind us till I come for you. You other two up on the roof and *watch the sky*. When you hear two blasts on the train whistle you get forward out of this car as fast as you can or you'll get left behind. Remember that, do *not* leave this position till you hear two horn blasts, then you hightail it to the next car."

The two cooks nodded then looked inexpertly at their rifles. One cook helped the other load his weapon, then began showing him how to aim and fire while the two professionals climbed up to the roof of the moving train, laughing at the two.

Gibbs made sure they didn't shoot the other two before they got up and out of a possible line of fire on the roof, then darted back forward. When he got to the central armory and sitting room for him and the mage, he found the room was stripped. "Good, good, I want every turret in the kitchen car manned," he ordered, then pointed. "You and you. Take the front pair and you and you the rear set. The conductor's boys will man the two at the back of the fuel car." He grabbed one of the men by the shoulder and locked eyes on the other three. "And watch the damned sky! You two wait here a minute."

He ducked into his cabin and hastily put a few extra things in his escape trunk, locked it, and dragged it out in the hall. "Take this up front and put it under my table."

Mr. Easton got the table on the right as he came into the dining room from his private car and Gibbs claimed the first table to the left, to better serve his employer as his chief of security as much as just because he could.

When the men carried the heavy chest away Gibbs loaded and locked the second crate since he had the time and some of the contents he would hate to lose if he didn't have to. When the men came back, he had them put the second crate with the first one, then help him with his final preparations.

"Sure seems like more than enough," the youngest security man, more of an older boy, said. He was a replacement for one of the men stupid enough to wear the ring of a man they'd killed after leaving the man's mage daughter alive. It was only a fluke he'd survived to leave with them, but if he kept asking questions Gibbs might need to kill him. Maybe he could get the kid to stay with the car and set off the charges from inside? No, the kid was surely smarter than that. His eyes narrowed as he thought of what he could do.

"It's just a diversion," he repeated as he wired another bundle of dynamite. There was no way he was going to tell the young man he had promised Firecloud to destroy his cabin if he ever thought he *absolutely had too*. If he didn't have to and Gibbs burned his source of power, Firecloud promised to make his death long and painful.

This surely constituted *had to*, and just maybe the recoil shock would cause the Native to lose his duel and solve the problem that way.

"Might only need single sticks instead of bundles of three," the young man observed helpfully then looked over Gibbs' shoulder. "What are those?"

Gibbs gritted his teeth as he placed another bladder of his special gel over the bundle of dynamite sticks, at the base of the wall to Firecloud's cabin. "Just something to help it burn so nobody tries to push the car off the track to chase us."

"Sure seems like more than enough," the young man repeated himself and Gibbs decided he needed to die.

"Firecloud's room is lined with four layers of heavy oak planks to keep all his magery from getting out. It'll take a little extra to do what we need to do," he said, then shrugged. "It won't matter if it's too much."

He wondered if that really *was* why the mage's cabin was layered in four, alternating angled, and individually charmed, two-inch thick planks of oak. He had never asked and Firecloud had never volunteered the information. All he'd done was even out the weight on the railcar's frame when he'd had his own cabin constructed on the other side of their shared railcar.

"Uh, Mr. Gibbs sir," Shane looked up at the cook's assistant wringing his hands. "Uh, sir, they's some kind of railcar under a balloon too small to lift it flying at us."

Just then gunfire erupted from the guards on the roof, then the heavy guns on the back corners of the kitchen car. In seconds the gunfire stopped.

"They keep dropping down out of the cloud cover, then back up where we can't see them," the cook added. "They's still over a mile behind us but they's catching up fast."

Gibbs pointed. "You! Finish this last bundle of dynamite and lay that bladder on top of it like I did the others, then go out the other way and haul ammo to the big guns. You!" He pointed at the younger man, the one with all of the questions and criticisms. "Come with me."

Without looking behind him, Gibbs rushed out to the rear stoop of the car he and the Native had shared for the better part of two, almost three years, the young security man behind him. The stoop was large enough all four men had elbow room as Gibbs searched the sky.

The heavier of the two cooks pointed. "There!"

Gibbs looked in the direction indicated. They had left the fog of the city and rail yard and the sky was clear below six or eight hundred feet.

He didn't see anything at first, then saw how the clouds swirled unnaturally in a line coming toward them. Then a railcar with bulbous wheels hanging off its sides and an oversized front stoop dipped below the blanket of gray lit faintly by the lamps of the city they were fleeing.

Only two shots rang out from above before the apparition rose back out of sight, the other gunners realizing the apparition was still out of range.

"They turn when they's out of sight and come down in a different place each time," the larger cook informed them. He was the kind of big that hid muscles in a seemingly soft, shell.

The other cook's apprentice was nearly as tall, but the kind of thin called *wiry* with a deep voice when he spoke. "They're getting closer by about a quarter mile every mile we travel. Should catch up to us about the time we hit that long downgrade on the other side of the ridge we're climbing now."

Gibbs thought furiously. "Okay, here's what we do. You!"

"Bernard sir, Bernard Franklin."

"Yeah, you," Gibbs said impatiently. "You stay back here with these two. You do the shooting unless you can get one of these two to figure out which end of a rifle is which. You two! You be his spotters and if you can't *use* the extra rifle at least keep it reloaded each time…" he waved his hand.

"Bernard sir."

"Yeah, Bart, reload the rifle Bart's not using every time he empties it. And Bart…"

"Bernard sir."

"Yeah, that's what I said. Quit interrupting me! Here's what we're going to do. We're going to slow down just before we get to the top of the ridge so they misjudge and come out of the clouds ahead of us where the bigger guns can get at them. You three stay here and fire as many bullets at them as fast as you can every time you see them and I'll have the other gunners do the same. Big target like that ought to be easy to hit once it gets in range."

"Yes sir," Bernard said.

Gibbs ducked through the door, shaking his head at the misplaced trust that was so useful. He scanned his former sitting room for anything forgotten, then ducked into his cabin to get one last thing. He donned the thin backpack with the only things he absolutely couldn't live without, then the rain slicker with the extra pockets filled with other necessities.

He left his room, checked the last bomb pack, connected the trip wire to the sparker that would set off the dynamite, and ran the wire under the carpet through the hall to the forward door. It only took a couple of seconds to connect the trip wire to the bottom of the door from the outside as he closed it.

Then he caught the other guard's eye and put his finger to his lips and whispered, "Go up top and tell them to fire as many rounds as they can the next time the railcar shows, even after it's out of sight. Guess where it might be and just keep firing. Do that twice, then when they disappear again get up and move *quietly* and over to the top of the kitchen car. Do *not* let those below know and do *not* get left behind. Two appearances by our pursuers and run as soon as the kitchen car stops firing the second time."

The security man nodded, then looked at the door, then rose to pass the orders to the others without asking questions.

The train's security men unloaded everything they could the next two times their pursuer dipped below the cloud cover and Bernard was sure they were starting to score hits. The cloud cover had fallen again as they traveled up the incline to the top of the ridge south of Memphis and it was only four hundred feet, well within the range of their big guns.

Just like Gibbs said, the train started to slow as it neared the crest of the ridge. If they calculated correctly, the sky railcar would come out ahead of them this time and all six of the big guns would be ready to fill the railcar and its puny balloon with hundreds of holes.

"Wait," he mumbled, then louder but still to himself he wondered, "What about the explosive diversion? I thought that was going to be before the ridge so we could already be racing down the other side to get away from it."

"What was that, sir?" the tall wiry cook said as he finally figured out how to hold the rifle properly. When Bernard looked at him blankly, he smiled. "I think I could probably join in the target practice the next time they show up, sir."

"Oh my god!" Bernard exclaimed and turned and ran through the door toward the front of the car.

The wiry cook was surprised at the departure and gestured expansively and knocked a small crate of ammo over the back of the rail. He lunged for it as it fell, spilling cartridges in a spray and dropped the extra rifle over the rail instead, then lost his balance and tumbled after it in an attempt to catch both.

"Rocky!" the tall, thicker cook squealed, then leaped over the rail. "I'm coming!"

Bernard looked in horror at the dynamite packs as he ran through the rail car. He *knew* they didn't need that many just to set the car on fire to block the rail. He picked up speed as he felt the railcar slow at a quicker pace than just backing off on the steam. He looked through the window of the car as he ran full tilt toward the hallway on one side and saw the other car getting further away.

Had he missed the signal? He was sure Mr. Gibbs told him there would be a signal. Two blasts on the locomotive whistle. That was it! But then he'd said that the whole train would slow down and to *stay put*!

The other car was getting further away! Maybe if he could jump, he could catch its rail? He ran full speed through the hall, angled just enough that his wide shoulders didn't bounce off alternating sides, and hit the door with the full force of his two hundred pounds. The door instantly broke away at the top and his shoulder lodged in the window as he soared out over the rail of the stoop. He was at the end of his heels-over-head flip when the force ripped the rest of the door away at the bottom and pulled the trip wire to the explosives.

Chapter 32

Liam walked Trouble into the opening made by four groups of strategically parked railcars. In the center of the arena stood the Native mage and two men in long rain slickers. The dark mage stroked an amulet and chanted a short phrase and the leather coats of the security men glowed with magery.

From just inside the shadow of the last cover he would have, he could see the three were facing at an angle to his position. He urged Trouble another step ahead and looked in the direction *they* were looking just as he heard the soft chugging of Heather's steam trike.

A second later the trike rolled out of the shadows between two railcars and Heather turned to stop and survey the dueling arena Firecloud had prepared. It only took her a few seconds then she twisted the throttle, spinning the rear tires as she spun the trike in a fast circle, spraying dirt and gravel into the air. After two circuits she stopped, threw her hands up and chanted.

The ring of dust and flying gravel never finished its fall back to earth. As Heather chanted the dust cloud began to spin faster and condense into a rope of spinning shrapnel as it moved toward the three men in the center of the arena.

The two flanking the mage flinched and dropped into a defensive crouch as the gritty dust devil approached.

Firecloud was ready and began his own chant as the swirling mass of debris bore down on them, and it dissolved and dropped in a heap a few yards away from him. But Heather had not been idle and she immediately started another chant, this one obviously hurried and he staggered as some of Heather's second spell got through. He retaliated to try to throw her off and gain the offense when Liam made his move.

Chanting the strongest deflecting spell he could muster with the defensive amulet Heather made for him, he kneed Trouble at the end of the third repetition. Pulling his pistol with one hand and the gun-shaped tinkering Fallon guaranteed him would make a man's skin feel like it was on fire – even though it wasn't – in the other. The boy insisted it didn't have any magery in it, but if it sounded like magery, it was magery – even if some insisted it was all tinkered.

He continued his shield chant as he raced at the trio holding his pistol in front of him directly over Trouble's head to keep the bullets from being deflected as they passed out of the spell. He fired all six rounds and was pleased to see one of the two flanking guard's recoil as the sound of impacts against his mage-armored coat jerked into him.

The man looked astonished for a moment then openly gloated as Liam holstered his pistol and pulled the second pistol from its holster forward of the saddle on Trouble's neck.

Liam was closer now and the mage was starting to turn to face this annoying intrusion and he kneed Trouble at a slightly different angle and lined the second pistol up and methodically squeezed the trigger six times. On the fifth and sixth shots the nearest guard's head jerked backwards once, then twice and he dropped like a stone.

It took only a second for Liam to understand the mage was square in his sights but the bullets hit the man next to him. The mage had used a variation of the deflector spell and was probably already drinking the dead man's life essence to renew the power he'd used.

This took only another second but by this time Trouble was halfway across the open area between the edge of the arena and the center where Firecloud waited patiently. As Liam raised the tinkering that was his most effective weapon if it worked, he noticed that Heather was racing her trike toward the mage from the other side of the open space while he was distracted

The other guard raised a pair of hand-and-a-half long pistols on neck straps and began firing a barrage of lead that Liam felt ricocheting off the angled deflector spell and go whistling into the night to either side. He kicked Trouble harder and yelled as he held the strange skin-burning-but-not-really gun and pulled the trigger as fast as he could to spin the tiny magnet that was somehow supposed to power the contraption.

The guard stopped to reload and Heather threw another spell as Firecloud flinched from Liam's assault. He roared in anger and reached into a pouch and pulled out an object and slung it in Liam's direction then twisted to face her as he snarled a chant at Heather.

Liam had just enough time to notice the object was a ring of tiny ears and drop the deflector spell, but not quick enough to chant the defense for that particular amulet. Heather had anticipated the need, but Liam just wasn't fast enough. The amulet reached him in its flight and he was instantly engulfed in sound from all around and all of it increased exponentially.

Sound battered him from every direction and every single sound *hurt*. His head was pounded as if with heavy, padded fists, each insect's chirp or bird's song or horse's hoof-beat was a physical punch jarring deep within his skull. He fought the sensations, but he knew what he was fighting.

Trouble didn't.

The stallion screamed and thrashed sideways and fell unconscious, landing hard and trapping Liam's leg beneath his body. Liam's head hit the ground and bounced and his vision went gray as the spinning ring of ears passed out of range. Just before it did, he heard the loudest noise in the world and the sky to the south lit up almost as bright as day, then everything went black.

There was pressure on his right leg and a ringing in his ears that wouldn't let him think as the black turned gray and he came out of the darkness. He blinked his eyes and shut them again as Heather threw a stream of fire at Firecloud, who'd sucked it into himself like water into a sponge. The sudden intense stream of light burned at his retinas and Liam blinked his eyes several times as he struggled back to consciousness.

He discovered the skin burner was still gripped in his left hand and he raised it and began pulling the trigger. The second guard decided Liam was not worth his attentions and turned his weapons on Heather but started jumping around as soon as Liam aimed the fake burner, his first shots going in random directions.

Then a dart sprouted in his eye and he dropped, or would have if Firecloud hadn't put a hand over the man's face. He raised his hand and even though he didn't grip the man's face with his fingers the body rose several inches and Liam could *see* the life force being drained. Using Trouble to shield him from the mage, Liam raised the fake burner over the stallion's barrel of a body and began repeatedly pulling the trigger.

On the other side of the arena Heather abandoned the trike and ran over to another position where she threw a rapid-fire series of spells at her opponent, staggering him backwards.

Liam couldn't get an angle on the mage where he stumbled to and stopped pulling the trigger on the fake burner and tried to get his leg out from under his horse. "Dammit Trouble! Wake up and get off me!"

Trouble wasn't listening.

He looked over the stallion's body just as Firecloud scored a hit and it was Heather who was staggered, dropping something to the ground as she took several steps backwards. The Native took advantage of his scored hit and stepped forward purposefully as he chanted his attack in a staccato of intermixed spells.

Heather raised a device and aimed it at the trike and an arm rose up out of the cargo box behind the seat and aimed itself at the beam of light

Heather shone on the dark mage with another of her brother's tinkerings.

In the second before it began firing, Liam noticed it was one of the arms of the former scorpion tinkerings he'd wondered what happened to when the wagon had gone airborne. But the business end no longer held a six-shot pistol. Now it held six barrels that were longer than a pistol but shorter than a carbine.

In the time it took Liam to identify the weapon it began spitting lead into the circle of heather's targeting beam. In two breaths, one in and one out, the entire thirty-six shot drum-shaped magazine was emptied into the circle of light.

Everything was quiet for just a second then Firecloud staggered upright from where he'd fallen – two spots of blood on his left sleeve – and sneered. Then he began to chant again and stalked toward Heather as Liam struggled to free himself.

Just then a shape dropped from the sky and another arm like the one on Heather's trike aimed itself just as Sesco rode down from the clouds in Fallon's flying harness. Sesco lined up with his target and within moments of appearing the mini Gatling gun spat its own thirty-six rounds in two seconds. Firecloud staggered forward from the impacts of the rounds that struck his neglected shields from behind and his spells were disrupted as three red dots appeared across his back.

The native mage coughed blood a moment, then dipped a hand into a pouch and pulled out a two-inch circular amulet made of two layers of soft leather with a design embroidered around the edge.

Liam growled and struggled harder to free himself. Heather explained to them the processes used to create certain powerful spells Firecloud might be creating if the missing children were his doing. The skin was from a baby with the embroidery using sinew ripped from that same baby's body while it still lived. Firecloud spun it toward Heather just like he'd spun the ring of ears at Liam then he reached into another pouch and pulled out a second embroidered disk of baby skin. He spun and tossed it toward the flyer with Sesco now firing a short-barreled shotgun as he dove out of the sky.

Both disk shaped amulets spun true, and a foot away from their targets burst into an explosion of sparks and lights. When the miniature fireworks dimmed Sesco was slumped unconscious in the flyer's harness and Heather lay in a heap on the ground.

Firecloud staggered again then squared his shoulders as he rose to his feet. He glanced once toward Liam and as soon as he felt the burning sensation raised a hand and chanted an alternating energy frequency to the one being projected toward him and the burning sensation stopped.

It took a few seconds for Liam to realize his weapon was useless and he concentrated on getting his leg free while the Native mage stalked toward Heather, slumped on the ground. Looking up, he saw Sesco hanging limp in the flying harness and drifting away with the air currents in the foggy night.

Trouble twitched and made a weak thrashing that served to let Liam pull his foot a few inches, only to catch the top of his boot on a part of the saddle. The stallion took a deep breath and came alert with a lurch, and Liam's foot was free.

He leaped to his feet and started running toward Firecloud who was bending down to grab Heather with both hands on her battle vest and lift her so her face was inches away from his.

Liam screamed as he raced at full speed toward the man that intended to kill the woman he loved, and Firecloud casually let go of Heather with his left hand and pointed it at him and chanted. Something grabbed Liam's legs and pulled them together and as he flew forward, he saw Firecloud smile and turn back toward Heather hanging limp in one hand.

Just before Liam fell headlong into the dirt of the rail yards, he saw Heather stir and her eyes met his. Then he hit the dirt and everything went gray just as he heard a banshee wail that cut off abruptly just as blackness engulfed him.

Chapter 33

"Coming around for the final pass before they cross the ridge!" Blackie yelled as he spun the ship's wheel then spoke into the talking tube. "Give me two ounces and five repetitions, Revis!"

"Two ounces water and five repetitions coming up!" Revis yelled back to the horn by his mouth and poured a measured amount of water into the steamer and began chanting the foamed steam as he fed it into the balloon above.

Those they were chasing began to fire into the clouds with those big fifty caliber rifles mounted on the corners of two of their train's cars. Most of those rounds had only pierced clouds, but a few had hit them, enough that Revis was having to replace steam foam at increasing intervals. But he was doing an exemplary job and seemed to be chanting foam better by himself than in tandem with his brother. His cadence had increased and now he could chant twice as much foam in half the time.

"Wait!" Maria yelled as the balloon cut to the left and gained altitude to lift back deeper into the cloud cover. "It looked like they were getting ready to cut loose the last car!"

Blackie didn't hesitate and vented foam as he flipped the rudders to aim them downwards and increased the power to the pusher fans. The air wagon did a smooth arcing turn downwards and seconds later they popped out from under the cloud cover nearly even with where the train should have been.

Instead they saw the train already cresting the ridge and heading down the long straightaway down to the swamps in the lowlands. Behind was a single car and behind that car something white rolled and tumbled.

Blackie jerked the controls and the air wagon lurched upwards and to their left. "Revis! No more water, but give me five more repetitions!"

"Five dry reps coming up!" Revis yelled back happily then started his assignment.

Rosa quickly hooked herself to a rope attached to a winch as the air wagon spun away from the intercept line it had been taking and gained altitude. The air wagon was graceful in the sky, not quick. They were in sight of the main train for only a second after they came back under the clouds, but the abandoned car was almost exactly parallel with them a hundred yards away and about two hundred feet below as the ridge grew towards the clouds.

But just as the main deck of the wagon's bow passed through the cloud, Maria yelled, "Down!" and threw herself against her daughter to get her away from the rail as a fireball lifted into the cloud cover to their right.

They looked in awe as the rising flames pushed them aside with the concussive force that vibrated through their bodies in a hard shockwave. As the heat of the wave washed over them the holes where 50cal bullets had punctured the balloon spouted steam puffs.

"Five more dry, please Revis!" Blackie yelled.

"Five dry reps coming up!"

A second tower of flame and concussive heat lit the cloud around them with unholy light but this time they were lined up better and the wave only pushed them faster. With Blackie stuck at the controls, Maria and Rosa rushed through the wagon to the aft deck to see the destruction through the blanket of gray and white.

"Madre Dios!" Maria said and made the sign to ward evil as she and her daughter gazed in wonder at the flaming red and orange apparition that rose into the clouds screaming in agony, then looked right at them before the cloud closed in around the aft deck.

They held each other for a moment then rushed forward to report. By the time they got forward Blackie regained control and was looping up and around. "Gonna be a while before they can fix that section of rail. It's up to us to finish this. Maria, you're sniper. Rosa, plot me an angle to come out at them about halfway to the swamps."

"Won't have to Pa." Rosa said and pointed just as they came out of the clouds at their low altitude. Behind them the clouds now formed a wall that climbed into the night sky straddling the ridge along its length. Above and ahead of them was clear sky with a blaze of stars above the blackness of the swamps in the lowlands.

The train was in clear sight only a couple of miles down the long grade to the lowlands. Blackie simply locked his gaze on the train's lamps and got a fierce look on his face as he piloted the air wagon. The train had picked up considerable speed and it took several minutes for the air wagon to catch up then pass them and move over in front.

With the sky so clear and the train running with lamps lit as if they had no fear, Blackie had no trouble getting into a position where none of the six big guns had a good angle on them. Maria and Rosa could begin sniping at the locomotive while they raced ahead of it and not much higher than the locomotive's smoke stack.

Blackie gritted his teeth with the sheer thrill of racing a train downhill as he gently angled the fans and let their balloon's wounds seep steam to reduce altitude.

"Revis, one dry rep please."

His voice was calmer than during the height of battle, but his heart rate was the same. Where one was dominated by fear this one had exhilaration as its main emotion.

"One dry rep coming up!" Revis was still excited to be a valuable member of the crew doing something he could do better than anyone else and his voice showed it.

Maria and Rosa continued to snipe at the locomotive, using the steel bullets Fallon had designed that were supposed to be able to pierce metal as thick as a locomotive boiler.

"This isn't working," Rosa said. "Fallon said these steel bullets are supposed to pierce metal but, well," she gestured toward the train racing down the tracks after them.

Maria started to say something then noticed how close the train was to them, then she let out a series of shrill coded whistles and grabbed for the tube talker. "Up! Up! Get us up! Runaway train!"

Blackie had already responded to her coded whistle but it took a moment for the air wagon to react. Luckily Revis anticipated the order and dropped an ounce of water in the steamer reservoir and began chanting foam. He was beginning his second repetition when the order came for an ounce and ten reps.

"No need to respond," Blackie quickly added.

As they pulled up and to the side, they saw the conductor throw a bag over the side then another, then he and his sons jumped just as the train passed a long wide ditch where land had been dredged to raise the rails above the uneven ground. One of the heavy guns started winking in the way a gun did when it was being fired directly at you, but Maria sent a couple of rounds into the cupola and silenced it.

They were quickly out of range again after another quick exchange then the train started shedding dark shapes. It continued to move faster and faster, then it began to rock on the tracks. It was still shedding dark shapes when it hit a cadence that lifted one side's wheels off the tracks momentarily. That side crashed down with a groaning sound, then the locomotive wrenched sideways and flipped.

The train had just been coming to a series of large manmade lakes on both sides of the tracks where a proper grade had been raised. The raised ridge was up to forty feet high in some places and fewer than ten in others. When the locomotive tipped on its side, the fuel car was thrown in the other direction.

Both skidded on the banks of the raised ridge and Easton's private car and the kitchen car with its four armored heavy gun nests continued on towards the long turn across the deep swamp. It wasn't a sharp turn, but it was long, and the two runaway cars were still picking up speed.

The first car began to lift its wheels on the inner track of the turn and two boxy shapes fell from the rear of the kitchen car, then both cars started to tip as another dark shape fell behind. They tipped over more, then faster and faster till they both toppled over the side of the rail and rolled down the bank and into the water. When it hit the water, inertia carried it over once more and the top of both cars were completely submerged. The heavy steel wheels carried the cars over again and far enough out from the bank they both quickly settled out of sight in the deeper water

Heather waited for her prey to get closer and when he grabbed her by the vest and lifted her, her hand fell to the bag that had fallen conveniently within reach. The effects of the spell Firecloud threw were anticipated and she'd chanted a special charm to take the effects of that spell and absorb the greater part of it.

She was knocked out, but only for a few seconds and she was quickly regaining control of her body. She remained limp to fulfill Firecloud's expectations as she waited for the right moment to let him know he'd lost by letting her inside his shield.

Her head lolled to the side and she opened her eyes just in time to see Liam fall to a tangler spell, then she struck and Firecloud let out an anguished scream.

She felt the link Firecloud had with his nest on the private train snap just as she pulled her mother's severed hand from her spell bag and thrust it up against Firecloud's throat. The scream came at the same moment the hand closed over his throat in a death grip.

His scream cut off and his eyes bulged as he tried and failed to chant. He clutched at the leathery hand and the bone sticking from the wrist where shotgun blasts had severed it in the middle of a death chant against those murdering her and her husband. Every touch of the severed bone and dried flesh was like the hottest fire stabbing through his fingers and hands as he tried to pry the death curse talisman from his throat.

Heather pushed the panicked man away and rose to her feet. "Mother says hello to her favorite instructor. You know, she always regretted that you blamed her for your addiction. She thought she was helping you with your choice of study material. She was trying to find you another tome to read, not turn you in. She didn't know the studies you were teaching were forbidden to her and you were breaking Guild Law by teaching her."

She walked casually around him as she talked. "What I don't understand is why you still blamed her even after you found that out. She even forgave you for the curse you put on her that harmed Fallon. You see, she saw what nursing a hurt could do to a person and didn't want to be like you anymore, no matter how much you continued to do to her."

She snorted as Firecloud clutched at the dead hand locked on his throat. "But that's all in the past. We're here because of the present." Her eyes grew fiery as he fell to his knees in front of her.

She went to her knees in front of him and took his face in her hands gently as it turned ashen white and his eyes bulged. "From the day she met you she wanted to be just like you, seeking new knowledge for knowledge's sake, till you turned on her for an honest mistake that was actually your fault. She spent the rest of her life fixing the problems people like you make. Then out of nowhere she's attacked and killed and she feels your scent on the men killing her and the love of her life."

She gripped his face. "She knew she was dead so she shifted her spell and set it for another target. Then when her hand was blown off, she infused the hand with *her husband's and her* life essences." She smiled warmly. "Kind of like you did with those children you murdered only this was done willingly instead of taken forcefully."

She released his face and stood up, brushing the dust from her trouser skirts. "But she added something. When I found the spell on her hand, I followed the training she gave me. Oh, thank you by the way. It was the same training you gave my mother without telling her it was forbidden."

"Anyway," she stopped and looked down as he put one hand on the ground for balance. His face was white and if he would have had a voice, he would have been screaming. "Hang on just a minute longer and I'll be finished."

"Where was I? Oh yes! When my brother and I and our new friends came after you we discovered the trail of death you'd left and we visited some of the families. We were able to gather some things from each child, hair from a brush, an unwashed shirt, that kind of thing. Found lingering essences of four children and some fella looked to have been run over by a train. With those five and my mother and father, that," she pointed at the hand strangling him, "has seven people's vengeance powering it."

She stopped one last time in front of him and pressed a special ring to his forehead. "Master Mage Firecloud of the Chawasha Tribe, I hereby strip you of all evil magery in the name of the Mage Guild."

She muttered several syllables and there was a flash and a sigil on the ring glowed for just a second, then Firecloud collapsed forward landing with his face in the dirt, the white bone of the severed hand protruding from beside his neck and his eyes glazed in a look of surprise. One hand clutched an unused amulet that flashed once mysteriously then began to smolder.

Chapter 34

"Found him," Fallon said smugly. "In about thirty feet of water wearing a coat with about fifty pounds of godstone coins and nuggets sewed into the lining." He shrugged. "Must have been hard to swim in."

"You think?" Liam laughed. "The rest?"

"Oh yeah. The main car had its own vault. We haven't opened it yet but some of the survivors have witnessed that all of the *new* godstone was kept in Mr. Easton's personal vault. That would be what was stolen." His face grew clouded. Those that committed the murder and those that ordered it were all dead, but that wouldn't bring his Pa and Ma back to life.

He took a deep breath. "Most of the guards didn't even know about the big piece. Most of the ones that did were the first on our list." He smiled. "It's still in Easton's master bedroom."

"Can you get it out?"

Fallon knew that Liam didn't mean the eight hundred-pound godstone meteorite or the vault with almost as much in ingots and nuggets. He meant the whole car, both whole cars to be exact. "Yeah, no problem. Already woke up three tentmakers and ordered a single balloon with panels cut so it can be separated into two a bit longer than that." He gestured toward the air wagon lifting the locomotive back onto the tracks.

"Think it's wise to show everybody how much you and Heather's mageried steam foam can lift?" Liam wondered.

Fallon shrugged. "Don't care. If more people can get around easy maybe they could do more without being beholden to somebody else. Besides," he added with a smile, "once people know something can be done, they'll figure it out themselves."

"Already applied to patent the process, though, so we won't have to pay somebody else to use what we invented. Congress done said new mage chants are like songs and books and can be copyrighted, and the tinkering is also new so we applied for the two individually and the process as a whole. Applied for the tinkered godstone paint sprayer too."

He snorted. "In fact, I've applied for so many patents the patent office is sending a fella down to fly with us for a few days so he can document everything and make sure we get proper credit."

"Even got a wire from that Tesla fella that wants some help with his own patent applications so they don't get stolen. Seems he's had that happen more than a few times."

"We're not going anywhere for a few days," Liam commented.

Fallon gestured. "Flying back and forth between Memphis and here to clean up what we don't salvage is still pretty exciting to most folks."

Liam made an agreeing face. "You okay?"

Fallon's smile got wider. "Yes. When Firecloud died his curse died with him, even that little backdoor thing he put in to get back into my head to shut me down when I got too close to him." He slapped his chest with both palms. "I'm not only good, I'm *cured*. I don't have any slow-motion hyper trances and all of my brain is unlocked and both halves put back together."

"I can also still take my memories and put them in *exact* replicas of a specific scene. The only difference is now I have to *concentrate* to memorize a scene and I can't add as much of the *feelings* as I did with my big book of pictures. Just like a normal person."

He seemed happy with the rationalization so Liam was happy *for* him.

He shook his head up and down. "Yeah, I really like painting and even though I can't do some of the things I could for a couple of weeks there, I'm not getting old too fast either."

He rubbed his hands together. "And you should see some of the things I wrote down before I got all *ner-mal*," he laughed at himself. "I can barely understand some of it myself anymore and I'm the one that thought it up."

"So, what are you going to do now?" Liam asked.

Fallon gave him a look. "Why help *you* and your sister, of course! That was the deal, you help us and if we live, we help you." He raised both hands to the side palms up. "We lived, Easton and most of his paid murderers didn't. We got our property back and extra salvage for damages."

"What are you going to do with those, though?" Liam wondered.

"Them? Nothing." Fallon said matter-of-factly. "I claimed the two cargo cars since one of them still carried the steam tractor with my very first godstone boiler system. Couldn't let that go. Might put it in a museum someday, though."

He pointed at the first air wagon setting the toppled locomotive gently back on the track under Blackie's expert touch with Revis chanting foam. "This is proof of concept on what mageried steam foam can carry. Sure, we had to strip the wagon of everything not attached to shed enough weight to be able to pick the locomotive up, but that means we now know *exactly* how big to make the next air wagon."

"The *next* air wagon?" Liam lifted an eyebrow.

"Of course!" Fallon exclaimed. "Do you realize we've built the most advanced flying machine the world has ever known? No? We did, and we did it with just a few pounds of godstone, a little tinkery and magery, and some pretty impressive people."

"But you know, those pretty impressive people? We just got them at random. Sure, we sometimes got some out of a small group, but they weren't really any different than anybody else." He made a face. "What I'm trying to say is there are a lot of people that could do what we did if they had the means and the will to do it."

He threw a gesture toward the air wagon as impressed crews checked the locomotive while others coiled all the ropes used to lift the massive steam engine back onto the tracks. Another group anchored lines to keep the air wagon from drifting off while Blackie vented foam.

"My sister and I laid claim to the two cargo cars and the barracks car," he gestured in the direction of the cars under water, "*and* those two. The local sheriff has already approved the whole battle as under the authority of our warrant and the contraband identified is rightfully our property. He just wanted to see the big piece once with his own eyes to have something more to tell his grand'uns when he's confined to a rocker."

Liam snorted. "So, again, what are you going to do?"

"Well, for one thing I already talked to Heather and we've agreed to give you and your sister one of the cars, your choice, and put a decent godstone balloon over it."

He waved a hand as Liam took a breath to speak. "Not right away. Already hired somebody to haul our salvage up north to Cleveland. Wired a shipbuilder on the coast of Erie Lake and he said to mail him my ideas and he'd talk when I arrive."

He gave Liam a wink. "So now Heather and I have to go up north with you to finish paying you a proper recovery fee for your help. And while we're up there we'll help you with *your* dark mage."

Liam nodded and changed the subject. "If you talked to a shipbuilder, why do you need more rail cars? Wouldn't you just build a ship under a balloon? We never did use the wheels for anything other than driving under better cover after we went airborne and a ship design could land anywhere if you made the bottom sturdy, land or water."

Fallon shrugged. "A lot of good wood in some of the better cars and they're already built. Plus, we can always remove the wheels and build a hull underneath later." He smiled wickedly. "Besides, if we're going to compete with the railroad monopolies we might as well take the best they have to offer at bargain prices when they're forced to sell off assets after we cut into their business."

At Liam's raised eyebrows, the young man exclaimed, "What! You don't remember? That big speech you gave in my secret cave where I tinkered where the voice couldn't interrupt. Oh, that was Firecloud by the way. Always in my head somehow except when I was inside my cave with its walls covered in shelves full of tinkerings made with parts coated in godstone." He gave a strange smile, then continued, "Anyway, the deal wasn't just to avenge my parents then defeat your mage and quit. Oh no! We pledged to help *anybody* and *everybody* that was being abused by those of power and these private railroads are an abuse of power." He tapped his temple. "I remember. There's even a picture of the scene in my memory journal."

Liam smiled. He hadn't forgotten but was hesitant to hold the brother and sister to the extended bargain.

Just then a man ran up and Fallon turned to talk with him a minute. "I have to go Liam, something about a railroad man asking if we can help fix the rails where Easton's people blew a hundred-foot crater in the rail bed." He rubbed his hands together again. "Time to generate good will."

Liam watched him for a moment then wandered in the last direction he'd seen Heather. He found her with Orlagh and the Fleetfoot youth. Then the rest of the crew gravitated their way as they talked.

"Did you hear what that fool boy's doing?" Blackie fumed. When Liam shook his head negatively, the big man ranted, "He's building a whole air wagon for Maria and Rosa and me," he snorted in disbelief. "Said it was fair recovery fee for what we helped him and his sister get back. Can you believe that?"

Liam laughed. "Yes, my friend, I can believe it because my sister and I seem to have earned the same reward. Personally, I'd rather keep my feet no higher than a horse's saddle, but I could get used to traveling *over* rough country, floods, and such."

Blackie laughed. "And lynch mobs."

"Yes," Liam agreed. "Definitely lynch mobs.

Blackie's face grew serious. "Mage Guild won't like it."

Liam shrugged. "They didn't help Heather's mama before Fallon was born, or after. They gave her *permission* to finish kicking Firecloud out of the Guild where they were too busy, but she could only do that *after* she defeated him in a duel, so they had her do the job they wouldn't do. Besides, it takes a Master Mage to make one of the amulets that lets one of us normal folk chant a spell, so the Guild will still get a cut. Maybe even more if demand grows."

He looked at the activity around the righted locomotive and its fuel car and pointed his chin. "Fella there was trying to start his own business. Bought that whole rig and got a loan to fix it up and make it legal for the tracks. Railroad men like Easton squeezed him till his loan came due then forced him to sell half his share to pay his interest-inflated loan. Then they forced him to take the contract offered and the pay was never enough to get back full ownership."

"Heather and Fallon forgave them their part in the last battle because they were defending their own investment as much as honoring a dishonorable contract. Gave back their full title and enough recovery fees for repairs through a generous contract to deliver the salvaged cars to Cleveland."

"That's where you and Miss Orlagh are from, isn't it?" Maria asked.

"Just a few miles northwest out in the Erie Lake. Puma Island. It's only a couple miles in any direction, a bit under five square miles total."

He smiled in memory. "Played on every square inch as a child. Knew every crack, crevice, and cave years before my first full forced change at human puberty when the curse kicked in."

He was pensive for a moment and didn't notice the gathered crew giving him a moment for that private thought. "But yes, that's pretty much where I'm from, Cleveland sixty miles to the east about eighty to the north and west to Detroit. My brothers and I did a non-stop race in beast form from home to Detroit and back once on the ice in the middle of the winter."

His face took on a melancholy look. "Dalton got mad because he thought Leander and I *let* him win 'cuz he was youngest." He snorted at the memory. "Fact is Leander and I got drunk the night before and were puking the first handful of hours and sicker than hell the rest of the race despite changeling healing. I made it back to our island but I was passed out a mile from the finish line and Leander took a wrong turn at the Otter Islands and got *invited* to a game of *pull the cat's tail*."

He was frozen in the memory of his two younger brothers, killed in the war over race slavery, changeling genocide, and mage rights in the southern and some western states.

"Gonna need more crew," Sesco opined. "I can't see an air wagon taking less than three, four people to operate full time. You or your sister one is always in puma form, so that's really only one of you to do everything even though there's two of you. Gonna need at least two more and that's really not enough."

Liam nodded. "You could do with one person with a lot smaller wagon, but one the size of a railcar, no, you're right. It would take a minimum of four to do a proper job of flying it."

"See! Gonna need a lot more crew and gonna need to train 'em," Sesco said. "That must be why young Mr. Fallon is puttin' a balloon on Mr. Easton's barracks car for his security."

"What?" Liam wondered. "I thought he was having the salvage claim hauled up to Cleveland by rail first."

"Yes, he is," Sesco replied. "All except for the barracks car. Already got carpenters hired to fix a walking deck around it. Won't have ground wheels, just more walking space around the railcar, a higher roof, and divider walls to break up the open interior into four separate rooms, two on each floor. Saw the schematics he gave the carpenter. Supposed to be finished and ready to pump up the balloon and spray it with godstone paint in two days."

"I don't think they're using godstone paint," Rosa interjected as she came up. "Fallon just told one of the new guys to take the carpenter over to where the air wagon is moored to look at how the balloon is attached to the upper deck and how the aft and forward decks are attached to the railcar frame. He also said something about *foaming* the sealant, whatever that means."

"Oh, that must be like when he made his one-man flyer," Liam explained. "He filtered the steam foam through melted godstone and the foam picked up just enough godstone to seep into the canvas and seal it with less excess. He must have figured out how to do it with a bigger balloon."

"Balloon's not bigger," Rosa commented. "It's smaller. He recalculated the size after the air wagon lifted the fuel car back on the tracks yesterday evening after he patched the wagon's holes. The drawing he showed me looks more like a sausage than a balloon but Mr. Fallon assures me it will lift the finished air wagon with full passenger limit of sixteen security and four crew."

"Fits," Liam mused. "Four crew and six gunners with two five-man security teams."

"He talked to you about it?" Blackie wondered.

"Not in so many words," Liam replied. "We talked about helping others and after our first expedition in justice we found that it sometimes takes more than you came to the party with. If not for the local changeling clans and the Master Mage and his students, it's fair to say most of us would have died and Firecloud and Easton might not have."

"Anybody find the bodyguard's body?" Maria asked.

"No," Blackie said. "All the dead were identified by all the survivors and the bodyguard and one other man are the only two unaccounted for."

"How about the patsy and the two cooks?" Maddy asked. "The others were just going to kill them but they got out alive."

"The one fella got lucky," Liam said. "Explosion blew him about fifty feet, but the cooks found him and one of them had some healing magery and kept him alive enough till Heather got a chance to see him. We let all three go free, offered them jobs with us in fact."

He snorted. "Cooks were on their last job because nobody liked their kind either even though they're both full blood white and the boy was just too full of questions. Didn't know what kind of person hired him to fill in empty slots we made in their ranks."

Blackie snorted. "Young kid trying to do his best and be the best he could and got hired by a man that wanted anything *but* that kind of employee."

He one-eyed Liam. "I'm thinking maybe he upgraded bosses this time around."

Liam snorted. "I keep telling people I'm not the boss, but everybody seems to keep getting that impression."

There was more than one skeptical noise from the gathered friends, even Revis chuckling as if he got the joke.

He turned and started in surprise as Rat appeared beside him. "Gods Rat! Don't do that!"

"What?" the wolverine asked innocently. "Real boss says to tell you to go ahead and set up the tent for the rest of the crew. Her brother is going to train a new crew by working them all night to lift the locomotive and fuel car up and over the bomb crater so they can get back to town and get repaired soonest."

Liam turned toward the others. "You heard, let's get it done so we can have some free time to harass the new students." He turned to say something to Rat, but the wolverine was already gone. "Wish he wouldn't do that," he mumbled.

"Hope I don't get a bunk with him," Revis whispered. "He smells funny." He thought for a moment. "Course I would smell funny too if I lived in tunnels under a trash heap." He brightened. "Maybe he cleans up real good."

"We can only hope," Maria said as she patted Revis' arm affectionately. "Speaking of which, it's been a long couple of days and *you* could use a new shirt at the very least."

"Aww, okay," Revis demurred, then let the woman lead him away.

"He's not the only one," Sesco said, then everyone agreed it was time to freshen up, leaving Liam with the tent to put up himself. He was inspecting the pile of poles and canvas when all of a sudden the others returned and swarmed the supplies, and the tent was erected within a half hour. Then they all headed for the line to the shower in the newly salvaged fuel car's rear cabin.

Chapter 35

"See, I got it all figured out," Fallon said. "You and Orlagh take my room, Sesco and Revis take the side of the supply room with the foam chanting station below your hammock, and Maddy takes the other. Revis chants foam, you or Orlagh pilot, Sesco is air cavalry or onboard sniper, and Maddy is chief engineer."

"What about Heather?"

"Master Mage and Boss," Fallon said smugly.

"And you?"

Liam glared at the device behind the young man with the features aged twice his actual years. Fallon had reclaimed the tractor he'd tinkered together for his father. It still maintained its robust frame and the water-fueled boiler but the boiler had been sprayed on the inside with godstone paint and all the tinker's parts between the water tank and the boiler were now godstone coated inside and out.

The wheels were gone and the frame with the steam engine sat on a narrow wooden deck that led back to a tiny cabin just large enough to hold the young Master Tinker's favorite tools and small workshop that doubled as a bunkroom. It had four of the in-line pusher fans that jetted air for thrust and the oversized rudders that looked like bird wings for maneuvering.

The balloon that would supposedly lift it looked tiny in relation to the relatively small air wagon. Especially considering the several weapons that projected from various places on the body.

The two, thirty-six shot Gatling's were now mounted just in front of his seat where the front wheel used to be. On either side along the sides of the airship was a line of ten, four-shot revolver shotguns that could be fired in three different patterns.

The way he held the control bars when he rode the sleek aircraft, he reminded Liam of Heather when she was riding her cycle or the trike she liked better. "Not much cover for all the weapons."

"I think I'll like the feel of the flight more than protection I can't see through," Fallon replied absently as he touched the frame of godstone sprayed steel. "Heather fixed me up with three types of mage shield and a memory spell for the syllables in their chants and I tinkered a synthetic replay disk using one of Thomas's ideas."

Liam had *sort of* introduced Fallon to Thomas Edison and now Fallon had both a regular written letter and telegraph correspondence with the other Master Tinker. Fallon had helped young Thomas get some of his ideas patented so the other Tinker could finance his insatiable search for knowledge.

He'd even begun correspondence with that other tinker, Nick Tesla, and coordinated with him on some other patents.

"How does that work?" Liam was genuinely curious.

"Sort of like a player piano," Fallon said. "I was able to duplicate the actual sounds of the mage syllables and when I charge the spinner with steam, it spins the disk and the holes in the disk cause the whistle to *chant* the shield spell in Heather's exact voice. It chants a shield just as strong as she could chant herself and all I have to do is spin it every few minutes to keep the shield active."

"Guild is *really* not going to be happy with you two," Liam chuckled as he shook his head.

"Already taken care of," Fallon said as he pulled himself up to the seat of his fifteen-year-old boy's idea of the perfect personal air wagon."

"The Master that helped us with Firecloud?" At Liam's acknowledging nod he continued, "Heather gave *him* Firecloud's body. They'll render the body down and use the material to form charms *against* just the kind of magery he practiced. They'll also be able to release the trapped life essences in the remaining dark amulets so the dead can rest intact."

Liam nodded again. Heather explained the whole thing to him when he asked, much more than he expected and enough to give him a wider window into the life of a Master Mage. Like changelings, they were rare in the world of what was referred to in some circles as *normal* humans. Like any group with a unique attribute, they tended to congregate with those of their own kind and protect the secrets of that uniqueness jealously.

Liam wondered how people with that rare of a power would not feel threatened by Fallon's tinkering competition, or the ability to copy and mass produce what another thought of as proprietary performances.

"Anyway," the young tinker explained excitedly as he sat sideways on the strange tinkering, "I can chant foam, throw up three different kinds of shield and two camouflage, and toss five different offensive magery weapons with nothing more than the twist of a steam valve." He reached up to indicate the panel of switches, gauges, and valves. "That's not including my tinkerings including a couple of new things."

"I'm not foolish enough to think I can face an army, but I've got enough to get me *out* of any difficult situation I'm going to allow myself to get into," he said, then shrugged. "Without plenty of backup of course."

"And that's where you come in!" He bounced around and settled into the comfortable, spring cushioned seat and began turning valves and knobs as he prepared his sleek aircraft for the sky. "You and my sister get to fly to your home in uncrowded comfort while the new recruits will be packed into tight quarters and given stressful training."

He gave a conspiratorial wink. "We can weed out the slouchers from the fighters on the way. By the time they get to your island you should have enough left to fully crew at least one of the next air wagons completed."

He watched as the large air crane moved Easton's private car and the kitchen car dredged out of thirty feet of water. The aircar balloon lifted the two cars at the same time and set them back down on the tracks in their old position behind the fuel car. The balloon remained anchored to the two cars venting foam while the two cargo boxcars were attached.

"Hate leaving Blackie and his family, and Brutus behind."

"Yeah, but it's the smart thing to do," Fallon replied. "We'll have four people we can trust watching our property and the conductor says he'll be ready to steam day after tomorrow so they won't be that far behind us. We'll fly faster than they can roll, but not by that much."

"You sure Fleetfoot can pilot the recruit barracks?" Liam finally asked the question he'd wanted to ask all along.

"Heh-heh," Fallon chuckled. "Heather told me about cat males. Deal with it my friend, your sister has chosen a consort and you'd best provide for him by giving him the training he'll need in his new station."

"How did you get so wise?" Liam snapped jokingly. "You may *look* older than me but you're still just a whelp."

"Ha!" Fallon laughed. "You're just mad 'cuz *you've* been chosen, too, and you don't know whether to rejoice or rebel. At least Fleetfoot is resigned to his fate and accepted the easy path. You keep fighting it."

Liam scowled. He knew that. But he also couldn't help it. He would *not* pass his family's curse to another generation. He was not free to act on his heart until that curse was lifted and he was learning the best way to do that was to challenge the origin of the curse.

Heather and the other Master Mage had investigated the Quinn Pride's Curse and given Liam and Orlagh bad news. There were only two ways to get the curse broken properly. The mage that had cast it must take it back voluntarily, or – like Fallon's – it will dissolve upon his death. All the special potions and chants they'd traveled across the country to find would do was *maybe* interfere with their forced change enough for them to stop the change at their warrior form.

The Quinn Pride of Puma Island would have to sell their island to the mage and his Family, or they would have to challenge him individually or as Family against Family. Or they could accept their curse and live a life stunted in their heritage knowing they would pass that deformity down to their children for as long as that mage lived. And Master Mages were the longest living people in the world.

Orlagh agreed with him it would be a challenge and Heather agreed to be their second if they could ever discover the source of their curse. That allowed her to ensure Liam was ready since it would have to be him that made the challenge. Despite his weak level of natural magery abilities, she found the ones he was most proficient in and concentrated on those to augment with her brother's tinkery.

In the two days since they'd served justice to Easton and Firecloud they'd gotten the original air wagon's holes patched and tinkered up two more flying wagons, the sleek, heavily armed racer Fallon called his own and the bulky air barracks and training wagon with its wide wraparound deck.

"You ready?" Heather said as she strode up to where Liam talked to Fallon sitting atop his new favorite seat.

"Just waiting for word from the boss to chant foam!" Fallon said, then pointedly looked at Liam.

Heather didn't help by copying her brother's look – but with and added mischievous smile. It took several seconds for him to give in.

"I guess the quicker we get in the air the quicker Orlagh and I can tell the world a crippled changeling is going to challenge a Master Mage even stronger than the one I love."

Heather's eyes grew wide for just a moment then she smiled and briefly touched his sleeve with a finger. "Then I guess Fallon and I will have to put our heads together and see if we can bring you up to a respectable level. So, I'll go loosen the mooring lines then."

She strode off with a happier gait than Liam had seen since the death of her parents. When he turned back toward Fallon the young man had a thoughtful look on his face. "You know, I put a lot into this cage." He reached up and grasped the nearest of the godstone painted bars in the open cage surrounding his pilot's seat then started mumbling as he pulled triggers and a tiny voice chanted foam. "Wonder if I could do the same with a smaller cage, or maybe like a skeleton?"

Fallon continued to talk to himself as he lifted the small sky tractor. He waved absently as he turned the sky tractor in a loop to fly by the rising boxcar barracks.

Shaking his head with a small smile, Liam marveled at how the young man had changed, more than once, in the few weeks since he and his sister had met the Richards family. Then the smile changed as he turned to walk the few steps to the air wagon. They'd met in friendship that quickly turned tragic then they'd grown together in adversity as they sought justice for that grief. Justice was served and now his and his sister's new friends were going to help them right another wrong.

He reached the wagon and scaled the boarding ladder with practiced ease to find Rat examining the controls. Liam didn't comment on the obvious in mentioning that the *information specialist*, as the wolverine changeling self-proclaimed himself, was supposed to ride the troop-carrying boxcar *if* he decided to come with them.

"Did you know there's a really nice *pocket* within the frame just under the aft deck? A couple layers of thick canvas and it'd make a nice comfortable private den," Rat commented, then pointed. "That is an odd device, what does it do?"

Liam smiled as he mentally added one more to the crew. "That's the trigger to power the sound echo horn on the front, there." He pointed, then down to the growing arc of tinkerings. "The sound bounces back and another horn hears it and then these tiny lamps glow where there's something in front of us. Twelve rows of lamps and each row stands for fifty yards."

Rat was engrossed with the lesson. "Why don't you take the right-side seat and I'll show you everything while we get up in the air."

Rat didn't reply but simply moved quickly to the right-side seat and began fumbling at the straps.

"We don't usually use those unless the wind is high or we're going into battle. Here, just strap this one across your waist till you feel more comfortable." Liam helped him secure the waist restraint then went through the process of calling the foaming instructions back to Revis who now sat that station by himself while Sesco manned the aft deck.

"Trouble is strapped in and munching an apple and the trike is secure," Sesco reported through the talking tube.

"Read where this fella up Ohia way dreaming of turning telegraph into talking tubes," Rat commented as he studied the valves and gauges arrayed in an arc in front of them. "Another fella says he might be able to do the same through the air *without* tubes or wires."

"Wouldn't be surprised," Liam responded as he continued through the checklist that Fallon had written down.

"What's that?" Rat asked, pointing at the small booklet.

"Startup manual and checklist," Liam replied as he mentally marked off the last item on the front page. He handed the manual across to what was turning out to be his new copilot trainee.

Rat read the front page, his eyes darting to all the things Liam activated in the startup, then turned the first page. "Whoa! What is this?"

Liam smiled as he called back to Sesco. "Release mooring lines."

Sesco repeated the order through the speaking tube and he and Maddy released the two aft lines. From their position on the ground Maria and Rosa could hear him speak to Sesco and responded as well as they released the two forward lines. Rat's eyes darted this way and that as the air wagon rose smoothly into the sky and Liam released all stations from liftoff duty. Heather hurried to coil the ropes as she pulled them up while Liam flew the air wagon.

They had delayed their departure for the better part of three days for two reasons. To finish repairs and quickly construct the two additional aircraft, and to complete the legal papers needed to close the warrant, reclaim stolen property, and claim the salvage of the Easton train in compensatory damage awards.

The courts would process the claims at their normal plodding pace but they were still allowed to utilize their new assets while the bureaucratic confirmation process continued.

Fallon flew his racy tractor back and forth between the lead wagon and the more cautious boxcar troop carrier, jabbering away across the yards between each airship. He yammered about things most of his audience had no idea what some of the words even meant, till Rat began asking questions and actually knowing what the tinker was talking about. Before they'd gone half a day Rat was hanging half over the side rail as he argued tinkering with the young man.

"How do we end up with people like that?" Heather said from the copilot's seat.

Liam ignored the *'we'* part of that accepting he somehow had no choice. She wasn't Feline Clan where that social norm held precedence. He wondered what the Mage Guild's rules were in these things.

"We're a magnet for people with inquiring minds is all and we enjoy answering intelligent questions. Combine the two and you get smart adventurous *interesting* people sticking around while the boring people wander off. Those kinds of people, just like all other kinds, tend to congregate, boring people get bored together and," he gestured toward Rat and now Maddy hanging over the rail having *discussions* with Fallon a half mile above the ground as the two airships flew side by side northward.

He snorted as he looked around. "Tiny space stuck up in the sky where you can't get away just makes it look like there's more than there actually is." He pointed his chin toward Rat. "Back on land he'd already be gone and digging new tunnels under some other town's dump yards, reading discarded books, newspapers, and personal writings."

They flew in silence for a while, listening in to the conversation on combining tinkering and magery. "Even if I didn't have Fallon for a brother,

I'd still say he was the smartest person I ever met and that one seems to understand what my genius brother is talking about," Heather observed after a while when Maddy returned to the aft deck.

Liam snorted agreement. "Sure is full of comments and observations and *comparisons*. Seems to always be comparing certain observations with two or three historical similarities and pointing out the endings. Calls it learning from history."

"Some people would call that an *advisor*," Heather smiled.

"Appears and disappears in a blink and seems to know everything going on within a mile radius at every minute," Liam added.

"Some people would call that a *spy*," Heather made a thoughtful face.

"Something just fell from the boxcar," Sesco's speaking tube reported just as Rat pointed back along the rail he'd been leaning over. "Maddy's putting the sniper scope on it. Says it's two people tied together face to face, *not* by their necks."

Fallon sped up and looped back around as Rat darted over the new framework constructed around the ground wheels in the beginnings of a wraparound deck like that of the boxcar. There were hooks for safety lines but the wolverine didn't waste time with them. The speaking tube continued giving the report.

"Maddy says it's those two boys, the wolf and puma that are always arguing," Sesco laughed. "She says they're tied face to face and they're *still* arguing. Got their arms wrapped around each other and leather mittens over their claws, but their muzzles are both in range." He chuckled again. "They both seem to be going in and out of warrior form and bumping snouts."

Liam smiled. "That Fleetfoot boy seems to be inventive with his discipline. Fallon says those two have real promise and asked they be given another chance to work out their species prejudices before we cancel their employment."

"Well that sure is an inventive way to keep the rest of the crew from hearing them while they work it out," Heather said as she peeked around the side of the wagon. "Well, up close anyway, as close as a thirty-foot rope."

After a while the two seemed to be enjoying their viewpoint too much to make it punishment any longer and they were pulled back up. Almost immediately another pair – these two strapped back-to-back – were lowered down.

Not long after that Maddy talked Sesco and Rat into attaching one of the emergency fall-stopping backpacks to the aft hoist line and letting her *ride the rope*. By the end of the day everyone – including Liam to everyone's surprise – had a turn, except Orlagh who made do watching from the safety of the aft deck with Trouble, who also seemed interested in the odd behavior from his people.

Chapter 36

"Big river," Fallon commented as they talked about the Ohio another two hours away. "I hear parts are as big as the Missip'."

Maddy flew the tractor ahead then made a big loop around behind them, two aeronauts chasing her on their sky cycles. He glared around the body of the wagon. "That girl better not…"

Liam laughed. "It's her birthday, or so she says, and you promised. Besides, what is she going to run into a half mile off the ground, one of the aeronauts? Just knock them senseless and not much more than scratch the paint on yours, and she won't come anywhere near us because you keep screaming over-the-shoulder piloting when she does."

Fallon continued to glare. "Listen Fallon. Maddy is thirteen now and Heather told me she's already hit puberty." He shrugged. "Happens early sometimes when the body is faced with certain kinds of stress. No signs of changeling in her yet but this one coming up is her first full moon since puberty and that's when latent abilities get pushed out. If she has any changeling in her we'll spot it and she can learn how to incorporate it into her life."

"What about that ancient heirloom she loaned Heather back a few nights ago?" he wondered aloud. "Heather says she can read *something*, but she can't actually tell if its changeling or repressed magery, or something else."

"What are you trying to say?" Fallon was genuinely confused.

"Well, actually, *that*," he gestured toward the young man. "Your *confusion* is the point I'm trying to make. Anybody else and you'd have already tinkered the riddle out of them." Fallon refused to get it. "You're afraid of how you feel about Maddy, her being just over *two whole years* younger than you and just a child, so you've actually succeeded in completely blocking her from your mind."

"That's not true," Fallon disputed. "For instance, I know right now she's," he leaned toward the tractor doing a loop a hundred yards in front of them, "*pushing the jets too hard*!" He gave Liam a *'so-there'* look.

Liam snorted. "Okay, whatever you say. Now, what is this new tinkering you want me to test for you?"

Fallon smiled devilishly then looked over his shoulder. "Hey Rat, you want to take the pilot's chair while I go torture our fearless leader?"

Liam ignored the standard joke that *he* was in charge of anything as he followed the tinker into the forward sitting room. Everyone only came to him because most things were too petty to bother the *real* boss with. When he got inside, he stopped short. "What in the..."

Standing in the middle of the room was a metal man, or at least the hint of the skeleton of a man and it was hanging from a rope hooked in the ceiling. "You built it."

"Obviously," Fallon smirked. "Want to try it on?"

"Me? But I thought."

Fallon shrugged. "Made it to fit you since you'll need what it carries before I will," the comment reminded Liam he would soon be presenting a challenge to the mage that cursed his family. "Here, let me show you how it's supposed to work."

"*Supposed* to?"

"Yeah," Fallon admitted. "Built the core before Firecloud's curse got snuffed. Doesn't fit me or Sesco and needs a body to power it so it actually hasn't been tested yet. Should work as well as any of the walkers I've tinkered."

Liam made a conceding gesture. "So, what do I do?"

They spent the next few minutes with Liam stepping into the skeletal suit and steam engine backpack. "Looks kind of flimsy," he commented as the arm braces were adjusted.

"Got to cut weight where I could. It's made of godstone tubing so it may be thin but it's strong. I was able to put a bit of flex in too, so they won't snap," Fallon mumbled his reply. "Now wave your arms around every way you normally would be able to. How's that feel?"

"Normal, just like the legs." He slow-motion trotted in place and made several rolling arm motions in the hand combat he'd studied over the years, then the same pattern at sparring speeds. "Good range without binding and not as heavy as I thought it would be even with my changeling strength. Steam engine is really quiet and I haven't sniffed any steam leaks."

"Power pack ain't on yet," Fallon chuckled. "You're moving all that by yourself with natural muscle power. Told you, I measured it to your body's dimensions. That's why it fits so tight and you wear it *under* your clothes."

"So, I can at least put my trousers back on?" Liam deadpanned. Fallon got busy with something else and waved dismissively to the question so Liam got dressed.

As he did so he discovered the skeleton suit had bulges at hips, knees, and elbows that felt odd inside his normal clothes but not so much as to take up all of the loose fitting. He looked a little lumpy but not where most folks would notice.

"Here," Fallon handed him an odd looking gunbelt and he glanced at it before strapping it on. Both holsters fit perfectly just below the bulges of the skeleton's hip hinges. "Right for your black powder pistol and left one for whatever new tinker's pistol I'm working on. Same tinker-magery things we already have, just in a more familiar application. Not everybody we face will be at Firecloud's level so I'll need you to test a few things for me."

Liam raised an eyebrow. The fake skin burning beamer had been moderately distracting to Firecloud and he'd eventually used magery to disable it, and him. A fake skin burner might not be any use in a one-on-one offensive fight with a mage if it was just a minor distraction, but there was no telling what else Fallon might come up with.

Liam nodded. He practiced shooting his pistol just as much with his left hand as his right, as he did with every other important task in his life. It was a simple survival trait his father drummed into him at an early age that saved his life more than once. He imagined several of the mage spells he'd learned with the help of Heather's amulets put in reach of a pistol grip.

"Okay, here," Fallon handed him a new leather rain slicker with godstone buttons, and rivets at all of the most stressful points, with a scattering of tinkerings and extra pockets and pouches. Closer inspection revealed godstone wires connecting in a grid pattern throughout the expanse of the inner lining.

Liam took the slicker. "Heavy."

"Yeah, well, you'll need all that at some time or other. Might as well get used to carrying it around with you all the time." He gestured. "Well, put it on."

Liam did so, then worked his shoulders. "Not really that heavy after all once I have it on. Sits on my shoulders comfortably and moves easy."

"It has special amulets that will wrap you in a three-way shield any Master Mage would envy. You'll be able to withstand anything he can throw at you and *you* won't get tired, as long as the suit's tinkerings don't break down." He made calming motions. "Not that they will! I've never made some things so small before and just don't have any endurance data to work with yet. That's why I wanted to make the dang thing relatively easy to wear in off mode."

He rubbed his hands together. "Now let's see what we get when we turn on the steam. I made the backpack when I was hypering in Firecloud's curse. Kind of curious to see what it can do."

"**No, no, *push*** down as you twist. Well, it would be up in your position," Fallon was pointing when his sister came into the sitting room an hour later to see Liam pinned against the ceiling. "Oh, hi, Heather. We've almost got it."

Liam twisted the indicated knob, and immediately fell, and just as quickly snapped into a ready crouch just as he landed.

"Wonderful!" Fallon exclaimed. "How did it feel? Was it natural like running in place or doing your hand combat forms?"

Liam rose to stand easy. "It happened too quick to see. I just instantly realized what I needed to do to not land on my face and *started* to move, then the suit finished the move for me so fast I almost overcompensated."

He moved around some more, flexing his legs and arms and moving about the room. "What happened?"

"Oh," Fallon released the grip on his chin to wave that hand, then resumed the thoughtful chin stroking habit as he explained, "The voice copy went about three times faster than it was supposed to and then got locked in the on position instead of the ten reps it was supposed to run. It was the pressure that made it so you couldn't turn the venting disc. I'll put raised ridges on the disks so you have something to grip to turn them easier and a better valve release system."

He stroked his chin. "I'll have to recalculate the lifting power though. I thought the foam tubes would just take half your weight so you could jump higher and farther. But this new information gives me some other ideas."

He looked at his test subject as Heather made a disgusted sound and went back to her piloting. "Anything else? Raised ridges on the control disks and a wider strap between the legs with more room to adjust. Is that all?"

"Yes," Liam said looking around at the broken furniture. "It's kind of hard to tell for sure inside this little room, but I did get a pretty good idea of what it's physically capable of."

He gave a small shrug. "Don't know about the magery. You're sure you tested the shields? Without that basic first defense I'll be charcoal in the first ten seconds."

"Yeah. Outside our ground camp last night while you were on Deck Watch," Liam replied with a smile.

He'd seen them leave but didn't know what they'd been doing, and since they didn't tell him, he figured it was none of his business.

"Heather blasted it with all she had in slowly prepared shots and it took everything she threw at it without a scratch. If it took what she threw at it under controlled testing, it should last as long as it needs to for you."

He gestured at the suit. "What did you do?"

"I was going for the *throwing* spell and had a dart ready and then stumbled when I hit that chair too hard and repeated the throw but mispronounced the tertiary syllable and then bumped into that post at the end of the wet bar. When I fell, I threw my hands out and just slammed into the ceiling."

Fallon *hemmed* and *hawed* as he inspected the chest plates and their little twisting plates that spun the artificial chanting voices. "Okay, take it off. I have to make some changes before we land and I don't have much time. Well, *hurry*!"

Liam got out of the tinker skeleton and was dressed and back up front in minutes. He took the copilot's seat and relaxed as Heather flew them toward his home. "He's tinkering."

Heather nodded, then pointed her chin. "Starting to see people. Cincinnati can't be far. I want you to take me out to eat in a restaurant with cloth sheets on their tables and waiters dressed in fancy uniforms before the full moon waxes tomorrow night."

Liam smiled. Things sure were easier now that he'd accepted his fate. "Yes Ma'am," he said it respectfully enough she only smiled in return.

She flew on and soon they began crossing tilled fields and additional crossing roads. Another half hour and they saw the first group of buildings on the outskirts of increased population. Then they were over the Ohio and Heather turned them toward the densest group of buildings on the Ohio side of the river, the flying boxcar trailing.

Heather flew them in an arc around one end of town and the keel brushed the top of a thick limbed tree. She recovered and brought them around the nearest docks to hover above a wide field between the docks and the business section of the waterfront.

Fleetfoot smiled as one of the spotters laughed when the lead airship brushed the trees and he saw the shadow that separated as the airship recovered and waited for him to land first to put security on the ground. He was still smiling at the sneaky way Rat had gotten off the airship away from where they would land, as he brought the boxcar in for a landing with growing expertise.

Several crewmembers swarmed over the side on fifty-foot ropes – using the controlled fall Fallon had shown them – and quickly drove stakes into the ground, then secured the lines they'd dropped from. As the troopship was tied down Heather brought the other airship around in a circle to set down between the boxcar and the riverbank.

By this time a crowd started to gather and gawp at the spectacle while Maddy took a guard position a couple hundred yards high and out over the water so she could see long distances up and down river.

Liam poked his head through the door to the sitting room. "We're here."

Fallon looked up. "Wear the slicker. Think of it as part of your uniform. If you're off the wagon you're in the slicker from now on."

Liam nodded and retrieved the slicker where he'd draped it over the wood and wire torso frame

Fallon used to work on it. "You do anything more to it?"

"Just filled the pockets with what goes in them." He tossed a small booklet and Liam snatched it out of the air. "Operator's manual for the suit and slicker in twelve, three by five memory charmed pages with half page pictures and half page text front and back."

Liam raised his eyebrows. "Burn after reading?"

Fallon snorted. "No, I'll need it to deactivate certain parts quicker when I change old parts with new and improved tinkerings and magery and charm a new manual. You can let the others play with the slicker if you want but the skeleton suit will only work with you and your body or the moving parts will get confused. Oh, and don't gain too much weight."

Liam nodded sagely, wondering if he only *thought* he knew what the tinker was talking about. He donned the slicker, then with legs spread shoulder wide looked at the first page of the manual and chanted the *memory* amulet he wore with his godstone necklace.

In a second the picture was printed indelibly into his brain as he read the tiny text instructions. A second later he turned the page, then again, then again for half of the manual then he lowered it and tucked it into its special inside pocket. "Same configuration as my vest only with inside pockets instead of outside. The other pockets match my heavier coat too, so everything is where I'm used to having it. Good thinking." He visually verified the contents of several of the pockets and pouches as he spoke.

Fallon nodded. "I do want you to check the holster slits before you go outside, if only to familiarize yourself with the way they let you get at your pistols."

Liam fumbled for the side slit behind the pocket and moved his hand from one to the other several times, then darted his hand into the slit and drew his pistol. "Slower, but that's to be expected. Goes back in harder than it comes out but that's okay too. Don't need to put it away fast."

He repeated the process with the left side's access slit, but didn't have a new tinkering pistol yet and muttered, "Wish I had my knife instead of some fancy tinkery."

Fallon smiled. "No problem." He pointed. "That holster comes off. I did it that way 'cuz I made several different designs and I didn't want to make a whole belt for each one. Here, here's the detachable sheath for your favorite knife and it has a couple of darts and a throwing charm sewn into it now, too."

"How long have you had *this*?" Liam held the offending sheath up in mock anger.

"Oh," Fallon waved airily, "it's the first one I made. But you already knew how to use a knife. I needed to get you more familiar with something a little more out of your comfort zone."

Liam shook his head as he attached the sheath, with his favorite knife already nestled inside, then practiced getting access to it through the slicker's left side slit. After a few draws he went for both pistol and knife at the same time while moving in different ways as he chanted the memory charm.

Satisfied, he stepped out of the sitting room onto the piloting deck to face a curious crowd. Just as he stepped out into the lowering sun Fleetfoot swarmed over the rail and came to attention in front of him.

"Sir! Guards are posted two to each side," he pointed with two fingers extended, "and one on each end of the barracks. We're giving the locals a look-see at the barracks to distract them from bothering you and Miss Heather and..." he looked down where Orlagh lay contentedly relaxing. She yawned and snubbed his plaintive look.

Liam couldn't tell him in front of his sister his mistake was in not mentioning her name *first*.

"The rest of the crew is building a pit for a night fire on the far side of the barracks so people take that as the public visiting part of our camp," the young puma resisted the urge to glance Orlagh's way, his bulging neck muscles attesting to the effort.

"Thank you Fleetfoot. Could you tell the cooks to see if they can get a rear quarter for the spit? We're early enough we should have a good bed of coals an hour before sunset. Tell the cooks to cut the fat end down for those choosing beast form tonight, then cook the rest over the open fire and let everybody else take what they want when they want it."

"And, Miss Orlagh and Miss Heather and yourself sir?"

Orlagh purred loudly, but Fleetfoot knew better than to relax.

"Miss Heather and I are going into town to eat but you can tell the cooks we'll *all* be at the main fire at some point before midnight curfew for those not on night watch. Tell them to go ahead and clean out the fresh produce bins and let them air out all night. Share with any of our guests that don't abuse the sharing, we'll get just what we need for one day before we leave tomorrow."

Liam gestured at the commotion at the nearest road. "Anybody I need to speak with?"

"Uh, a sheriff's deputy, and another fella *insinuates* he represents the mayor. Got a couple of the boys talking to them with all kinds of *official* sounding words long enough for me to fetch you."

Liam smiled as Orlagh perked up and he scented *smug pride*. "Good job son!" He gestured. "Then let's don't let your boys' diversionary efforts go to waste."

Fleetfoot turned a brief bow to Orlagh, *then* to Heather, then scampered over the rail with Liam quickly behind.

On the ground he strode quickly without appearing to and was soon the focus of turning eyes as he rounded the boxcar. The guard on that side gave him the simple nod he insisted on when too many had snapped to attention – and sometimes saluted – in his presence.

"Ah, sheriff?" Liam's voice held the question as he approached.

"No, no, Deputy, Deputy Fields, uh, sir, and this is…"

"Terrence Hamilton the Third at your service. I've worked with the mayor's office." The man looked around as Fields made as if to say something, then stopped. "Don't know why he isn't here yet, such an important visitor coming to our city out of the blue so to speak."

"Well, we did come unannounced," Liam stated.

"Nonsense, my good fellow!" Hamilton said expansively. "In the age of telegraph there's no such thing as surprise when people travel through the sky for anyone with eyes to see."

Liam tried not to flinch. That was certainly true and some of the people interested in such comings and goings might not want them to get where the newspapers already said they were going.

Hamilton craned his neck. "What would the chances be of getting a look at one of those wonderful tinkerings or meeting the tinker what tinkered something so grand."

"Seems to me I read people have been making flying machines since just before the start of the war," Liam observed.

"Not like *that*!" Deputy Fields exclaimed with finger stabbing toward the boxcar with its diminutive silvery colored balloon and odd pusher fans.

Just then a large wagon came into view and Hamilton wilted.

"Ah, here comes Mayor Parsons I think and maybe, yes, that's Sheriff Hooper and Deputy Wilson horseback behind the mayor's coach," Deputy Fields sounded relieved at the reinforcements.

The opulent coach with the team of four horses rolled up and stopped at just the right spot to let everyone see the occupants emerge. First came a man that was not portly, but still on the thicker side of fit.

Liam was just stepping forward to introduce himself when the other man stepped out of the coach and turned with a smile.

The scent that lingered with the torture he'd felt ever since his family had been cursed assaulted his nostrils and his attention locked on the source of the stench he associated with torture.

It was the mage that had cursed his family, smiling and reaching into a pocket.

Chapter 37

Liam *almost* grabbed at the pistol on his hip but just as he took a breath to chant a shield the *rest* of the man's body language and scent registered.

He instantly adjusted the paths of his hands and put his left over his chest and the right one to come up horizontal *without* a pistol as a greeting. "Liam Quinn, Mayor Parsons."

The mayor shook his hand reflexively then he turned to the sheriff. "Sheriff Hooper, Deputy Wilson." Wilson's eyes grew wide at Liam already knowing their names.

Then Liam looked the mage directly in the eyes, eyes that mocked him behind a fake smile. Liam realized the mage didn't know his secret had been exposed, didn't know the necklace that allowed his family to maintain their sentience also allowed them to *scent* the source of the curse.

"Master Mage Hammersmith, at your service," the mage bowed but did not extend his hand to shake. Master Mages didn't like to be touched – especially one who'd cursed the one he might touch.

Liam nodded minutely as he tried not to let his animosity become too apparent.

The mayor was oblivious as he craned his neck. "I have read of your exploits, young man. So, these are the warships of the sky? Is that big armored one the one that blasted that train off'n the tracks and killed all them scoundrels? Heard the fireball rose a mile into the sky and weren't no survivors."

Liam kept his eyes on the mage and only Hooper and Fleetfoot noticed the tension.

"I would like to invite you to my home for the evening sup young man and that sister of yours too," the mayor continued as he threw his hands out expansively.

"I'm sorry, mayor, there's been some sort of mistake. I am Liam *Quinn*. It is Heather and Fallon *Richards* that own these vessels," he gestured toward the boxcar as he spoke.

The mayor turned toward the mage. "But I thought you wanted the pumas?"

Hammersmith rolled his eyes and gave Liam a suffering look as Parsons turned and blurted, "That's okay, they can come too."

Despite the anger seething within him, Liam gave Hammersmith a sympathetic look and the man almost smiled naturally. "I am afraid Miss Richards and I have plans to eat in one of your city's fine public restaurants. She is getting properly attired as we speak. I only interrupted my own preparations so as to meet you properly and apologize for the missed opportunity to speak more."

Parsons looked frantic for a moment, then recovered. "Splendid! Might I select the establishment and serve as your dining host? I am sure the city would be honored to treat such celebrities to their best! So? Will there be four?"

"No, I'm afraid, just Miss Richards and myself. My sister and young Fallon will be remaining in camp." He left it at that and wondered if the mayor would prod.

Hammersmith saved them all. "I have an idea. Why don't the mayor and I return to town and send the coach back for you. That way you will not have trouble finding us. It is a half hour each way so the wagon should return in one hour?" And so, he slipped himself into their company unless Liam made a point to exclude him.

Liam dipped his head, maintaining eye contact and Hooper's brows creased. "In an hour and a half then, gentlemen. Sheriff, Mr. Fleetfoot can show you and your deputies, and Mr. Third the boxcar," Fields snickered at Liam's words. "Let 'em hang out on the forward deck as long as they don't touch anything, Mr. Fleetfoot."

"Yes, Sir!" Fleetfoot almost saluted but Liam's eyes stopped him. "Gentlemen, if you would come this way, I want to show you the future of air travel."

Liam hurried back to the wagon and let the others know what had just happened. Heather was almost ready but said she had to change into something more *appropriate* and disappeared back into her room. Fallon and Maddy grew frantic over a dinner jacket they had been preparing for Liam.

Liam turned to his sister. "In an hour and a half, I will be having a *civilized* supper with the Master Mage that cursed our family. I plan to give him Formal Challenge at that meal. Heather says as Challenger I get to decide the time and place."

He sighed. "Killing him will end the curse but killing a son of a powerful Old Mage Clan holds its own path of revenge curses. And if I die it doesn't necessarily hold the rest of you to abandon our island. I am not challenging him for the island, only for the curse. I *will not* make that bigger challenge without a *full* Family consensus."

He looked in the direction of Heather's room as she changed into a more official dress. "I have five days to specify time and place or the Challenged gets to choose. I am choosing Clawstone Park as the dueling grounds five days from the time of our supper tonight. Both entire families will be in attendance as witnesses and they will then decide whether to accept the verdict at the end or continue the fight till one family gives ground or is exterminated.

Orlagh waited till he was finished then rose and gave him a playful head butt, gave the paw signs for *we will prevail*, then yawned and lay her head on her paws and closed her eyes.

An hour later the coach pulled away from the boisterous party the crew enjoyed around the large fire pit lined with river stones and dripping beef juices into the steadily fed bed of coals. Men sat their mugs of ale and bottles of wine down just long enough to cut steaming slabs away and eat heartily while the heat singed another layer.

The ride was considerably bumpier than riding the sky and Liam gave Heather an apologetic smile while the mayor's wife rambled on incessantly. Liam wondered if Heather's ears would start bleeding as he was thankfully ignored by the jabbery woman.

The half hour eventually passed and a footman helped the ladies down first, Liam stepping down himself last, then offering an arm to each. The mayor's wife blushed at the courtesy and made a show of accepting as she preened for those lucky enough to see her on the arm of the man whose story was showing up in dime novels.

As they paraded through a natural cordon of admirers some of the whispers were loud enough to hear.

"Are those Master Mage's robes she's wearing? At *her* age!"

"Killed her Master to get 'em I heard."

"Heard she can fly without a balloon."

"Without a *broom* you mean," one voice cackled and was warned of being cursed.

"He don't look like that much," a man snarled.

"He's got nice shoulders," one woman opined.

Another man added. "Wouldn't want to face a warrior puma at night in a body that size with shoulders like that."

"I would," a female voice whispered too loudly just as the crowd grew silent.

Heather snorted and gripped Liam's arm reflexively as she started to turn in the direction of that last voice and he diverted her impending targeted response. "What a grand place you have brought us to Mrs. Parsons! Isn't it, Miss Richards? Such a beautiful outside must surely be exquisite on the inside."

He carefully didn't mention the quality of the food. An opulent setting didn't always ensure a competent kitchen.

The mayor's wife preened as Heather leaned forward, laying her head against Liam's chest. "I am sure we could find no finer place to dine or company to keep," they heard several swooning sounds from the crowd as she cuddled against him.

A nervous man in an elaborate uniform with a particularly harried look escorted them inside and toward a cleared area with a table big enough to seat a dozen. At his height Liam was able to look across the wide-eyed crowd as an usher was trying to get a couple to change tables with another. The clothing of the couple being moved showed this was probably a special treat for them instead of a normal place to eat while the other couple's dress and attitude spoke of a higher social level.

As they came to their table Liam spoke aloud, "This is much too large for just the five," he made as if to just notice the Guild man with Regional Guildmaster Knots next to Hammersmith, "six people."

"You there, you two, yes you!" He made *come here* motions to the two being moved. "Will you join us? We have plenty of room and I noticed there was a mix-up in your seating." When they hesitated, the usher tried to intervene.

"Nonsense!" Liam said cheerfully before any objection could be made. "I insist!" He leaned forward toward the mayor's wife and shook his head up and down. "*We* insist."

And the mayor's wife shook her head up and down. "Yes, please join us, we insist!"

The mayor made fish imitations, his mouth opening and closing without any sound coming out, while Hammersmith glared and the Guildmaster failed to hide a smile.

"See! It is settled, you two will join us for our meal and we will talk about the wonderful hospitality your fine city has shown Miss Richards and I." He looked at the tables pushed together after introductions were made and put his chin in his hand. "There's still too much room. I know!"

He motioned for the harried doorman. "You sir! Yes you! There were some people outside I heard were waiting for just the right table for the odd number in their group." The man began to look panicked as he looked to the mayor for help.

The mayor was too slow.

"Yes, you know the one's I'm talking about. Youngish looking mother with two boys about fifteen, sixteen." The doorman almost fainted. "Yes! You *do* know the three! Would you ask them to join us, please? Ask them politely, but if they demur you must insist. Do *not* disappoint me!" Liam said sternly then smiled and touched the frozen man on the arm. "Quickly now, and do not return without them!" The man jumped then ran to get the three new guests.

"Wonderful!" Liam continued exuberantly before anyone could react. "That fills every chair but one. You there! Yes you!" Another man froze. "We have one chair too many. Will you please take it away so we may spread our elbows a bit more?

Thank you, thank you, ah here are our last tablemates."

More introductions were made before Liam continued, "Please, everyone, sit down. Could one of you boys come over here and sit beside Mr. Dover. With your mother sitting beside Mrs. Dover your brother will have a Master Mage to talk with while we eat."

Nobody had the nerve to object and whispers flowed outward like ripples in a pond as Liam expertly put the two mages between young men and mostly opposite him and Heather.

The mayor and his wife were thrown off their stride, but Mrs. Parsons quickly regained her form and became the perfect hostess even though she was not in her home. Liam cajoled the mayor into helping him help Mr. Dover and the Martin boy order something they never heard of. Liam made sure to order double portions and gave the waiter a stern look with the order.

Heather helped the others with the mayor's wife beginning to relax with the wine and make honest suggestions. The mayor's face grew whiter with every expensive dish they ordered.

The Regional Guildmaster didn't hesitate and dove in with the rest experimenting with selections from the menu with the boy next to him while his mother looked on in wonder.

"What are you folks celebrating Mrs. Martin?" Heather asked once the first round of orders was taken.

The diminutive black woman sat proud in her chair. "Saved enough to send my boys to university Miss Richards. They both sent in papers and passed all the entry exams and I paid their first two years tuition in full," she held up an official receipt. "Had enough left over to buy my boys a going away meal they won't soon forget. Almost didn't get a seat because we're an odd number and all the tables are for two and four and up.

Her boys had the grace to look abashed at not telling their mama the truth while the mayor sneered.

"Well then it was lucky for you we had enough room we could afford to sit an odd number," Heather reached over and patted the woman's hand.

The mayor saw Liam's glare and realized what he was doing and took on the smell of prey – avoiding Liam's gaze from then on.

The plates of food kept coming and after a while the mayor's wife noticed her husband's reactions to the continued largess and she gave him several pointed looks. He finally got it through to her he had offered to foot the bill and she blanched.

She was trying to get a waiter to put the cork back in a newly opened bottle of wine when the Regional Guildmaster cleared his throat. "Excuse me, please. While I admit this is one of the more entertaining nights I have ever had the pleasure to enjoy, I still have a duty to perform."

"I have been *encouraged*," he gave a smiling Hammersmith a nod, "to bring the subject up, despite the public setting."

He faced Heather. "Miss Heather Richards. You are accused of using dark magery in the killing of a Master Mage and stealing his life essence for personal gain. Furthermore, I have documentation that places you at Fifth Level Acolyte and yet you come here wearing the knots of a full Master. The penalty for the first two is death and the last the loss of all Guild status. How do you plead?"

The rest of the table grew quiet as the charges were spoken and the Guildmaster drew forth a subduing wand of the blackest wood and casually held it at the ready.

Chapter 38

Heather smiled and calmly reached into her hip bag lying on the table between her and the mayor's wife, who nearly fainted when Heather only pulled forth a roll of papers. "First, here are the papers that advanced me, signed by my new Master and the Phoenix Guildmaster."

"This absolves you of the wearing of full Master's Knots," the Guildmaster said as he read the papers. "How do you answer the other charges?"

Heather again reached into the bag and drew forth another set of papers. "That is the written record of the inquiry into the incident that got Firecloud thrown out of the guild. He taught my mother forbidden knowledge to use her as a worthy sparring partner. She was unaware the chants she was learning were forbidden because she was a *special student* and had no other instructors, nor did she have the opportunity to associate with other acolytes."

"The only reason she was caught was because she innocently went to another Master to get additional training *to impress* the Master she idolized. The inquiry determined she was without blame but had learned too much to stay an acolyte. They did not kick her out of the Guild, only ended support for her. Without guidance and no one to explain why she was being shunned she taught me all she knew."

"By the time the Guild Council discovered their *second* mistake, I knew too much and to avoid further scandal, they gave me to a new Master," she gestured to the first set of papers, "who taught me Guild Laws and eventually approved my rise to full Master."

"Those papers attest to my authority in using dark magery in both the awarding of Master status, because *all* Masters are authorized to learn *all* forms of magery, even that forbidden to Acolytes of all five levels."

"That absolves you of another charge, but there is one more charge and it holds the penalty of death," he tapped the ebony wand against his sleeve and the mayor's wife tried to move her chair closer to Liam.

Heather smiled and reached into her bag and pulled out her mother's hand – and the mayor's wife fainted against Liam. Mrs. Martin crossed herself and Mr. Dover looked curious while Hammersmith glared.

Heather gestured toward the papers in front of the Guild man. "Copies of all of those papers are in the Regional Guild offices in Phoenix and another copy in the national offices in the Capital. I'm surprised Master Hammersmith didn't inform you of that fact before he *suggested* you make your charges public."

She pointed at the cursed hand. "My mother created that curse with her dying breath and compelled me to seek all those that murdered her and her husband, and avenge their deaths. She saved the last death for herself, that of the Master that cursed her children with forbidden knowledge *after* he had been supposedly stripped of that knowledge when he was banished from the Guild."

"No, I did not kill a Master Mage. My mother came back from the dead to drag her enemy back there with her because the Guild failed to do their duty."

The Guildmaster shuffled through all of the papers while Hammersmith continued to glare. Then he looked up. "That covers everything but the stealing of a Master's life essence." He didn't quite let go of the wand in case he still needed it.

Heather smiled and removed a ring of solid godstone. "I hereby officially return the life essence of the Dark Mage Firecloud to the Guild to be purified and disposed of properly."

"Ha!" the Regional Guildmaster exclaimed with a wide grin. He grabbed the ring and looked at Hammersmith, who was obviously deflated. "Well, Master Hammersmith, we have done our duty and discovered not another dark mage but a shining example of our unique membership."

He bowed in his seat as he admitted, "The Guild has been watching Firecloud for months but maybe we should have been watching him more closely." He looked pensive. "But we are so scattered and our organization so disrupted by the war, both in deaths among our highest ranks and those who have lost their faith in the Guild protecting them from…"

He realized he was rambling – in public – and stopped. "Master Mage Richards, as the Regional Guild representative, I thank you for the service you have done for us. I will make sure this," he put a hand to the pocket where he'd put the ring, "is properly dealt with and your Guild membership is properly updated and annotated with the relevant awards."

He pointed his chin at the severed hand. "Uh, may I ask what you are going to do with that?"

Heather picked it up and held it out just as Mrs. Parsons raised her head from Liam's tolerant shoulder, saw it waving in front of her, and passed out against him again. "I will perform the final rites now the death curse has been completed so Firecloud's victims can rest easy, then I will render it down to its useful parts."

"Be careful young Master, those types of uses are as dangerous to the user as to the use," the Guildmaster said then sighed. "But you know that. Just be careful. Now on to one more thing." Hammersmith regained some vigor. "There is the matter of these amulets you are making. You are endangering the livelihood of hundreds of mages with these new ways *normals* can wield strong magery."

Heather smiled again and reached into her bag and drew forth one last bundle of papers. "There are all the syllables for each of the new spells to create amulets normals can activate."

"You're *giving* them to the Guild," the Guild man was incredulous.

"No, not *giving*. We already copyrighted the amulet charm and the spell syllables but we're authorizing the Guild to act as distributor. It takes a Master level to make the amulet, maybe some fifth level acolytes can, but not many and only the easiest ones. That way the power still rests with the most powerful of us."

"My brother and I are asking only a one percent user's fee to be paid directly into my personal Guild account. The Guild can charge individual Masters what percentage they want to craft the amulets, but I always get one percent of that fee. I'll even let you keep the papers but I get one free unannounced financial audit per year upon demand, non-accumulative, to inspect your books."

Hammersmith looked eager. "Oh, and one last condition that must come with an Oath Promise." As Hammersmith's eager look turned to a glare, she added. "No one… *no one*, is allowed to see those papers for exactly five days and two hours from this moment. Say now, do you accept in the name of the Guild?"

"Gods yes, young Master!" he chuckled. "You don't bargain very hard and the Guild welcomes the largess, but in the name of the Guild, I agree to award Master Heather Richards with a one percent licensing fee. The fee is to be collected by the Guild and deposited in Guild coffers to be withdrawn by Master Richards at any Guild sanctioned bank. I also give Guild assurance the contents of the new spells will be put under secret lock for five days and two hours from this moment. So, let the contract be witnessed by three Guild Members."

Heather said, "Witnessed."

"Witnessed," Liam said as he touched the Novice's braid he laid on the table.

Hammersmith sat rigid as the Guildmaster looked puzzled at his hesitation, then he gritted his teeth. "Witnessed."

"Master Mage Hammersmith," Liam intoned seriously before anyone else could speak. "I accuse you of placing a curse on my family to gain lands refused through rightful offer, but refused nonetheless."

"How?" Hammersmith stuttered.

Liam placed a hand under his buttoned shirt and drew forth the godstone necklace. "The curse robbed us of sentience during our forced changes. We went to several Master Mages but only one was able to help by creating these so we retained sentience while in our full beast form."

The Guildmaster looked at the necklace, then at Hammersmith, then at Heather, then at the necklace again and his brows creased in a frown as Liam continued, "You sent several letters demanding our island in return for ending the curse and the curse had your scent on it. We have those letters in a safe place as evidence of the attempt."

"None of us would have had the mind to note the scent *every single time we changed* if we had not retained our sentience because of these," he flicked the necklace, then let it drop. "Each of the four of us wears one of these and we've always been looking for that scent, the scent of the mage that cursed us with bestiality during our forced change. The scent I smelled the moment you stepped from the Mayor's coach."

He gestured toward the braid as their guests' eyes bulged at witnessing the challenge. "As you can see, I have applied to the Guild as a Novice level one and been accepted. I have *also* voted as a *witness* in Guild matters, and my vote has been acknowledged by three Masters, so I am a Guild member in active standing."

Liam locked eyes with the mage. "Under Guild bylaws I hereby give you *Formal Challenge*. I accuse you of using dark magery for personal gain at personal danger to an innocent victim, my entire family."

"I demand redress in full. You will remove the curse and publicly apologize and pay reparations, or face me in a duel to the death."

"Oh god are they going to start killing each other?" the mayor's wife whined and tried to scoot her chair away from Liam and closer to Heather.

Heather patted her hand. "No dear, they will finish eating like civilized men, then they will drink and brag to their friends how brave they are… *then* they will start killing each other on a sanctioned duel grounds in five days. Now eat that ice cream before it melts."

"I must say Master Richards, things don't seem to stay uninteresting around you for long, do they?" the Guildmaster said with a laugh, then turned to the other mage. "Well, Master Hammersmith, this *Novice* has challenged you to a duel to the death. Do you dismiss his accusations with a quick truth chant to prove your innocence, admit the charge and apologize, or will you punish his impudence by accepting his Formal Challenge to a duel to the death?"

"Why doesn't he just take the truth chant and prove his innocence?" Mrs. Dover asked. "If he has nothing to hide what does it hurt?"

"That's one of the reasons so many folk died in the war," Mrs. Martin said. "For the right of folk like me to be free of another man's chains and my boys to go to a good school and folk like Mr. Hammersmith to not be searched without due cause. One man's nose don't meet that standard, beggin' your pardon while sittin' at yer table and all, but won't let a free meal interfere with the truth."

"And I wouldn't put you in that position," Liam stated. "Mrs. Martin is correct and by the Constitution's Fourth Amendment, Mr. Hammersmith does not have to submit to any truth enchantment and to use that refusal as evidence of guilt is not what so many died to protect."

Mrs. Martin looked pleased to hear that as Heather added her say. "But Mr. Hammersmith is also a Master Mage and a lifelong member of the Mage Guild. He has other oaths than to our Constitution, oaths that follow other rules. He may not *have to* submit to a truth enchantment, but he *does* have to answer a Formal Challenge or forfeit Guild membership!"

Heather smiled at the petit woman. "He can also do that by *voluntarily* submitting to a truth enchantment, but yet again he can refuse. But if he refuses to accept a truth enchantment, or admit the charge and face the Guild's punishment, he *must* meet his challenger in a duel to the death. It is the only way he can put the accusation to rest. It won't matter if the accusation is true or not, the challenge will have been answered with full legality."

Hammersmith looked like he was about to burst a blood vessel and Liam was enjoying his discomfort when one of the waiters jostled his elbow. He glanced at the man and had to keep from showing his surprise as a restaurant-uniformed Rat filled his wineglass with a wink, then a pointed look to the side of the room.

Liam looked away from Hammersmith when the mage looked to see the Guildmaster's reaction and saw Fallon with that look he got when he was memorizing a scene. He looked back at the mage just as Hammersmith looked back at him with a glare.

"Well, Master Hammersmith? What say you? The young *Novice* has made a scandalous accusation *in public*, just like you asked me to do with your earlier *information* of Miss Richard's crimes. Do you *submit* or will you prove your innocence on the dueling field?"

Hammersmith gritted his teeth then shook a finger at Liam. "I will meet you on the field, *Changeling*!" Then he got up, throwing his chair into the occupied table behind them, and stormed off.

"My, my, yes indeed, Miss Richards, things sure are interesting around you," the Guildmaster chortled at the abrupt exit. "I take it you will be acting as Mr. Quinn's Second? Yes? Splendid! And I am further predicting the mage copyrights and patents I accepted the licensing to with a five day's secrecy grace are what this young Novice will be using to risk his life for the truth?"

Heather nodded her agreement and the Guildmaster turned to Liam as the rest of those at the table openly gawped. "Are they that good?"

"Not without my brother's tinkering, and you'll notice I didn't put that in the offer," she said.

The Guildmaster hurriedly looked through the papers then snorted as he looked at her with more respect.

"So, I only got half of what I thought I was getting?"

Heather shrugged. "I gave you what I said I was giving you and the price. If you want to haggle with my brother for a licensing fee for the tinkering half, he is standing right over there." The Guild man looked where she gestured and Fallon waved. "I'm sure he will give you a fair deal in return for a few minor concessions."

The Guild man put his head in his hands. "I'm going to give away the library, aren't I?"

Heather laughed. "Actually, no, you'll just have to trade some syllables for free Guild copyright usage and he'll give you two new ones without fees, free and clear although he'll still own them."

The Guildmaster was shocked but after a moment stuttered, "T-t-t-two *n-n-new* syllables?"

"Yes, free and clear to you with our use of the syllables he'll designate *we* can use free and clear in any of our future endeavors."

"Oh yes, oh yes indeed, you do make life interesting," the Guildmaster chuckled, then motioned and Fallon sauntered over to take Hammersmith's chair after apologizing to the lady it had hit.

Fallon signaled a waiter and the mayor groaned.

Heather finally had mercy on him and motioned for the maître d', then looked at the mayor. "Mayor, I would like to thank you for the offer of picking up the tab, but since we ended up with five extra diners we invited at the last minute, I feel it is only honorable I pay for this wonderful meal."

Mayor Parsons brightened and his wife signaled the waiter for more wine.

Heather gave the maître d' a godstone ingot. "Mr. Quinn and I will be leaving with the mayor and his wife, but my brother and our other guests will be staying. Make sure they all get anything more this will cover," she closed the man's hand around the small godstone ingot. "Make sure all five get one of those beautiful silver mugs I saw for sale in the lobby, engraved with their names as well as all those present at our table, and today's date."

The man was effusive in his thanks then his eyes bulged when she gave him a tiny leather pouch full of godstone beads. "I think there're enough in here to give one to each of the wait staff, servers, cooks, *as well as dishwashers and busboys, too*," she shook her finger at him. "*Every single one.*"

She glanced up and Rat signaled, then she looked the maître d' in the eyes again. "All twenty-three waiters, twenty-three servers, twelve cooks, six dishwashers, and six busboys. One bead each for all seventy of them, and two for you. You may give the remainder to Mrs. Martin and tell her to split the rest among the five guests."

The man's eyes looked ready to pop out of his head. He would never have imagined such a gratuity, but the stories told and his own witnessing of this mysterious Master Mage barely old enough to be a three-braid Acolyte was staggering. The stories were already spreading outward from their restaurant of what he witnessed close enough to hear every word and this latest act only made the tale all the more amazing.

She, young enough to still not be married and named spinster, and her dashing champion had calmly *taken over* through pure character radiance, showing even the harried employees grace and respect while making them proud to serve them their best. Then she and her suave companion calmly humiliated an elder Master Mage by naming him a dark mage in public and driven him from their table with righteous determination.

And *then* had calmly taken on a debt they didn't have to claim, and expanded it to make sure five total strangers got the night of their life. His mind reeled. They had instantly picked out the five people present tonight who everyone else was most likely to dismiss out of hand, befriended them on the spot, and drew them into lengthy and meaningful conversation with those that thought themselves above the normal person in class, opinion, and relevance.

And now they further rewarded *every single* hardworking man and woman that made all of those other insufferable, self-important people feel better about themselves with more than each one made in a season.

"Oh Miss, I don't…"

She closed his hands around the small pouch. "You and your people deserve so much more for putting up with…" she glanced around the opulent room then back at him, winked, and smiled warmly.

"I'll let my brother know, and we have *eyes and ears in the walls* that will make sure management doesn't try to cheat you… are you ill sir?"

"What? Oh, nothing, yes, I am well. It's just when you said *eyes and ears in the walls*. I once heard about…" he shuddered. "Just another story in a dime novel about a notorious spy from New York and D.C. Stories say he came through Cincy once about five years ago. Left a trail of dead politicians, crooked lawyers, lawmen, and assorted other ne'er-do-wells that cater to that sort. Dime novel said this spy had eyes and ears in the walls and no crooked act was not revealed to him or gone unpunished."

He shuddered again, then gripped the small pouch and looked up at her. "Thank you so much Miss Richards. You don't know how much some of our people need just this to get out from under the debtor's thumb. I'll make sure each one gets his or her godstone bead from the Sky Mage."

Heather patted his hand again and bent down to whisper in Fallon's ear while one of the Martin boys asked the Guildmaster a question. Then she said good-bye to her dinner companions and offered her arm to Liam.

They walked through a pool of quiet that flowed through the restaurant with them, bubbling with whispers as soon as they were a dozen feet away. Every employee they passed bade them goodnight and they spoke to each one as if they had known them all their lives. Outside they quickly gained anonymity in the bustling early evening crowds just as the sun set behind the buildings around them.

"You do this city thing like you've done it before, Mr. Quinn."

He smiled. "Went with my Pa to Cleveland more times than I can remember to meet with bankers and politicians and others that breathe rarified air. My sister and I traveled from home to Chicago to Denver, then San Fran and Los Angeles on down to San Diego and crossed paths with more of that particular species. They all respond to the same cadences and social *chants*."

Heather giggled. "Yes, they do, don't they? Oh, look at the scarves in that window. Let's go in and get something for Maddy."

Chapter 39

Mrs. Martin wrung her hands. "I just didn't know who else to talk to, Mr. Quinn, sir. I don't mean to be a bother, but my boys was so excited to get to go to a real university."

"What exactly happened?" Liam asked.

"Well that nice young man Mr. Fallon escorted me and my boys home hisself. Rented a coach just like we was important folk and gave us a ride home. Then this morning I went down to the railroad station and, you know they got a telegraph station there? Well, they do and I was going to buy my boys' train tickets up to Columbus to go to school and the feller there says he has a telegraph fer me."

"Can you imagine, sumbody sendin' *me* a telegraph message. Well, I just had to see what sumbody had to say to me so I pays the man for my message..."

"Uh, excuse me for interrupting. You said *you* had to pay for this message?"

"Yes sir. I always paid to *send* messages, didn't know you could do it t'other way 'round. Anyways, I paid for my message and it says the school made a mistake and my boys *ain't* been accepted to the university. I don't know what to do Mr. Quinn. They's so excited they's both likely to wet themselves and I ain't got the heart to tell them they can't get to learn like they should, like any other folk's chil'ins," her voice cracked at the end.

"And now Mr. Beatty says he don't need me no more. I been keeping his three houses clean most all my life, didn't even tell nobody his boy is my boys' daddy from before the war like he asked me not to and now he just up and says he don't need me no more."

"I don't know what to do Mr. Quinn," she wrung her hands as she talked. "One minute I'm on top of the world with pride about to bust my chest, then I meet folks like you and Miss Richards and I think things can't get no better. Then the whole world turns on its head and what was good is now so bad I'm at my wits end."

"Now don't you worry a bit Mrs. Martin," he put an arm around her shoulders and felt the tremors she barely held back. "Tell you what, Fallon has been grumbling about how all these stories about us are getting so much wrong people are getting a distorted idea about us. He's been complaining he doesn't have time to do it himself but we sure would like somebody to write our stories truthfully."

"You said your boys wanted to be newspapermen, and write dime novels and newspaper articles on things that really happened?"

"Yes sir, one does sketches and the other writes, and both can do both. Earl writes when Samuel sketches, Samuel writes when Earl sketches, and they both write about their own sketches."

"Well then its settled, Earl and Samuel can write and sketch dime novels Fallon will edit for truth and since Mr. Beatty doesn't need you any more maybe you could take employment with me."

"Mr. Quinn, sir, it don't take nuthin' to clean one of these air wagons," she scoffed. "You jes funnin' me, ain't ya?"

Liam smiled. "No, Mrs. Martin, I ain't funnin' you. I don't mean the air wagon though. I mean the main house at home. Half of it is closed up right now cause my sister and I were out west, but it'll need to be opened back up and we've been away almost a full year so there will be repairs to be made and new purchases to make. Oh, there will be more than enough for one person just to manage the work crews. In fact, my sister and I will probably have to hire one or two more house staff to help you do it all right."

She gave him a penetrating look. "Okay, Mr. Quinn, and what would you be willing to pay?"

"A dollar a day wages with room and board."

She thought seriously. "Dollar a day and *free* room and board, not a dollar a day and a dollar and a penny in fees?"

"Nope, dollar a day and *free* room and board. That includes a private bedroom and three meals a day from the main kitchen and whatever *paid* day off you choose each week."

She thought about it some more. "Three bodies for one dollar wouldn't be worth it but with free room and board I s'poze we can accept. I'll have to talk to my boys first though."

"No, not all three of you for one dollar a day," Liam corrected her. "I mean a dollar a day for *each* of you, and free room and board and a paid day off for *each* of you. You will run the house and your boys will write and sketch our story truthfully and take classes at the city college when we're not traveling."

"Heh-heh! Mr. Quinn, you sure don't bargain like any businessman I ever heard of! Okay, you have yourself a deal, but you'll have to wait for me to travel on the ground like God meant people to travel. I ain't gettin' on no flyin' wagon!"

Liam smiled understandingly and leaned forward to whisper conspiratorially, "I don't blame you Ma'am. When we're up real high, I don't go anywhere near the rails. In fact, most of the time I just sit inside and it don't feel like I'm doing more than sitting still since the car isn't rattling down the track."

The youngish mother gave Liam a measuring look. "My mammy used to try that on me. Didn't work then. You doin' it ain't going to work now."

Liam pursed his lips. "In that case, got a man coming through here in a day or so driving a locomotive pulling some cars Miss Richards and young Fallon own. You can ride up north with them if you'd prefer, then take a boat to Puma Island."

"Mighty convenient," she said openly as she continued to give him a skeptical eye.

Liam chuckled. "That's one of the reasons we landed here in Cincinnati. The train coming will be using Cincy's railroad bridge to cross the river."

"The other reason is your change," Mrs. Martin observed. "The curse what made you challenge that mage."

"Yes," Liam looked reflexively at the part of the earth hiding the waxing moon. He could already feel it passing behind the earth as the sun rose on this side. "My family is cursed with a forced change during the three days of the full moon, half of us locked in our full human bodies and half locked in a full beast form, body *and* mind, with a complete lack of human sentience. The curse is like a hydra, as soon as wedding vows are taken, if either is not a changeling then the curse simply passes to the children, then the children at their normal forced change at the first full moon after human puberty."

Mrs. Martin gasped as he continued, "Yes, Master Mage Hammersmith was not able to *purchase* our land but he figured if he could kill us through other means the land would become open for purchase through the courts."

"He is a not an old man, but he's not young either," Mrs. Martin argued. "What good is such a curse if he won't be alive... oh."

"Yes," Liam said. "Mages don't age like normal folk, something to do with healing chants. Some say the great mage Myrddin is still alive. Changelings live a little longer than most human types because of their natural healing attributes, but not near the age of a Master Mage. He will most likely look the same when I am an old man leaning on a cane."

He smiled wryly. "The only way to get around the curse is to father or birth a child out of wedlock and certain courts don't recognize bastards inheriting," he said as he looked in her sympathetic eyes, and her own sons' heritage.

He vowed to himself to make Mr. Beatty – and his rapist son – pay for what they had done to her and her sons.

"No," he continued, "we must either leave our island or kill the mage that cursed us. And old mage Families don't like it when you kill one of theirs, regardless of the reason. Causes some of the less tolerant among them to let loose with more curses."

He patted her arm. "But that is not for you to worry about," he said as he motioned for one of the full human student troopers from the boxcar. "Could you take Mrs. Martin up to the wagon to see Miss Richards, please? Mrs. Martin, Miss Richards is sending some other new hires over to the hotel till the train gets here." He smiled at her look. "Yes, you are not the only one we've offered employment to. In fact, if we don't slow down on recruitment, we'll have to get rooms at another hotel."

"But, my boys and my things at home."

"Not to worry. Son, as soon as Mrs. Martin sees Miss Richards, you get another man and take her everywhere she needs to go to do whatever she needs to do to move north on our train, understand?" He dug into a pocket and pulled out a small pouch of silver coins. "Use this sparingly, but don't hold back if you need it. Make sure Mr. Beatty knows who her new employer is, and I *will not* be pleased at any interference from him or his staff! Now go."

The young man took charge of the woman and as they walked off another person found something for him to do. Later in the day after supper he saw her again with two very sad looking boys and he walked up with a big smile.

"Hello boys. Did you hear the good news?"

"We got kicked out of school afore we even got there," Earl mumbled. His twin looked about to cry.

Liam waved the comment away. "But that made you available for something even better! I sent my Pa a wire to let him know where we are and what we're doing and he sent three or four telling me what he and my Ma have been doing since Orlagh and I last wired."

He eagerly commenced to divert their attention from their disappointment. "You were going to go to school to learn how to work in a newsroom so you could eventually be reporters, then start your own newspaper. Right?"

Both boys bobbed their heads, but with sad eyes.

"Well, seems my Pa has been selling pieces of property on the south shore of our island and building a little village with just one street and beachfront parks. He even hired a newsman from New York City that owns his own printing press. Problem is, the man needs at least four assistants to do all he can with what printers he has. It's a problem of too much machinery for one man to operate and be a newsman at the same time." Liam shrugged. "He has four openings in a working newspaper and says he'll apprentice you both and will let you print your dime novels of our travels for a fifth of the profits for using his printers."

Three sets of jaws dropped. Their mother was the first to recover. "This newspaper fella going to pay a wage, or make his teaching the trade his pay?"

Liam replied as the brothers looked at each other with unabashed glee, then back at him. "Don't actually know that part. I only have the few lines on a wire from my Pa. Lots of other news from home that pertains to what's going on here. I did get the chance to inform him of my joining the Guild and my Formal Challenge after identifying Hammersmith, so we had other things to talk about."

The boys looked ashamed they'd put their excitement over his more tragic problems. Here he was helping them with their lifelong dream in the best way imaginable, all while facing imminent death in only a little more than four days. Being twins, their shame was evident to each other even if nobody else suspected. Of course, their mother knew and Liam had the benefit of changeling senses, so he knew as well.

As if nothing had happened, Liam continued happily, "The indications I got was that Pa decided since the Quinn Pride of our Clan is going to die out or move, he would put a claw in the eye of the mage that did this to us. We only had the one main house at the base of the tail overlooking Sandy Cove all these years and the dockhouse built on one side of the pier on the south side. The rest of our island was all wild and natural."

He smiled with the memory for a few seconds, before adding, "That's probably why

Hammersmith wanted it. A completely unspoiled island and only the two structures. More than enough room for him to build a fancy Mage Castle for him and his offshoot family."

"Pa is changing that. He's building a village that will only be the one street west from the South Dock and two streets of residential homes for permanent residents. Named the village Puma and he's selling parcels for businesses and housing further from town and a couple of blocks back from the main shoreline road. One long business strip and two parallel residential roads and a mile-wide lake coast, just enough to fill one whole side with people and waters to disturb a pompous mage's fantasized solitude."

Mrs. Martin snorted, nodding sagely. "Could even abdicate and still score coup."

"But we're not going to do that!" he declared. "We've been concentrating so hard on keeping our island to ourselves we were in danger of becoming just like those that mark their property lines and snarl at any that would dare cross that line on a casual walk."

"So!" He rubbed his hands together. "What that means, boys, is there's a town being built on the south shore of Puma Island and the townsfolk need a working newspaper so they can learn all about their new neighbors. You can have a job and go to school at the same time as Newsie Apprentices."

He shot their mother a glance. "But remember, you're still in Mr. Richards' employ sketching and writing dime novels from what we write in our journals. The apprenticeship is something being offered *in addition to* Mr. Richard's employ and you can work any other things out with the newspaper's owner when you get there. How does that sound?"

Both boys and their mother agreed it was serendipitous and put them on the path of their dream much quicker. When he left them, he hadn't gotten ten steps when another problem found him.

He was walking toward the wagon when Rat *appeared* by his side. He matched step cadence with Liam and began without preamble, "Hammersmith is preparing to test your defenses to get a chance to see what surprises Miss Heather and young Fallon have cooked up. He has people setting up to attack at sunset and moonrise when you and your sister are most indisposed. He wants to see what he's up against since the Guild is holding to their bargain and refusing to let him see the papers Miss Heather gave them."

Liam nodded as he approached the wagon's ladder. With one foot on the lowest rung, he said, "Get with Mr. Fleetfoot if you would, please. And try not to leave a trail of bodies like you did the last time you were here."

Rat's eyes narrowed. "Dime novels always exaggerate."

Liam shrugged. "Get a writing team to set records straight next time."

Rat looked over where the Martins were talking animatedly about their good fortune. "Just might consider the option."

Liam turned to put a hand on a rung, then turned back to add another thing – and Rat was nowhere to be seen. He shook his head and climbed up to the main deck. "Evening, Mr. Lawson."

"Evening, Mr. Quinn," Sesco said from his Duty Watch station. The faint sound of the pusher fans on Fallon's tractor came from above. "Miss Orlagh is in Miss Heather's room and your things are ready in yours."

Liam smiled. Fallon's old cabin was now officially *his and alternatively, his sister's*. "Thank you, Sesco." He looked at the lowering sun as the pain began to tug at him. It was still a few minutes before the moon would crack the horizon, but the pain, like always, didn't wait for the moon to show.

Passing into the sitting room he kept his features calm as Heather looked up.

"Fallon is up about five hundred feet with a half-dozen spotters with sniper rifles," she said. "Took off about ten seconds after Rat talked to him, just before he talked to you."

Liam nodded. Rat told the person he needed to tell first, *first*, *then* had come to Liam, having already set in motion exactly what Liam would have ordered.

"I sent out the silent alarm," she pointed to the nearest switch that would put the entire camp on heightened alert specifically designed to not look like an alert. A panel's lamps began to flicker and she read the report. "Fallon has spotted several teams of people moving into position around our camp."

"They'll attack as soon as the moon cracks the horizon," Liam said, and she nodded.

"Our people will be ready for them, and I've sent word for team leaders to collect all tinkered amulets and talismans so none are used. That's all this is, just a way for Hammersmith to see our mageried weapons in action. I should have…"

She trailed off and he spoke into the pause, "No, you *shouldn't* have. You had to face Firecloud alone, well, except for all those times when you didn't."

He pursed his lips. "We've both checked all the Guild's dueling rules and there's no way you can help me. I have to do this from start to finish by myself or it will devolve into a family against family all-out war till one side is all dead."

"It doesn't stop with me if you die!" It was out and he could see she felt better. "Don't think they're stupid enough to want my brother and me doing to them what they're allowing one of theirs to do to you and yours."

He hid another flinch of pain as the moon rose closer to the horizon. "You think if Hammersmith's Family Elders know that's what they're facing they might intervene?"

She shrugged. "That has a better chance than if *our* Hammersmith has the moral fortitude to back down now he's been exposed."

She held up a newspaper. "Only one day and word is already getting out. Some other Hammersmiths are being asked embarrassing questions and not reacting well. Seems they're all a bit standoffish and like to surround themselves with lots of open space and all of this attention is unwelcome."

She gestured. "The local Hammersmith Housemaster has a place west of here on the other side of the river. Our Hammersmith seems to have come calling after our direction and most likely destination hit the wires before we left Memphis. He just wanted to see his handiwork in person in a neutral place, didn't know about our Magecraft amulets to allow us sentience during our change, and now he's embarrassed a related Family Household Head."

Liam nodded as more pain knotted his insides.

Her brows creased as she realized his pain was coming sooner than it should. "You go ahead while the rest of us entertain our new friends."

Liam smiled through another spasm, nodded, and went into his room. In seconds another twist wrenched its way through his torso just as he unbuttoned his shirt and the worst pain he'd felt in all his years of changes threw him to his knees.

Gasping for breath and throwing his shirt off and to the side he looked at the window to see the sun was still up enough the sky was still fading to twilight. The moon was not up yet and he'd already felt the worst pain of his life. As another spasm wrenched him against the wall, he heard his sister yowl wretchedly from the other side of the wagon.

Then the world turned red as his body seemed to catch fire, and he screamed *before* the moon cracked the horizon.

Chapter 40

Beanpole crept through the growing dusk as silently as a shade, just like he'd learned when stalking invading bluecoats back home. He sneered as he moved silently, his partners flanking him. They were reminiscing about the war over mugs of ale when that mage had offered them a hefty sum for a quick job.

He froze when he thought he heard a single note, like someone tapping the edge of a wine glass. He waited several seconds then started to move again.

He'd gone several more feet, marking the position of his four teammates every foot so they all maintained the proper line, when two of the most horrible screams he'd ever heard made all five of them freeze. After a few seconds he breathed again. The mage told them to expect the screams just as the moon rose and they were supposed to attack as soon after that signal as they could get into position.

Damned animals were changing their skins already and the moon wasn't even up yet. He sneered again. Well, these two animals weren't going to like where *their* skins ended up after tonight.

In the distance the darkness of intervening trees thinned enough as they crawled, each foot punctuated by those unearthly screams, when he saw the first lamp being lit. The screams continued and he sneered as he got closer to earning some serious pay. Verifying the precise line of his team, he started to slide forward when the dirt a foot in front of his head thumped and he froze.

He waited, then exhaled and started to move forward again, and the ground thumped in the same spot, now only a half foot from his head. He turned his head to look at One-ear on his right and saw him slide a foot forward, and his head slammed down to the ground with the sound every veteran recognized and the smell of released bowels drifted his way.

On the other side of One-ear, Paddy was hustling backwards, frantically looking up at the sky, making no attempt to muffle his retreat, his weapon left behind. Beanpole looked to his left to see both his left flankers retreating just as noisily. He reached forward and dug into the earth till his fingers found warmth and he pulled out a steel bullet still hot from the barrel that had spat it out.

He was looking at it in fascination when another spot near his head thumped. "Okay, okay, I get the message," he muttered as he tucked the bullet into a pocket and worked his way backwards. The back of his head itched like it had never done before in his career as a stalker and by the time he rejoined the other survivors he was having a hard time masking the shaking.

Only then did he realize he no longer had his sniper rifle and the front of his trousers were wet.

Sesco watched through the amazing tinker scope as the last man finally decided to leave the field of battle. "One casualty, four retreating," Rosa whispered. "The other team reports three didn't get the message and the two survivors running faster without their weapons." He could hear her smile in the dark. "Ground teams are moving in to clean up."

The tractor shifted position and seconds later they heard the soft phfft of the sniper rifles with the tinkered tubes over the ends of the barrels. Rosa's wrist signaler flashed dimly through the thin cloth she wrapped around it to not interfere with her night vision. The tinkered lights were bright enough to read the dots and dashes through the fabric. "One more casualty and four retreating. That's all three stalker teams neutralized. The perimeter is now clear."

The tractor moved around again and they came in above the road that ran along the riverbank. Sesco lay in what Fallon called the starboard aft sniper's sling, with his rifle in its harness so he didn't have to bear its weight. He peered through the tinkered scope, amazed at the clarity once you got used to the otherworldly look of things as he looked for danger to their camp.

As they patrolled above the riverbank road, he watched the guards retrieving the bodies and their weapons, and the survivors putting as much distance between their camp and themselves as they could on foot in the dark.

On the other side of the tractor's smaller cabin, in the port aft sniper's sling, Rosa tapped in the report on her wrist signaler. Four more snipers crowded the forward deck around Fallon's control seat.

"At least the screaming stopped," Rosa whispered as she scanned the ground below with her scope.

Sesco didn't need to look at her to talk and kept his eyes on his duty as he responded, "Hope that's a good thing."

They were silent for a few minutes then the tractor started moving toward the end of the riverbank road away from the city. That put Rosa and Sesco aft of what was actually happening but didn't stop them from scanning the ground below.

"We just passed over some hiders," Sesco whispered. "I counted three."

"I saw two," Rosa added as she tapped her signaler. "Fallon says he saw them but there's worse ahead."

Sesco looked back along his legs in the direction the sky tractor was flying to see a large wagon piled high with loose hay. "Oh, you've got to be funnin' me," he whispered with disgust, then twisted around to look at Rosa.

She turned from looking at the wagon toward Sesco and whispered, "Attempting to sandwich us."

"Yep," he replied softly as he looked back down to scan the ground as the sky tractor slowed and lost altitude to investigate the supposed farmer and his wagon of hay.

After a few seconds, he whispered, "I have six, maybe seven moving in an arc just behind us around the wagon. There are two more, total nine confirmed. They're splitting up into three-man groups and one in each group is all lit up with natural magery." He didn't bother looking at her as he reported in a carrying whisper, knowing he was spotter and she was signaler till the shooting started when they would both be shooters.

They both knew to take out the mages first.

"On my mark," Sesco said, "we begin thinning the mages first, then their backup."

"Mark!"

Orlagh lay panting as the screams finally stopped and she realized she had been the one screaming. She whimpered and felt a light touch as a soft sheet was lain over her naked, shivering body.

"Ohh, that hurts," her throat felt raw and her voice sounded like a rusty hinge.

"There, there," a soothing voice said as her hair was brushed from her face.

"Heather," she gasped, still too weak to move. "What?"

"Hammersmith," Heather spat, then her eyes caught fire. "He sent a little present to you with the moonrise. Problem is he didn't anticipate just how much *forbidden knowledge* I've been exposed to in my life. Our Mr. Hammersmith was so engrossed in his little act of arrogance and petty revenge for the public Challenge he neglected to entertain the idea you would allow anyone to witness your change under current circumstances."

"But I didn't…"

Heather patted her arm. "Yes, I know, you *didn't* allow me to witness your change. In fact, I had to break down the door to my own room to get in here."

Orlagh looked to see the door splintered down the middle and charred on the ragged edges as

Heather shrugged and continued, "Been thinking about remodeling anyway."

Orlagh looked back up at her then realized her head was in Heather's lap with her back against the drawers under her friend's bunk. "Thirsty."

She closed her eyes for a moment, then when she opened them a cup had magically appeared and she sipped greedily.

"There, there, not too fast. Drink all you want but in slow sips to let your body settle where it needs to go."

Orlagh let her friend set the pace and before long she felt much better. When she could sit up on her own and hold the cup herself, she finally asked, "My brother?"

Heather's face fell. "I could only help one of you at a time. He's okay, he's okay!" she rushed at the panicky look on Orlagh's face. "But his pain lasted longer and was more intense. He's sleeping but it won't be till morning before he'll be able to do much more than rest. Revis is dribbling rabbit blood on his lips and he's licking it, but he won't wake up. I chanted a healing spell and he appears to just be sleeping very deep."

Orlagh smiled. "Yes, he does that when he's hurt bad, has since he was three. Scared me to death the first time it happened when we were little. I was oldest, and female, so I was always *in charge* when all four of us stayed out all night. His first all-nighter he was so exhausted," she snorted. "I thought I'd killed him and carried him all the way home crying so hard I couldn't see and kept running into trees."

Then she realized she was rambling. "If he's licking blood from his lips, he'll take a straw." She looked at the darkness outside the window. A shaft of moonlight lay across the wall. "How long?"

"An hour after you quit screaming the first time, another half hour after your first few drinks of water."

Orlagh breathed deep and flinched. Every muscle, every bone, even her skin hurt. She rolled her shoulders and looked around as her head began to clear.

"I heated the water again just a few minutes ago if you want to freshen up while I check on Liam," Heather nodded toward the privacy screen where Orlagh's clothes were laid out.

Orlagh began to move more and each movement hurt, but also helped her settle into her body. It was harder for her in human form because she only got to do it three days out of every twenty-nine and a half as the phases of the moon moved through the sky. She stumbled into the screen, almost knocking it over before catching her balance.

The water felt good as she washed away the clinging sweat, each washcloth full of soothing moisture bringing her more and more awake. In minutes she was quickly pulling her clothes on and buckling the gunbelt when Heather stepped through the shattered door.

"Whoa! And where do you think you're going?"

"To kill that son of a demon!" Orlagh spat, then couldn't get around the mage without putting a hand on her and got a flustered look.

"And what will that solve?"

Orlagh snorted. "I'll feel better!"

Heather smiled. "Still can't."

"Why not?"

"He's been *Formally Challenged* to a duel to the death," Heather explained. "Both he and your brother are *untouchable* by anyone else in their extended families. To do anything would declare blood feud and only one family would survive that."

"Then I'll go kill the brother or cousin or whatever that owns the place where he's hiding," Orlagh declared.

Heather shrugged. "Could do that, but Liam would still have to face his Hammersmith. Then you've got two dead, one on each side or, my personal favorite, two of them and none of us. And make no mistake, it's *us*, and more than just my brother and me with you."

Orlagh wilted. "It *hurt*! More than I've ever hurt before and I could hear Liam screaming in pain and… and… he's my *little brother* and I couldn't do anything to help him!" She broke down and Heather gathered her in her arms and held her till the shaking stopped.

"Are you ready?" Heather said when she finally stopped.

Orlagh sniffed, then shook her head. "Ready."

Heather nodded once then turned and led the way forward to the sitting room.

When Orlagh came out of the hallway she saw the lamps were turned down and the steel shutters with the gun slots lowered. She was glad the low light hid her tear-reddened eyes.

Then her eyes locked on Fleetfoot's gaze as she firmed her spine. "Could somebody give me an update please?"

Fleetfoot started before she finished, "We have repulsed a three-pronged stalker attack with one third losses to their side and none on ours. Then we repulsed another probe with a camouflaged wagon full of irregulars backed up by three sniper teams with rockets. Mr. Richards' sky wagon took some burns on the underside but he had it lined with iron plates when he built it, so it survived and nobody on board was hurt 'cept Herb and all he got was the hair burned off his left arm. Nobody on our side used any of Miss Richards' magery."

"Thank you," Orlagh said when it was obvious he was finished. "Anything else?"

There were several glances toward Liam's cabin, but nobody said anything. "Okay, I'm going to guess that was only their first attempt to get us to show what my brother is going to carry when he faces their embarrassment." Several eyes sparkled at her description of Hammersmith.

She scanned the crowded sitting room and her eyes locked on Earl and Samuel. "You two!" They jumped and their eyes grew round. "You're the reporters, right?" At their synchronized head shake, she continued, "Have you talked to any prisoners?"

Their heads again bobbed in tandem. "Get their statements, get statements from the guards and whoever goes through the bodies and their possessions and write it up in long form with sketches and a one-page short piece for the local paper. Then I want Mr. Fleetfoot to assign two men to escort you into town to the newspaper office and see if you can roust somebody out to take your story."

She waggled a finger at them. "And make sure the newspaper story has *your* by-line on it. Mr. Fleetfoot, have your people stay with Earl and Samuel until the first sheets come off the printer. I want the first ten in my hand with the ink still wet."

"Yes, Ma'am," Fleetfoot said, then ushered the brothers out the door.

She turned her eyes on Fallon. "You ready?"

He simply nodded.

"The rest of you already know what to do," she let her eyes wash across them as she continued, "I'd appreciate it if you had something good to say when he wakes up... tomorrow." Then she led Fallon back to Heather's cabin.

"She was going to remodel anyway," he muttered as he stepped between the charred halves of the shattered door. "How do you want to do this, difficult and glare-y, or calm and efficient and over quick?"

The glaring started, then she sighed in resignation and calmly removed most of her clothes.

"That it?"

"Don't push your luck, tinker boy!"

Fallon wisely decided minimal small clothes was as close as he was getting and quickly and efficiently took dozens of measurements.

He took a measurement, jotted down the numbers, then moved to another spot. In the process he twisted and bent her in several different poses, taking measurements and writing each around a rough sketch of a human body. He was totally engrossed in what he was doing until Orlagh began quivering.

"Stop that! Hold still!"

She didn't, and the quivering got worse. He stood up straight, glaring as he took a breath to admonish her, then saw she was struggling to keep from laughing. She was looking over his shoulder at the doorway with the privacy door shattered in half and hanging wide open.

He glanced at the barely dressed young woman in her small clothes, and turned around to see her favored suiter standing in the doorway with a mixture of horror and rage as he flickered between human and puma warrior forms.

Chapter 41

"You're *sure*?" Orlagh wondered.

"Of course I'm not sure!" Heather wasn't helping. "It's *magery*, and somebody *else's* magery at that. I got a look at it while he was pumping himself into making this change extra painful but it wasn't aimed at *me* so I only got a sideways look at it."

She shuddered. "It was like a little child pulling the legs off tiny animals to hear them scream. Your screams *fed* him, but I was able to follow the link back without him knowing because he was so infatuated with your pain."

Orlagh found it hard to believe what she was hearing, but she knew her friend's power and didn't doubt her reading.

"I was able to find out some interesting things, oh, and those herbs and spells you brought back from San Diego will still come in handy." She sat closer and got her serious face on. "Here's what I want to do."

When she was finished Orlagh sat back with her mouth hanging open. "You're crazy." She looked over at Liam lounging on a pile of cushions. "She's crazy." Liam yawned and put his head back down and she looked back at Heather. "You know you're crazy, don't you?"

"Well, yeah, most Master Mages are to one extent or another," Heather agreed as if it were a given. "But that's beside the point. What I have in mind is just one part of a comprehensive battle plan."

"Pretty sneaky one too," Fallon observed.

Heather acknowledged the compliment with a nod. "It'll be a couple of days before we can live test it so we might as well go on to other things. Fallon has decided that instead of trying to come up with new tinkerings he's just going to concentrate on making the ones we already have work the best he can."

"He's already got the size of the signalers small enough to fit on a wrist and the echo detector's picture is getting better."

"The sky cavalry," Fleetfoot said.

"Yes, definitely the sky cavalry," Heather agreed. "Fallon, you want to take that?"

Fallon nodded and rose from his seat. "I finished the two new ones before we landed in Cincinnati and I put new tinkerings in the original. All three are basically the same now with the original one having just a slightly different frame. All three have the same weapons and tinker-magery shielding amulets."

"Everybody did a really good job not using any mixed amulets when we got probed last night but we're still not giving back the amulets we collected except for the basic shield spell. Don't want to tempt people. Tell your people to try not to use shields but if you *have to*, don't hesitate to activate it. I want everybody to have both deflector and gas filtration. Those are the two that will best defend you against bullets and knives and even fire because it's either sprayed or thrown. Gas shield keeps your air clean inside puke gas or in a smoke-filled, burning building and it'll cut down on the heat transfer for a few seconds."

When you're on patrol make sure your activation trigger is handy. Shield isn't any good if it isn't on, but don't keep it on because then it could be examined, and counteracted, even from a distance."

"How far?" Fleetfoot asked.

"With our Hammersmith, somewhere around fifty to a hundred feet. His host relative, probably about twice that if not more. He's an old guy, close to a hundred thirty years. We know the local Hammersmith is backing off helping his nephew, it is a nephew, but only in action, not voice. Some of the cousins have also backed off after the first newspaper story came out, but again they're still Family and aren't actually speaking out against him, just not being silent."

Fallon smiled at Samuel and Earl rapidly taking notes and sketching the gathering. "That was a good job you two did on that quick back story, then the restaurant challenge and the way the Quinns are being tortured by their changes. That was a nice touch with the picture of Hammersmith's demented face through the link as he tortured them."

"Newspaper feller printed one hundred copies of the dime novel we started with and a couple hundred of the newspapers reporting the battle the night of the change," Samuel informed them. "We have ten copies of each run. The rest are already sold, so the printer is printing another run on the dime novel with two hundred this time. Want us to get ten more copies?"

"Yes," Fallon replied. "That way we can compare the two to see if there've been any changes. Protect both us and the printer from accusations later when others start printing their own runs to keep up with demand."

"You think there'll be a demand?" Earl wondered with wide eyes.

"You sold a hundred novels in one day in just one town and got twice that number clamoring for their own copy, I'd say you boys are going to start getting royalties any day now," Fallon said as he looked around the room. "For those of you wondering, we're not shying from telling things exactly like they're happening and we're using names when we can get signed releases or the incident is so public multiple witnesses easily identify the principals involved."

Orlagh waited till he hesitated, then she cut in, "I'm going to the train station with Mrs. Martin and the others. You going to send somebody up in the tractor as sky watch?"

Fallon looked at his sister then back at Orlagh. "I was going to do it myself, but I'll be busy with a special tinkering I'm trying to finish before tomorrow night. Maddy will be sky watch."

Maddy smiled, then blushed when everybody looked at her.

The meeting didn't last much longer and Orlagh caught up to Maddy as she was getting the sky harness ready to lift. "Thank you for watching over us."

Maddy smiled as she tightened the last strap then put the checklist in its pocket. "Flying is the most peaceful thing in the world and watching all those people from so high up is like watching ants scurrying about. You watch for a few minutes and you see the patterns where most of them go to and fro. In a few more minutes you can see where the pattern is broken and that's where the interesting things usually happen."

"I'll follow you with long and short glasses and getting messages from several ground sources and you'll have your signaler," Maddy pointed to the gauntlet on Orlagh's left arm, "in case anything happens you need to know about."

Orlagh helped her adjust the hang of the sky harness and then Maddy engaged the steam engine and it chugged silently while they swung the heavy frame toward the rail gate. Maddy's toes barely touched the aft deck as Orlagh and Revis extended the rail to put the sky harness out from under the overhead.

"Your steam is good," Orlagh said then began separating cables and safety lines as Maddy opened the valve to the steam feed and pulled the trigger of the amulet to chant foam into the vertical sausage of the balloon. The new tinkered chanting foamed a measured amount of steam and the sky watch flyer lifted smoothly from the deck just as Orlagh disconnected the hook on the top of the balloon. "Good luck!"

As Maddy flew up and over the riverbank road, Orlagh dropped over the aft deck's access ladder and directly onto Trouble's back. She kneed him around as she put hands on the stock of the carbine then the spare pistol and the tinkered pistol and ammo pouches.

She walked Trouble through the edge of camp to the hellos of several of those she rode by. She returned greetings and smiles and in moments was approaching the road that ran in either direction along the riverbank to and from the city. The camp was remote but the nearby road was fairly regularly traveled.

Heather was waiting for her on her steam trike, the cargo box piled high with bags. They matched speeds as a couple of their guards on rented horses followed at a discreet distance but close enough to come to their aid in an instant.

The ride into town was uneventful and they quickly arrived at the hotel that had accumulated seven new employees for the village being built on Puma Island. Heather dealt with the front desk while Orlagh assembled the seven new employees in front of the hotel as porters loaded their luggage onto a large wagon. When the last crate, chest, and bag was loaded the seven people were helped up on the wagon and driven the several blocks to the train station.

As the wagon rumbled away, Orlagh fed Trouble an apple, then tied him near a water trough before gathering her brood around again. "Our train is still twenty-five, thirty minutes away so if you have anything you want to do you have that long to do it. Leave somebody to watch the luggage."

Heather came riding up on her steam trike and parked it away from the line of water troughs on the other side of the steps to the raised boardwalk. The two women then went to the station office and picked up the wire that was waiting for them.

Heather read it, then looked up. "They left the last stop on time and say they should be on schedule or a few minutes early since there's nobody else on the track ahead of them."

They were early and came chugging into view only ten minutes later.

"Is that them?" Heather mumbled absently. "I didn't think we had that many cars."

The train pulled up slowly with the salvaged locomotive and its fuel car and owner's cabin on the next car. Easton's private car and the kitchen car salvaged from under thirty feet of water were third and fourth. But the next cars weren't the ones they expected. First came a passenger car filled with people, then a flatcar with a rough railing wrapping around the edge. It was covered in revelers with a wet bar in the center.

Blackie raised a hearty hand, the bottle he was pouring into a customer's mug held high as he called out a greeting. "Hello Miss Heather! Well hello Miss Orlagh, glad to see you up and about." Then the train moved on and another passenger coach and then another, both full, came by.

The platform signaler waved his day lamp as the conductor pulled slowly forward past Heather and Orlagh. Then came their other cars by the end of the platform, but an extra cargo boxcar and a fancy caboose trailed at the end with the caboose stopping directly in front of them at the very end of the platform.

Brutus stepped down from the last steps directly onto the platform then placed a wooden step under it for people with normal length legs. "Miss Heather, come look at what Tinker Fallon bought," he declared proudly.

Heather and Orlagh exchanged looks, shrugged their shoulders, and accepted the invitation. Inside Brutus pointed. "Got four bunks up top there and each one has its own wide windows to let the night air in. Got its own privy and small kitchen and sitting room and I had it all to myself!"

They looked around at the scattered trash of discarded food containers, gnawed bones, and several unidentifiable somethings.

"Can you believe it? All those people and they just left me alone with all of this. Oh, I need to tell the conductor the cold closet is empty." He headed for the door, ignoring the trash he kicked aside. "Make yourself at home. I'll be back after I get something to eat, I mean, tell the conductor he needs to restock the pantry."

Orlagh and Heather looked at each other with wide grins, then dashed out of the caboose. They intercepted Mrs. Martin just coming up the steps to the back stoop.

"There you are," the feisty woman said as she pulled herself up on the deck of the caboose's stoop.

"This is not our car," Orlagh said in a rush. "We know the occupant and said hello. Our car is further up."

"What is that smell?" Mrs. Martin curled her nose. "There's a *bear* in there, isn't there?" She clucked her tongue and shook her head and turned to climb back down the railcar steps to the train platform mumbling, "Gonna be livin' in'a menagerie."

In moments she gathered the other six and hustled them and their luggage, in three trips, to the cargo boxcar, then to the passenger car with their seats all together.

They were getting settled when the stationmaster came running up with the conductor.

"Problems?" Heather asked as the two men came to a stop in front of her.

"Yes'm," the conductor said. "Unscheduled private train left north of here and we won't be able to have clear track after it gets here so we'll have to stay the night."

There was nothing they could do. There was only so much track and it was owned by several different organizations with agreements for shared and unscheduled usage. Their train was part of that scheduling but without the clout of ownership. They would have to wait their turn for open track and that opening was rescheduled for the same time the air wagons were scheduled to lift.

They made hasty changes to their plans and the wagon returned to take their seven back to their rooms but with one bag each, the rest staying with the train. Even though the passengers were subjected to an extra day's expenditure on their adventure, they were all thrilled.

"Every one of them only bought a ticket on the chance they'd get to see the famous flying railcars," Blackie explained when he could finally reach them through the chaos. "Most every one of them has several of those dime novels that have been cropping up and they all heard there's a new novel being sold here in Cincy."

"Anyways, I had the two passenger cars filled up with passengers that only wanted the *chance* to see our air wagon," he shrugged. "Then I near filled a third car, could have filled it too if'n you didn't need seats for your people here not flyin'. After a bit I got to wondering what if the air wagons weren't *in* the air when we trained on through. Couldn't very well say to near a hundred forty people, *'sorry you didn't see the flying railcar, thanks fer yer money, good day'*, and not expect a few of them to take exception, 'specially me being dark and all."

"Then when we was pulling the siding away from the kitchen and private car to let the frame dry out on the way we found our Mr. Easton liked all kinds of fancy liqueurs and wines and whiskeys and such. And there was more in the cargo boxcars. Mr. Easton liked his spirits and made sure his employees was well lubricated to make them agreeable."

"So, I'm thinkin' to get a flat car and wrap a safety rail around the edge so people don't get drunk and fall off. And every time we stopped, we'd fill one of those balloons up with that foamed steam and cart cases of spirits and kegs of beer and wine back and forth to that little one-man wet bar in the middle. Thrilled the paying passengers to no end and they emptied the bottles and kegs as fast as we could float out full ones. Already made more selling Easton's hootch than I did selling tickets and I didn't expect to sell tickets, just deliver empty cars."

"And all this after having one foot in the grave and my neck in a noose," he shook his head in wonder but his smile didn't get any bigger only because it *couldn't* without splitting his face in two.

Mrs. Martin found them. "Miss Richards, the conductor asked me to tell you they're moving the train to the side track to get out of the way of the two trains going the other way before we can be on our way."

"Thank you, Sophia," Heather replied. "I thought you were back at the hotel?"

"Some of the folks on the train didn't want to sleep in their seats another night and I was able to get most of them rooms in some other hotels. I just came for another group of four men wanting a room near a saloon. Found just the right accommodations for 'em then I was going to go to my own bed."

"Tell you what, Sophia, you tell us where to take these young men and go ahead and go to your bed now, you've more than earned the right with all the help you've been today."

"Oh, that would give me time to have a hot bath and I shore do need one. Thank you, Miss Richards." She gave them their instructions then she was gone so fast it took Heather and Orlagh a moment to recover.

"I think she was waiting for one of us to dismiss her for the day," Heather mused. "Gonna have to break her of that so it doesn't turn into a habit. She needs to end her workday earlier and on her own. Come on, let's go see what kind of lazy men would send a little old lady off to find them a saloon and a room to pass out in."

"Don't let her catch you calling her old," Orlagh quipped. "She's not that much older than me." Then she thought to herself, *"And her boys are almost full grown and I don't even have any children yet."*

They found the four at the Flatcar Saloon with Blackie telling stories to all four as they nursed empty mugs.

"Ah, gentlemen, I wager this is the escort Sophia promised so you would not be accosted on the way to further revelry."

Heather one-eyed him and he confessed, "These fine young lads were ready to lend me an ear *all night long* but I have other duties. Sophia suggested an alternative, then went on a mission of sorts, and here you are. What did that genius woman come up with?"

Heather laughed, then hooked a finger at the four youngish men. "You four, come with me. We found you a single big room with floor room for all four above a saloon that has poker tables. Here, she said this is the change."

"Change? You mean she didn't *keep* what was left?" the spokesman seemed dumbfounded.

"No young sir. Ms. Sophia Martin would never dream of taking any more than what she thought was fair. She has already paid for the room and baths and breakfast in the morning with a wakeup call in plenty of time to catch your train." She held out the pouch. "And this is what was left over after she took the dollar you offered her for the service."

The man finally took the pouch, handling it like it would bite. "She gave us our change back?" He still couldn't fathom the integrity of the act.

"Unless you would like to give her an earned gratuity," Heather suggested with a raised eyebrow.

"Yes, please do that," the young man said as he handed the pouch back.

"Well come on!" Orlagh bellowed as Heather snatched the pouch from the youth's hand.

It took a few seconds but the four finally followed and were soon introduced to a skeptical hotelier who eventually accepted the young men as paid guests.

"Well, that takes care of everybody on the train that has issues," Heather said as they left the hotel saloon. Behind them the four young men were already ordering mugs of the local ale and encouraging others at the bar in singing bawdy songs with them.

Orlagh just shook her head at the off-key caterwauling that accosted their ears. "Saw Rat inside, in the corner under the stairs by the side door. Winked at me."

Heather snorted as they reached their transportation in front of the saloon and checked the still hot steam level. "That man sure does get around."

Orlagh untied Trouble's lead from the post and gave him a pat and a kind word before stepping into the stirrup and throwing her leg over the saddle. Settling her split skirts, she looked down at Heather now sitting astride her cycle. "Wouldn't be surprised if he beats us home with a full report on what those boys already got themselves into."

Heather snorted as she fed steam to the trike and turned toward their camp. "Not foolish enough to take that bet. Let's go home, I'm all for my bed."

Orlagh just nodded as she kneed Trouble to follow. She only had three days in human form and wasn't about to waste the last night of it with sleep. She planned to be relaxing on the aft deck of the wagon when Rat finally *did* return to his own nest. She intended to get some honest talk time with the secretive wolverine.

Chapter 42

"What's that?"

Liam looked up. "Morning Miss Heather, I'm doing well after another tortuous change, and how are you this morning?"

Heather smirked. "Don't remember the hour *after* the change much do you, the hour I held you naked in my arms while you babbled *all kinds* of secrets?"

Liam took a stare-at-the-campfire look. "What secrets?"

She pointed at the letter in his hands instead of answering.

"Oh this," he waved it in the air. "Letter from my sister. Wrote it just before moonset and gave it to Rat to give to me." He smiled. "I could tell he was *very* curious about its contents but resisted opening it."

He paused dramatically. "It mentions some dates from five years ago we should check certain old newspapers looking for the words *mage* and *hammer* in the headline, not Hammersmith, just *hammer*. Then another group of old days and the reason will be obvious, and her *source* wouldn't tell her, just gave her the dates and word search."

He made a wry face. "Sounds like her *source* has intimate knowledge of the particulars of the events in reference and the background would help us, but wants us to dig the clues out ourselves from public records and put it together with current events.

"Oh great!" Heather rolled her eyes. "She stayed up all night cause it was her last night in human form for a month and cornered Rat and squeezed him dry."

Liam snickered as he tucked the letter in a pocket. "Even talking to her through a crack in the aft deck above his nest he still wouldn't actually admit the person depicted in his *story about a fella*, is him."

He tapped the pocket with the letter. "Said she spent an hour with her ear to the crack in the deck and her rear in the air scribbling notes by moonlight. She put the sheet of notes with the letter so I could check it for anything she might have missed."

Heather snorted. "That sister of yours is some woman. I can't wait to spend more time with her in a form where we can talk more."

She put her hands on her hips. "And that means you have to start training for your duel."

He sighed and – although he not only knew she was right, but had insisted on the regimen himself – gave a theatrical whine. "Awww, do I *have* to?"

She ignored him as he rose from the bench sofa against the wall of the air wagon and followed her out on the forward deck. Liam passed the information on dated newspaper articles to both their resident reporters-in-training, then scampered down the ladder to the ground and made their way through the crowd of people striking camp.

Mooring spikes were being pulled up and lines looped over and around tree limbs and trunks.

They skirted the boxcar troop wagon and the fire pit being filled in and mounted the steps into the coach, sitting opposite the last of their *official* visitors.

"Well Sheriff, Mr. *Smith* was it?" Heather raised an eyebrow.

Smith smiled. "Yes, Ma'am."

"Well then, Sheriff, Mr. Smith, have all the proper forms and documents been presented for me to sign?"

The two men looked at each other then back at her and the sheriff said, "Yes Miss Richards, they have. My office would also like to thank you for the delivery of three very wanted men. Ah-hem, uh we are confident of their identity despite the condition of their faces due to the exit wounds. You have received the requisite bounties to your bank, have you not?"

"Yes, we have, and no you may not know the names of our snipers. The bounties went to my account because I am their employer. I will distribute the bounty funds as appropriate to *company* regulations, and those are private."

The sheriff made an accepting face and nodded his head once. "There! Then that is settled and I have an authorized witness for those that keep badgering *me* for an answer I don't have!"

The Pinkerton man scowled but didn't say anything as the coach driver and the two coachmen hanging onto their rear standing post tried unsuccessfully to appear to not be able to hear the purposefully loud words of both the sheriff and Heather.

Sitting backwards next to the driver Earl scribbled furiously while Samuel sketched the open coach.

They continued mixing friendly banter with *official* topics all the way into town with Deputies Wilson and Fields escorting them on horseback to the train station.

As they mounted the steps to the platform, they saw diminutive Mrs. Martin shaking her finger in the faces of four very contrite young men as they hovered over her like massively limbed trees.

At a raised eyebrow, Sheriff Hooper snickered. "Spent the night as my guests and didn't need the room she lost rest to find for them."

"Ow!" Liam said with a theatrical laugh, then pointed his chin toward an equally dejected Brutus. "What's with him?"

Nobody knew, so Liam and Heather went that way while the sheriff and the Pinkerton man went to *Smith*'s office in an upper room above the train station.

"She made me clean it," Brutus muttered miserably. "And it was just starting to get comfortable."

Liam looked at Heather, and she excused herself, sounding as if she had a hairball caught sideways as she turned her back and put her hands on her knees.

"Miss Richards? Are you okay?" Brutus came out of his funk with a concerned look.

"She's okay, Brutus," Liam said as he steered the boy to the steps of the caboose. "Just a little out of sorts at the moment."

Brutus nodded knowingly. "Yeah, I heard some women gets like that in the mornin' someti…"

He stopped then looked at Heather, then at Liam, then at Heather, then at Liam, and his jaw dropped and his eyes grew wide as he mouthed the phrase, *morning sickness*.

Liam wasn't actually paying attention as he was already in the process of mounting the steps. When he turned smiling wide to look back, Brutus was staring at him with eyes bulging.

He waited a second. "Well, come on, lad, it can't be that bad. Besides, you're going to get some company for the ride up to Cleveland."

"Well, I've been wrong before," Liam mumbled as he stared at the inside of the caboose. Every closet, cabinet, and drawer stood open, and stuffed to overflowing with every scrap of trash one could imagine. Some of the drawers and half the cabinet and closet doors had been broken in the attempt to close them on bulging contents.

Liam was standing in complete stunned silence when Heather bounded through the door with her face under control… stopped dead… and had to turn away as she choked again.

Brutus leaned to look around Liam and he tried to block the bear boy's view. "Miss Richards? You sure you're okay?"

"She's fine, Brutus," Liam snorted. "Uh, I take it you cleaned it all by yourself?"

Brutus smiled. "Yep! Sure did! Asked Mrs. Martin where I should put everything and she said…" He then mimicked her pose, one hand on his hip and the other wagging a finger. "And she said," then *he* looked upwards because Mrs. Martin was a tiny woman and looked up at *everyone*, "*I don't care where you put it. Just get it off the floor!*" Brutus looked smug and proud in equal measure. "So, I did!"

Liam walked into the caboose's sitting room. "Yes, you sure did get it all off of the floor." He picked up a very stained cloth napkin, with the initials JE embroidered in gold thread in all four corners. "Most of it anyway."

Brutus pursed his lips. "Missed a couple, three, uh four things," Brutus' eyes swept the room with fresh eyes, "but a person would hardly notice, huh Mr. Quinn, sir?"

Liam kept a brave face as he stepped cautiously into the middle of the room, watching where he put his feet. "So, I hear you're getting some roommates."

Brutus' face lit up. "Yeah, four fellas what got throwed in the hoosegow last night for bein' rowdy cause of *singin'*. Can you imagine bein' throwed in jail for havin' fun *singin'*?"

Liam closed his eyes and sighed just as Mrs. Martin stuck her head through the door. Liam froze and Brutus smiled as Sophia's eyes went wide, then she took on a suffering look and turned around to motion behind her. "Come on in boys and meet your new roommate."

Four contrite young men shuffled inside the caboose as Sophia spoke, "Mr. Quinn, let's let these five get acquainted. Brutus," he beamed at her, "you did a good job getting *most* everything off of the floor."

"It weren't nuthin' really," the adolescent male bear changeling exclaimed. "But I shore did work up a powerful hungry," he ended the statement with a note of pure hope.

Sophia sighed. "Tell you what. You did such a good job of cleaning the floor, why don't you clean all the drawers and cabinets and closets too. We're leaving within the hour, right Mr. Quinn? See, about an hour. I'll go get one of those big trash wagons to come over here and you can just chuck everything you don't need… no, make that *everything* into the back of that wagon."

"You can put everything you absolutely *have to keep* in that one closet without the broken door. That's your closet for your possessions so don't break the door." She stood in front of him looking up at his great height, then waved her hand in a sweeping motion toward the door as she finished. "Everything else goes!"

The diminutive woman then turned toward the other four, put one hand on a hip and wagged a finger on the other. "You four got kicked off all three passenger cars, out of four saloons, *and* all of Cincinnati in just two days. You pay all your bills but you got more money than sense! This is the caboose, the end of the train. You get kicked off and it's rolling along the tracks behind us as we keep going. Last chance boys, now help this young bear rediscover the blessings *and requirements* of civilization."

"I will return just before the train pulls out. You! You're the oldest! *You* will tell me if the caboose is ready for me to look at before I step inside. If it's not you will ride on the roof to Cleveland." She glared at the others. "And if *you four* cause him to have to ride all the way to Cleveland on the roof then *you four* will ride up there with him. Do I make myself clear?"

There were several mumbles she accepted, then smiled. "If I am pleased with the progress, I will have the cook send back enough food to satisfy five growing boys. Come on Mr. Quinn, let's let these young men make us proud."

Liam didn't comment till they got outside. "Did you see Heather?"

Sophia snorted and pointed toward the train station's office. "Went running that way looking like she was choking. She see the caboose?"

"Yes, before *and* after."

"Ah, explains the choking sounds," she shook her head and snorted. "You ever meet a bear?"

Liam thought about it. "No, but I never met a wolverine before either. Knew both existed, just never met one. Pretty rare breeds."

"All changelings are pretty rare breeds, Mr. Quinn." Sophia commented as they walked toward the front of the train. "All of your kind put together only make one in a thousand after the War purged so many. And that's taking into account all those that just got enough changeling blood to change just their face or a claw hand. Changelings at the level your family is, is another one in a hundred of the first one in a thousand. Well, the level you *would* have if'n y'all weren't cursed."

"Did you know some places they torture people to see how pure they are? Changeling blood could show up as one tiny patch of skin turned to fur, or a single fingertip changing to a claw. Some cultures, even in this country up to the Civil War still cut off any changeling part they found through legal torture."

Liam knew. All changelings knew. If torture brought out a patch of changeling skin, that patch of skin was cut out. If a finger turned into a claw the claw was removed, or the whole arm if the percentage of changeling blood allowed the change to concentrate in that one body part.

People thought that was how you *purified* someone.

Changeling blood, like that of mages, existed in most every human but in traces so small as to be able to be ignored. There were still quite a few in the world of pure human stock and those sometimes displayed traits that got the unlucky person booted from the species purist's rolls.

That was also why Heather's new amulets allowed supposedly *normal* people to use them. Magery ancestry, like changeling blood, was scattered so far and wide everybody had a little of each. Purists from all three sides didn't like it, but most rational scholars agreed it was a basic truth. The one-in-a-hundred, or a *thousand*, were those that actually *manifested* their heritage.

"Some kinds of changeling were more hated than others. Those that didn't reproduce quickly and provided special trophies got thinned out more than others. Wolves, cats, 'panzees and all their kin bred in numbers and formed clans for protection, but others didn't fare so well. Natives here killed most of the oliphants and camels, but not the bison folk. Europeans killed most all of them and the Native wolfen folk till they numbered no more than your own folk. Others got treated worse 'cuz there weren't that many of them to begin with."

She shook her head in disbelief. "All for *trophies* or out of pure stubborn, willful hatefulness. No, ain't many wolverines or bears left in the world except hiding in places most normal folk ain't set foot yet. Here's Miss Richards. You okay now sweetie? Saw what you saw. Sure was a sight, weren't it?"

Heather made a whoofing noise then the two of them wandered toward the front of the train as they talked in the hushed voices women used when they didn't want men to hear them. Liam simply trailed close enough they knew he was still with them but far enough back to not be drawn into their conversation when they saw fit to put him on the spot, like womenfolk tended to do to men.

People on the platform started pointing and everybody looked up to see Fallon bring his tractor wagon around to hover beside the train just as the three of them came even with Blackie's open-air Flatcar Saloon.

"Hey Liam!" Blackie yelled from his bar. "Got a full shelf for the big air show! Ya want a drink?"

Liam looked at Heather and Sophia continuing on and yelled back, "Give me a few minutes to get a look at the late Mr. Easton's private car and get Sophia settled and I'll be right back."

"I'll hold you to that!" Blackie yelled, then got busy making drinks for the rowdy crowd that was boisterously thrilled to *finally* see the famous flying balloon railcars.

As they walked a cheer went up behind them as the barracks boxcar came over the tree line in the direction of the river, then a louder cheer as the original air wagon lifted into view and flew at a steady pace towards them.

By then they were at the partially refurbished private car and Liam followed the ladies inside. It had changed.

When the private car and the kitchen car toppled off the tracks and rolled into thirty feet of water, they hadn't sat submerged for long, but they *had* been completely submerged. Heather quickly decided to rid herself of the interior decorations of both cars along with all the interior wood paneling and furniture. The insides of both cars were stripped down to the sturdy outer shell and robust frame including talking tubes and gas lines.

By the time the train arrived in Cincinnati both cars were well ventilated and the heavy wooden superstructure dried out. The stripped insides of both cars were ready to be remodeled.

The two rescued cooks beamed when the trio stuck their heads into the former table section of the kitchen car. The dining room was just as stripped as anywhere else in the two cars while the huge ovens and cookware had been cleaned and returned to service.

"We are ready to go, Miss Richards, and we've prepped that special meal you mentioned to us Mrs. Martin. A meal fit for a starving bear!"

"Thank you, Rocky," Heather said with a sideways look at Sophia, who simply shrugged. "I hope you made enough to feed five instead of one, he's got some new roommates."

Rocky put his hand to his heart. "*Five* bears?"

"No, no," Heather laughed. "The new four are human, just big and young."

Rocky waved a hand negligently. "Four *humans* I can handle, even four more changelings of a different sort, just not four more bears." Then he chuckled. "Would have to tow the caboose with a two hunnert foot rope too. *Whew-w-wie*! I'll just double the portions and it'll be ready in a shake."

"Fine, Rocky," Heather said. "Do you want me to have someone carry it back?"

"No Ma'am. Frankie and I like to present our own meals to those we make 'em for. You folks are a lot easier on the ears and skin of our backsides than our last employer and it has become a joy again."

Heather smiled. "Okay then Rocky. We'll let you get about your business. We're scheduled to leave in…"

"Forty-seven minutes," Sophia said as she glanced at an impressive pocket watch tied to a bodice pocket by several colored pieces of yarn.

"Forty-seven minutes," Heather repeated. "Can you deliver the meal in forty-five and come back through the cars? You might want to stop and talk to Blackie on the way back. He tells me Frankie had a birthday a few days ago he didn't get to celebrate because Mr. Easton had you working every waking minute catering to all the new security he thought would save him."

The two looked at each other and their faces split wide.

Liam led the way through the door and back into the former private car, through it and into the first passenger car where he gestured toward the thickly padded seat with the built-in desk and side table. "Here you are Mrs. Martin."

"Oh my. I said just someplace I can do some paperwork, not, *this*," she gestured feebly, stunned by the luxuriously padded window seat when everyone else had only the simple lightly padded bench seats standard on any railcar. She planted her hands on her hips and glared up at Heather. "I said I'd help you catch up on paperwork so you better have enough for me to make *this*," she threw her hand toward the fancy leather chair, "worth the effort!"

"Oh, don't you worry, I'm *way* behind what my accountant and my business partner tell me I should be reading and arranging and approving and signing. You just sit right down and dig in. I'm sure by the time the train pulls into Cleveland later today you'll be thankful for this chair."

"Okay, where is all this paper *work* you say you have for me?"

Heather pointed toward a large bin in the front-right corner of the car, in front of the newly installed desk and comfortable chair. Sophia leaned forward and lifted the lid on the bin to reveal a haphazardly stacked pile of scattered papers.

"I just sort of started tossing them into that box when they began coming in faster than I could read them, and then there got to be so many that I couldn't bring myself to start."

"Well," Sophia demurred, "good thing I got a comfortable seat to work from cause this is going to take more than one little train ride to the other side of the state to get straightened out."

"Oh, thank you, thank you," Heather said effusively. "I didn't realize how bad it had gotten till Fallon asked me about something I had no idea what he was talking about. Turns out it was patent papers that could have cost us millions if we'd have missed sending them in."

"You mean thousands, of course," Sophia muttered as she pulled the bin closer to the chair.

"No, I mean *millions*," Heather said. "Here, let me help you with some of that." Then she bent to help Sophia arrange the first handful of loose papers and Liam took that opportunity to casually head back to the Flatcar Saloon while both women were distracted.

"Liam, my boy, over here!" Liam could hear Blackie's voice and after shouldering between two large men, he saw his friend in the one-man bar he'd built in the center of the flatcar.

He waved, then worked his way between the revelers to the nearest edge to the standup bar.

"Here, here, make some room for Mr. Quinn. That's it, thank you fellers." Liam could hear the whispers moving out in a ripple as Blackie continued, "We've got whiskey and scotch and bourbon and *lots* of brandy, and we've got red and white wines, and another double handful of kegs of this fine ale." He patted the large keg that rested on a low enough platform Blackie could see the door to the next car back.

"I just ate breakfast," Liam said. "Ain't even halfway to lunch yet."

"Well, I ain't drinking either, but these folks paid good coin to party and now they getting everything they paid for," he gestured toward the three famous air wagons that circled the train station. Several people nearby pointed to sketches of those very same air wagons in the dime novels they carried.

Then he saw a woman looking from her novel and at him then back at her novel several times as her jaw dropped further and further.

"You might want to go find Miss Heather's arm to hold for protection, son," Blackie advised just as Liam noticed another woman eyeing him.

"Ah, speaking of which. Hello Miss Richards," Blackie exclaimed loudly as Liam sighed in relief. "Sorry, I would offer you a drink but Mr. Easton didn't seem to carry anything that didn't have a kick to it and we didn't get any mixes for ladies' drinks when we bought supplies today."

"No thank you, Blackie, we're flying," Heather answered gaily, then she moistened a handkerchief and dabbed at a smudge on Liam's cheek as she spoke, "I signaled Fallon and he's going to hop on down here and pick us up. Here he comes now."

To the defeated looks of one woman and the near swoon of another, she offered Liam her arm and he took it. They said their good-bye to Blackie and Liam walked her to the edge of the flatcar.

It took those on the flatcar a moment to realize what was happening as the two of them casually moved to the side of the car. When they reached the rail, four of Fleetfoot's men formed a casual cordon around Heather and him against the flatcar's side. As he scanned the area, he saw Earl sitting on top of the back end of the car ahead of the flatcar writing, and Samuel sitting on the top front of the car behind the flatcar sketching.

Looking up at the approaching balloon, they could see Fallon at the controls as he sat in the old tractor seat and flew toward the train. Everyone on the flatcar moved toward the sight they paid good money to see, causing the flatcar to lean toward that side. Then, as the heavy wood and metal flying balloon seemed to loom large, several of those pushing to get closer started moving away and the flatcar leaned the other way.

Fallon turned the pusher fans this way and that, to bring his air tractor alongside the flatcar with his forward deck in front of Liam and Heather as he coasted to a gentle bump against the rail. "Can I give you a lift?"

Chapter 43

Liam leaned on the rail of the forward deck – Maddy had them using nautical terms for uniformity – and watched the train pulling into the Cleveland rail yard below.

From their vantage point he could see a forest of smokestacks in one area, and a sea of coal cars in another. Another section had the newer locomotives that burned diesel gasoline instead of coal or wood and next to that group stood fuel tankers that were huge gas tanks like the kind of gas that burned in the lamps on the busiest streets of many large cities.

Each used a different fuel to burn, but they all used that fuel to create steam. Steam powered the world, not the wood or coal or gasoline or lamp gas that fueled each.

There were also a few that looked to be the same as the small ones underneath the original wagon, the kind that burned water to boil water for the steam that magery made so light. War had created a surge in inventiveness, and not just for new and better ways to kill other men.

There were other craft in the skies around them, all of them suspended below immense balloons of hot air, light gas, or the steam foam invented during the war. The difference was that with all of the other vehicles the balloons were huge in relation to the cargo being carried below.

Their three air vehicles were different. None that knew the history of flight had seen their like before. The structures they carried were as heavy as they looked and the balloons they were suspended beneath didn't look big enough to lift a horse much less a house.

As usual with nearly everyone they flew in sight of, fingers jabbed from the end of extended arms and shouts drifted up to them. They flew above a sea of pointing fingers.

"There's Fallon," Maddy said, pointing with her chin.

Sesco was taking a turn at the helm and flew them in a circle until Fallon came up alongside. Liam threw Heather a rope and she looped it over a cleat, then threw the end back and he pulled the two airships together. Maddy snagged the rail of Fallon's airship with one of the new hooks made just for that purpose when the two airships were close while airborne, and the waif held on as Heather crawled across the rails.

"Okay, I'm onboard," Heather said as she got her footing, a hand on Liam's arm for balance as the two airships bobbed.

Maddy unhooked from the rail of Fallon's airship, then used the small reverse hook to help push the airship away as Liam let out the rope he'd been pulling till the end flew through his fingers. As Sesco pulled one way, Fallon veered his airship the other, and the rope sang as it spun through the cleat and fell free to hang below. Liam began pulling it in and coiling it over the cleat on the rail as Sesco moved them toward home.

"Got the carpenters working on the new airship gondolas starting first thing tomorrow,"

Heather started without preamble. "The tentmakers were there and saw Fallon's airship's balloon and know exactly what he expects from them. They all say they can be finished in a week despite their trepidation the sizes aren't sufficient."

"I can't wait to see them all in flight," Liam said without a trace of doubt he wouldn't.

They hadn't had much opportunity to test the tinkered amulets and talismans Heather and Fallon constructed for his duel, but many of the components were among the first tinkered magery for the airships, he'd learned to use. The new suit was just an accumulation of most of what he'd already had experience with, just a bit more energetic than before.

He wore the full suit and practiced the muscle memory of its weight while reaching for and drawing specific charms or amulets all day. The exercise of running from one end of the airship to the other and back again and crawling over the new frame around the outer hull was much needed after the change this morning. By lunch he was having fun and by the middle of the afternoon he was ready to take a break from constant practice.

Heather jumped to Fallon's airship during lunch to go ahead while Liam continued to practice, pushing himself hard till he started making fatigue mistakes. One poorly thrown dart ricocheted and flew over the rail instead of into it to land in the bar of the Flatcar Saloon chugging along below them at the time.

Blackie got several ridiculous offers for the souvenir but messaged he would return the dart when able.

Liam knew when to quit and when they came to the Cleveland rail yard, wore a clean shirt under the rain slicker battle coat when Heather jumped back aboard.

They turned northwest and stayed low as the Cleveland skyline began to reveal Erie Lake, one of the seven Grand Lakes stretching from the thousands of interconnected fingers of Minnesota Lake halfway across the country to the massive Hudson Lake that fed into the Atlantic at North, Central, and South Hudson Falls.

"Ohh, it's beautiful," Heather said as they came up over the city proper to see Erie Lake over and through the Cleveland skyline.

Liam had to agree, and all the more so because he recognized these waters. His eyes found the docks his father always used when coming here. There was the shack where he lost his virginity two months after his first change and over there was where he saw his two younger brothers on their way to school. Before their first year was over, they were embroiled in the war, one fighting for the south and the other for the north.

Neither had come home from the war. As far as anyone knew they were buried in one of the hundreds of mass graves or their bodies lay undiscovered near one of the thousands of battlefields. Changelings were highly prized as scouts during the war, but their lives were valued more as mounted trophy heads, pelts, teeth, and claws to whoever on the opposing side caught them.

The three airships flew directly over Cleveland's main street, and Sesco let loose with their horn, steam shooting forward like the breath of a dragon. The other two airships quickly responded and all three bugled their calls with breaths of steam as they crossed from above land to over water with pusher fans on high speed.

They turned more to the west and flew on across the open waters of the Grand Lake. After a few minutes Liam lifted a hand to point. "There, that crooked line on the horizon."

Heather watched the crooked line begin to grow upwards till it was a definite thick line. There were dozens of ships in the water below – from small one-man rowboats or sailing skiffs on up to sleek three-masted tallships. There were even a few balloons in the distance taking advantage of the early evening calm, but none had as large a passenger cabin below as theirs.

Liam's heart began to race as the line thickened to the point he could see the difference between the trees and the limestone cliffs and narrow beaches on the southeast side of the island. The rest of the island sat on a ragged shelf of limestone jutting an average of between thirty and forty feet above the lake's normal highwater level.

"There, see to the right," she followed the line of his finger. "That's the tip of the tail. We just call it Tailtip. The entire tail is about a mile long, maybe a little less. The main house is on the cove side at the base of the tail. If you keep looking, you'll see the top of the lookout tower over the trees, there, see it?"

"Yes, thatched roof?"

"Yes, from water level it just looks like part of the forest canopy. Sure does look vulnerable from up here."

She turned and smiled at him. "No more than from anyone else except from the air, and only those from ground level who know it is there, *will* know. Fallon and I saw two days' worth of papers with our story filling up to two pages, and details like that are kept confidential."

"Earl and Samuel are getting some good coverage with their by-lines and those dime novels they're printing by the hundreds. That level of detail of your eagle's nest wouldn't be in their reporting."

Sesco steered them around south of the island to give Orlagh and Liam a first long view of home after a year away seeking a cure for their curse. As they came in close enough to see individual trees, he turned on a southwest heading and skirted the southeast corner of the island.

"See!" Liam pointed. "It looks like a puma about ready to pounce except you can tell it's not an aggressive pounce because the tail is straight up."

Heather tilted her head and smiled. "Could also be a sleeping cat that just got scared out of one of its lives."

Liam swatted playfully at her and they swayed together as a gust of wind caught their airship.

"Sorry Ma'am," Sesco apologized. "Not used to air currents around islands and warm waters."

She smiled at the pilot, then up at Liam, then reluctantly moved away from his embrace to lean again on the rail.

"There's the dock," Liam resumed the aerial tour. "Hunh, it's about three times as long as it was last year. That wooden pier is new too."

He pointed again. "All those buildings going up are new. Look at that! Three, four, five, seven, nine new buildings under roof in one year. Ma and Pa must have started soon after Orlagh and I left seeking the cure for our curse."

"There are another half dozen with at least one story finished and another eight or nine foundations being leveled," Heather commented as Orlagh stood against the rail to better see the home where she had been born and raised for the first twenty three of her twenty four years.

"Pa said in one of his lengthier wires he was building a one street village facing the south shore," Liam gestured at exactly that facing them as they skirted the south edge of the island at a half mile above the water.

"That's at least twenty three, twenty-four buildings for a main street for sure and they don't look like small buildings," Liam continued to tell them what they could all see. "All the ones I see are at least four stories, or will be."

Heather pointed as they drifted along the southern coast of Puma Island. "See that line there where the trees thicken again? That looks like where the village buildings will stop. I see three of those big mansion hotels with one community floor and three apartment floors above that. They might have open space and trees between them but they'll hold a lot of people. And look, there are already residential homes going up in two lines behind the main street. Your Pa sure is showing Hammersmith he wasn't going to get a peacefully uninhabited retirement home if he won their battle."

Liam looked on with both horror and elation. Horror the privacy he had known since birth was being invaded and elation his father and mother had come up with such a fitting claw in the eye to the mage that cursed them. It was all they could do because the mage remained anonymous, until the godstone necklaces they wore returned their sentience and they were able to *know* the scent of their torturer.

Until Liam crossed paths with Master Mage Hammersmith in Cincinnati, the Quinn family only knew they were cursed, not by whom. Now they did. There was no mistaking the scent. Each of the four of them smelled it from the beginning to the end of their forced changes every full moon.

Before they had gotten their godstone necklaces to at least give them their sentience during their time in forced change, they would never remember that scent or its relevance. But with the necklace amulets they all wore, they *did* remember.

And in his arrogance Hammersmith wanted to stand face to face with one of his victims and have that victim not know who he was. He hadn't known about the side effect of the amulet, only what it did, but that still didn't break the curse and being long lived, he could just wait for the four of them to die of old age or the effects of violent times.

Now he was undone, exposed and openly accused as a dark mage. The epithet was bandied about loosely by those that didn't know what magery was or feared it so much they needed all magery to be dark. He might be able to legally eliminate the stain to his honor by killing Liam, but there would still be three Quinns alive that all knew his dark secret.

And they had already spread that word to the four winds through the words and sketches of two mulatto boys with a dream realized decades sooner than expected.

Sesco flew them around the southwest corner, the part Liam assured them was the front legs of a crouching puma, and headed north along the western shoreline.

"There are a couple more buildings out this way but they're not as tall, only a couple of stories, but they all have those rooftop gardens," Heather commented as she pointed toward the ground. "And I think I see a big loop turnaround in the road."

They came in closer as the shoreline edged further west but Sesco maintained a due north heading. They crossed the westernmost point of the crouching front legs of the cat-shaped island and came back over water as the shoreline now ran in an easterly drift off of due north.

"Doesn't look like much of a head from this angle." Heather teased but Liam wasn't taking the bait.

They continued to loop around and he pointed. "Sandy Cove. Twenty, twenty-five yards wide, mile long white sand beach with a smooth bottom no more than six feet deep out almost two hundred yards from the shore. Best swimming beach in the whole world."

He watched it from a new angle, memorizing the new perspective with focused intensity.

"Well?" she asked.

"Yes, it's working," Liam replied. "Everything is really full of detail and I can barely talk slow enough for you to understand. You can, can't you?"

"Yes," Heather replied. "You sound a little wooden, though. "If you have to talk to anybody while hypering they'll know something is wrong, right, whatever."

"Won't need to talk to Hammersmith."

Heather made a wry face. "Point. Go ahead and drop hyper so you don't fall asleep."

"Sesco," Liam turned toward his friend as he dropped the hyper spell, then took a swallow of one of Fallon's energy drinks, "take us in a loop to the left around the main building there. There's a clearing east of the main house with a notch into the woods. Put her down on the north side of the notch with her nose toward the house. Signal the boxcar to set down south of us in the same orientation."

"Yes sir," Sesco replied as he looped the airship around to get the angle, then expertly vented foam as he spun the pusher fans in reverse and backed them down and into the cleared notch into the denser woods.

Liam prepared to go over the side in one of the rope slides Fallon had tinkered, watching the ground come up slowly as Sesco backed down and in. "My brothers and I used to play kickball on this field when we were restricted to the main grounds."

"Restricted?" Heather raised an eyebrow as Orlagh let out a feline chuckle

Liam glared at his sister. "We had free run of the whole island but we sometimes got bored and had fun with the neighbors."

"Neighbors? What neighbors? You lived alone with just the four of you. The nearest neighbors were on other islands... oh."

"Heh-heh, yes. We played tricks on the neighbors, things like sneaking boats out of one port and switching it with another boat in another port and not always on the same island. One time we spent an entire night pulling an otter's raft and hauled it all the way to the mainland swamps, with him sleeping on it. Took him half the day to figure out where he was and drag his raft back home."

"Cats tricking otters in the water was the most fun things we ever did, but we sometimes got caught," he said with a grin, then leapt over the side and played out his drop rope till he touched lightly on the soil of Puma Island just as he ran out of rope.

After more than a year... he was *home*.

Chapter 44

He didn't have time to enjoy the feeling as a gust of wind caught the airship and he had to pull hard to keep from being dragged to the side.

On the other end of the ship, Revis got a chance to ride-the-rope down to the ground and had done admirably. The two of them easily held the airship steady as they walked their ropes backwards. As soon as they reached the trees, both of them threw the end of their ropes around the trunk and tied them off. By this time Sesco had vented enough foam the airship's wheels were touching on the high side.

"Hold up!" Liam yelled. "Revis, release your rope so we can push them forward and out some where the ground's less sloped."

"Loosen my rope and follow your lead coming up," Revis called out happily.

The airship was still bobbing enough they were able to manhandle it forward and a little further from the trees where the ground was more level. "Okay Revis, that's good." Then he yelled up to the airship. "Set her down right there Mr. Lawson."

Sesco vented foam and the airship settled, its ground wheels groaning as they took the weight on their tinkered shocks. As soon as the wheels began creaking, Liam and Revis walked their ropes toward the airship as the boxcar troop ship began its approach.

They hurried over to help the boxcar but two crewmen had already rappelled down and were pulling the airship into a position to sit level and partially close off a private camp for the crew.

Liam watched for a few seconds, then turned to help on the ground as Orlagh was quickly lowered in a sling. When her feet touched, he loosened the sling and she darted out and ran around them and yipped her pleasure at being home then she walked up to stand beside Liam as she looked pointedly toward the main house.

Liam turned in that direction, and coming across the open field where they'd landed was his father and mother. His father was dressed in buckskin trousers and a hemp-cloth button-down shirt, while his mother, like his sister, was in full puma form. They still walked regally, side by side as they approached their surviving children.

Liam put his hand on his sister's head as she pushed up next to his leg, then Heather was standing next to him on his other side and one step behind. Fallon was standing behind and beside Orlagh in the same supportive position.

Liam stood tall as his parents walked toward the four of them. They stopped in front of Liam and Orlagh, the two cats purring and gazing into each other's eyes. Liam locked eyes with his father's.

"Father, we are home."

"Son, daughter, welcome home." Then the tightness left both men and they embraced while the two pumas beamed feline smiles and rubbed heads.

"Father," Liam said when they finally quit pounding each other on the back and grinning like fools. "I would like you to meet my very good friends, Miss Heather Richards and her brother, Mr. Fallon Richards. Miss Heather, Fallon, this is my mother, Sinead Quinn and my father, Dillon."

"Mother, father, these are the two people who have made it possible for us to break this curse and begin to grow our family like you intended when you and father made your wedding vows."

Dillon held up a dime novel with a wry grin. The three airships behind him were drawn in detail on the cover. "We know. Couldn't do it a little quieter, eh?"

Liam blushed as the boxcar's crew scampered around behind them securing the airships. Fallon had the great idea to send somebody north with the Martin boys' findings. The presence of the latest version of their odyssey in his father's hands told him Fleetfoot's chosen pilot had arrived safely. "Uh, well sir, uh things kind of got a little interesting there and we had to do *something*."

He looked sheepish but his father simply shook his head and laughed. "Yer Ma and I couldn't begin to count the number of times we've heard those *exact* same words as soon as we asked you about certain things you and yer brothers done."

Dillon looked at Heather. "Welcome to our home Miss Richards, Mr. Richards."

"Thank you, Mrs. Quinn," Heather gave a slight bow to Sinead in her full puma shape, *then* to Dillon, "Mr. Quinn. We thank you for your hospitality."

She gestured toward the three airships. "I hope we are not intruding *too much* on your idyllic privacy. Our people will try to be unobtrusive till you can give us a more remote spot to moor while we help Liam prepare for his duty."

Dillon frowned. "Your mother and I have talked about the wires you sent, well, I talked, she signed then we swapped twice." He looked at Sinead and Orlagh with loving eyes. "Although we agree your challenge was reckless, the publicity created by your two writers," he opened the dime novel to a page near the end and held it up for them to see, "has put our island, and your challenge for the entire nation to witness."

The picture sketched on one page was of the table full of people at the restaurant in Cincy and the text on the other page proclaimed Liam's Formal Challenge word for word.

He turned to Fallon. "Mr. Richards, the man you sent is in town showing off that wonderful flying system you tinkered. He sold out of the dime novels he carried in addition to that thick mail packet he delivered directly to Puma Island's new Post Office."

Fallon nodded his thanks as Dillon turned back to his son. "Your mother and I had already begun the process of relinquishing a considerable portion of our privacy but we encountered some resistance in certain business communities."

"Hammersmith!" Liam spat.

Dillon nodded assent. "The Hammersmith Family is quite extensive. You met just one son of the Patriarch of the Cleveland branch while he was visiting the Cincinnati branch. Pittsburgh, Chicago, and Boston all have their own Hammersmith

Houses that are larger than both Ohio Houses, but the largest House is in northern New York, state, not city. There are at least nine other small Houses that are just getting started west and south."

Liam pursed his lips in consternation as his father continued, "We didn't find out about the source of the interference at first, not till after that resistance evaporated, right about the same time as this came out," he waved the dime novel at the page with the sketching of the Challenge. "I doubt if anyone in the Family even knew why our projects were put on a Family *do-not-assist* list. Just that it was."

Sinead let out an impatient snarl.

"Oh my! Where are my manners?" Dillon exclaimed and gave a slight bow to Heather as he gestured. "We can talk in the house. Come, come, and please be welcome in our home."

As they walked to the house a couple hundred yards away, he continued talking. "Like I said, the trouble started almost immediately. At first, we couldn't find someone reputable to come out here and survey the south shore to see if that would be the best place to build a village. Then the people we hired started having trouble getting any other contracts and other contractors started backing out."

He shook his head as they walked. "What we finally had to do was expand our limestone quarry and offer building sites for free to anyone that could pay for the rest of the building costs up front."

He smiled wryly. "We actually ended up with about six times more applications than we had spots offered, both business and residential. After we received your information through that air mail flyer, we found out that more than half of those applications were submitted by people with close Hammersmith connections."

Liam scowled and gritted his teeth as he let his breath out through his nose then breathed in slowly to calm himself as Orlagh's tail lashed angrily.

"We checked with our lawyers and construction hadn't reached the point where we couldn't cancel the parcels that were already paid for if no construction had begun. But we still ended up with three Hammersmith parcels, one business and two residential parcels that were too far advanced to legally cancel."

They neared the first ring of low walls that surrounded the main yard of the sprawling Puma House and both pumas jumped the step ahead of the rest. The walls were short and did nothing more than arc between high points and had been back-filled to create patches of level grass leading up to the main house. Each arc wrapped around the house was about twice the height of a normal stair step and covered two or three dozen square yards of manicured grass bordered by landscaping of shrubs or flowerbeds.

"Luckily, before we even got your information, part of every contract we wrote for the village investors included the stipulation they had to build all outer walls with limestone from our island's quarry and interior walls with wood from the land we cleared for the village," Dillon continued as they mounted the last pair of steps to the entry patio.

"In the meantime, some, not all, but some of the contractors that wouldn't talk to us before, are sending people to apologize after finding out they were unknowingly abetting a dark mage." He chuckled. "Seems they want to make it up to us by cutting their profit margin if we won't talk bad about them for being duped by Hammersmith influences. Told them no."

"You told them no?" Heather asked with some surprise.

"Yep!" Dillon exclaimed. "Told them I'd still pay them my original offer as long as they guaranteed a quality job, half up front and half after completion if I'm satisfied. Also said I would *publicly* answer any question about reactions to Hammersmith influences with the truth as I see it. Have more respect for a man that can admit a pressured mistake and go on, than one that would pay to hide their mistake by fancy words."

Heather nodded appreciatively.

"Here we are," Dillon said as they reached the wide patio that wrapped around the main house. He grabbed the doorknob and opened one of the two wide doors to the interior.

They trooped inside the main building, a tower of native limestone that rose four stories but only contained three actual floors. The bottom floor was two stories high and open for most of the diameter of the tower except for a ring of closets, bookshelves, and cozy little niches that might be relaxing for any feline, many of them located on top of bookshelves and closets. One of the ground floor niches contained a large couch beneath its wide window.

As they entered, Dillon gave his new guests the tour. "This is the main sitting room and there are two more floors above. Orlagh's wing goes that way, north parallel with the beach, and Liam's goes just a bit south of due east toward the eastern cliffs a couple hundred yards away. They used to share with their younger brothers, but Leander and Dalton never came home from the war."

His face was haunted for a moment before he continued, "Come this way and I'll show you the lookout tower."

He resumed his earlier topic as they climbed the series of stairs and puma friendly ramps around the fifty-foot room. "After your challenge and the revelations the Hammersmith Clan of Mages was responsible for our curse, we've had rival Mage Clans offer to help us, but we're not sure we need to get involved in mage politics in addition to our curse, my apologies Miss Richards," he bowed slightly in Heather's direction.

"No apology needed, Mr. Quinn," she gave a slight bow in return. "I am fully aware of the dangers of mage politics as my entire life was molded around the effects of their version of compromise and accountability."

Dillon nodded in understanding. "We were able to acquire the assistance of some low-level mages without too much of a problem before your discovery of our curse's source, but all of them were scared away by what they found."

He flicked his necklace. "These were the only successes we've had in over a decade of torture."

"I'm sure my brother and I can more than make up for any assistance you have lacked due to Hammersmith interference," Heather assured them as they passed through the door that led up to the roof. "Oh my, what a beautiful view!"

"It's a lot better up there but I don't go up often since I can't share it with my wife," he pointed to the lookout tower then looked at the puma standing on her back feet with front paws holding her head above the wall around the roof – her daughter beside her doing the same. "Come on up if you think you can make it." He began climbing the ladder up the side of the two-story lookout tower.

The rest followed and when they crowded inside the walled circle, Liam let his father proudly continue the tour without his contributions. "The tail of the island goes up that way," he pointed north. "You can see the lake on both sides all the way till it flares at the end about a mile away."

He turned to the left and pointed. "That's Sandy Cove with the head on the other side," he said as he continued his turn. "The main quarry is over that way, and that way is the village and the docks. You can't really see much from here except the tops of the trees at the edge of the island. There are two spots, there and there, where enough trees were cut down you can see the chimneys of some of the mostly finished buildings. We saved only the best lumber and used the rest for the village."

Fallon didn't bother trying to see with his natural sight, knowing changeling sight was better, and whipped out a looking glass. Heather raised her hands in front of her face with fingers and thumbs bracketing a circle a half foot in diameter and chanted the air to form a natural magnifying lens.

Liam looked with the rest. He had experienced this view his entire life and could easily see the difference. There were several of the largest trees that were missing from the horizon he remembered. And the chimneys were not all he could see that were different.

"Is that Fleetfoot's airmail carrier?" Heather wondered, just as they all recognized the object that came up over the tree line and headed in their direction.

It took only moments for Heather to let her air lens dissolve and Fallon to lower and collapse his looking glass. With only a little more than a mile of forest to cross, the flyer came into shouting distance within a couple of minutes.

The godstone saturated canvas balloon was not much longer than a tall man, seven feet, and just two and a half in diameter. The gondola below it held a reclining seat in the middle for the pilot's comfort and a cargo basket in the front with the steam engine and steam powered pusher fans behind the pilot's seat. Twin pontoons gave it a stable landing base on land or water.

The craft had carried copies of all of Earl and Samuel's research on the Hammersmith Clan's public notice from Cincinnati to Puma Island in a night flight before they left for Cleveland escorting the train. His father was reading about their findings at the same time the air and rail convoy left Cincinnati.

Liam leaned over the mid chest high wall around the lookout tower as the flyer swerved to the east so as to come in against the wind.

"Sir! I stayed in town tah git a feel of what the locals was saying when they saw the fleet circlin' 'em," the pilot called out immediately. "Seems there was a whole boatload of new people come in on this mornin's ferry and another half dozen fishing boats with more'n twice the crew numbers they needed. They's all down at the docks agitatin' people and they's all carrying torches and ropes and guns just like changeling and slave lynch mobs before the war."

"That didn't take long," Liam commented. "Wilson, right? Cobb Wilson?"

"Yes, sir, Cobb Wilson, sir!"

"Okay, Mr. Wilson, here's what I want you to do." Liam pointed. "Pop on down there and tell everybody to prepare to launch. Tell them I'm declaring riot control status and outfit six men in full combat gear to remain here on the ground and defend the house from any and all unwanted intruders. Defend only and do not fire unless fired upon. I expect everybody to be ready to cast off mooring lines by the time I get down there."

He turned to his father as the pilot simply spun his aircraft and jammed the fans on full power as he vented steam to drop lower. "Our people will manage things here with directions from mother and

Orlagh but you'll need to come with us because they know you."

Deferring to his son's authority, Dillon simply nodded and they followed the others, already at the bottom of the ladder down to the roof.

Chapter 45

As they came in over the trees, they could see the gathering of loud people crowding around the base of the dock's main pier. There were several large fishing boats – some showing low maintenance and questionable appearance – docked along the pier and a crowd of men carrying staves and torches at the base of the pier. Another arc of people with shotguns and pistols and long handled fishermen's gaffs blocked them from leaving the pier.

Fallon brought his more maneuverable airship around and down by the docks behind the defenders and the rowdy *fishermen* and their supporters who'd secured the pier for the coordinated docking, began shouting louder. When the other two airships, bristling with armed men lining the decks, came over the trees in a delayed appearance the crowd of agitators broke off in shock, then resumed their shouting even louder.

Snipers on the decks of the airships marked the men that led the renewal of the yelling, then awaited orders.

Fallon brought his airship down with practiced ease. As the frame settled to the cobblestone of the street at the end of the docks, the troop ship took position two-hundred feet directly above the smaller airboat. The deck facing the crowd was lined with men sighting through the scopes of sniper rifles at the crowd, or down the lengths of odd tinkerings that *resembled* rifles of a strange sort.

Fallon set a last lever then rose from the pilot's seat to be quickly replaced by one of their best pilots from the troop ship. Fallon and Heather fell in behind and to the side of Dillon and Liam, and just as they got halfway, Sinead and Orlagh came dashing out of the woods and running up to join them.

Liam gave his mother and sister a look, but his father just chuckled. "Didn't think they'd listen to you. We're a family again, boy, time to stand up to what we face united and open to what we are."

Liam nodded in agreement then turned and set his eyes on the growling crowd of agitators.

As they came closer a man from the defending side separated and approached them. "Welcome home Liam, Orlagh. My name is Henri LaForte. I'm the owner of the General Store," he pointed in the general direction of the main street.

LaForte then turned to Dillon. "Mr. Quinn, sir, these *men* claim to be nothing more than tired fishermen looking for a port for the night before they sail up through the Grand Lakes back to their home port on Minnesota Lake. We told them the only accommodations are private homes that are more tents than houses and the quarters for the construction crews. They say they just want to have a couple of drinks at our saloon and they'll sleep in their boats. Say they know we have a saloon 'cuz they heard it from another fisherman."

Dillon looked at his son and shrugged. "I like a good card game every once in a while, and a man can't play cards without wetting his whistle with his winnings. I needed a place for the crew expanding the pier so I built the saloon and hotel. Hired a couple of fellas to brew me a good ale and their wives cook for the hotel. It isn't the only saloon and we've only got nine finished buildings."

"We told 'em we ain't lettin' 'em off the pier, Mr. Quinn," LaForte continued. "They ain't fishermen and we told 'em so, but they won't change their story. Told 'em again, they can dock but they can't leave the pier, but they's insistin' they be able to go to the saloon and get a hot meal like other fishermen brag is so good."

"Okay, Henri, thank you. I'll see what I can do."

They made their way the last few yards to the confrontation and the crowd of defenders melted aside to let them through. The false fishermen started to surge forward at the breech, but came up short when faced with two pumas in full beast form and four people in human form.

The agitators outnumbered the six by more than seven to one, and they and the defending construction crews and new residents put together by at least two to one. But the confidence of the four humans and two pumas made the agitators pause long enough for the crowd to reform behind them.

One man stepped forward from the rest. "You the cat what claims he owns a whole town, and kin tell folk they can't visit public businesses?"

"No, I'm not."

The man looked startled and confused for a moment. "What? You mean we can go into town?"

"No. What I mean is, I *am* the cat that *does* own the whole town until each building is completed and the new owners have paid for it in full, and that *my* village is in fact *not* a public town as yet. As a *privately owned* community, we can, and do, claim the right to deny entry. As any maritime community, we do, though, hold to maritime courtesies. Therefore, you will be allowed to dock for the night for your safety."

He gave the big man a penetrating look. "It would be criminal of me to send you out on the lake at night with storms brewing since you are so clearly not a fisherman."

"You callin' me a liar," the burly man bristled and the crowd behind him growled.

Dillon smiled as Heather softly chanted a shield she could throw up in a heartbeat if the agitators surged forward. "Any good fisherman, whether sail or steam, knows his knots. Tell you what, have one of your men go get a ten-foot length of shoreline and show me some knots and I'll let you into town."

The man glared at Dillon, then those beside him, then at the grinning faces of the townies blocking whatever he had planned. After a moment he gestured to another man and whispered to him frantically and pushed him toward the boats docked at the end of the large pier. The second man ran to one of the boats and disappeared inside and moments later came back with a coil of rope and a knife.

"Ten feet ya say," the burly *fisherman* sneered.

"That's *rope*," Dillon said patiently and the sound of stifled snickers could be heard from the crowd behind them as the majority tried hard to keep straight faces. "I said shore-*line*. Tell you what, you bring me a ten-foot length of shoreline and you won't even have to do any knots."

"Bring you ten feet of shoreline and we can go into town?" The man was suspicious.

"On my Honor," Dillon proclaimed seriously. "You bring me a single, unbroken ten-foot length of shoreline before sunset and I'll buy your first two drinks. Don't bring it before sunset and you agree to stay on the pier or leave if you think you're waterman enough to deal with lake storms."

The man spat in his palm and thrust his hand out. Dillon spat and seized it in return and easily resisted the pure human's attempt to crush his hand. Then the man turned on his cohorts and after brief consultation three of them went to three different boats. After a few minutes of waiting and conspiratorial whisperings and some open laughing among the townies two of the men returned with nervous looks.

They refused to say anything, just pointed to where the old captain owner of one of the boats in the supposed fishing fleet was pointing at the lapping water at the edge of the lake as he talked to the third man. The old man then took a shovel and made a line across the line of debris at the water's edge. He then paced off three normal walking steps and the length of one of his boots and made another cross line. Then he handed the shovel to the fake fisherman and walked away laughing loud enough everybody on the pier could hear him.

"You trying to make me look like a fool," the burly man was livid when he realized how he'd been exposed as a liar and a fraud.

There were more snickers from around them, as Dillon tried valiantly not to stab at the opening the man left.

Fallon didn't have that ability and mumbled too loud in the ensuing silence. "Doing pretty good all your own rockhead."

Liam stepped forward just as the man took a breath to explode and began to step forward. The two of them came up face to face with only inches between and he spoke before the other could. "Sir, you and your *associates* have been proven no fishermen and we have informed you this is still private land and you are not invited to visit."

"Some of you carry weapons," he pointed at the staves several of the men carried, "and others carry torches. Combined with your deception it can only be suspected you have more than a normal sailor's shore leave planned."

He threw a thumb over his shoulder. "There are three snipers on the deck of the airship behind me and seven more on the one over the road leading into town."

A few of the men in the crowd began to look nervous and some of them at the rear of the pack began to move closer to the docked boats behind them.

They hadn't noticed that Fallon had been signaling the two airships and were surprised when

Liam turned his back on them and even more so at his words. "You people can either go back to what you were doing or stay and watch the show, but if you stay, I need you to move back a little so you don't get mistaken for a target. That's it, the rest of you get completely off the pier, now please."

The fake fishermen were caught off guard and Liam cleared a space between the two groups over ten feet wide when they reached the spot where the pier and the rest of the dock met. Before anyone could react three thumps blew bullet holes in a line across the dock end of the pier. The troop ship was not that far away and the rifle cracks were fairly loud and right behind the loud impacts. Almost immediately another three shots poked holes in the planking two full strides away from the first line.

"This is private property and you are not welcome," Dillon's voice boomed loudly in the silence as he pointed at the six bullet holes. "The area inside those six holes represent *no man's land*. Any man stepping into that six-foot wide boundary, from either direction, will be shot dead, no questions asked."

"We would prefer you leave but since you arc obviously not watermen, we do not want to be responsible for sending you out on the lake at night with possible storms coming, so you may remain docked till morning. But remember, the men in those airships have the ability to see at night well enough to pick you off one at a time even if cloud cover blocks the light of the waning moon."

"Oh, and I shouldn't have to warn you but seeing you up close I feel I must. If you stay, those men watching you tonight will also shoot anyone seen causing damage to the pier." He started to turn away then turned back. "Also, a handful of our otter friends from a neighboring island have agreed to sleep under the dock this one night in exchange for one of the hotel's soon-to-be-famous fish platters for each of them. We told them they could play with anyone they find under the pier or docks tonight."

He smiled devilishly. "Don't know if you know it or not, but if otters don't take kindly to someone, they tend to play *rough*."

Dillon gave them one last beaming smile. "I would advise not giving the otters or my son's snipers a reason to find fault with your actions. Otherwise, have a nice night."

He turned his back on them and shooed the watching townies. Most of them did return to interrupted activities but a few stayed as obvious guards in addition to the floating airship. The fake fishermen returned to their boats and all but two of them released mooring lines and sailed or steamed away.

The townies had only partially dispersed when the two remaining captains came back out on the pier and stood at the edge of no man's land. Curious, Dillon went back to talk to the old man that had shown the fake fisherman where to get ten feet of shoreline.

The old man one-eyed them suspiciously then stuck his hand out in a belated greeting. "Bjorn Torhild."

He jerked his head in the direction of the woman beside him. "Millie Eriksson. You those people we bin readin' 'bout, ain'cha? The ones what chased that murderin' railroad man halfway 'cross the country an' kilt him and his devil mage?"

"Yep, that's us!" Fallon blurted with a laugh. "Regular Sky Rangers is what we are!"

"Told you Millie."

Then the old man's brows creased. "Don't recollect no mention of sky rangers in the newspapers or those dime novels coming out, though. But no matter, Millie and I bin a bit down on our luck the past couple of years what with bigger companies chasing little boats like us outta the best fishing spots."

He jerked a thumb at the departing boats. "Was hired to carry a bunch of men from Cleveland to Puma Island. Millie heard about Puma Island building its own fishing village and thought maybe we could get work here after we delivered our cargo of workers."

At the raised eyebrows, he explained, "That was what they told *us* they were, new workers hired for security and labor. Looked the part so we didn't turn down the money." He frowned. "But half of expected pay is still better than nothing and we did get the half up front to bring 'em here."

He smiled through a half-dozen remaining teeth. "Ten feet of *shoreline*?" He cackled and slapped his leg while Millie just shook her head and chuckled ladylike.

Both were tanned and their leathery skin roughened by decades on the lake. Both their boats looked older than they did.

When the old fisherman caught his breath, he said, "Just thought we'd tell ya those folks was talkin' 'bout comin' back around t'other side of tha island and *'finishing tha job we was paid fer'* in the exact words of tha man in charge of tha *job* they was hired tah do."

He looked at the sky and sniffed. "Gonna be a big one 'bout midnight or so."

He looked at them with a big smile. "Bit of otter blood back a couple of generations gave me good weather sense and really good hearing." He breathed in deeply and back out again. "Don't mind if we accept tha offer of a dock ta tie up through tha storm tonight. Bin a long day and I am a bit tuckered and don't feel like fighting tha lake when she's of a stormy mood."

Liam smiled and looked at his father and Dillon offered, "You want to come into town? The hotel really does make an excellent fish platter as well as several other kinds of dishes. We have a native deer that is good and we get bison from the mainland on a regular basis. We also have pigs and cows and chickens so the choices are not limited."

"Appreciate tha offer, but we'll probably fix something together and turn in early," the old sailor replied with a sideways look at the old woman standing next to him. She blushed and leaned to brush his arm softly.

"As you wish," Dillon replied. "We'll still leave the ground guard in case the others come back, and the otters will still be under the dock. Thank you for the warning. We'll send one of our airships up for sky watch in case they do try to come ashore somewhere else."

The old man looked at the sky and sniffed again. "Otter blood never wrong. Mebbe you should land yer sky boats a'fore the storm hits. Gonna be a doozy wit lots of lightnin'. Yer sky boats take lightnin'?"

Liam didn't know and looked at Fallon who shrugged. "The only storms we saw so far were just rainstorms, no lightning except that one and we were on the ground in a forest and no lightning hit close so we couldn't test my lightning rods. Don't know if they work or not. Theory is sound but no actual strike yet to see if we get fried or not."

He stroked his chin as several sets of eyebrows were raised. "Godstone should absorb any lightning but I don't know if it'll find a human body to go through somewhere along the way."

He turned to Heather. "You have any ideas?"

She thought about it for a few seconds. "I think so. There are two spells I can chant that should shoot the lightning away from the railcar underneath the balloon." She thought for a bit more. "Yes, two of my chants on the rods you already put in, interwoven with a connector syllable should be more than enough to protect the crew. The rods we've always used should be enough but can't believe we never thought about it more than that before."

"You that good, girl?" Millie wondered as Fallon shrugged. "Mebbe you could teach me a couple of chants to make old bones less stiff in the mornin'?"

Heather smiled. "Yes, Millie, I could. In fact, why don't I do that now? I thought I felt a little bit of ability in you, plenty to learn a memory chant and use it to memorize a handful of others."

"Handful?" Millie wondered as Heather stepped across no man's land and took her arm and walked her back to her boat. "I can learn more than one?"

The two women walked away and the old man watched lovingly. "She hurts so bad some mornings its almost high sun before she can even lift anchor or untie a mooring line. Little pain relief would sure make her last days less of a chore."

"That offer of a meal still holds," Dillon said. "For both of you, even if you wait till breakfast to take it."

"Mebbe Millie and I will make it fer breakfast," the old man mused thoughtfully. "Been a while since we had a real sit-down meal together at a table what didn't sway with the waves." He looked Dillon in the eyes. "If your boy's mage can ease Millie's pain enough to walk to the hotel before high noon we'll be there."

"Good!" Dillon smiled. "And while you're there we'll talk about hiring you and Millie to fish the designated private fishing grounds a mile out in any direction from the shore of Puma Island."

The old man tried unsuccessfully to hide his instant interest. It would be the perfect place to fish the last years of his life with the woman he loved, who seemed to love him in return. He and Millie would have access to *prime* private fishing grounds they *couldn't* be chased from, wouldn't have to go far to get to a safe port, and wouldn't take nearly the effort of just staying alive in the waters around Cleveland.

"I'm sure Millie and I will be eager to hear what kind of offer might get us to leave the Crooked River watershed," he tipped his wide brimmed hat. "Mr. Quinn." Then he turned and meandered back to his boat.

"Well, I don't know about the rest of you, but I want to check out this fish platter everybody's talking about," Liam declared. "Heather's going to be an hour or more if I know her, making sure Millie is proficient in her healing magery. By then she'll be hungry too, and we can start planning for my duel while she eats."

Chapter 46

"I hear only the two largest of the five boats of our visitors from yesterday made it back to port," Liam said conversationally as he held his arms out to the sides.

"Yes," Fallon replied as he checked another set of tinkerings on the new battle suit. "There! That should be the last one, see if it moves easier. The troopship lost them when the worst part of the storm hit. The winds were so strong the airship barely made it back to port themselves. Wouldn't have if it hadn't been for the lightning rods keeping those three strikes away from the crew."

Liam moved in the hand fighting motions he had practiced since he was a cub. "Feels good, so good I don't really feel it any more. Do I finally get to check it out for real?"

Fallon pursed his lips. "We're in the middle of a private island a mile from any shoreline or prying eyes with a private airship guarding the sky above us. I think we're safe from the eyes of any Hammersmith spies."

Liam smiled as he loosened up inside the special suit his friends had tinkered and charmed together to keep him alive against a powerful dark mage. The *suit* was nothing more than a series of joints and hinges connected by wires, cables, and steam-actuated pulleys and pistons that looked too flimsy to bear their own weight, much less add to the wearer's strength. But the flimsy look was belied by the twin facts of being made mostly of godstone and infused with magery.

Liam donned the rest of his clothing over the suit and the equally augmented rain slicker and performed some more physical motions to feel comfortable with the full extent of his movements, then smiled. "How do I look?"

Fallon shrugged as Heather commented, "I can see it in magery sight, and I can see you look *bigger*, but that's only because I know your true size."

Liam nodded. "Good enough. Okay, let's do this." He moved around a little more, then stepped over opposite to where Heather moved as he pulled the tinkered goggles over his eyes. "Okay, I'm ready to…"

And Heather shot him with a spell he'd never encountered and everything went black.

There was pain, then again, then he narrowed it down to his head, then his face, then Heather slapped him again. "Come on Liam wake up. Come on just a little bit more."

He tried to speak and it came out as a rough growl. He tried to swallow and that didn't work either, then he felt sweet wetness cleanse his throat of the fire that filled it. "There you go, just a few drops, not too much," Heather's voice was soothing.

"So, you didn't kill him?" Fallon's voice made Heather clench him tightly for a moment.

Heather almost sobbed. "He said he was ready and that meant he'd chanted the shields."

"*Was going to say, 'Okay, I'm ready to turn my shields on'*," he tried to say but it didn't seem to want to make it from his fuzzy brain to his mouth.

"Lucky you only chanted your attack at one third strength so he could see what it did better when it hit his shield," Fallon muttered. "But it gives me some ideas for some more tinkerings. Hey, Liam, you about ready to try again? I've got things to do and I still need to *see* the suit in real action."

Liam groaned and made an effort to rise but he felt as weak and limp as the time when Fallon had tested one of his tinkerings mixed with magery by shooting everybody and studying them to see how they were affected. It took him a couple of tries, but he finally made it to his feet.

The first thing he did was pull out one of the stoppered nutrition pouches from a coat pocket. He pulled the stopper and downed the liquid, replaced the stopper and put the empty pouch back in its pocket. Then he ate one of the grain, nut, and fruit squares that was soaked in honey to help pack the mixture into a solid cake. He pulled up his water flask and took a single swallow to rinse his mouth, then chanted his shield into place. "Okay, shields up, *now* I'm ready."

And Heather blasted him with yet *another* spell he'd never seen before. This time it splashed off his shield and he was able to *see* its structure due to the addition to the shield spell and the tinkered lenses in the goggles.

"Again," he said as he staggered backwards, then recovered, and Heather immediately shot him with the same spell again.

He watched the spell as it washed across his shield and used what he saw to devise a counter. Touching the proper amulet, he quickly chanted a defensive response that set up a counteractive resonance. The spell lashed out and wrapped around Heather's third attack and twisted it into shreds that quickly dissipated.

Then she attacked him again, this time with two spells chanted almost at the same time and within seconds he was returning fire with one counter while laying a shredder trap for the other. Heather cast the spells again and his counter shredded one into nothingness by converting it into something harmless while using the energy to help him throw the other back to its source with a small boost in strength. The returned spell bounced off Heather's shield.

"Excellent!" Fallon exclaimed as the two combatants turned to look at him with smiles. He locked eyes with his sister. "Would it have gotten through?"

"Yes," she confirmed. "If I hadn't already known it was coming it would have penetrated, not enough to do any harm, but more than enough for a distraction that could increase the probability of the *next* attack getting through deeper."

"Good, good," Fallon muttered. "Okay, we've sent all the required papers and gotten the proper responses, so the duel is definitely on."

Liam turned toward Samuel and Earl. "I want one of you in the air as quick as you can and the other one on the ground to meet our hosts' guests at the dock. Each of you will have to sketch and write both. Heather and I are going to the dueling arena and will meet the Guild observers and Hammersmith and his Second there. Then the Guild observers will inspect and secure the arena while my family tries to host Hammersmith and his people with *civility*."

Earl and Samuel both pursed their lips but didn't comment. Everyone had gotten a surprise in the crash course in Guild politics and couldn't believe the Quinn Family would have to *civilly host* Hammersmith and his Second and a minimum of three additional *guests*.

The Guild Observers would ensure the cordiality of the pre-duel banquet where both sides would have the chance to resolve their dispute. They would also ensure the sanctity of the dueling arena from sunset the night before till the time of the duel.

Liam looked at the angle of the sun, then at the twins. "Their ship should be arriving within the hour. I want you to witness all the way up to the banquet then I want you to deliver your sketches and words to the two printers we've chosen as soon as the banquet ends. One publisher will distribute locally and the other will ship all his copies east, south, and west on each mail train."

He gave a small shrug. "You should be back in plenty of time to witness the duel, then you can write up a special edition issue. I expect you'll have enough from sunrise to sunset to put out another whole issue."

He gave a wry smile. "If I don't like *that* issue, I might have to rethink our employer, employee relationship."

The two young men had grown relaxed enough they recognized the ironic joke. The only way he *wouldn't* like the next issue would be if he lost the duel, in which case he wouldn't be reading that issue.

"Oh, I'm sure you'll like it, Mr. Quinn," Samuel assured him. "Got some juicy information from a couple of sources we've already confirmed, will be of some help."

He pulled several papers from inside the shoulder bag of reporter's supplies he and his brother had begun carrying and handed them to Liam. "Got some things that have been verified by at least three written sources on the first page and information with two sources on the second page. The third page is a rough map of the U.S. and Canada where Hammersmith Houses are located and how many Family members live at each. The last page is the list of all the Hammersmith Houses and the names of every member we could identify and their primary duties. Mr. Rat has the same pages and said he would fill in any spots we missed as he gets new names."

Liam snorted a laugh as he looked at the third page. The *rough* map was so detailed every major city and town was placed where it belonged and to scale. The sections the two Martin boys had personally seen were sketched with forests, hills, waterways and railroad tracks all in remarkable detail for their small size. Then he looked at the last page and saw each House was ranked and who each Housemaster reported to in the overall, extended Family.

His Hammersmith was actually fairly low on the overall Family hierarchy, thirty-seventh in seniority by age and being only a level three Master, was forty-ninth in magery. Mr. Winchester Hammersmith was the youngest son of the Cleveland Hammersmiths and was forty-eight years old and still living at the Family mansion on the banks of the Crooked River.

Winchester Hammersmith had a wife and two children, both grown and also still living with their grandfather and grandmother in the Family mansion in Cleveland.

He also had two older brothers and two older sisters, the eldest twice his age, and all of them had wives or husbands, and children. There were even a handful of the next generation of Hammersmiths, and the paper Liam held indicated every one of the elder relatives had considerably more magery than he did without his tinkered augmentation.

He turned to the first two pages and read several entries while the two Martin boys waited patiently. "Good, good," he said with a smile. "This should give my father and me something to talk about during the banquet."

"Gonna make an enemy of the whole damn Cleveland Branch of the Family if you put even a tenth of that in the dime novels," Fallon observed as he read from beside Liam. He looked at the two young journalists then back at Liam, who pursed his lips in thought.

"We know they might come after us too," Samuel said as he lifted his chin in stubborn defiance. "That's the price of being a journalist. The truth is too important to be afraid of the revenge of power when their crimes are exposed. The Hammersmith Mages are not the only ones abusing their status."

"We found a number of links between the Hammersmiths and several other known names," Earl took over the revelations. "Names that are known to represent wealth and power many distrust due to nefarious actions alluded to with minimal proof of alliance. Their names seem to be linked all the way back to long before the war."

Samuel spoke as soon as his brother paused for a breath, "Some of the names on the first two pages are linked with the Hammersmiths since before their Clan Head fled their homeland in Europe nearly two hundred years ago."

He gestured toward the papers in Liam's hands. "His name is on the top of the list of names for the Catskill House north of New York City. Echhardt Hammersmith, two hundred thirty-four years old and one of the most powerful mages on the continent."

Fallon one-eyed Liam. "Your family couldn't have picked on just one mage with no Family like my sister and I, could you? Had to pick on a mage with a hundred vengeful relatives."

Ignoring Fallon's comment, Liam looked up at the angle of the sun, then at the Martin boys.

"You two go ahead and meet the envoy ship and do what it is you do best while I get in some last-minute training out of sight of prying eyes."

The two young men dashed off to witness the arrival of the steamer carrying the Hammersmiths and all their guests and the Guild representatives. Fallon and Liam and Heather relocated to the clawstones where they went through several more practice sessions with Heather throwing known and unknown spells at Liam in varying groups of two and three at a time to keep him in practice.

After an hour they stopped and Liam ate a prepared meal while Heather cleansed the arena of magery residues. Then she joined him as he sat on one of the ridges created by whatever had carved the clawstones.

She pointed as she spoke. "I think the little valley here in front of the clawstones will work best. What do you think?"

Liam scanned the area again. The two of them had run all over the thirty acres of Clawstone Park and he'd felt most comfortable in two spots. This one had the benefit of a natural stone formation that gave the park its name.

Local Natives said changeling gods sharpening their claws made the parallel grooves in the limestone bedrock of the island. University people like his father said rocks grinding away at the bedrock caused the grooves as they were carried along by a great blanket of ice from the north in the distant history of the island, like an enormous sheet of sandpaper.

Liam leaned toward the latter with a small voice reminding him the existence of some of the old gods had more than credible evidence despite what science claimed. And if the multiple proven evidences that many of the minor gods and demons surely existed, and in some cases still do, then why not an over-god like that of the three faiths that each believed in their individual, One True God.

The central area of Puma Island's, Clawstone Park consisted of a sixty-foot-high ridge that, from the air, looked like a long oval of stone seventy yards thick in the middle, thirty on either end, and a couple hundred long. The oval of scoured stone ran in a north south direction and was covered with grooved lines its full two-hundred-yard limestone length except for the central ridge at the top of the outcrop.

That top ridge had still been worn smooth but a ten-yard-wide strip at the highest point didn't have the claw marks of ancient changeling gods. Native Lore said that was because the ancient gods sat at either end of the main Clawstone when sharpening their claws and *of course* they didn't use the top of the stone ridge as they raked their claws along the sides to sharpen them.

To the east and west of the main clawstone ridge were similar outcrops that were not replicated on the respective east and west slopes. Longer than their central cousin, the three-hundred-yard long outer clawstones were just as high as the ridge they flanked by fifty yards to each side.

The result was a natural amphitheater that was over two hundred yards long and a hundred fifty yards wide with the main clawstone sitting in the center.

They chose the side with no trees as the *official* dueling grounds on Heather's experienced advice and Liam did most of his practicing in that space since they'd arrived.

While he was contemplating the events that brought him to this spot, the horns sounded telling him the Hammersmith steamer was inbound to the dock. He took a deep breath, then disrobed and removed all of his tinkered magery, from the augmented rain slicker down to the skeletal godstone suit outside his smallclothes.

He was dressed again in normal clothing, except for a non-augmented rain slicker, when the Hammersmith retinue walked through the woodlands to the south of Clawstone Park a couple hours later. Taking a deep breath as Heather moved up beside him, he moved forward as Winchester Hammersmith walked toward him from the other end of the natural arena.

Dozens of people walked with Hammersmith while he had only his mother, father, sister, and Fallon behind him, and his Second beside him.

Then a portion of those with Hammersmith split away from the central group, fanning out to either side in a flanking move.

Chapter 47

"Guild reps," Heather whispered. "They will move in ahead of us and then the two duelists will advance and be introduced and the Challenge voiced aloud for witnessing."

Liam nodded as they walked toward the center of the East Arena. The Guild men and women, five to each side, stopped at almost the exact center of the open space. Even without his tinkered magery, Liam could feel the magery being expended as the Guild scanned for evidence of the breaking of Guild Law.

It bolstered Fallon's contention that magery could be learned and small potential increased through augmented use over time.

As they grew closer, the magery focused on him and those with him. Heather advised him the Hammersmith group would have already been scanned in this manner and he would get their *full* attention till both groups were in place.

The last few dozen paces were almost like walking through a crowd that moved slowly out of one's way, there was *some* resistance but it melted before steady pressure.

Following Heather's advice, Liam kept his eyes mostly on Hammersmith's Second. By Guild Law, as soon as they stopped walking *neither* of the two duelists was allowed to look at the other or their Second could interpret that as an attack and issue an immediate counter-attack. *After* he stopped walking, if Liam were to turn his eyes from those of

Hammersmith's Second, that one would be justified in immediately attacking Liam to defend the sanctity of the duel.

Heather would provide the countering defense of that sanctity by watching Hammersmith and killing him if he looked at Liam after they stopped.

Guild members watched all four to ensure the rules were kept... and would kill any of the four breaking those rules.

Liam and Heather walked at an even pace and he could see Hammersmith's face go red as they purposefully slowed that pace to make the Master Mage and his Second wait several seconds. They sauntered up slowly and Liam used the last few paces to openly study Hammersmith and the Guild observers.

Hammersmith's face grew redder and redder at the open taunt, as Liam and Heather measured their pace to make the challenged party wait. Liam especially noticed the interest shown by one of the Hammersmith party, a slight smile on his lips that was somehow different than the sneer on the faces of most of the others.

One step away from stopping Liam snapped his eyes to Hammersmith's Second's eyes and put on his poker face as he raised the personal shield that was all his natural abilities allowed. Heather had spent most of her time forcing him to improve on his natural abilities and proven to him that practice had increased the ease with which he used his tinkered magery augmentation.

Without hesitation the lead Guild observer said, "Master Mage Winchester Hammersmith of Hammersmith House, Cleveland, you have been presented with a *Formal Challenge* by First Level Novice Liam Quinn of Puma Island. Novice Quinn, you may present your challenge for witnessing."

Although the challenge was from Liam, he was not allowed to acknowledge the accused in this ceremony. His Second did that for him. "Novice Quinn accuses Master Hammersmith of using dark magery to curse his family with forced changes linked to the lunar cycle and with non-sentience during the forced beast form change."

"Novice Quinn further charges that Master Hammersmith has cursed his entire family for no other reason than personal gain in acquiring land ownership of the entirety of Puma Island," Heather continued. "Novice Quinn also accuses Master Hammersmith of magery torture since the Challenge was issued by using additional dark magery to inflict extreme pain through subsequent forced changes."

This unexpected additional charge drew some looks from the Hammersmith retinue, not all of them sympathetic or supportive to their relative. Liam didn't have to look to be able to *feel* the anger pouring from his opponent.

"Novice Quinn demands only that Master Hammersmith admit his transgression and remove the curse and apologize in front of Guild observers," Heather finalized. "Novice Quinn assures the Guild that if the accused *submits* to this demand, he and his Family will Pledge to allow the

Guild to exact *all* other disciplinary actions they deem fitting for the crime committed."

The chief guild observer nodded and turned toward Hammersmith. "Master Hammersmith, you have been Formally Challenged and the Challenge has been stated and witnessed. How do you respond?"

Hammersmith's Second was about Winchester's age and had similar enough features that Heather proclaimed him most likely the next older brother. "Master Hammersmith scoffs at the outlandish imaginations of this *changeling* masquerading as a Novice. Only a Guild Member in good standing may present such a Challenge. Where is the documentation that has elevated a *changeling* to the level of a legitimate Guild Member?"

Heather was ready for the question and immediately pulled a sheaf of papers from within her Second's Vestcoat. The Guild Chief accepted the papers and with two others read through them in short order. Liam could feel their magery as they scanned the signatures for falsification or forgery.

The papers were passed to other observers as the Guild Chief spoke, "The authenticity of the awarding of Novice Level One to Liam Quinn is verified. The Challenge therefore is supported and requires an answer."

Hammersmith's Second didn't hesitate. "Master Hammersmith demands that the Accuser present credible proofs for his outlandish hallucination."

"Novice Quinn and each of his family wear godstone necklaces infused with Master Magery that allows them only to retain their sentience during their forced changes," Heather responded. "This retaining of sentience allows each of them to utilize their changeling attributes to *smell* the source of the curse as it forces them to change form. All four of the Quinn Family members can easily identify the source of this smell. Novice Quinn smelled it on Master Winchester the instant he came within scenting range when they met in Cincinnati."

"So, this *changeling* thinks he smells an innocent man's mage-scent on a spell that has been altered by the magery of yet *another* mage?" Winchester's brother openly scoffed. "Is the Guild now going to accept the alterations of traditional evidentiary methods in the presence of unproven *tinkery*?"

"The Guild is not here to explore the factual basis of the accusation," the Guild Chief reminded the Hammersmith Second. "The efficacy of the method will be explored in due time, but the outcome will not be found before tomorrow's duel. Does Master Hammersmith wish to defer the duel until the next full moon?"

Heather had explained that Hammersmith could ask for an extension to the five-day limit, as could Liam if he wished. But Hammersmith was unlikely to do this as anyone and everyone could investigate the accusation using magery, and he would surely be exposed. It would be better for him to admit his crime now than to ensure capable Guild investigators found him out.

Another unlikely scenario that would actually save Hammersmith's reputation and tarnish that of Liam would be to ask for the delay, then simply remove the curse. He would lose the leverage he attempted to get to obtain Puma Island, but the accusation would be a cloud over Liam's credibility forever after. That would open the Quinn Family to *justifiable vengeance* by the entire Hammersmith Clan.

Heather proclaimed that as the least likely scenario due to the information the Martin brothers and Rat had accumulated. Winchester Hammersmith was the kind of man that barreled through opposition even when proven wrong. He lacked the ability to accept a subtle approach.

"Of course not!" Hammersmith's older brother sneered. "The insult to the entire Hammersmith Clan is too great to allow to go unpunished! We… I mean Master Hammersmith demands Dueler's Justice!"

The Guild Chief nodded. "So be it!"

He turned to Liam. "The Challenge has been accepted. I take it this natural arena will be the dueling location?"

"No, Guildmaster," Heather still was the only one allowed to speak for the Challenger's side. At the surprised looks, she explained, "This spot was chosen for the Confrontation because it is open."

She gestured. "The proposed arena is on the other side of the central clawstone. If you will all step this way, we can view it from the height of the spectators.

Liam led the uneven march to and up on the central clawstone ridge with Hammersmith and his brother belatedly flanking them on the other side of the lead three Guild observers. Walking seven abreast with the Guild members between, they approached and scaled the central ridge.

When they reached the top of the wide oval ridge, they looked upon a much different landscape than the one behind them. Instead of a level expanse of grazed grass, the western half of Clawstone Park was filled with a mixture of large old trees and huge boulders seemingly lowered gently from the sky. Two of the immense boulders were as large as the trees nearby while others were only as large as an oliphant, the natural kind, not the smaller changeling version.

The arena Heather presented was filled with open space between the boulders and the scattered trees. As a dueling arena it would provide a plethora of hiding places and battle cover. It was the perfect arena for an inexperienced mage of limited ability facing a much stronger opponent.

"Ahh, good choice considering," the Guildmaster said, then turned to Hammersmith. "Master Hammersmith, the Challenger has presented the formal arena. You have one last chance to decline the Challenge. How say you?"

Hammersmith's brother sneered. "The Challenger attempts to show gallantry and courage by making false accusations and ridiculous challenges, then attempts to cower behind mage-proof obstacles like a coward."

His sneer grew. "Master Hammersmith invokes the Change of Venue Clause in the Guild Law books. The accusations made in the Challenge are so egregious, Master Hammersmith demands the right to determine the dueling arena!"

Winchester added his sneer as his brother continued, "Master Hammersmith demands the duel take place in the other field," he pointed behind the gathered crowd. "The arena is over a hundred yards long and more than fifty wide and is devoid of obstacles to a *proper* duel. There is also an uninterrupted view for the spectators to witness justice."

"Done!" Heather shouted so quickly all those listening could not help but imagine Liam and his Second had scored some sort of trap for the accused.

The Guildmaster spoke before Hammersmith's Second could object to his objection of a Change in Venue. "The Change of Venue has been accepted by the Challenger. The duel will be held an hour prior to sunset tomorrow in the eastern arena of the area of Puma Island known as Clawstone Park."

He then turned to Liam. "By Guild Law I am allowed to give the Challenger one last opportunity to withdraw the Challenge. If you withdraw your Challenge you will be expelled from the Guild and will be subject to forfeited compensation to the aggrieved party. Novice Quinn, do you wish to withdraw the Challenge?"

Heather had instructed Liam that this was the only time where he was not only allowed, but *required* to speak. "No Guildmaster, the Challenge stands as spoken."

The Guildmaster nodded and turned toward Hammersmith. "Master Hammersmith. Your demand for a Change of Venue has been awarded and the duel will be held in the eastern half of the area of Puma Island known as Clawstone Park. By Guild Law you are allowed one more opportunity to accede to the demands of the Challenger. How do you respond?"

Winchester had several insults to respond to as well as the suspected trap he'd fallen into at the end of the formal introduction meeting and the venom dripped from his lips as he growled, "This *changeling* has insulted me and my entire House and Clan with his filthy accusations. He has printed false witness in the rags *normals* read for *entertainment* to inject interest into their petty existences. Those hundreds of individual insults can never be withdrawn but *can* be refuted."

He openly sneered at Liam as he ranted, "After I rid the world of the lies from *your* filthy animal mouth, I will deal with those that helped you manufacture those insults and spread them to a gullible race of fools too stupid to understand the lies your lackeys have fed them about their betters!"

Several of the Guild observers reached for subduing wands as Hammersmith took a step toward his accuser. "For compensation for the outlandish slander and libel you have committed I demand the Compensation of my accuser's entire family legacy. I demand *one quarter* of the island known as Puma Island as soon as I kill this," he gestured angrily and three Guild observers drew their subduing wands, "*annoyance*!"

He turned to the Guildmaster but the three Guild observers didn't put their wands away. "As soon as I win tomorrow's duel, I demand my Compensation as the southern coastal village and docks with another quarter of the island upon the death of each of the other three in sequence."

He sneered again as he gave Dillon and Sinead a look of disgust. "They might outlive a *normal*, but they won't outlive me." He turned to give Orlagh a leering smile. "Maybe I'll take you on as a concubine to breed me some half-breed servants."

He looked around to see if his barbs were getting him any revenge for his earlier embarrassments but nothing more than a couple of clenched jaws met his gaze. The serenely confident faces of the majority gave him another twinge of doubt that he let slip, and he reacted badly.

Raising a finger to jab at Liam, three more Guild observers drew their subduing wands as Hammersmith snarled, "I accept your Challenge *changeling*, and I promise I will make your death as long and as painful as Guild Law allows. I will make your friends and Family watch you suffer and if any of them so much as *think* about interfering with Guild Justice, I will kill *them* in front of you before I end your miserable existence!"

Hammersmith's face was turning so red Liam wondered if his head would explode and he tried and failed to hide the smile the thought produced.

Hammersmith saw the smile and took a step toward him and three more Guild observers drew their wands, only the Guildmaster remaining unarmed. Several of the Hammersmith supporters reached for pockets or inside clothing or bags, but none openly pulled forth amulets or talismans of magery.

Hammersmith jabbed a finger at Liam. "Tomorrow at sunset I will make you pay for the insult you have given, *animal man*."

Then he turned toward the Guildmaster. "Finish this!"

The Guildmaster was not the only one to show surprise at the break from civilized protocols and it took him a couple of seconds to finish the formal proceedings.

"I remind you that declarations of a change to the particulars of the Challenge do *not* change those particulars. The Challenge is not changed from the original declared basis from the Challenger." He calmly faced Hammersmith. "The Challenged can make no alterations as to ownership of lands or property *if* he wins the duel."

The Guildmaster took a deep breath before continuing, "Both parties have indicated their intention to proceed with the *declared* parameters of the duel to decide Justice," he intoned as he returned to scripted wording. "Let it be known that from this moment forward the arena will be monitored and the spectator's viewing section charmed for safety and will therefore be forbidden to anyone but the five Guild observers charged with maintaining Dueling Arena Sanctity."

Without another word, five of the Guild observers trotted down from the central clawstone outcrop and began spreading out to inspect and secure the arena grounds.

The Guildmaster turned to Dillon. "You are the Master of this House. Do you offer hospitality to the Challenged and his retinue?"

Dillon knew the consequences of refusing and didn't hesitate even though he hated the prospect of hosting the very man that had tortured his family for a decade and spewed such hateful bigotry and vengeful threats only moments before. He would not only have to serve that man and *his* guests but supply them with comfortable lodging for the night.

The five remaining Guild observers would ensure the two parties maintained civility.

"Yes, Guildmaster," Dillon replied respectfully. "The Challenged and his Second and three witnesses will be quartered in my home and will attend tonight's banquet with the Challenger, his Second, and their three Witnesses. The rest of the Challenged party will be awarded the accommodations in the village their purses allow."

"What?" an indignant voice called out from the nearby crowd. "We're being treated like common *tourists*?"

The Guildmaster turned to face the crowd. "I do remember the announcement before the steamer left Hammersmith Docks that the duel banquet would be open to the *minimum* number of people by Guild Law. That is Challenged, Second, and three Witnesses. I also remember the announcement that accommodations would be limited and would be charged for at market rates for demand for those that did not wish to remain aboard ship for the night."

There were no more comments despite the low rumble of several unsatisfied people among Hammersmith's supporters.

The complaints ceased as a strange craft appeared over the trees, floating majestically and serenely against the gentle breeze, and Dillon spoke into the silence. "We may not have the room to accommodate more than the required minimum number of Guild guests at our home, but we do not wish to inflict another mile and a half hike through our beautiful island."

He gestured as the airship approached. "For those that wish to return to our partially completed village in a more leisurely manner, we offer to *fly* you over the forest to return to the village."

The crowd that had been pushing closer to hear every word of the challenge confrontation, now drifted in the direction of the airship as it floated to the ground in the middle of the largest open space south of the dueling arena. The five Guild observers tasked with the sanctity of the arena approached but did not leave the space they were marking off with their chanting.

"I know the trek through the woods to Witness the Formal Challenge was not easy for some of you and would like to offer a less strenuous way back to the village," Dillon continued. "Any of you that wish a ride back to the village and your ship or your hotel room are welcome to ride for free this one time."

Several of Hammersmith's supporters dashed to be the first to choose a spot on the decks of the boxcar troopship while the rest tried to show continued support for their relative or friend and still hurry to get a choice seat. Only a couple of them stayed long enough to personally wish Hammersmith good luck before they dashed off to get the ride of their lives.

Hammersmith and his Second, as well as two of the Witnesses scowled openly at the unexpected largess while the fifth, the oldest man Liam had ever seen, gave a different facial expression, one of restrained respect, and nodded to Dillon, then to Liam. Then he turned to one of the other Witnesses who had begun talking animatedly to him.

"If the rest of you will come this way the main house is only a couple of hundred yards up the beach."

He didn't tell them the beach was two hundred yards away and they reached it about the time Winchester began to complain.

"Ah, here we are," Dillon said an instant after Winchester gave out an exasperated puff of air and demanded. "How much further is it?"

They all looked up the curve of Sandy Bay to see the limestone tower that was the main house. Through the trees surrounding the four-story tower they could see the two, three story wings, one that pointed eastward across the base of the island's upraised tail, and the other paralleling the beach northward. Railed balconies open to the outside lined the four-story central tower and its wings.

"My, what a quaintly beautiful home," the elder female Witness said as if in surprise. At a snarl from Winchester, she gave an exasperated snort and took the other Witness' arm and whispered, "Instruct your sons on the etiquette of Duel Guests before they embarrass us any further in front of our hosts."

All four of the Quinn family members smiled in their own way as they realized Winchester's mother was not familiar with changeling senses. The snort and negative sad shake of his head of the eldest of the five told them at least *he* knew their hosts had heard the admonition.

As they trooped along the white sands of the beach toward the massive limestone castle, the third Witness casually moved to his two sons and engaged them in some verbal lessons in Mage Guild Etiquette. The elder Witness continued to snort softly and roll his eyes at the Guildmaster as the two sons continued to speak loud enough for the four changelings to hear every word.

Liam offered his arm to the woman from the bay side. "Sometimes this sand can be softer than it appears. It is not uncommon for one to momentarily lose one's balance."

The mother of his enemy smiled with genuine warmth and accepted the offer of support. "Why thank you, young man."

The group was halfway to the main house before the two brothers finally realized they were talking loud enough for all four of their changeling hosts to easily hear their every word despite the distance. Their father did not try to hide the fact he was continuing to berate them for their inhospitable acts and attitudes… including his threat to invoke *Parental Authority* and demand a halt to the duel and his own *Truth Questioning* as Family Head.

Even the Guildmaster's ears perked up at that loud proclamation.

Chapter 48

They entered the wide double doors of the limestone tower and the Hammersmith matriarch gasped. "It's *beautiful!*"

Sinead, even in her full puma form, was able to strut proudly into the expansive, two-story entrance sitting room with a toss of her head in invitation and a soft purr.

"This way please," Dillon said as he followed his wife and led them to the ramps to the roof. In moments they were on the roof and facing an enormous round table covered in every imaginable dish.

There were steaming platters of several types of fish as well as an entire roasted piglet with the skin removed, a pair of wild turkeys roasted golden brown, and several platters each of thick grilled beef and bison steaks. Between the platters of meat were dozens of platters of raw and steamed vegetables and separate platters of fresh fruits.

Even the two youngest Hammersmiths were surprised and impressed by the banquet offering.

Rocky and Frankie stood proudly by their masterpiece as their two new apprentices watched nervously.

Sinead paced a wide circle out onto the roof as Dillon gestured. "The weather is so nice we thought our guests might enjoy the view we cherish so much as we dine."

The Patriarch of the entire Hammersmith Clan bowed low, before replying, "The Quinn

Family shows great honor in their duties as Duel Hosts and the Hammersmith *Clan* is honored in return."

Dillon performed the seating flawlessly following Heather's advice, and soon had them arranged properly as the Guildmaster chanted an insect repelling charm.

Following Guild etiquette, the duelists would sit across from each other with the others sitting in alternating chairs, Challenger, Challenged, Guild observer, then repeat. Because of the odd number of diners this put half of the table's occupants a little closer, but the size of the huge table still gave that group plenty of elbow room. The two gaps between the Families gave the cooks access to the center of the table.

Sinead and Orlagh lounged on raised platforms that put them so their heads were at the perfect height to eat at the table with the others. The meat placed in front of them was cut to bite-sized pieces and placed for easy access one piece at a time.

When they were all seated, Fallon touched a control under the table where he was sitting and the central section of the table with all of the dozens of choices of the feast began to slowly turn as Dillon spoke.

"I know many of you are used to having paid staff serve you but our culture has a different tradition in that we serve ourselves from the dishes our cooks present," he smiled and reached forward to pick up a small platter of grilled fish fillets as the center of the table brought his favorite dish in front of him. "Just pick up anything that catches your eye or tempts your nose and take what you want. Rocky and Frankie will replace any platter we empty till all of us have eaten our fill. Please help yourselves."

As several people reached for platters, the Hammersmith mother spoke as she eyed the platter of bloody meat Frankie placed in front of Sinead at her place on the raised platform that brought her up to table height, "You do not give thanks to your changeling gods before eating?"

"Our family acknowledges the existence of some of the beings referred to in the histories as gods, but we do not worship any single one of them," Dillon replied. "But we will not interrupt you if you choose to pray to any god *you* may worship."

"You will not wait in proper silence while we do so, if we so choose?" the youngest Hammersmith tried to keep the sneer out of his tone but wasn't completely successful.

"We could if we so wished," Dillon responded with a smile, then traded the platter he was holding for another as it came by on the rotating table.

The Guild observers were getting the hang of the moving banquet and seemed to be ignoring the table talk. That was not the case as each was doing their job and *remembering* every single word and facial expression as part of their duties.

"When it is expected, or demanded, as *proper*, then it is not done freely in the feeling of equal respect," Dillon replied casually as he dipped a large spoonful of steamed vegetables onto his plate and placed it in a gap in the offerings as the center of the table continued to slowly turn. He paused a moment and plucked up a small bowl of grapes and spooned several next to his vegetable side dish. "Respect is shown, in my opinion, by not interrupting those that wish to give thanks in their own way instead of *forcing* respect."

"For instance," he said as he stabbed a large grilled bison steak and placed it on the remaining space on his plate. "Your Patriarch, Master Mage Echhardt Hammersmith and two of our observers gave their private thanks to their individual gods while you and I spoke."

"None of them were insulted by an interruption *of them* during their private moment with their god and they did not insult anyone else by *demanding* silence while they prayed. In that way all differing beliefs were given and showed respect to all others."

The Hammersmith mother thought about that a moment then nodded and closed her eyes to speak with her personal god while the rest of the table began selecting dishes and socializing with those not currently praying, and not interrupting her during her private time.

The noise rose and fell as the diners ate and listened or spoke while their table neighbors ate. Rocky and Frankie continued to bring out fresh platters to replace the ones emptied the fastest, while their assistants removed those empties. Mages and changelings both had more active metabolisms than normal humans and the amount of food consumed would have fed more than three times their number, but the two cooks never faltered.

"And you just force the steam through a godstone tinkering that has a magery chanting implanted inside like any other amulet or talisman and the tinkering turns the steam foam into, what?" Echhardt asked as he cut into his third bison steak.

"It's still steam foam, it's just so insubstantial it is lighter than hot air or hydrogen gas or even normal steam foam," Fallon replied as he waved a kabob stick with several vegetables and meat cubes impaled on its length. "The godstone turns the steam into foam that is pumped between an inner and outer shell to make a cold closet that will stay at freezing temperatures in the middle of summer, for up to a week or more, depending on how often you open the door."

"But only with a good Master Mage's cold charm on the interior," one of the observers commented.

"Yes," Fallon replied, "but a cold spell performed with normal steam foam only lasts a day. A cold closet with mageried and tinkered steam foam in the walls will last seven or eight times as long."

"Putting the possible earnings of all Novices and Acolytes in jeopardy," Winchester observed.

"Actually, no," Fallon contradicted him. "It actually *increases* their job opportunities."

"How so?" the Guildmaster wondered.

"The tinkering that turns steam to foam is only a portion of the insulation and *lifting power* that magery puts into the foam," Fallon explained airily, waving the kabob stick. "Any Fifth Level Acolyte would be able to hire out to seven times as many clients in the same time period. They could cut their prices in half and reach many more clients and *still* make more profit."

"But only if they purchase one of your mageried and tinkered foamers," one of the Guild observers commented.

Fallon smiled. "But of course! Godstone is not an inexhaustible resource. My sister and I may have a considerable amount now, but we are using it up at a prodigious rate building our fleet of airships and supporting my experiments. The amount of godstone in a single personal tinkered foamer is more than some of our own employees make in a year and we pay more than many employers."

"I hear the foaming chant includes a new syllable and *you* are the one that discovered this new syllable," the Guildmaster stated.

"Yes, that is true," Fallon dipped his head.

"Then that means every time we used it, we would have to send a portion of our Guild fees to *your* accounts!" Winchester was scandalized.

"Actually, to *my* accounts," Heather interjected. "My brother may have discovered the two syllables, but he is not a member of the Mage Guild. I am, so he relinquished possession to me and I will pay him after keeping a one percent handling fee."

"Hunh! One percent!" Winchester snorted. "It is worth *half* if not more just to keep the Guild from claiming them outright without reimbursement.

He is not in the Guild and therefore is not *authorized* to claim ownership."

"Actually," the Guildmaster replied as he paused with a large strawberry on a tiny, finger-long spear of silver, "the Guild Council signed on to the new laws after the recent war between our nation's states."

He eyed Heather and Fallon both. "Since then, the Supreme Court has determined the Guild does *not* own all new magery. SCOTUS has ruled that normals and changelings can copyright new chants and new syllables they create, and incorporate them into tinkered patents."

He smiled as he turned his eyes on Fallon. "Tell me young Master Tinker, has the Guild confirmed your ownership of the new syllables?"

Fallon nodded. "Yes, my ownership as discoverer and my sister's role as my Guild proxy and chief financial auditor."

"I also hear you only asked for a one percent fee on the Guild's use of your new syllables," the Guildmaster commented as he dipped the speared strawberry into a bowl of chocolate melting over a small candle and plucked it from the silver spear.

Fallon shrugged as Heather answered, "We have already done the work and should make more from the increased use by bringing the cost down for both Novices and Fifth Level Acolytes as well as customers. More people will be able to afford freezer closets that last longer than a day, and less food will spoil, thereby reducing the waste we all abhor but usually can't do anything about."

"Then there's the flying thing," Echhardt commented as he dipped a speared sautéed mushroom into a small bowl of a white, tangy sauce.

"Yes, well, we figured it was better to simply license the tinkered magery to anyone and everyone for a smaller fee than what is traditional rather than try to hoard the method and have everyone trying to steal it from us," Heather said, then gave a shrug. "Besides, once people know something is possible it doesn't take them long to figure out how to do it themselves. If we hadn't gotten patents and copyrights somebody else would have eventually discovered how to do it and we'd have to pay *them* to use our own inventions."

Fallon examined the properly charred cube of meat on the end of the kabob stick he waved about. "We gave the Guild the right to charge the rest of the *traditional* licensing fee we could have charged so the price won't be *that* much lower."

"But… but…" Winchester stuttered. "That means the Guild is *indebted* to you and to…" he jerked his head to stare at Liam. "How can the Guild be fair?"

"Winchester!" his father boomed. "I have remained silent while you have shown disrespect for your Challenger and the Host Family, but I *will not* tolerate your insulting the neutrality of the Guild in this matter."

Heather cut him off before he could say more. "The Guild is beholden to my brother and me, not to Liam Quinn. To insinuate that I, a First Level Master Mage would use Guild indebtedness to influence a Formal Challenge is worthy of a Challenge in itself, even during a Duel Banquet!"

She glared at him as she said, "Be careful what insults you spout from here on out *Master Mage* lest you make more enemies than you already have."

She turned to the Guildmaster with fire in her eyes. "My apologies, Guildmaster."

Then she turned toward Dillon and Sinead. "My apologies, my hosts."

She locked eyes with Winchester Hammersmith again, and gritted her teeth. "My apologies Master Mage Hammersmith. The post-duel banquet is supposed to be cordial and respectful. I apologize for my outburst, Master Hammersmith."

All eyes went to Winchester Hammersmith. His next words would set the tone for the rest of the banquet and he showed wisdom for the first time since his arrival. He dipped his head in return. "Apology accepted, Master Richards."

Two of the observers unobtrusively moved their hands away from holstered subduing wands and the meal got slightly louder than before as the diners tried to smooth over the tension. It took a few minutes, but a more relaxed conversation eventually resumed.

As the diners slowed their pace, Rocky and Frankie deftly switched out all of the meats and vegetables and replaced them with fruit bowls and confections as they judged the diners' moods.

"You say you found a Master Mage to alter the curse so you could all retain sentience during your full beast forms," Echhardt stated. "I know of very few Masters that could accomplish such a feat without detecting the identity of the source of the curse or being detected by the source."

"I am surprised the one that made those," Echhardt gestured generally toward the necklaces at his hosts' throats, "did not offer to sell you that bit of information."

Liam wondered if his father would practice the teaching he'd been given as a child and was not disappointed when Dillon didn't take the bait and reveal information on the one they had finally gotten to help them.

"That detail is not relevant to the fact all four of us would be able to detect the mage scent of the one that haunts us every cycle of the full moon," Dillon said as several sets of eyes locked on a visibly nervous Winchester Hammersmith.

"And yet not one of you has pointed an accusing finger at the Challenged," one of the observers *observed*.

Liam was prepared and took this one by simply *releasing* the containment spell he'd been holding around himself and every mage at the table except for Heather perked up. "You see, holding one's mage scent inside oneself is one of the first spells a Novice is taught. It seems that even with my limited abilities I was able to learn that common courtesy before I was taught to look for the mage scent of another with magery instead of my changeling senses."

He locked eyes with the man that had tortured him since puberty, and his parents and sister for longer. "I thank you for the courtesy of holding your mage scent within yourself *Master Mage* Winchester Hammersmith, but we have supped together and spoken to each other courteously. I feel we have gotten to know each other enough you could relax that courtesy if you so desire."

"A courtesy you did *not* think to hide," Liam added, "when you and I first met on the banks of the Ohio River outside Cincinnati. The lapse in control that allowed *me* to identify *you* as the source of the curse on my family!"

The youngest Hammersmith gave his father a panicked look, then firmed his face. "That will not be necessary. After all, with all that is being claimed our young Master Tinkerer can do, for all I know he has tinkerings arrayed around this very room that could learn how to defeat me with a single syllable."

"True," Heather replied. "Guild Dueling Laws do not forbid such a thing."

"What? You mean I could have lined the place with scanners? How could you keep that from me?" Fallon was scandalized his sister had not suggested the ploy.

"Because I didn't want you doing exactly what you would have done," she replied bluntly, then turned to their host's other guests. "Guildmaster, Master Echhardt, I give you both my word of Honor I purposely kept that information from my Master Tinker brother to avoid even the suspicion we might use such a tactic during this banquet."

"But the tactic would have been legal, and by the way, its future use will be covered in the Laws as soon as I can contact the Council," the Guildmaster replied as Echhardt narrowed his eyes at the youngest Master he'd ever met.

Heather nodded her head in a tiny bow. "I was going to suggest the change before you left the island in any case, and will support it when it comes up for a vote *unless* objectionable amendments are attached."

"Even after I kill the one you are Second to?" the Challenged asked with surprising calm.

Heather looked at the middle-aged Master Mage and gave him a pitying smile. "I'm sorry to disillusion you *Master* Hammersmith, but *Novice* Quinn will *not* be dying tomorrow."

Her smile grew brighter and she examined a large red strawberry she'd just dipped into heated chocolate. "Of course, you might not either."

Then she bit the strawberry in half and looked at the Hammersmith Patriarch who was gazing intently at her as she chewed and swallowed. "Umm, that's good! Have you tried the strawberry dipped in chocolate, Clan Master Hammersmith? It is hard to get better than strawberry, but strawberry coated in warm chocolate does so."

Chapter 49

"Why in the world would I do that?" Liam wondered honestly. "The place will be crawling with his supporters."

"For one thing, that's *precisely* why," Heather fumed, then pointed toward the south where they could see the line of lights that marked the growing village less than two miles away. "All those people that came here looking for a new life with patrons that treat them like they matter will be on *our* side of the arena tomorrow. They *need* to see you walking among your enemies with confidence in tomorrow's outcome."

"But what if I *don't* succeed," Liam blurted since she was the only one near enough to hear.

Heather put her hands on her hips. "You *doubt* my magery combined with my brother's tinkery?"

Liam made like a fish as he tried unsuccessfully to voice his doubts without giving insult, then the words came out in a rush. "It's different facing you with Fallon there to fix anything I break."

"You and the suit took everything I could throw at you without harm, well except for that time you didn't activate your shields," she punched him on the arm. "Don't do that again this time, okay?"

"But that was in *practice*."

Heather planted her hands on her hips again and Liam shut up, already learning one of her most readable body signals as she spoke softly and doubled down. "Liam Quinn, I hurled my spells at *full strength* during those last two *practice* sessions. Every one of those attacks was stronger than the ones that staggered Firecloud when he and I dueled, and your suit withstood them all with no harm to you."

She smiled sweetly. "I can ensure you, Master Winchester Hammersmith is no Firecloud."

Liam thought fast. "But I won't have the suit with me if we go into town."

Heather snorted. "You'll be safer in town than anywhere else on the island."

At his baffled look, she explained, "You and Hammersmith are the two safest people on the island, I should say. If you are injured by one of Hammersmith's supporters then that person and any associates will be executed, as will Master Winchester Hammersmith if it is discovered he had prior knowledge of an impending assault and did not stop it."

She locked her eyes on his in the light of the quarter moon. "The same would be true if one of *your* supporters assaults Master Winchester you have prior knowledge of, and *he* will be in the village celebrating and showing his courage and lack of concern for the duel's outcome. And don't worry about suicide assassins, there are spells the Guild can do to determine exactly *who* violated the sanctity of the Challenge."

"If a hundred are involved in violence toward the other, without the knowledge of either of you, those hundred will be hunted down and executed by the Guild."

Liam looked at the sky where the troop carrier floated above the village on Sky Patrol.

"Don't worry," Heather consoled him. "Fallon already briefed all the troops on Guild Law and there are only a few onboard the troopship. Six of them are guarding the castle grounds in three roving pairs, two ground, and one airborne. The rest are in town with shocker batons to break up any fights."

"I thought you said..."

Heather laughed. "Oh, you and Hammersmith are the safest two people on the island, but everybody else is open to doing what their liquid courage allows. That young man of Orlagh's, Fleetfoot, even sent the troopship over to the mainland a couple times today to pick up a couple dozen hoe-boys looking to make a couple dollars to wear security sashes and stand by storefront doors in pairs with their arms crossed till the streets clear."

"I have a feeling we're going to need more than that," the Guildmaster said as he crossed the roof toward them. "Another ship of fools just docked."

He looked at them with suspicion. "Somebody seems to be telling people on the mainland about tomorrow's duel and about half those coming to see have their own copy of the last dime novel you folks printed."

"There is no telegraph line on the island but *someone* got the message to the Regional Guild office in Cleveland and they sent ten more observers to secure the arena and provide security for what seems to be turning into a major event," he observed, then glared at Liam. "And you, young man, if you don't wish to see your father's brand-new village burned down before sunrise, I suggest you make an appearance on those streets," he threw a hand toward the lights of the village as the growing sound of hundreds of noisy people began to be noticeable.

"Why..." Liam started.

"Because, my naïve Challenger, as of now only one of the duelists seems to have the courage to show his face," Heather crooned, her lips brushing his ear. "As they fuel themselves with liquid courage, Hammersmith's supporters will begin the taunting and *your* supporters will not have your presence to help them ignore those growing taunts or throw their own with any confidence. Eventually a fist will fly, then another, then a chair will be broken, then a window. Before long the chaos will spread and fires will be started."

"Hammersmith will have long since been whisked back here to safety, where *your family* will be *required* to protect him, but your father's village will burn," the Guildmaster snorted a laugh. "Of course, not near as much as any other less well thought out construction, but the wooden parts of the village will burn. Okay, maybe just the furniture and all the windows broken since your father thought ahead and most of every structure is made from native stone, but there will be some measure of destructive, embarrassing chaos."

"Unless I go into town and show that I am not afraid of tomorrow," Liam muttered with resignation.

The Guildmaster beamed. "Precisely! And if the updated information I received from the serendipitous reinforcements are any indication, you won't have to *act* confident."

"I'm wearing my gunbelt," Liam complained as he followed the Guildmaster and Heather to the ramp into the house. "And one of those shocker wands, neither of those will give away any battle secrets before tomorrow… right?"

The other two ignored him and he grumbled to himself down into the house and to the front door where he retrieved his gunbelt and knife and put one of the smaller shocker wands in the pocket of the light rain slicker he donned. He put on his hat and gave a brave face. "Okay, let's go parade in front of the cheering and booing masses so they don't kill each other."

"That's the spirit," the Guildmaster exclaimed with a hearty laugh… then looked around curiously. "Uh, what're the chances of getting to ride on one of those airships instead of having to hike a mile and a half or more?"

Liam smiled. "Let's go see."

He led them toward the moored airship he'd almost begun to think of as home and called out at the bottom of the new boarding stairs, "Night watch, permission to come aboard."

Sesco stuck his head over the rail. "Permission granted."

Liam led the way with the Guildmaster next and Heather following last. When they got on the forward deck, the Guildmaster quickly looked around.

"It's more like a ship than the hot air balloon I rode in once," he commented as he peered up at the silvery shape above them, shining with the light of the gibbous moon. "Balloon looks too small. You say it's the magery that makes the foam so buoyant?"

"That and the godstone in the shell," Liam replied.

"Ah," the Guildmaster mused cluelessly as he inspected the control panel while Sesco secured the entry door in the side of the rail and locked it. "I knew regular steam foam was better than hot air and even hydrogen but your balloon is so small it almost seems impossible to believe it could lift something as *substantial* as this remodeled railcar," he patted the heavy wood of the pilot's console. "Especially with the steel frame and rail wheels still attached."

Sesco took the pilot's seat and pulled the plug on one of the talking tubes. "Pilot to foam chanter."

After a few moments Sesco took a breath to repeat his call when Revis' voice came through the tube. "Foam chanter to pilot. Sorry about the delay. I was peeing off the aft deck. Do you want to talk to take your mind off not going to town?"

"No, Revis, I'd rather stay here with you on Watch," Sesco replied with a smile. "I called because we have three passengers who want us to deliver to them to the village."

"Oh. *Oh!* Foam chanter ready for duty, sir!"

Sesco smiled at his brother's voice. "Foam chanter, give me four ounces and fifteen reps, please," he requested as he turned valves and tripped switches to feed steam to the pusher fans.

"Four ounces and fifteen reps coming up!" Revis called back and they could hear him chanting a perfect cadence through the open window of his duty station.

Already on standby, the airship quickly achieved full steam and began to make the mooring lines creak. Liam and Heather released the aft mooring lines and the Guildmaster excitedly darted from rail to rail as two of the guards secured the ropes by hand while also watching to see he didn't endanger himself.

Liam and Heather loosened the forward pair and played them out till they were holding the ends, then when Sesco signaled, they released the forward mooring lines. The hemp ropes sang as they whipped through the hoops of the mooring stakes and hung below the airship as it rose smoothly into the night sky.

The Guildmaster didn't try to hide his glee as he darted from rail to rail to see all he could despite the night's darkness. Sesco got the pusher fans going at full revolutions and looped around to give the excited Guildmaster a full view of the main house. Then he flew over the dueling arena and the two mages aboard were able to clearly see the active magery of the Masters guarding the arena from tampering.

"You can see so much," the Guildmaster spoke softly as the silence of the sky surrounded them except for the faint hiss of steam and the whirring of the pusher fans.

"There are two boats in the northern bay," he said, pointing.

"Bjorn and Millie," Heather said with a smile.

"Our own private fisher folk," Liam explained, then smiled. "Got exclusive fishing rights to our island's one-mile border territory and free docking at the pier. They don't much like big crowds."

"I see more than just two people."

Heather pulled down a pair of tinkered tubes with glass lenses and looked through them. She flipped a couple of lenses in front of the tubes, twisted the ends closest to her eyes, and stared into the night as Sesco took them in a continuing loop as they rose into the sky. "Bjorn has some changeling blood, not much, but enough for some good weather sense. Ah yes, some of our otter neighbors are visiting kin."

"They're using one of Fallon's tinkerings to grill," Liam sniffed the night air five hundred feet above the bay, "bison steaks to go with their fish."

Heather handed the twin scopes to the Guildmaster and showed him how to adjust the lenses to see in the dark, then let the man be as he looked at *everything* they passed above as Sesco looped them around toward the southern shore.

"See," the Guildmaster said as he pointed. "Here comes another ship full of people wanting to see a real mage duel and watch a man die."

"People don't always get what they want," Heather said softly, then said over her shoulder, "Sesco, can you put us down against the side of the pier just like we were a regular ship so we can step directly from our deck onto the pier?"

"I'll do my best, Miss Richards," Sesco replied with a confident air. "But you and Mr. Quinn might need to spot for me so I can put the mooring lines in the dock workers' hands."

In the end he didn't need them. He flew the airship directly toward the docks at only a couple dozen feet above the lake's gentle waves on the calm night. Then at the last minute he turned the airship on its side and killed the fans and drifted slowly in the still night air. Two burly dock workers easily grabbed the still dangling lines on the starboard side and pulled them closer as Sesco vented foam.

"Foam chanter, two dry reps please."

"Two dry reps coming up!" Revis responded, then chanted the remaining foam into an even thinner substance.

"The addition of magery does *that* much?" the Guildmaster's astonishment was evident.

"Yes, Guildmaster," Heather replied. "But like anything, it has its limitations. We're still learning what they are."

They drifted closer and the two dockworkers pulled the lines as Sesco vented steam just as Revis completed his chant, and they bumped into the side of the dock with their deck at the same level. Sesco smiled smugly as the Guildmaster openly gawped at the precise maneuver.

Liam didn't give him a chance to recover and opened the rail door. "Thank you Sesco," then louder, "thank you Revis!"

"You're welcome Mr. Quinn," came the reply from aft. "Have fun in town!"

"Thank you Revis, I will."

Then he looked at Sesco. "I'm sure a couple of the others would take their own duty so you and your brother can visit the village."

Sesco looked back at the aft end of the airship. "No, sir. I think I'll take the extra duty with my brother."

"Why don't you take him with you?" the Guildmaster wondered.

"Oh no, sir," Sesco shook his head. "Revis don't much like crowds since that drunk bull beat his head so bad and some people full of drink in big crowds always seem to pick at him till he gets mad. Then we end up in the hoosegow till I can calm him down. No, my brother and I will take the duty so six others can enjoy the whole night instead of having to come back sober."

He smiled. "Besides, taking all those other men's duty gave my brother and me a chance to practice precision night flying and we got to impress all them rubes," he gestured and Liam saw the curious crowds finally beginning to lose their fear of the odd airship's dockside landing, and come closer.

"Right," Liam replied, "Guildmaster, Miss Richards, let's disembark so Sesco and Revis can get back in the air."

The Guildmaster finally regained his air of authority in the face of the wonderful airship ride – and the nearing crowd – and nodded to Sesco. "Thank you for the ride, Pilot, and thank your brother for me."

"You're welcome Guildmaster, and he heard you," Sesco tapped the end of the speaking tube.

"You're welcome Guildmaster," came faintly through the flared end of the tube.

"Revis, give me four ounces and fifteen reps please," Sesco said as he added fuel to the boiler and began to increase steam pressure.

"Four ounces and fifteen reps coming up!" Revis hollered back and began his measured chant.

Heather stepped from the deck to the dock just as the airship began to pull against the mooring ropes, followed by the Guildmaster, then Liam who shut and latched the rail door.

He was the last to step on the dock, and signaled the dockworkers to release the mooring ropes just as they grew taught, and the dockworkers released them. Before anyone on the dock could react, the lines sang through the cleats and the airship lifted smoothly into the night sky. The two free-hanging mooring lines on the port side shed a stream of water as they rose out of the lake while the two on the dock side hummed through the cleats as dockworkers stood away for their safety.

The three looked at the airship rising in the night, then turned to face the crowd that had come onto the docks at the base of the pier to see the strange sight.

Loud voices shouted.

"It's her!"

"It's him!"

"It's *them*!"

Then the crowd surged forward and they realized they had no avenue of escape.

Chapter 50

Liam signed the last dime novel and looked down at the grandmotherly looking woman who fairly jumped in place. "There you are Mrs. Johns."

"Oh, I'm not Mrs. Johns, that's my sister. I'm Mrs. Willum and these ones are fer me," she pulled forth several dime novels. "I got every copy of the adventures of the Sky Rangers, even the ones everybody knows is fake."

Liam smiled. "And how do you want me to sign them, Mrs. Willum?"

"Oh, the same as you did for the one for my sister, to Mrs. Willum from, and then sign it. 'Cept for the fake ones. You might want to say they're fake."

"I think a collection like this should get more than that," Liam declared. "What's your first name?"

"My, oh my, that would make them so much more *personal*. Oh, thank you so much." After a moment she gushed. "Oh, oh yes, uh, Veronica Willum. Used to be Baker, but its Willum now."

Liam smiled and started writing with the tinkered quill Fallon had given him earlier in the day to help him catch up on the seemingly growing stacks of paper Mrs. Martin presented to be signed. "How about, to my friend Mrs. Veronica Baker Willum, from Liam Quinn of Sky Ranger One?"

Mrs. Veronica Baker Willum gasped daintily and fluttered her arms like a bird for several seconds then gushed politely, "Is *that* the name of your airship? Nobody I know knew! Oh, wait till I tell everybody."

She fluttered a bit more, then took a deep breath and got her excitement under control. "That would be so nice of you, sir. Thank you so very much."

Heather stuck her head over Liam's shoulder. "I've finished with mine. Would you like me to add something after Liam signs them?"

"Oh, Miss, that would add so much more meaning to them. I don't know how to thank you," she fanned herself with the single copy she'd gotten for her sister. "I can't believe I met the Sky Rangers in person. Wait till I tell the ladies at the quilting circle."

"You quilt?" Heather perked up. "I need to get some new blankets for the coming winter and I can think of nothing better than thick, hand sewn quilts. Will you walk with us so I can see if you would take the commission?"

"Oh my, yes," the woman gushed, fanning herself with the dime novel.

They had taken only a couple of steps when Rat appeared beside the two women. "Hello Ronie, it's been a long time."

Veronica flinched once, barely enough that Liam's changeling senses detected it, and then she said smoothly and with much less airiness. "Hello Arthur, or no, you go by the name *Rat* now, don't you?"

Rat gave her a slight bow. "Ever since a certain debutante broke my heart."

Veronica snorted. "You never had a heart Arthur, and I refuse to call you by that silly name so don't expect me to."

She turned toward the others and seemed to grow taller, and less fluttery. "Evening Guildmaster Phillips, Miss Richards. Oh, do finish signing my novels Mr. Quinn. My excitement was not all an act," she said with a smile, then leaned close. "The President is a fan too but didn't want to risk asking for his own signed editions. Got some opponents would use it for political benefit since there are *some* that resent the service you recently provided."

"Oh, do close your mouth and try to act more natural Guildmaster."

The Guildmaster shook his head and muttered, "I was warned about this assignment, but no-o-o, I said I had it all under control." He snorted as he looked from one of them to the other. "Veronica Baker Willum, also known as Ronie Baker, and Grant's ears in some quarters if I'm not mistaken."

Ronie gave a slight bow as the recovering Guildmaster continued, "And the infamous, notorious, etcetera, etcetera, Arthur, no known surname *acknowledged*. The Family still hasn't forgiven you for saving them from annihilation?"

Rat shrugged as Liam finished signing Ronie's novels and handed them to Heather to add her own words. "Actually, having fun for the first time in too many years."

The Guildmaster gave Rat a look, then at Liam and Heather. "Yeah, haven't been here more than half a day and already been better entertained than the entire past year."

"Yeah," Rat agreed, "seems to be like that most days with this bunch."

"We're right here, you know," Liam grumbled.

Heather patted his hand. "The more they talk the more *we* learn dear, now hush."

"So, what does bring you here, Ronie?" Rat asked.

"You in charge of intelligence with this bunch, *Arthur*?" Ronie countered.

Rat scowled and looked at Liam, then Heather, then pursed his lips.

"Yes, he is," Liam stated. "Doesn't want the job but won't pick one of my people to take it over from him and just keeps doing it himself."

Ronie snorted. "Yep! That's our Arthur. Loves what he's doing till he has to follow through with cleaning up other people's messes. Then he goes and hides under a trash pile till he feels better about himself."

Liam saw the way Rat scowled and it wasn't anger at Ronie's words, but more at the memories those words brought back.

"The President has been reading about this group of people who were wronged and forced to seek justice on their own against all odds," Ronie returned to the main topic. "Somehow these regular folk turned into something else entirely and managed to clean up an entire section of the country that had begun to fall under the sway of evil with more power than sense."

Rat made opening and closing motions with one hand and mimed talking at the same time, then stage-whispered, "Once she gets started, she don't quit."

Ronie just glared at her fellow *information specialist* as she continued, "The President is trying to clean up the mess caused by the war but there are too many folks think this is the perfect time to increase their own wealth and power without the *gub'ment* looking over their shoulder. A lot of them are going to succeed for no other reason than there's more of them then there is of us."

"Your Mr. Easton and the dark mage Firecloud, for example," she said. "The man you intend to kill tomorrow is another. In fact, there is no shortage of their kind infesting our country. The President and his administration would love to help all those people, but he can't. Besides not having enough resources, he is limited to which ones he can *openly* help as well as those he can *openly* oppose without ironclad evidence."

Liam and Heather, and the Guildmaster as unwilling Witnesses, listened as the president's field agent continued, "The President is capable of ending this duel without either of you dying. You say the word and by morning the entire Hammersmith Clan will be on ships headed home with the full knowledge they are aiding their country by allowing you to live."

"What makes you think…?" Liam started only to be interrupted.

"Oh, come now Mr. Quinn. Winchester Hammersmith may not be the most powerful mage in his Family but he *is* a Level Three Master," Ronie chided. "Your Master Tinker has already proven he can augment natural abilities with tinkerings, but there's only so much he can do."

"We can lift a fully loaded railcar into the sky with five gallons of water," Liam commented.

"Can foamed steam stop a stream of fire as thick as a man's wrist?" Ronie charged on, not noticing Heather's thoughtful look or Fallon's smirk.

"No, Mr. Quinn, it would be smarter to let your government make this little duel problem go away, then you can be free to assist your country in ways the president can't do openly, and a bit more on your competence level."

Liam glanced at Rat but the wolverine was as stone-faced and unreadable as always. "Why don't we wait till after tomorrow evening to decide what we're going to do and what offers we're going to make."

"Silly boy, can't you see you need to be *alive* to help others," Ronie snapped, then stabbed Heather with her piercing glare. "You girl. Did you try hard enough to talk your man out of volunteering to die young?"

Heather ignored the *'your man'* part as she responded, "No, I didn't try to talk him out of it at all. In fact, we've been working together day and night the past handful of days along with my brother to make sure Liam finishes the duel alive and with his honor intact."

"So, I'm sorry to have to say, Ronie, but that includes *not* accepting an offer of *employment* from the government," Liam stated emphatically, adding,

"Already turned down the same offer from Alan Pinkerton. Don't want a stronger noose around my neck."

Ronie pursed her lips and breathed out in exasperation, then took a breath to resume when Heather cut her off, "Mrs. Willum, Ronie, if Liam dies tomorrow, we'll talk."

"Hey!" Liam objected, but Heather waved him off.

"If my brother and I are so incompetent we let you get killed tomorrow, then *gub'ment* work is all we're good for anyway," she said, as Rat tried unsuccessfully *not* to snicker while Ronie glared impotently.

"That's better," Liam grumbled and Heather batted her lashes at him.

"You people are *crazy*!" Ronie exploded quietly to not be interesting to the crowds that had finally drifted away after the boring book signing.

Rat snickered and patted her arm. "Told ya they was interesting. Now why don't you and I leave these young folks to *their* night while we go catch up on each other's adventures?"

"But President Grant…" Ronie started to complain.

"What?" Rat cut her off. "Does our old friend Ulysses really want every one of these young folks or does he just want one of these fantastic flying machines. I bet he sure wishes he had one back when he was takin' orders instead of givin' 'em."

Ronie clamped her mouth closed and shot a glance at Heather and Liam, who both smiled back innocently.

"Come on, luv, let's go have a pint or two and talk. We have plenty to catch up on and both of us can earn our pay."

"He *pays* you?"

Rat snorted. "No, luv, you know me. Just being in the game is pay enough for me, besides, my way I don't have to submit spending receipts like you do."

"Plus, you get to keep what falls your way," Ronie muttered as they walked away.

Rat laughed aloud. "People lose things, I find things. That makes 'em mine." Then the two entered the crowds of the village's burgeoning population and their voices blended into the overall noise.

Liam looked around and saw Heather smiling as she watched him. "Oh, sorry, did you say something?"

Heather snorted. "No, I was just letting Rat keep you informed through your changeling hearing and didn't want to say anything to drown out what he might be passing to you," her smile broadened. "So, what was it?"

Liam snorted. "Letting me know why the topic of pay has never come up. Did you know the only reason he even stayed around is because we're *interesting*?"

"He does tell us a lot of *interesting* things about the people we want to know about, too," Heather reminded him as she took his arm and turned toward the end of the pier. They walked toward the under-construction village and in moments the crowds were thick enough no one knew who they were.

They passed through the edge of the crowd coming and going from the three ships currently lined up at the docks and in moments were walking the wide walkway in front of the line of new shops, hotels, and saloons.

At the end of the pier, the blacksmith's shop and the main stables were at the eastern end of the road next to the two large warehouses and three grain bins. The pier sat flush with the stables with the warehouses and grain bins on a dead-end road to their right. Going left, west along the main street they first passed the blacksmith shop and next to that was one of only four of the completely finished hotels on the island, and it was used entirely by the construction teams hired by Liam's father.

Of course, the first saloon on the single main street of the new village was next to the first full hotel and it had three floors of rooms above the open first floor. The crowds on the boardwalk around the wide double doors showed that both were full of guests. The next building was also a four-story hotel, but it had a restaurant on the entire first floor. Its boardwalk and side patio were also crowded.

The General Store was next but only two of the three upper floors were completed under the finished, flat roof. The next lot contained a small park that wrapped around a stone outcrop being sculpted by several serious looking young men and women.

Liam recognized its future shape just as Heather whispered, "It's a crouching puma with its tail upraised, just like the shape of the island, somewhat."

They stopped and watched the artists conversing and measuring and cutting lines to be finished with detail later. The entire outcrop was not being sculpted. Instead, the artists were sculpting a crouching puma in raised relief on each side of the outcrop. The front, between the twin lion halves, they were shaping a stone bench wide enough to sit five adults.

"It looks like they're duplicating the clawstone grooves on the top backrest between the tails," Heather said as they walked in front of the park sculpture.

"Can't wait to see it when it's finished," Liam said earnestly.

They continued walking along the street of the growing village with crowds of people all around and none of them knowing who they were.

For the most part.

"Good day to you, Mr. Fleetfoot."

"Good day to you as well, Mr. Quinn, Miss Richards. Uh, Mr. Quinn, I was instructed to tell you the saloon with the sign of the crossed wands on a drinking mug, Myrddin's Mug, is full of Hammersmiths. Emptied their House in Cleveland to see the show as they tell it. All of them and some others from other Houses are staying in the hotel above the saloon."

"Yes," Liam replied. "It's the building *our* Hammersmith purchased through a second party. He doesn't actually *own* it because of the way my father wrote up the contracts to those settling here, but it is still his place."

Liam shrugged. "Figure any man should be able to celebrate his last day of life in the way he chooses."

Fleetfoot looked to the sides and tried to stare down the few people that had moved close enough to hear the words of one of the men in the duel they had all come to see. But the young Sky Ranger didn't know Liam purposely said his words loud just so those close by could not mistake them."

He was doing what he'd been *instructed* to do. Show everyone he was confident *he* would be alive at the end of the duel, but not in a bragging way.

He glanced around furtively and spoke more softly, "Besides, if I did start to wander in that direction, I'm sure one of the four men and two women you have shadowing us will make you proud."

Fleetfoot opened his mouth to deny the accusation, then snorted. "The other man and two women just got promotions."

"Good," Liam said. "Thank you, Fleetfoot. We'll stay clear of Myrddin's Mug."

"Thank you, sir. It's the building just after this next one. There's a nice little patch of beach in front of it and across the street you might want to look at."

Liam smiled. "Yes, I played there as a child before any of this," he gestured toward the village, "was built."

"In fact," he pointed at the building that housed Myrddin's Mug and three floors of hotel rooms, with a rooftop casino that was still unfinished, "there used to be the oldest, largest black walnut tree on the island standing right there where that building is now."

Heather stiffened at his side and he was instantly alert. "What?"

She chuckled softly. "Do you know where the lumber from that tree is now?"

Liam thought a moment. "Most of the best lumber harvested when my parents cleared the strip the village sits on is supposed to be used remodeling the interior of Orlagh and my wings. The rest was used in the buildings that were built," he nodded toward the line of four and five story structures.

"He kept it? *All* of it?" Heather was excited.

"Well, *most* of it. The best cuts of lumber and some whole limbs. The rest he used for interior work and beds and such. I think he even kept all the root balls intact."

Heather gasped and clutched at his arm and whispered intently as she leaned close, "Do you think he kept the root ball of the old walnut tree that stood *directly on top* of the site of the building now owned by the Hammersmith Family?"

This time she made it a point to only whisper loud enough for *his* changeling ears to hear.

Liam smiled as he caught her meaning. "I can take you to it right now if you want."

"No," Heather purred as she snuggled closer. "We really *do* need to be seen to keep riots from happening. I have all night to destroy Cleveland's entire Hammersmith House. For now, let's have some fun. I think I hear music down toward the other end of the street. Let's go see if they're dancing."

Chapter 51

"But I need to talk to Miss Richards! She's the only one can sign these papers," the excitable man waved them in the air for emphasis.

"Not the only one," Liam commented. "*Mister* Richards can sign them."

"The *boy*? Heard he ain't old enough to shave despite looking like near thirty. Can't be responsible for no minor signing something he don't know nothin' about. Prolly break sumpin' and blame it on me. Say I broke it in shippin'. Nope! Ain't letting no boy sign."

He took a bullish stance and glared as he crushed the papers in his hand. "*Miss* Richards needs to sign before I hands it over soes I can make sure the boy don't break nuthin'."

Liam tried another track. "What is it anyway?"

The man straightened the sheets and read. "Sum kinda' tinkering things. *Del-eye-ket* things that prolly break easy so I ain't lettin' no boy git his hands on 'em."

"I know!" Liam held a finger up. "What if I get the Master Tinker that *ordered* the parts and let *him* sign for them?"

The man pondered that for a minute. "Guess that would do."

"Excellent!" Liam exclaimed then turned to see Mrs. Martin at his side.

"I already told the Master Tinker, sir. He said he'd be right down."

"Thank you, Sophia. Could you see this gentleman to a waiting room, please?"

"Yes, Mr. Quinn."

The man's eyes grew big but before he could say anything, Sophia had him by the elbow and was steering him into a side room. "Would you like something to drink? Tea or maybe lemonade?"

"I sure could use a big glass of lemonade, Ma'am," the man gasped. "Had to use that bag of metal parts as a club to push my way through the crowds at the dock then dragged it the whole length of the street to yer airship. Sure glad I didn't have to drag it through the forest we flew over to get to this side of the island."

Liam snorted as they passed through the door to the outside. The crowds continued to grow during the night as people came to see the duel to the death between a Master Mage and the Novice that challenged him. Several of Fleetfoot's people were needed to patrol the grounds to keep the curious away.

But some business still had to be taken care of and it was easier to bring those problems to him instead of him flying all over the island. Besides, he had more people to block for him at Puma House.

Both the pier and the shoreside dock were completely lined with ships and boats when he and Heather called for a ride home the night before, with more than half of them serving as hotels for the overflow. Several more were anchored further out and were being serviced by energetic boys in rowboats charging exorbitant prices to drunken sailors and revelers to get them back and forth.

As it was, there weren't near enough rooms and more people kept coming. The result was dozens of people sleeping in the woods behind the main street along the south shore between the private houses going up. More than a few of those made it all the way to the main house in their nighttime wanderings. When he and Heather flew home, there were two of them at the house, one sitting at a table with Sophia and the other one tied to a tree.

Liam noticed the one that had been tied to the tree was no longer there. The other had taken employment and was currently with Fleetfoot's recruit class.

"Liam! Over here!"

Liam looked to see his father motioning to him and walked over to sit at the limestone table with his father, and Echhardt Hammersmith.

"Good day to you Master Hammersmith."

"And to you Novice Quinn. I hear you had some excitement in your little village last night."

Liam looked at his father who was busy pouring another large glass of lemonade. He accepted it and sat before answering. "Couple of fellas with liquid courage thinking they could get their sketches and names in a dime novel even if they did get beat to a pulp then thrown in jail and fined. Fleetfoot's people stopped them before they got within swinging distance of us."

"No, not that one," the eldest Hammersmith said softly.

"The other time we were in a saloon with some folks and a few of your kin came in and well," he shrugged, "words were passed and challenges made. The next thing we knew we were out in the middle of the street and I was using what natural magery I have to make crawdads dance. Could do one, but not two, and only had to do one to win the bet."

"Yes," Echhardt sighed. "I've already heard. My great nephew insists you had to have cheated but all his brothers and cousins say they were watching the whole time and they all agree you were using just your natural magery."

He scowled. "Trouble is, your father says none of his children *has* any measurable magery. And when the messenger came from the hotel where the rest of my family is staying, he said you never heard of the test."

"No, Clanmaster, I hadn't. One of the young men just said he bet I didn't have enough magery to make a crawdad dance and I said I did. Then we made a bet and when we went out in the street and somebody got the crawdads, I asked them what I was supposed to do and they laughed at me and then told me what I bet I could do… so I did."

"So, Miss Richards did not include the exercise when she trained you?"

"No, should she have?"

Echhardt snorted. "The practice exercise is to focus one's magery and can use just about any of the lower life forms. It usually takes children several weeks to master it. They first start with earthworms, then graduate to flies and mosquitoes. It is actually the basis of the insect repellant chanting."

He gave a small smile. "It's a game we use to get the youngest children interested enough to start training early. The earlier you start and the more you practice the greater your power as an adult."

"The Cleveland House sits on the banks of the Cuyahoga, Natives call it the Crooked River, and there are a lot of crawdads on their shores. The adults don't even have to entice their children to practice their magery, simple sibling rivalry does it for them. They have contests to see how many crawdads they can dance. I think the record for a child not yet a Novice is two. I can do fourteen."

"I can do three pair of scorpions. Good day Clanmaster, Mr. Quinn, Liam," Heather said, as she walked up looking like she'd just awakened. "But that was ten years ago. I don't know how many I could do now."

Dillon raised an eyebrow at his son at the familiarity and Liam smiled in return.

"Good day, Miss Richards," Echhardt rose partially along with the others at the table.

"No, no, stay seated," she plopped herself in the last chair. "Where is, oh hello Sophia. I wonder if you might do me a favor."

"Rocky and Frankie already prepared something Mr. Richards suggested before he locked himself in that room with you all night. Ah, here comes Frankie now."

Frankie was carrying a tray that looked too heavy for one man, but the burly chef showed no sign he was having any difficulty. He deftly switched it from above a shoulder to a two-handed hold while Sophia quickly transferred plates and pitchers and glasses from the platter to the table. In seconds the platter was empty and Frankie was headed back to the kitchen with Sophia making one last check of everything before following.

"I must say Mr. Quinn, your home is nothing like I was led to believe."

At Dillon's raised eyebrows the eldest Hammersmith continued, "The last time I had correspondence with my son that lives in Cleveland he said his youngest son claimed to have *finally* found a site for his own House instead of continuing to drain his father's coffers without much input to the accounts."

Echhardt cut into the bison steak he'd been served and took a first bite. "Umm, that is just delicious. Cooked *exactly* the way I asked! Anyway, I was told it was an uninhabited island except for the two owners who just wished to live out their final few years and then my son's son would simply move his family in."

He took another bite as Heather drained a glass of Fallon's nutrient drink. "Then I hear that same grandson had been *formally challenged* by a Novice, accused of dark magery and would I like to Witness the Hammersmith Clan defending its Honor on the dueling field."

"Then on my way to witness this mystery I discover I am reading about those same events I had heard second and third hand from gossipy kin, but from a completely different perspective. Oh, and I wonder if I could get you to sign my latest copy, you know, the one where you formally challenged my grandson in a restaurant full of people in Cincinnati."

"If you have it with you, I can sign it now," Heather quipped, then pulled out the tinkered quill.

Echhardt swallowed another bite of his steak and chased it with lemonade. "In my room."

He cut another bite and speared a sautéed mushroom before chasing it with lemonade. "But to get back to my story, when I get here, I find the elderly couple on death's doorstep are changelings still young enough to bear children who have two adult children that *also* call the island home. On top of *that* there is a thriving and lively village of several hundred people, all on what I was told was a nearly *uninhabited* island, *and* my own Family owns a lavish hotel tavern in that village."

"I asked my son about these puzzling discrepancies and he said *his* son's secretary gave him the original report and he trusted these reports without verification and unknowingly passed on the discrepancy to me."

He shrugged as he stabbed a strawberry in a bowl by his plate. "With a Clan as large as mine, it is not unknown for lower-level people to report things with a rosier view than facts would support."

"Doesn't excuse those lower-level people when they abuse the power of their Clan and Family," Liam observed, as he waved his kabob stick then pulled the grilled onion slice that was next in the row of meats and vegetables with his teeth and chewed.

Echhardt smiled as he chewed the last bite of his bison steak, then he swallowed and took a drink. "That's what people like *you* are for, young man! Pity it takes death to bring forth misdeeds, but those misdeeds usually include pain, misery, and death. Sometimes an honorable death is needed to stop further pain."

He turned his eyes to Dillon. "I can assure you, sir, after today my gaze will be thorough on my grandson's habits. In the spirit of that pledge, I will tell you something few know."

He took a preparatory breath, then looked at Liam and back to Dillon. "As Master Richards can attest, many Master Mages keep certain tomes of a *questionable* nature. These books contain difficult magery, including knowledge that should never be *used* but should be *known* so it may be recognized and countered if it *is* used. After one of the large Gatherings I hosted at my Catskills House, I discovered one of my most dangerous collections was missing. I couldn't openly search for the culprit, but I did narrow it down to two Houses and honestly, Cleveland House was not one of them."

He took a long pull from his glass of lemonade, draining it to the lemon slices in the bottom. "Ah, that was a superb lunch and does your House proud. My compliments to the staff."

He took a deep breath as he toyed with the empty glass. "One of the more dangerous chantings in that particular grimoire dealt with a curse remarkably similar to the one that has claimed your Family. It is a curse that requires death to chant into being as it requires the assistance of a true *daemon*. If my grandson has acquired my missing grimoire and *is* the one that cast your curse, then he will face Clan Justice."

"You are anticipating his victory then?" Heather was smiling tolerantly.

Echhardt snorted. "My grandson may not be one of the more powerful of my line, but young Liam here," he gestured politely, "is a Novice who could only make *one* crawdad dance. Young Winchester was dancing three crawdads by the time he was six and quit playing the game at nine when he was dancing six in a double pattern of three each."

He gestured toward Liam again. "He barely glows even in the dark and that is with his aura shield *off*. I am sorry if I give insult, but I cannot fathom mere *tinkering* can overcome such a gulf in abilities."

Heather shared a smile with Liam before answering as Frankie and an apprentice cleared the table. "I assure you Clanmaster, the duel will be a surprise to all."

Echhardt snorted as he looked at Liam with a seeing chant on his lips to reveal he was using his strongest magery.

Magery was a vocal science that required the chanting of special syllables that controlled the energies being manipulated. The syllables were strung together in phrases and sentences that were *commands* and *instructions* in the mystery that was magery.

Beginners and those with limited natural abilities needed to *chant* those magery formulae aloud and in a measured cadence, while Masters with years of experience could simply *think* the cadences. It was still verbal, but it could be done with just a thought. The ability was one of the five requisites to moving from a Level Five Acolyte to a Level One Master. If you had to speech chants aloud – even in a subvocalized whisper – you couldn't *be* a Master.

Echhardt Hammersmith was a Level Five Master, one of less than a double hundred known in the world, and almost never would need to move his lips silently without expending a considerable amount of energy in the chanting.

He snorted and shook his head again in disbelief. "I'm surprised you could even make one crawdad dance. I can only say I admire your confidence to the point *if* Novice Quinn is victorious and Winchester *is* the chanter, your Family's curse will dissolve immediately upon his death."

"If Winchester wins, the result will be different as Clan Law forbids us from killing our own. But dead, his incarceration will not be the lonely, lengthy, and miserable existence he will live if *he* were to be the victor. And believe me, if he lives and is guilty of this curse, *that* will be his fate!"

"We agree there is a *miniscule chance* my opponent will be victorious," Liam admitted as he gestured toward Heather. "But if you had seen our sparring sessions you would not think so."

"I am surprised you are giving me this much information so far in advance of the duel," Echhardt commented as one of the kitchen apprentices refilled their lemonade glasses and put out plates of Heather's favorite energy squares.

Echhardt tried one and his eyebrows raised. "My, that tastes good. I wonder if your chef would share the recipe with my man."

"I usually make them myself," Heather admitted. "But they are so popular I gave the recipe to Rocky and Frankie just last night before my brother and I did some important collaborations. This is their first attempt at the energy squares."

"I can see why you call them that," Echhardt admitted. "I can feel the energy being converted to replenish what I have already used today." Then his eyes grew wide and he licked his lips. "They're *enchanted*! Preserved from going stale and flavor and taste enhanced!"

"Yes," Heather admitted. "But just tiny chants over the raw materials when they are freshly harvested and at their best. The chant is too small to interfere with the roasting of the nuts and grains or the drying of the fruit bits. Then the whole thing is mixed with honey and some other things and baked, then cut in squares and a *fixing* is chanted. We're going to start issuing wrapped squares to all duty Watches to help make our employees better able to handle the increased stress of their responsibilities."

Echhardt chuckled. "That wouldn't have been so hard to do if you hadn't printed dime novels of your exploits and sent them all over the country."

Dillon made a face and shook his head in agreement as Liam replied, "True, but then the island would be flooded with nothing but Hammersmith supporters and no one would know of your Clan's embarrassment. It would be much easier to brush into a corner and covered by more complimentary social role models."

"Good point young Novice," the Clanmaster sighed. "It's a shame I was not made aware of this long ago. I might have been able to stop it before it became an embarrassment."

He shook his head sadly. "But that is a lifeline out of reach."

"There is another problem you should know about," he sighed again. "Guild rules allow a duelist to request energy from Family and Master Winchester Hammersmith has requested an energy transfer chanting from all Clan attendees since the duel is not *within* the Clan. It is up to my discretion whether or not to do that, but in all respects the refusal would be a grave insult to my son and *all* his sons and daughters. There are also several representatives from other Houses in attendance. To refuse my grandson's rightful request would make them wonder if I would refuse to support *them* if their need arose."

He looked Liam square in the eyes. "I hope you realize, Novice Quinn, I *cannot* refuse to be the conduit to give him all the extra energy every single blood relative in the spacious arena you have provided is willing to give him."

"Yes, well, good luck with that," Liam chuckled and Echhardt scowled as Heather and Dillon joined him with silent smiles of their own.

His face went neutral but before he could speak, Heather leaned forward in her chair. "Clanmaster, can I tell you a story that will show you why we act as if we have a secret that will both surprise and dismay you?"

Echhardt pursed his lips and sat back, crossing his arms defensively. "Please do."

Heather smiled her thanks. "When Mr. Quinn here," she gestured toward Dillon, "and his wife decided to violate their wish to keep the island uninhabited except for their progeny they chose the spot with care and planned well."

She gestured around them. "As you can see, the forests here are old, many of the trees on this small island are even older than you. When the Quinns chose the south shore for their claw in the eye of their hidden torturer, they determined just how much of the shoreline's magnificent trees to harvest and which to keep to beautify the spaces between the size buildings they wished to allow to be built."

"These choices were based on a quick study and one of the choices was the desirability of the trees as good lumber or magnificent shading for citizens restricted to a single public strip." Heather took a dainty sip of the thick energy drink Sophia was serving before continuing, "One of the more magnificent trees, an ancient black walnut tree, stood on one particularly desirable location for a commercial and residential building."

Echhardt's interest went instantly from casual, to focused. "Yes, Clanmaster. Before the building where all the highest-ranking members of the visiting Hammersmiths with the most natural power slept last night was constructed, an ancient black walnut tree stood in that *exact* spot only a year ago."

The Clanmaster exhaled slowly and deliberately, and couldn't help but release a hint of fear as she continued, "I just found out last night and to my surprise I also discovered the *root ball* of that ancient tree was still on the grounds of this House."

Heather pulled a gnarly wand from inside the bag she carried over her shoulder and placed it on the table in front of the Hammersmith Clanmaster.

"My brother and I made that last night," she gestured to the wand on the table. "You may have it, Clanmaster Hammersmith."

Echhardt didn't touch the powerful talisman. "You are so confident you would *still* give me this?"

"That wand contains considerably more than what the contributors would have *voluntarily* offered and it can be recharged *at will* from any of those that slept in Myrddin's Mug's rooms last night," Heather explained, then at his growing anger quickly added, "Never more than a quarter of what is available within each contributor in a single month without volunteering more and only within a few yards distance. About the distance to the public walkway in front of Myrddin's Mug."

She twitched a shoulder. "The combination of my magery and my brother's tinkery does have some limits. Other than the extra amount of drainage from the donator, we seem to have reduced the leakage to almost nothing."

Echhardt gazed at the wand, then after a few seconds his lips moved as he chanted a stronger *seeing*. "It just looks like a stick, even with my most powerful *seeing*. It doesn't even show the potential that of newly harvested ancient root wood should have. You say you do this with the help of your brother's tinkery and present me with an example hours before the duel between my grandson and the man that makes your aura glow brighter?"

Heather blushed, as she looked sideways at Liam. "Yes. You may be able to discover its secrets in a week or two of intense and continuous deep scrutiny. But even then, without my brother's genius you will never duplicate it because the masking chant is what keeps the vampire chant from evaporating. Breaking the masking chant improperly will cause the rest of it to unravel."

"How long does the vampire chanting last?" Echhardt's scholarly curiosity was getting the better of him.

"Don't know," Heather admitted. "Just made it last night. Normal vampire talismans last two weeks to a month depending on the level of the Master chanting them, but their leakage is always visible to a Master and even some Fifth Level Acolytes."

She gestured. "Take it and use it as you see fit."

"Even if I use it to give my grandson two and a half times more energy those same kin would have given willingly?"

Heather and Liam shared another smile before she replied, "Yes, even so. But you do not have to give him any of it if you don't wish."

Echhardt snorted. "If I *refused* it would be the same as inviting a Familial War for a new Clanmaster."

"On the contrary," Heather responded. "The dueling Laws say only that you act as a conduit for the *voluntary contributions* of those of your Clan in attendance."

She let slip a derisive snort. "I'm wondering how many of them will not even bother to attend the duel knowing they will be asked to give energy."

She shook her head sadly. "They will blame it on excessive celebrations in the night, but even if they do show up to the duel, they will be reluctant to contribute much of what energy remains to them and *they* control the amount they give."

"So legally and politically, you do not have to give your grandson energy from that," she gestured toward the untouched wand still lying on the table between them. "You could simply honor his request and take only the voluntary contributions of those of his kin that manage to make it to the duel."

"You *could* do that," Heather stated calmly. "But *we* are asking you to give your grandson *all* the energy that," she gestured toward the vampire wand, "contains."

Echhardt looked at Heather in shock, then at Liam who smiled and shook his head yes. "You people are crazy! You're serious, aren't you? You stole a quarter of the energy from my entire line through dark magery then turn around and *give* it back to me to use against you!"

Liam shrugged. "Won't matter."

Echhardt turned an accusing eye on Heather. "You made more than the one talisman, didn't you?" He stabbed a finger toward the wand, then at Liam. "You said this was the only *wand* you made. You made another amulet that *isn't* a wand and any borrowed power Winchester throws at him," he twitched a hand toward Liam, "will fuel his own energies through *his* vampire chanting."

"Actually no," Heather replied. "I did make three more amulets, one each for Sinead, Orlagh, and Dillon, but their vampire chant isn't linked through the Myrddin's Mug location. You see the best lumber from clearing land for the village went to Quinn House. Your grandson slept on a bed of the best walnut last night and my brother and I made three vampire amulets linked only to Master Winchester Hammersmith."

Echhardt slapped his thigh and cackled, "Now *that* is how that particular dark magery is *supposed* to be used! Catch someone cursing you and drain them every time they activate it."

He one-eyed Heather. "Sometimes makes the *daemon* link a little testy, though. You up for that, girl?"

"Won't know till it happens, if it happens," Heather replied. "But it won't because the *daemon* will be madder at your grandson than me or the Quinns and will get his or her revenge during the draining along with the Quinns when the curse activates at the next waxing of the full moon."

"Yes, if Novice Quinn does lose tonight, then poetic justice will befall my grandson at the rising of the next waxing full moon," Echhardt nodded. "But you still wish for me to contribute all of this wand's stolen contents to my grandson?"

"Yes, please," Liam replied with a smile as Echhardt finally picked up the powerful talisman.

"You are that confident you will live, and my grandson will not?"

"I am confident I will live," Liam stated with conviction.

Chapter 52

"But you said you would see the Laws were amended!" Winchester fumed as he glared at Liam in his suit of tinkered magery. "Look at him! He glows brighter than my Clanmaster!"

"You did not seem to mind yesterday when your attributes out-glowed his feeble shining," the Guildmaster forced neutrality into his voice and face.

He sighed. "There was nothing in the Laws that stopped tinkery of this kind before we arrived because we never anticipated it. The oversight will be corrected as soon as it can be, but not before this duel. You did get a considerable energy contribution from your kin as Guild Laws allowed. I have known you since you were a toddler and I can rightly say your own aura has never looked so strong."

Winchester Hammersmith pouted. "And where *is* everybody? Half my favorite aunts, uncles, and cousins are not in the reserved priority seats."

"It is my understanding they are still at the special banquet the host Family is providing to make up for their lack of housing amenities," the Guildmaster informed him.

"Well, they better hurry," Winchester fumed. "I'm not going to play around. With that much power I'll have to finish him off quickly before he figures out how to use what he's got, however he got it. If they miss my victory it's their own fault."

The Guildmaster tried not to roll his eyes.

Liam moved inside his special suit. "It still feels like there's a catch in the left shoulder. I noticed it as soon as you tightened it before I put on my shirt."

"And you're just now telling me?" Fallon fumed. "There's no place to get you undressed enough to fix it that everybody can't see."

"It'll be okay," Liam said as he moved that arm. "It's just a small thing that might have always been there now that I think about it. It's just I'm a little more nervous and, well, it'll be okay. Don't fret it."

"There's the signal from the Guildmaster," Heather cut in. "Let's go Liam."

"Don't worry, Fallon. I'll be fine. You'll see. I could disconnect that arm and still beat him into submission, metaphorically speaking, of course," Liam said as he stepped up next to Heather.

Heather took the time to wink at her brother. "I'll be right back, then we can plan how best to smooth the ruffled pomposity of a *very* surprised and riled up Old House of mages."

Fallon snorted. "Still should have told me so I could check it out before he goes into serious combat. Oh, go on, they're waiting to see a show. Don't make my suit look bad because you couldn't tell me about a defect before you demonstrated it in front of a few thousand people for the first time."

"Sure thing my friend," Liam said and finally got a smile in return. He gestured toward the small table with the after-duel energy squares and thick nutrient drink that awaited his victory. "Don't forget to keep the pitcher cold, it tastes nasty warm."

Fallon snorted. "Go, they're starting to look impatient."

Liam turned to look at the Guildmaster waiting calmly while the Hammersmith brothers fidgeted under the gaze of nearly five thousand sets of eyes. "Good. Okay Miss Richards, let's do this."

"Heather, Liam. I think we can dispense with the honorifics till we get near the people who worry about those things."

"Okay, Heather, my luv," he smiled mischievously, "let's do this."

She gave him a fake glare but the smile ruined it, nodded once and they set out in step the forty yards to where the Guildmaster and the Challenged and his Second waited.

Liam's smile was as bright as Winchester's frown was dark. "Good evening Master Hammersmith!" Liam said loudly, then gestured toward the sides. "Look at all the people who came to see my Family's curse dissolved. I hear there are nearly five thousand people sitting on the slopes of the clawstones."

He narrowed his eyes and smiled. "I was sure we saved the proper number of seats for your favorite kin, but half your reserved section is still empty. Are they well?"

"They are refreshing themselves after the unselfish way they contributed to our teaching you a lesson," the Master Mage sneered as he released the hold on his aura to show the gift he'd been given by his Clan through his Clanmaster.

Again, he forgot the heightened senses of a changeling and didn't notice when Dillon, Sinead, and Orlagh all three focused feral attentions on him. He also didn't notice his Clanmaster *did* notice their reaction to him dropping his aura shield as he continued, as did all of the nearest Guild members. "After I teach you a final lesson, my Family will make sure more abominations like the *tinkerings* you wear will be outlawed so only *pure* mages may practice the art!"

Liam smiled pleasantly. "Didn't you hear? There's no such thing as a *pure* mage. Magery is dominant in certain Families, yes, but *anybody* can be taught, can *learn* magery."

"Didn't you know I have been tested for magery several times in my life and it wasn't until *after* using Master Tinker Richards' tinkerings and Master Mage Richards' magery combined did I ever *show* any sign of natural ability. I was declared *mage-free* as a toddler, when I first attended school, at both puma and human puberty, and twice in my travels looking for a cure to your curse."

"I have taken one test since then and that was the one where I was awarded the Knot for Level One Novice that I needed to teach you a lesson you will remember the rest of your life."

His smile grew feral. "However long or short that life may be."

"You dare threaten me…"

"Uh, *Master* Hammersmith," Liam interrupted with a chuckle. "I have *already* threatened you. It's called a Formal Challenge. That is why we're here, in case you've forgotten. Try to keep up, *old boy*."

Hammersmith glared at Liam, then at the Guildmaster. "Get on with it!"

He gave one last evil glare at Liam. "I was going to make it quick but I've changed my mind. I'm going to make you suffer before I kill you."

"And you," he glared at Heather. "When I'm finished with him, I'm going to take you as my bedservant while my wife is bloody as compensation for your insults."

Liam barely restrained himself but the Guildmaster didn't see it because he was glaring at Hammersmith with disgust. "The Seconds will escort their charges thirty yards in opposite directions, that way for Master Hammersmith and that way for Novice Quinn," he bit out with barely restrained anger. "When you achieve your positions, you will remain facing *away* from this spot. Either duelist turns to face his opponent at this time will be immediately killed by all perimeter observers." He gestured toward the increased number of observers the crowds had precipitated.

"When I am satisfied both duelists are ready, I will move to the priority seating area where I will then give the signal and both Seconds will withdraw another twenty yards. Again, if either duelist turns toward his opponent, that duelist will be immediately executed by the observers."

"I will then give the second signal and both duelists will turn and face their opponent. When I am satisfied both duelists are ready, I will give the last signal and you will be on your own, but remember, there are only two normal outcomes to this duel, either one of you dies or one of you submits *and the other accepts* that submission. If either of you attempts to voluntarily leave the marked arena," he gestured toward the colored flags and the observer midway between each, "you will be immediately executed by the nearest observers."

He looked toward each of them. "Master Hammersmith, do you understand the instructions?"

"Yes, yes, just get on with it," Hammersmith muttered. "I have important things to do later tonight."

"Novice Quinn, do you understand the instructions?"

"Yes, Guildmaster, I do. Thank you," Liam bowed his head slightly and the Hammersmith brothers both glared at the Guildmaster when he returned the respectful nod.

"Seconds," the Guildmaster intoned loudly for all those in attendance to hear as his magery boomed his voice to the seated spectators. "Take the duelists to their assigned positions."

Liam offered his arm as if he and Heather were walking through the village and she smiled at him as she accepted the gesture. They could both hear the chatter from the spectators as they walked the thirty yards to the marked position talking as if on a stroll.

"Are you ready?" Heather whispered as she maintained a pleasant smile and happy demeanor.

Liam's back itched as he expected Hammersmith to break all rules at any moment and blast him from behind despite the speech given by the Guildmaster.

He still found it hard to believe the civility that was required by everybody from host to guest in the day leading up to the duel to the death and flinched inwardly at every unexpected noise.

Without Heather's council and the combination of her brother's tinkery and her magery, they would not have had the confidence to maintain that charade. *He* would not have been able to maintain that charade!

"As ready as anyone in my position could ever hope to be thanks to you and your brother," he smiled as he gazed warmly into her eyes.

She laughed gaily and the spectator's chatter increased as they smiled at each other and spoke without concern to the gravity of the situation. Her soft words belied the relaxed nature of her outward appearance. "Just don't forget to keep your focus. Fancy tinkering and magery won't get you through this if you don't stay focused and use the suit properly."

He smiled and patted her arm and leaned so close their breaths mixed. "I had the best teacher in the world. I don't think I could mess this up unless I got stupid and forgot to chant my shields, and even then, it would be interesting to see what happens."

"Don't even *think* that, much less *say* it," she glared at him with her eyes as her face maintained the charade of friendly banter as if the two were unconcerned that one of the two duelists was supposed to die.

He patted her arm and kissed her on the temple so quickly she didn't have time to react as they reached their mark. "Here we are, show time."

The spectators buzzed and his relaxed demeanor dissolved as he looked straight ahead. "I promise I won't do anything stupid."

Seconds later the Guildmaster gave the next commands in mageried loud-voice and Heather marched away from him to a spot twenty yards away where his table of after-duel refreshers awaited. He smiled and winked at her and a few seconds later the Guildmaster gave the next loud-voice command and he turned his back on her and faced his enemy.

His face hardened as he chanted his shields followed by the *special* chant his friends had created.

Then the Guildmaster gave the final loud-voice command and Liam darted to the right three steps before leaping toward his enemy as fast as his changeling body and his godstone suit could sprint.

The move was completely unexpected and Hammersmith's first chanting flew wide and missed by a full pace to Liam's left. They were sixty yards apart at the set-off and Liam had both his natural changeling speed and strength as well as that of the tinkered suit. He covered half the distance before Hammersmith could chant a follow-up to what he'd thought would be a disabling first blow.

The next chanting caught Liam square in the chest and he was stopped dead in his tracks by the force of the attack, but his shields held. Hammersmith's face went from momentary surprise to a sneering gloat as Liam was halted then back to surprise as Liam leapt toward him again, apparently unharmed.

Liam was fast, but so was Hammersmith. He grew up in a Family where he needed to react fast to the attacks of siblings and cousins, all of them practicing to control the masses through competition with each other.

He threw chanting after chanting at Liam, each one stopping his adversary but not getting through the shield Liam surrounded himself with. At one point, Hammersmith threw his chantings so fast Liam was forced backwards several steps, but none of the strikes penetrated.

Stopped from getting any closer Liam began throwing his own attacks. He wasn't as fast as Hammersmith, only throwing one chant to his opponent's two and three, but he was concentrating on his shields, his true strength. With each strike he was hit with, he felt the silently chugging miniature steam engine strapped to his back increase its vibration through his torso as the mysterious godstone tinkering absorbed the magery Hammersmith bombarded it with.

He marveled, as he chanted himself into a *hyper* state and was able to *see* and *hear* Hammersmith's chants and devise counters and responses so quickly he was able to detect a variable pattern. One specific chanting seemed to always follow another in a sort of predictable one-two punch. Another was a three-punch combination his opponent used twice.

Hammersmith's face contorted as he hammered away at Liam's shields, relentlessly pounding away with more than Liam and Heather had ever put the suit through in their tests. In his *hypering* chant Liam verified all three of the pattern groups and identified two more in the next few moments of the fierce battle as the suit absorbed what was thrown at it.

Only ten yards separated them and the magery sent flashes of fire and light and gusts of explosive air displacement in all directions as they pounded each other.

"*Is that all you can do?*" Hammersmith screamed and increased his assault. "*I can't even feel your gnatty attacks!*"

Liam smiled as he taunted his enemy. "I don't seem to be feeling yours either. Does that mean I'm as strong as you, or you're as weak as me?"

"*Gods damn you!*" Hammersmith screamed at the sky in frustration and began throwing chants Liam recognized as in the realm Heather had designated as being *dark magery*. Of course, he'd been given tinkered defenses for those as well as he drove closer to his enemy. Hammersmith was surprised by the successful counters and hesitated a moment. Liam took the respite to advance another five yards before the furious Master rallied again with even stronger chantings of dark magery.

Liam didn't have time to see the reactions of the spectators with enough magery to *see* what was happening, as the chants thrown his way were more complex than what Heather had taught him. It was no concern of his that Hammersmith was breaking Guild Law by using the dark magery restricted to Masters in the open view of Acolytes, Novices, and those without magery.

He was able to shred or deflect the chants his shield didn't absorb as he used the duel to *learn* what was thrown at him using the *hyper* chanting Fallon and Heather devised to *memorize* every spell and how it was used tactically. He watched in fascination, as Hammersmith seemed to move as slow as he did when he was teaching Heather the dances of hand combat.

As Hammersmith continued to chant his even more complex dark magery, Liam studied each one in hyper and what didn't get absorbed into his shield to regenerate his energy he used in his counters and deflections. He stepped another pace forward and Hammersmith snarled in hatred and lunged forward.

In a second Hammersmith moved within physical grappling range and had him by both upper arms and lifted him from the ground and threw him with magery augmented strength.

Liam twisted catlike but landed just enough crooked on his left arm he felt the small strut connecting the shoulder and elbow hinges snap. He rolled with the fall but his left arm was foremost when he came up to face Hammersmith and it didn't work as he expected. The throw also caught him enough by surprise his hyper chant was disrupted and he slowed to normal speed in a rush just as he rolled to a stop facing his opponent.

As he recovered, it was only the new phrasing protecting him from the resulting lethargy of a hyper crash that kept him from falling. But as he focused and slowed to normal speed he realized with a foe like Hammersmith, normal speed could be dangerous.

As a changeling he was fast but still couldn't move in time and the mage's quick strike caused his left arm to go limp and pain to shoot through his entire left side. The pain was evident as he turned so his left arm was behind him but Hammersmith marked the weakness *and* the quick wound and circled as he blasted Liam with more of his dark magery. Seeing his victory in Liam's pain, Hammersmith pushed to get within grappling distance again as he hammered at the exposed weakness.

Liam tried to keep away while still keeping his left arm behind him and chanted attacks of his own as he struggled to regain his balance.

Hammersmith finally grabbed onto Liam's rain slicker with one hand just long enough to pull him closer and latch on with the other as he dragged Liam closer with a snarl. "Now I'm going to make you pay for embarrassing me in front of my Family."

"You forgot something," Liam said as he chanted the final trap in the only spell he had learned that he could *think* into existence. "One, we're in contact," he glanced down at Hammersmith, who had him pulled close with his arms trapped between them. "And two, we're *inside* each other's shields."

"So," Winchester snarled.

"We still have all the power we have. How much have you got left?"

"Enough to snuff out your miserable life, *animal*, and your fancy tinkering can't stop that."

"Really?" Liam said as he silently completed the final chant and prepared the activation command in his mind. "The thing about my *tinkering* isn't that it blocked your attacks. It's that it *absorbed* all that energy you've been blasting me with for the past minute and whatever."

Hammersmith's eyes went wide and he tried to throw Liam away from him, but his arms were locked.

The blast of magery Liam released into his foe with a thought threw Hammersmith back ten yards. Of course, his arms were still locked, as were his meaty fists, in Liam's coat.

There must have been some sort of magery laws broken, but instead of blowing the two apart Hammersmith carried Liam along with him as he flew backwards thirty feet and more. Then Liam landed full on Hammersmith's stomach when they hit the ground and Hammersmith groaned explosively and his hands relaxed.

Liam didn't hesitate as he quickly rose dragging his enemy upright with one hand as the feeling came back in his left arm. He steadied Hammersmith with his left hand as he began to pummel his enemy with several suit-powered punches to the stomach and ribs with his right fist. Hammersmith grunted with each punch, his reactions a perfect display of a complete lack of magery in defense.

After several meaty punches Liam steadied the Master Mage with his left for a moment until Hammersmith was teetering on his feet. Then Liam reared back and slammed his fist into the Master Mage's face to topple the dark mage unconscious on his back – with blood pouring out his shattered nose and split lips – spread eagled on the ground with arms and legs akimbo like a human X.

Liam walked up to stand over the prone body and looked down. By Guild Law he was supposed to end it now by killing his foe, and when he did, the curse would die and his Family would again be able to make their changes consciously. It would be the proof they needed to vindicate his Challenge.

And all he would have to do was kill a man lying helpless and unconscious on the ground in front of him.

He looked down at Hammersmith, then around at those that came to watch such a spectacle. The Family of the defeated man had not all shown up, but their section was no longer as empty as it was at the beginning of the duel and all of them were on their feet. Some showed complete surprise at the outcome while others had the look of anticipation.

Liam marked the owners of both.

A third group just looked sad, mostly the oldest of them, but two in particular. Liam had dined with those two the night before and enjoyed their company despite the circumstances.

Liam looked around the arena and saw thousands of faces on both sides and all looking at him in complete silence. Then fists were raised and thumbs were pointed up or down, mostly down. He couldn't believe it as even some of the Hammersmiths in their reserved section rose from their seats and pointed a thumb up or down as if *he* was the arbiter of life and death, and he froze for several heartbeats.

He blinked his eyes and looked back down at the man that had tortured his family for so many years. Then he looked around at the expectant faces and stepped away from the defenseless man.

"No! I will not kill him!"

He pointed at the prone figure. "You *saw* the dark magery he threw at me! You *saw* the chants he broke Guild Law in showing to Acolytes, Novices, and non-Guild witnesses! Let *those* be his crimes that you," he stabbed a finger at the Hammersmith section, "investigate as is proper."

He crossed his arms. "As a Guild member in good standing I defer my Formal Challenge to Guild Justice as written in the Guild Laws that states I may do so with five witnesses to the use of dark magery in the presence of those not authorized to witness such chantings," he glared at the Hammersmith entourage.

"Do I have five Master Mages who will Witness the use of dark magery in the presence of those not authorized to see such displays and demand a *truthsaying*?"

Almost immediately the Guildmaster moved out of his traditional position and stood with arms crossed and palms flat to his chest. The rest of the observers were a heartbeat behind. Slowly, but steadily, members of the Hammersmith Clan all rose and most crossed their arms over their chests.

Liam made note of the few that crossed their arms below their waist. Those weren't in actual objection to his demand, but were instead those who truthfully *witnessed* nothing wrong, either because they didn't actually *see* the chants or thought the chantings *shouldn't* be restricted and given the designation of being *dark* in the first place.

The vote was sealed as soon as five of the observers of Master level status voted to accept his deferral – there were dozens more than the needed number – and Liam gave the prone body of his torturer one last look then turned to go back to his side of the arena.

It was over and he didn't have to kill his adversary, and there would still be a truthsaying to expose the curse. He smiled as he walked toward his friends.

He had taken only a couple of steps when those in his direct sight grew wide-eyed and the observers lunged toward their subduing wands.

The reactions of those in his line of sight told him something was happening behind him and the only thing behind him was Winchester Hammersmith, flat on his back and totally unconscious.

In automatic response to their expressions, he *thought* the hypering chant as he strengthened his shields. Before he could complete another thought, something slammed into his back and everything went black.

Chapter 53

"He is unharmed even after what hit him?" a voice said as he began to feel his body again.

"Yes, especially since he learned an earlier lesson and didn't drop his shields even though he *did* turn his back on a downed foe that wasn't dead," came another voice, one he also felt through what he was lying on. Then he recognized it as Heather's lap and voice, and he sighed.

"There, see. Just got the wind knocked out of him," said another voice. His sister's, but she couldn't talk in puma form.

He opened his eyes, blinked several times to clear his vision, and smiled. "Hi sis," his voice sounded like a rusty door.

He swallowed and tried again, "Nice dress. Looks good on you."

"Why thank you little brother. Just happened to have it on hand, you know, just in case I had to make myself presentable real fast."

Sinead moved within his view and his smile widened. "Hello mother. I see the curse is broken."

"Yes, just as Master Hammersmith turned to ash. We thought he'd taken you with him for a few minutes. Welcome back to the living."

"He wasn't dead," Fallon objected. "Well, not all the way, and not for very long."

"More of this tinkered magery of yours and your sister's no doubt," Echhardt complained as he looked around Heather, who held him in her lap and against her chest.

He snuggled closer.

"No, actually all tinkering," Fallon replied. "Funny how a jolt that can knock a man down could also start him back up."

"So, he *wasn't* really alright till *after* you tinkered him back to life making him jump around like a puppet like you did when you poked him with that security baton?"

Fallon peered at Liam like he was examining a bug. "You got all your faculties? Hello-o-o, are you in there or did your brain die?"

Then he muttered, "Don't know if I can tinker you back to normal if you ain't."

"You poked me with a security baton," Liam croaked as he pushed feebly in an attempt to sit upright.

"Repeatedly," Echhardt confirmed. "It would have been funny the way you jumped around if Miss Richards hadn't looked about to call up a *daemon* to bring my grandson back to life just so she could kill him again."

"Wouldn't have wasted it that way," Heather breathed softly. "Would have traded mine for his."

More than one person gave her a look she didn't see, as she was distracted when Liam tried again to rise. With a little help it only took him a couple of tries, but in moments, with her to lean against, he was on his feet, then a terrific roar engulfed them.

He flinched but saw the smiles on the faces around him. It took a moment to realize the roar was coming from nearly five thousand voices as the

Guild observers and Fleetfoot's security people kept the spectators in their seats. They were standing and jumping up and down and screaming, but they stayed in the ridges of the clawstone embankments to either side of the arena where each of them had claimed a seat.

He looked to the side to see a smoldering pile of ash with a vaguely human shape. "So that's what those subduing wands do."

"Actually, no," the Guildmaster said. "That wasn't done by us."

"What do you mean?" Liam asked.

The Guildmaster clamped his mouth shut for just a moment then made a coded signal with Echhardt in finger talk, then gave another signal.

Three observers immediately closed around them and began chanting a privacy dome as Echhardt spoke, "My grandson was not the one controlling his body when he rose to attack you from behind. The chanting that was sent through him to kill you used every scrap of energy in his body to fuel itself."

The Guildmaster pointed. "He looked like that before anyone could shoot him with a subduing wand. Subduing wants can easily kill if you're hit by too many at the same time, but even when they kill, they don't leave, *that*."

He pursed his lips as he looked at the charred remains on the ground, then up at Liam. "The chanting that makes such a thing possible requires a death and it was also in that grimoire I told you was missing. That particular chanting is only known to a few Mages of my own age or older."

"Myrddin almost killed me when he caught me in his private library," the Clanmaster's face took on a distant look at the memory before he continued, "I told him I'd just got there but that was *that* time breaking in so his truth chanting proved I wasn't lying. I was able to succeed seven other times during my apprenticeship. Two of the chantings I stole from Myrddin were in the stolen grimoire."

He shook his head sadly. "He will be very disappointed in me when he discovers how shabbily I have protected the secret knowledge he *allowed* me to steal. I hope he lets me live to make it up to him."

The centuries old mage brightened again. "But that is another day. Sadly, I *do* have new information I have not even had time to share with the Grand Lakes Regional Guildmaster as yet. Just as our victorious, *living* Novice was regaining his wits a runner from Myrddin's Mug came to me."

He sighed. "We now know who stole my dark grimoire. Do any of you remember a frail looking, quiet boy? Heh-heh, boy. He *was* such a beautiful boy when he was younger, but in mind he *stayed* a boy even into his fifth decade. Or so it seemed. Anyway, you may have noticed a frail man that always stood behind my second eldest son's wife. Bernard is his name. A member of the Baltimore Hammersmiths."

Echhardt looked at Fallon. "Read those dime novels about your Family being cursed. Before we'd ever heard of you, all of us thought maybe he had been cursed too, but no matter how we looked we couldn't see anything wrong with him. After a while we just thought he was like that. It happens sometimes, and the mind just don't grow with the body. All his life we just thought he was addled from sometime young, just reached this certain point and never got any older if you know what I mean. Happens more in Families that don't seek out fresh blood."

"Bernard is, *was*, all shy and withdrawn. Never looked up and if you tried to look him in the eyes, he'd close his and make gods-awful noises. The other children used to do that to him for fun."

He was lost in thought for a moment. "Was seen *talking* to one of your Sky Rangers, one of the ones that flies your one-man airships, the sit-down kind with the cargo space in front. Boy, man, don't talk to *anybody* and nobody thought it strange he was talking to someone not Family."

"He was one of the ones seemed to be drained the most by Master Richards' little vampire chanting and stayed back at Myrddin's Mug and Hotel. Just about the same time Winchester was being turned into a charcoal briquette, Bernard was killing your Sky Ranger to power the control spell, then Winchester to double its power. Then he stole the airship and flew off toward the mainland while we were all running around here in a turmoil."

There was a commotion outside the privacy dome, and the Guildmaster signaled and the observers let the dome collapse. As soon as another messenger was let in, they raised it again.

"Go ahead son," Echhardt said to the young Acolyte. "It'll save me having to repeat it."

The young man dipped his head. "As you wish, Clanmaster. Uh, Bernard killed his brother Jacob and his cousin Frederick, too, and stripped both of rings and necklaces and personal purses."

He hesitated as he looked at the attentive faces and Echhardt motioned for him to continue. "Raided the lockbox and took all the godstone coin and ingots, gold and silver too. We're completely broke Clanmaster 'cept what we left back home, or each had in our pockets or on our fingers, wrists, and necks, including all the Clan Heads from the visiting Houses."

"He took it all and is gone," the young Acolyte's voice broke as he delivered the last words of his devastating news.

The young man gulped once, looked around, then whined, "Everybody alive is stompin' 'round and makin' threats and most of 'em are too weak to do more than make noise anyway and nobody knows what to do so they's just yellin' at each other."

When the young man took a breath Echhardt cut in, "Thank you, Acolyte. Now here's what I want you to do. Are you listening? Good. Run back to Myrddin's Mug and tell every Master you see I said they better have a complete report for me when I get there and I will be there in one hour. Now *run* but remember to save enough breath to report so they can understand you."

"Yes, Clanmaster!" Then the young man was gone without waiting for the observers to break their privacy chanting. A pair of Fleetfoot's better runners quickly flanked the Acolyte and ran with him to make sure he delivered his message safely.

"So that's that," Echhardt stated bluntly. "Guildmaster, I can't begin to express my apologies for the actions of *two* of my progeny. I trust you will not begrudge me the haste with which I wish to scrub both their names from Guild roles as well as from any share of allowance or inheritance."

"Of course, Clanmaster," the Guildmaster bowed to Liam and his family and friends, then gestured to Echhardt and the two men walked to the other side of the park where there were no people and chanted another privacy dome so they could talk.

As soon as the Guildmaster moved away, the three observers moved to help the others maintain the sanctity of the duel arena. Two observers chanted over the remains of the late Master Winchester Hammersmith as another two prepared the bag they had thought would be for Liam.

"We need to leave the arena so these men and women can make their reports and relax after a job well done," Heather spoke louder than she needed to for the benefit of the observers and they helped the quartet move to where they could rejoin Fleetfoot and their own security outside the arena's secure boundaries.

They moved as a group to the airship and were soon up the access ladders fore and aft and Revis was happily chanting foam to lift them into the sky. As they rose into the night sky, they could see the observers taking the charred body of Winchester away and the restless crowds finally swarming over the deserted arena collecting souvenirs when the observers released the area from sanctity.

"What could they find in a deserted field in the dark?" Liam muttered as he and Heather leaned over the rail watching the crowds swarm the arena as Sesco flew them in a loop once around Clawstone Park.

Heather just shook her head in bafflement.

Sesco took them in a wide loop around Clawstone Park then toward the village in another wide loop that would take them over the main house so he could signal the Watch to give them a quick report.

"There's something wrong with the signaler," Liam said as they came over the house slowly so Sesco could tap out the message in Morse code.

"What do you mean?" Heather asked. "How can you tell?"

"It's too loud," Liam said. "Can't you hear it?"

Heather gave him a measuring look, then took on the look she had when she was silently doing magery.

"Whoa! Your aura just flared."

"You saw that?"

"Yes," Liam said. "Looked kind of like when the suit's on and I can see a person's aura. But this is different in a way. With the suit I see a kind of glow *around* somebody, just like you always said. But this is more like an *inner* glow."

"Maybe it has something to do with whatever it was Bernard hit you with," she looked at her brother talking animatedly with Fleetfoot on the other side of the forward deck. "You were down, dead, and it was only Fallon's poking you with the shocker baton that brought you back to me," she leaned against him.

"He said something about the body using the same kind of energy and the heart might just need its trigger pulled. If he wasn't my brother, I would have throttled him the first time he jabbed you and pulled the trigger and you jumped like a puppet."

"Well, I don't remember anything but waking up with you holding me," he confessed, then smiled. "It was the most wonderful feeling in the world, felt safe."

They were quiet for a few minutes as Sesco flew them in a slow loop along the southern coast of the island, the waning moon reflecting off the water in front of them to the east.

"Your aura's stronger than it was before the duel," she commented as they turned the southeast corner to head toward the docks. "You're as bright as a Third Level Acolyte."

"I feel different too," Liam said with furrowed brows.

"Have you tried to change yet?"

He swallowed. "I'm afraid to try." He made a face as she looked at him in surprise.

Then she nodded and answered her own initial thought, "You never had a chance to learn more than the basics. Hammersmith cursed your family before your full change at puberty."

"Yes, I don't know if I have a warrior form or if I'm one of those that is *naturally* tied to the full moon. All I know is I have a full beast form. Just don't know how to *change* to it yet. And I don't want to try it dressed like this or with our current passengers."

"What if I get halfway in between and can't figure out how to change back again? It's happened before. People get stuck and it takes serious *therapy* to get them unstuck. That would be a fine ending to *that* dime novel!"

Heather chuckled. "Your mother and sister have both already gone back and forth to full beast and in between to warrior form. Orlagh had a little over a year after puberty to practice controlled change before the curse. But even after the curse your mother spent more time with your sister *talking* the process through when they were in human form than your father and you."

She snorted. "They had less time together in human form than you and your father so never put off important talks because they always had time later."

Her smile took away the sting of the truth. "Orlagh already talked to Fleetfoot and he would do just about *anything* for the female that chose *him* as consort and protector when she was cursed."

"Even teach a change-blind changeling how to change?" Liam muttered.

Heather laughed gaily. "Yes, even that tongue twister!" She patted his arm. "Relax. I talked to Fleetfoot and a couple of other changelings, including Rat, and changing is not much different from magery."

"Children *chant* themselves into whatever change they can accomplish while adults just *think* themselves into change in seconds like a Master Mage *thinking* a chanting."

Liam shrugged in agreement. He had talked to enough changelings in his life other than his father to know all about the *theory* of willful change.

He wished he had the nerve to try to change just enough to present his warrior form to the world when they landed. "I'ow 'ry 'ar'r." He tried to say but his mouth wasn't working

Heather looked over at him and snorted. "See? That wasn't so hard, was it? You might work on the muzzle a little so people can understand you. Not very impressive if it sounds like you're trying to talk around a hairball."

Liam snorted and concentrated on his mouth, and it shifted. He twisted it around, then spoke hesitantly. "I... I'll try harder, is what I was saying."

She looked at him critically. Then she looked down and smiled.

He raised his hand to see his forearm was furred and muscular but in his human shaped arm and hand, with just the hint of cat's claws at the tips of his fingers. He still had the pads of his fingertips but his human fingernails curved around just enough to make them claws instead of fingertips and nails.

He instinctively dipped his hands into the slits in his rain slicker and out again, then to several pockets to check their contents. "Hunh, never felt it before but it feels natural."

"Ah! Got yer cat man on I see," Fallon said as he turned around from looking over the rail on his side with Dillon. He nodded complimentarily. "Looks good. Can you talk?"

"Go tinker yerself!"

"Yes! He *can*! And like a real person too," the young man laughed as he looked him over critically. "How about the hands."

Liam dutifully showed Fallon his hands with their human fingertip pads and fingertip claw combinations and the young tinker pulled out a measuring tape and measured him from elbow to partial warrior's clawtip.

"Make your claws bigger!" Fallon ordered and Liam complied, more out of curiosity than following the command. Fallon measured again.

Liam put up with the indignity because he was trapped on the foredeck with the Guildmaster and Echhardt in the sitting room still getting their story straight for their Guild, and it was over five hundred feet to the ground below.

"Now full human. Good, good," Fallon muttered distractedly as he measured again then started on Liam's head, measuring the placement of his ears and the length of his muzzle with changes till he couldn't talk but had battle teeth, and back to the warrior shape he felt best in and could talk plainly.

Then Fallon grabbed a particularly long hair at his temple and yanked it out.

"Ow! Hey!"

Fallon held it out and Heather calmly took it and placed it in a locket in her *special* bracelet.

"You could have asked," he grumbled.

"*I* would have," she said then shrugged. "Got one now, so I don't have to. Now the collection is complete and I'll always be able to send you power if you need it, no matter what form you're in."

"I'll get more measurements later to see how it all fits together," Fallon said as he measured Liam's shoulder width and arm length. "Does it feel any different?"

"Reach for things is off just a bit," Liam said as he moved through several hand combat motions, then touched his pistol, knife, and several pouches and pockets. "Not enough to mention except I *do* notice the differences."

"He sees auras different," Heather said.

"He does?" Fallon said then darted away. He was back before either of them could comment with a bulky tinkering of tubes and lenses he put over his head and looked at Liam. "Watch Heather do something magery."

Liam smiled. "That's easy," then he ogled her with bulging eyes.

She hit him and Fallon exclaimed, "Whoa! Your aura *is* different! Everybody else's is like a covering *around* people. *Yours* is inside of you!"

"That's what he said mine looked like," Heather said.

Fallon took off the odd eye scopes and handed them to his sister and she put them on. "Do some magery," she ordered.

Liam snarled and she exclaimed, "You're right! That sure is different. Oh, I bet that's Forth Level Acolyte for sure, maybe Fifth Level. Did the suit do *that*? It didn't look that strong before we left the arena."

"No," Fallon said as she removed the tinkered twin scopes and handed them to him. He didn't put them back on. "I think whatever that chanting was that burned Winchester to a crisp did it, or at least, whatever dark magery it was that leaked through the compromised suit's shielding and killed him for a minute or two there."

"Right here ya know," Liam muttered.

Fallon shrugged and looked his sister in the eyes. "Won't know till we can get his coat and shirt off and check it out and can't do that with prying eyes and ears aboard." He nodded behind them toward the sitting room and the two highest level mages for this entire section of the nation in private conference. "Can't wait to get those two ashore, or better yet, get aboard my own boat and let you two deal with politics."

He looked where Sesco was bringing them over the eastern end of the docks. "Hey Sesco! Pilot! Whatever! What's the chance you can set us down right on the roof of your construction barracks hotel building?"

Sesco stood up in his Pilot's seat and looked over the rail at the village on their left. He sat back down and spoke into his talking tube. "Revis, boss's brother wants us to show off. You want to earn a day off?"

"Ain't had a day off in'na while big brother. Let's bet 'em!" Revis sounded happier than any of them had ever heard since they'd met him.

"Give me a spit and two reps little brother!"

"A spit and two reps comin' up!" Revis called out and they heard him spit, then chant out two reps at the same time Sesco turned the fans into the wind and vented foam.

"One rep, three spits, and two reps!" Sesco called into the speaking tube as he angled the airship toward the roof of the construction workers' hotel.

"One rep, ptooi-ptooi-ptooi, two reps comin'up!" Revis called out. He chanted one quick foaming rep then they heard his steam valve inject steam into the balloon above them through the foaming tube in three short bursts coinciding with each vocalized *'ptooi'*. Then he chanted two more reps at the same time Sesco vented foam and angled the pusher fans against the gentle night breeze.

The airship drifted silently and slowly till it settled its ground wheels on the roof of the building that housed most of their construction workers.

"Vent balloon!" Sesco called out and Revis blew some sort of farting *noise* into his foaming tube. The nearest foam exhaust port spewed steam and the airship settled on its wheels.

Liam looked over the rail to see them sitting directly in the center of the roof of the construction barracks hotel.

Eyes showing white all around, the nearest Roof Watch cowered in a corner with his weapon pointed half at Liam and half at the balloon looming over him.

Chapter 54

"I think next time we might want to *schedule* any rooftop landings ahead of time," Liam muttered, then raised his mug to his lips and took a sip. He'd changed from his warrior form back to full human while removing the suit after Echhardt and the Guildmaster left the airship after giving him odd looks. It was easier to drink without a muzzle. "Lucky the watch didn't quit right then and there."

"Not lucky at all," Fallon contradicted him smugly. "Told 'em there would be surprises and we delivered."

Liam snorted. "Yes, we do deliver surprises."

He sighed. "Okay, what do we do now? First thing is make a regular rooftop dock watch on the dockside hotel with special warnings so we don't stop the heart of the next recruit stuck on boring duty and shooting one of us with his last breath cause he thinks he's being attacked from the sky."

"Just take a few training sessions and standard coded hailing calls and responses," Fallon beamed. "Shouldn't be too hard."

Liam groaned and Heather patted his arm. "I believe Fleetfoot has already taken care of everything. When we got down to the street I looked up and there were a couple dozen recruits and veterans all up on the rooftop pointing and gesturing. He'll probably have docking cleats installed before we get finished with whatever it is

Echhardt and the Guildmaster have cooked up for us."

"Bet you it's another offer to work for them," Liam changed the subject before taking another sip from his mug then frowned at it. "This ale tastes different than it did yesterday."

"It's the new magery that's gotten into you from whatever it was the suit or Bernard's death chant did, or both, whatever," Fallon waved it off.

He tapped the tinkered twin short scopes hanging from his neck. "Shows up different than any other mage I look at through these. It'll fade or it won't. Ah, here comes our new best friends."

Liam looked up as the Guildmaster and Echhardt walked up to their table in Myrddin's Mug. They were followed by several of Echhardt's progeny, some of them looking sheepish and some glaring balefully at their Clanmaster's guests. One of them carried a box he dumped on the table. Several crawdads tumbled out and one of the Mages kept them in the center foot and a half of the large round table.

Liam looked up and one-eyed Echhardt who was smiling. "You want me to make crawdads dance? Seriously?"

Echhardt smiled and gestured toward the Guildmaster. "Your Regional Guildmaster does not believe me so the only way for me to prove what I claim is for *you* to make crawdads dance in front of sufficient Masters," he said, then gestured toward those in attendance.

Liam scowled at Echhardt, then at the Guildmaster who stood with his arms crossed and a skeptical look on his face. He breathed out through his nose and looked down at the crawdads on the table being held within an eighteen-inch circle by one of the late Winchester Hammersmith's scowling relatives.

Liam concentrated on the tiny arena and the glows of living beings came into his *sight*. Unlike the outer glow he'd come to be used to, these were the same inner glows he had seen since waking from being dead.

He reached out and touched one of the crawdads with a chant on his mind and made it move toward another. He touched that one with another chant and brought the two of them together and facing each other till their waving claws touched and he held them in that general pose.

Then he made them dance in a circle, first one way then the other. He reached out to another crawdad then another then backed off. Did he want these people to see what he could now do? Instead of bringing the other crawdads into the dance he set them randomly exploring the arena as he wondered at the difference in how he perceived magery.

As he wondered at the change in his perception, he kept two of the crawdads in the center doing their circling dance while he moved the other five around the edges of the chanted arena in a random manner. After a couple of seconds, he noticed he could *feel* the edges of the chanting and, curious, he had one of the crawdads *poke* at the invisible wall.

He had a second crawdad touch the arena wall on its side, then another and the third one found a tiny crack in the chanting. Curious, Liam *pushed* at the crack... then lost his concentration when Heather ground her boot onto his foot.

He started to turn to see what she was doing when he looked at the crawdads just as his hold on them slipped. The two in the center weren't just circling a common center with their claws touching. They were standing half upright in each other's grasp. The other five crawdads were at equidistant points around the perimeter also half raised from the table as they probed the chanted wall with glowing claws. One of them seemed to be crawling *through* the chanted wall.

As soon as he lost concentration, they all resumed the normal actions of wild creatures, except for the one halfway through the crack he'd seen in the chanted wall. That one hung in the air, trapped by the chanting as it waved its claws and legs feebly, half in and half out of the shield.

Liam closed his eyes and groaned.

"See!" Echhardt crowed. "Told you!"

The Guildmaster scowled. "You were right. So, what do we do?"

Echhardt ignored the question as he looked at Liam. "Explain yourself *Novice*. How is it you know that particular chanting of *dark magery*?"

"What? I don't know any dark magery!" Liam automatically defended himself. "I hardly know any magery at all unless I'm wearing Fallon's suit."

He opened the lighter long coat he wore instead of the battle slicker. He'd purposefully left all the accessories in his room except for the shields and energy storage tinkerings. "I don't have any more magery than I had before, do I?" He looked at their faces, then at Heather. "Do I? I *do*?"

"You just performed three of the five tests to be a Master," the Guildmaster accused him then counted them off. "You chanted multiple castings *without moving your lips*. You did not just make the creatures *dance* with a moving shield box you *took control* of a living creature's body. He looked at the table with the six cowering crawdads and the one still trapped within the chanted arena wall. "*Seven* living creatures' bodies. That is dark magery number two."

He held up a third finger. "And three, you not only performed the dark magery of taking control of a living creature's body, you performed *another* dark magery chanting by using that creature to pierce a *shield*."

Liam made like a fish, his mouth opening and closing with nothing coming out, as he looked at the arc of faces around the side of the table open to the room, then blurted. "I didn't *mean* to. When I felt the edges of the shield, I just got curious, then I *felt* the crack and just sort of *pushed* at it because it was softer in that spot than the area around it."

"Impossible," a voice from the looming crowd snapped. "He's just a *Novice*!"

Echhardt beamed like a proud parent. "That's four. How many more do you need?

"Five is the threshold," the Guildmaster reminded the eldest Hammersmith.

Echhardt scowled, then jabbed a finger at the arena. "They serve crawdad gumbo here don't they? Cook those Novice!"

Liam responded more to the tone of authority than the actual order. Without thinking he formed a thought and *took* the shield around the seven crawdads away from the Master holding it and reshaped it into a sphere."

"He *took* it," an indignant voice objected. "He took it away from me!"

"Shush, shush," another voice hissed.

Liam ignored the voices and lifted the seven crawdads inside a chant he didn't remember learning. He looked for a mug or pitcher of water he could drop them in to boil but he didn't see one. Well, he would have to boil water anyway, why not just heat the inside of the floating bubble of squirming crawdads?

Fallon had told him once about heat being nothing more than the stuff that made up things *moving faster*. He *thought* the concept and in an instant the pressure inside the bubble increased, and in a flash the seven crawdads were steamed in their own fluids.

Heather scooted a plate to the middle of the table and he set the meal down gently with another mental chant he didn't know he knew and released the shield bubble. When he looked up most of the Hammersmiths surrounding him had moved back a bit and their expressions now included nervousness and fear. More than one of them held a hand close to a weapon.

"Ha!" Echhardt boomed and several of his kin jumped, then looked sheepish.

For the first time Liam noticed the room contained nothing but Guild Masters, except at the table with his family and Fallon.

Echhardt turned to the man that had chanted the arena shield. "He *took* it from you? You didn't pass it to him?"

"No, Clanmaster. He *took* it from me!" Then he looked sheepish. "I didn't even feel it happening till it was just... *gone*. Happened so fast I was halfway to chanting a new one cause I thought I'd just mentally drifted before I realized that it was just... gone."

"Ha!" Echhardt exclaimed. "That's five! And he used the shield to lift weight. That's six, *and* he cooked a meal inside a shield. That's seven, and two more of those are dark magery."

He crossed his arms and looked at the arc of Hammersmiths. "Did any of you see his aura when he performed all of these feats of Masterful magery? Huh? Not one of you? I'm glad none of you claimed the lie because I could not see his aura as he chanted *multiple* dark mageries no one taught him, and all of them *at the same time*. That's *eight*, eight lines he has crossed. And of that eight, all but two of them were dark mageries that are forbidden to all but Masters."

He crossed his arms with his palms facing his chest. "I vote yes."

Heather stood up and crossed her arms with palms facing her chest. "I vote yes."

Then the Guildmaster copied them and in seconds the entire room full of Master Mages were likewise voting yes. Not one held their arms crossed below their waists in the *no* position.

"Stand up Novice Mage Quinn!" Echhardt snapped.

As he did so the table was whisked out from in front of him and Echhardt and the Guildmaster moved in on him as he blinked in momentary confusion. "What?"

Echhardt pointed at the Novice knot he'd attached to the shoulder of his coat. "Remove that knot!"

Liam was stunned. Heather told him more than half of all Novices were kicked out of the Mage Guild and another half of all Acolytes, but he never imagined he would be one of them.

He was *proud* of his Novice's Knot!

With clumsy fingers he numbly fumbled at the Guild ranking knot on his collar in a daze. It happened so fast he didn't think, only reacting to a Master's *order*.

His mind reeled as he realized Heather had voted with the rest to strip him of what he'd begun to be so proud of. Not only voted with them but was the first after Echhardt condemned him for casually chanting dark magery. He finally got the knot free from his shoulder and hesitated before handing it to Echhardt.

Was this the Clanmaster's revenge after leading them all to think he was different than the first Hammersmith he'd crossed paths with?

Echhardt made a *gimme* motion and Liam placed the knot in his hands.

Liam began to slump when Echhardt turned and traded the knot for one the Guildmaster gave him.

"Novice Liam Quinn," the eldest Mage intoned. "You have honored the Guild by exposing a *crime* of dark magery, then you openly chanted *eight* acts of Master Magery yourself, six of them of the dark levels, and all of them cold and without prior preparation."

Liam hung his head in shame, and Echhardt smiled tolerantly as he continued, "Dark magery is not termed so always because it is inherently evil. It is termed so because it has the most *potential* to be used in an evil manner. It is, in effect, considered too dangerous to teach to those of limited abilities, but also of those of greater ability but a lacking of moral character."

Liam felt like he could melt into the floor but held his head high instead. He would take this and do his family proud in his humility.

"Everything you have done, every public act you have displayed for those with eyes to witness, has been of the highest moral character."

"As a Fifth Level Master, I hereby award Novice Liam Quinn with First Level Master's knots. I would give him a two or even a three, but that would require additional testing and we have not the time for that."

Liam's jaw hung open and his eyes bulged as Echhardt stepped forward and attached the Master's Knots to his shoulder.

After he stepped back Liam reached out with shaking fingers and touched the knots. "Thank you Clanmaster, Guildmaster," he nodded to the other man, who would have been doing the duty if a Master of Echhardt's standing had not been present.

Heather brushed the knots with loving fingers then leaned in and gave him a peck on the cheek. "Congratulations."

She was smiling warmly when Echhardt boomed. "Master Heather Richards! Step forward!"

In surprised shock she did so automatically. Echhardt turned to the crowd and crossed his arms in front of his chest. "I vote yes." The process was done just as quickly and Liam smiled as the room full of Masters all voted yes again.

Then they all looked at him and held their votes in front of them. "Oh, right, sorry," he smiled as he looked at Heather, and crossed his arms in front of his chest. "I vote yes."

Echhardt reached forward and removed her First Level knots and traded them to the Guildmaster for Second Level knots, which he then attached.

"Again," the oldest person she'd ever met whispered, "I asked for a jump up to Third but I was told you should spend a few months at this level first."

He stepped back. "I present First Level Master Liam Quinn and Second Level Master Heather Richards, who also is now the youngest *Second Level* Master currently alive and only the second youngest in recorded history."

Liam leaned in and pecked her on the cheek. "Congratulations."

She beamed as several Masters moved forward to congratulate the two as Dillon and Orlagh and Fallon gaped.

"So, this is what you people do behind closed doors," Orlagh said as she moved in to congratulate her friend and brother.

"It can happen anytime five Masters get together, actually," Heather commented as the saloon's tables were moved around and a buffet quickly set up. They looked at an entire room full of Hammersmith Masters.

"I'm having more of a problem with all of these people wanting us dead not three hours ago and now they're slapping us on the back like old friends and serving us free drinks and food," Fallon complained. "What's up with that?"

Heather snorted a laugh. "Mages live the longest of all the human species, two, three hundred years or more in some cases if they avoid the difficulties of duel challenges. Others just get tired of living and end themselves in one way or another."

"Our Master Echhardt Hammersmith is one of the oldest and he knows Myrddin personally. You heard him admit that and in a way that says the mythical Myrddin not only existed but is still alive."

"The traditions in magian society are scripted much more than that of changelings or the shorter lived, dominant human species. The rest of the Family was actually *required* to support Winchester whether they liked him or not. He's

Family and Clan, and Family and Clan comes before any and all personal feelings."

His eyes bored into theirs meaningfully. "Even in the case of truth in some instances."

"And we openly broke one of those unbreakable traditions by allowing you three to witness these events," the Guildmaster said as he and Echhardt rejoined them with their own drinks and a finger food selection.

"Six," Echhardt said and pointed his chin to two spots in an upper balcony where Earl and Samuel were busing sketching and writing. "Those two I invited," then he tilted his head toward an open upper window where a face peered in from outside, "that one seems to go where he pleases."

"Clanmaster Hammersmith assures me the results of this break from tradition will benefit instead of harm our Guild," the Regional Guildmaster explained. "He seems to think the entire country needs to heal by becoming a *Nation Clan* and to do that we need to know each other better, *all* of us. I hope he is correct because once we travel *this* road there is no getting off."

He turned his gaze on Fallon. "That brings us to you, young Master Tinker. The Guild is wondering what to do with your marvelous and dangerous tinkerings. Clanmaster Hammersmith and I are wondering if we should immediately declare your example of tinkered magery on the restricted list and declare it *dark magery* of the second level."

"It may be only part magery and part tinkery, but as I understand it, it does require both. Since only the Guild can regulate magery, your tinkering comes under our jurisdiction whether you yourself are Guild or not."

"Didn't help much with Firecloud," Fallon reminded the Guildmaster.

"No, it didn't," the Guildmaster admitted. "To our shame we did nothing even knowing people were dying around him." He hung his head. "Including children and babes."

He raised his head. "But that will not happen again while I am in this office!"

He glared a moment at those who might doubt him then relaxed his body language. "And I also know about your other deals with other Guildmasters, Master Tinker, and I can tell you the information you presented has already been restricted to Master and above."

"So where is this tinkered magery you created, that allowed a Novice to defeat a Third Level Master and then turn its wearer into a Master Level mage?"

Fallon smiled and displayed upraised palms. "Bernard melted it."

"What," the Guildmaster's face fell. "But you can rebuild it can't you?"

"Actually, no," Fallon admitted. "You see, I built the core backpack part of it when I was still messed up with Firecloud's curse and I've never been able to build another one *exactly* like it. And believe me, I tried. I built the one Liam always wore first and it worked different than the ones I tinkered for Orlagh and my sister and even the one I tried to build for myself, and I paid special attention to *that* one. None of them can do the things Liam's could."

"Whatever it was Bernard blasted through the late Winchester Hammersmith hit the center of my tinkering and melted the whole thing into an unrecognizable lump and left a pretty nasty burn on Liam's back. If it hadn't melted to absorb the energy that blasted through the shield, Liam would have had a hole burned through his torso big enough to stick a clenched fist through without getting bloody."

The young tinker gestured his helplessness. "I never could duplicate *that* particular tinkering and now the best invention I ever made is just a lump of melted metal. I can't even take it apart to see how it was different from the other ones I made from the same schematics 'cuz there's nothing recognizable left to study even if I *could* figure out how to study it."

"Besides, it wasn't the tinkering that turned Liam from a weak Novice to a strong Master. It was that grandson of *yours* and whatever it was he chanted through your *other* grandson trying to kill Liam," he glared at Echhardt, "and ruined my best tinkering ever in the process." He feigned indignation.

"There was a lot more than just a backpack tinkering," the Guildmaster pointed out.

Fallon shrugged. "Yes, and I couldn't get any other copy of that design I tinkered to work the same as Liam's original suit did. I spent twice as much time on my own suit and I couldn't even get it to *do* half the things Liam's suit could. It was all in the back plate with that *one special* steam engine and its surrounding mageried tinkering. I made every one of the parts when I was hypering my life away at a month a minute and I ain't doing that again for any Mage Guild."

"I'm not sharing those dark chants that were in the tinkering either," Heather added. "And don't bother trying to steal my grimoire with them written down because that's one group of dark magery I'm not writing down. Besides, they also didn't work in the other suits like they did in Liam's."

She copied Fallon's shrug. "Like Fallon said, Liam's suit's godstone steam engine backpack was different and it changed my chants just like it changed all the tinkerings it controlled. It was an actual one-of-a-kind tinkering with magery infused in it we could *also* never duplicate. We've all seen chantings like that, famous wands and talismans and amulets that show up once in a lifetime and never again."

She gave Echhardt a measuring look. "If I'm not mistaken, Catskill House has an entire floor devoted to Family Heirlooms that are one-off chantings."

He acknowledged the truth with a tip of the head as she continued, "We all know sometimes things just can't be duplicated no matter how many times we try. We can do something that *resembles* the one-off chanting, but we can't duplicate it."

She gestured toward Fallon. "Tinkering is no different and the combination of magery and tinkery is so unexplored it's not surprising it contains one-offs as well."

"Like she said," Fallon said. "Believe me, if I could tinker that same backpack again, I would be wearing it right now and not, this," he plucked at the light, long coat he wore. Liam could see the glow it displayed with the magery the tinker's sister had infused into it and was quietly impressed.

"That brings us to one last thing," Echhardt said. "We may not get your tinkering, but we can make you a Guild member."

"No, you can't," Fallon crossed his arms. "And if you do that vote thing, I'll turn it down."

"You can't," the Guildmaster started, then stopped. "Oh, wait, yes you can. It was part of the Emancipation Proclamation."

"Right," Fallon declared. "I don't have to join your little exclusive club to practice magery as long as I honor Guild copyrights concerning *profits*. And I already got agreements for that in writing *and* the Guild pays *me* for syllable licensing on the two syllables I discovered and hold the copyrights to."

There was stunned silence for a few seconds till Echhardt spoke. "Well, I guess that settles that. Then there really is only one last thing to talk about and that will have to wait for more privacy." He eyed the room full of Master Mages, all but two of them *his* progeny and their spouses.

"No," Liam said.

"What?"

"I said, *no*," Liam repeated. "I'm not going to work for you."

"But Bernard tried to kill you," a voice from the crowd yelled.

Echhardt rolled his eyes. "That's why I wanted to talk in private."

"Doesn't matter," Liam said. "I'm not chasing after Bernard for you. That's what we've been waiting all this time for, not this fancy celebration we ended up with. You were supposed to be telling us what you found out since your grandson tried to kill me and *did* kill two of our men and steal one of Fallon's most advanced tinkerings."

"He killed two of his own family, too, young man," another voice growled.

"Three, if you count Winchester," Liam corrected. "But the answer's still no. Those deaths make him your problem, not ours."

Echhardt turned toward Heather. "Master Richar…"

"No," Heather cut him off. "The same Proclamation accepted at the end of the war that freed human and changeling slaves also freed me from being *required* to perform Guild duties I object to. I *also* have the right to relinquish Guild membership at any time if I so choose with nothing more than a notarized, written request and still retain all previous Guild contracts *and* without even the need to explain why."

"But he killed two of your people and stole an expensive piece of equipment," Echhardt persisted.

"He *also* killed *three* of his own Family, members of *your* Clan and *your* blood, and stole valuable restricted grimoires and considerable Family treasure worth more than the equipment he stole from me," Heather countered then smiled sweetly.

She relaxed her body language. "My brother and I came north to aid the friends that aided us in our time of grief and need. We have paid that debt in full and more and now we four, and those that wish to follow us, will embark on a new quest."

"I hate it when young folks can't be manipulated properly," Echhardt muttered darkly. "Okay, but I still win."

"How is that?" Fallon raised his chin as if inviting a punch.

Echhardt smiled. "I read all your dime novels, even the ones written by people repeating rumor and gossip that are full of lies before you got those two mulatto boys to do it right. One thing every one of them has is your Pledge to each other to keep rooting out evil after you help each other break your curses."

He smiled broadly. "And I can't think of anything more evil than a man that would use dark magery to kill five people, three of them his own family, and steal treasures potentially worth well over a million dollars."

He chuckled. "The only difference is the Guild won't have to pay you to hunt him down for us. Oh, I will definitely finance my own search for my wayward grandson but I won't have to pay *you*."

Fallon smiled. "Won't have to take orders from you and get to claim a bigger finder's fee when we snatch him out from under you."

Liam and Heather traded a smile, then caught Orlagh's eye just as she started to say something and waved her off.

"Bet we catch him before you do," Echhardt challenged.

"Ha!" Fallon snapped back. "You've got what, eight, ten major Houses and the same number of satellite Families full of kin in your Clan and twice as many in non-magian staff *and* the resources of the entire Guild."

He sneered. "*I* have the Sky Rangers! You don't stand a chance!"

"I bet you one of those tinkered suits and I supply all parts against this entire building and I will pay for the final construction if you find him before it is finished," Echhardt wagered, then shrugged. "Not that you could."

"I get to change the schematics on any unfinished floors at your cost if I find him first," Fallon shot a counter offer.

"Done!" Echhardt spat in his palm and thrust his hand out.

"Ha!" Fallon spat in his palm and they shook on it. A room full of half smiling Master Mages, Orlagh and Dillon, and a pair of furiously sketching and writing journalists, and Rat watching from yet another hiding place, witnessed the entire exchange.

Fallon puffed his chest as the Guildmaster and Clanmaster drifted away shaking their heads and chuckling.

"Thought you weren't going to work for them," Liam smiled.

"I'm not, *we're* not," the young tinker replied. "What I said was true. They have their own resources but I can't trust them to keep us informed and they'd still expect us to give them our information *and* take orders from them."

"And what they said was true, too. That son of a daemon killed two of my personal friends and stole one of my best tinkerings. I'm not letting him get away with that," Fallon was firm.

"Echhardt was right about our Pledge, too. We did make that pledge and I can't think of any better way to start now that all four of us are curse free, than to hunt down the dark mage who thought he could kill our friends and we'd let him get away with it."

"Plus, we get to keep a bigger finder's fee on *their* treasure instead of having to pay them a finder's fee for our Sky Ranger air bike. Plus, number two, since we win, they won't have time to take the flyer apart before they bring it back to us and *I'll* have time to check out their grimoires before I give *them* back," the young tinker was proud of his faultless logic.

"He has a point," Liam reluctantly admitted.

"Yes, like *you* need to learn more dark magic," Heather quipped.

"Hey, it's only dark magery if you do dark things with it. Besides, I didn't know I was doing dark magery when I chanted it. He told me to do something and he's a Fifth Level Master. I'm only a lowly Novice, well *was* a lowly Novice, but that's beside the point."

He smiled. "Now I'm a Master and I can pretty much do any magery I please."

Heather snorted. "As much as any other Master Mage *allows* you to get away with."

"As much as anybody allows *us* to get away with," Liam said, then looked through the windows at the crew readying the airship for launching. "You know, if we want to win this bet, we'd better do something a bit more constructive than standing around arguing about how much we *intend* to do."

...END.

From the author: Thank you for taking the time to read *Godstone Mage*. If you enjoyed my Sci-Fi Steampunk adventure, please consider telling a friend or posting a short review, as word of mouth is an author's best friend and greatly appreciated.

Thank you,
Rick A. Mullins

ABOUT THE AUTHOR

Rick A. Mullins

 When I was twelve, my older brother, Randall, turned me on to his copy of the Hobbit, then his Edgar Rice Burroughs' Pellucidar series, and thought… 'I can do that'… and I've been writing ever since.

After high school, I served four years in the Air Force, a year at Ohio University, two years of working travel, four years in the Navy, then another couple years of working travel before I finally returned to northern Ohio to become a factory drone. I retired in July of 2015, and now get to devote my full attention to my two favorite passions: writing my own sci-fi and fantasy adventures, and reading those from other authors.

I hope you, the reader, will enjoy the many worlds I have visited in my dreams and converted to sci-fi and fantasy adventures as I allow my imagination to entertain me at night, and you on these pages.

~Rick A. Mullins

BOOKS BY THIS AUTHOR

Circle of Magic

Magic has come to a four-hundred-mile circle centered over northern Ohio.

Confrontation is inevitable as old ideas clash with new powers.

Is the Circle of Magic a gateway to hell… or an alien invasion?

Final Extinction

Mankind has been driven into hiding inside walled cities to avoid a Final Extinction.

The new genetic science of CRISPR, combined with off-the-shelf tech, has allowed gene hackers to build dinosaurs and creatures of mythology in their basement or garage.

At the end of civilization, a caravan of elves, giants, and were-folk travels west through a world of monsters to a mountain sanctuary to escape persecution by purebred humans.

BOOKS BY THIS AUTHOR

Mustang Riders

An alien invasion has begun!

Super genius, flying aliens have opened portals between Earth and thousands of parallel worlds in the multiverse.

Ravenous flying predators have followed them to our skies, and their hunger is insatiable.

Zombie Labyrinth

IS-42 made everyone immortal. The only problem was, it killed nine out of ten people first, and the dead ate half the survivors before things settled down.

Three years after the end of the world, a team of salvagers has discovered a mountain Labyrinth full of military equipment… and hungry zombies. Is an almost unlimited treasure worth the risk of being eaten alive?

Also by Rick A. Mullins

http://www.dreamquestbooks.com

WORLDHOLE SERIES

DRAGONHOME
MAGI
FLOATSTONE PIRATE
CRYSTALLINE DREAMS

T.F.T.M. BUNDLES SERIES

TALES FROM THE MULTIVERSE: VOLUME 1
TALES FROM THE MULTIVERSE: VOLUME 2
TALES FROM THE MULTIVERSE: VOLUME 3

NON-SERIES

CHANGELING MOON
CIRCLE OF MAGIC
CREATACEOUS ANOMALY
FINAL EXTINCTION
GODSTONE MAGE
MUSTANG RIDERS
TEMPORAL ZOO
TEMPORAL ZOO 2: ALPHA CENTAURI
ZOMBIE LABYRINTH

www.ingramcontent.com/pod-product-compliance
Lightning Source LLC
Chambersburg PA
CBHW021832010726
47493CB00005B/1361